Head Above Water

Head Above Water

Hugh Shankland

Matador
9 Priory Business Park,
Wistow Road, Kibworth Beauchamp,
Leicestershire. LE8 0RX
Tel: 0116 279 2299
Email: books@troubador.co.uk
Web: www.troubador.co.uk/matador
Twitter: @matadorbooks

ISBN 978 1788034 401
British Library Cataloguing in Publication Data.
A catalogue record for this book is available from the British Library.

Printed and bound in the UK by 4edge limited
Typeset in 12 pt Minion Pro by Troubador Publishing Ltd, Leicester, UK

Matador is an imprint of Troubador Publishing Ltd

The ditty does remember my drown'd father

KICK-OFF

Stories abound. When I was a lad it was Nan, Nan even more than Mam, who filled my head with him. How tall he was, and strong, and always how good to her, for kindness no one could touch her Robbie. For musicality too. He played the cornet in his school band up in Glasgow, and the ukulele she said he played as good if not better than George Formby. And what a marvellous whistler. When hurt he'd whistle to beat the pain, whistle and whistle and whistle she said, 'Tipperary' non-stop a whole half-hour one time he cut his foot on an open tin. And he could whistle two tunes at once, imagine, that's two parts to the same tune, and at an age when the most I could do was a kind of kettly hiss through the gap my milk teeth left here. This chipped front tooth's nowt to do with that, it goes back to a summer's evening in the Lane when all we had for a cricket ball was a stone.

For my sister's birthday, her first, guess what he did. Cut a penny-whistle from an old bit of bamboo and played 'Happy Birthday' for her all day long! Because he could turn his hand to anything, my dad. His own dad up in Scotland was a pigeon man and from him he must have already picked up the basics before Nana took him back down to our town where she was born, having had enough of the old man's ways, the Quadruple B. Anyhow, what happens when one day from Glasgow comes a surprise present of three racers in a basket? My dad builds them a cree and breeds row on row of regular winners. Descendants of them three originals are flying round still, and making good money by all accounts, if you hear the racing men.

In the next-but-one street to ours only a couple of weeks back I happened to be passing the door of this old chap I've half-known all my life, and he says to step inside the front room a moment and help pull out this battered owd couch sitting there. Get on the end of that, young Felix me lad, not saying what for. So when I'm holding up one end he crawls underneath and from among the heaps of old stuff lying there he pulls out this particular pre-war magazine where it's printed that third place out of nigh-on three thousand birds in the Up North Combine went to a red check hen, bred and raced by R. Rowan. And next before I know it old Mr Jackson's telling the whole saga like it was but yesterday they were out there at the allotments, him in his own garden right next to me dad's, eyes on the sky for the first dot of a bird, and suddenly there she is winging in over all the gardens way ahead of a big long line of them, and all the neighbouring men are up on their feet as well whistling and rattling the feed tins. The trick is to get the ring off quick and get that ring in the clock. They have their own now, they have their own clocks, but back then before the war there was just the one big clock on the table where the officials sat, so a lot used runners, any bright lad extra-quick on his pins to fly with the ring. Of course Robbie Rowan, old Mr Jackson says to me, your dad Robbie did his own running, his legs were longer than anyone's.

And that's only the start of his many talents. Unless you're good at people, or such I believe is the case, there's not much of a living to be had out of being a painter. But that's the thing, he was good, better than good, and by any reckoning could have made a fortune at it. On my bedroom wall at home hangs this beautiful big picture, a pencil drawing he made the momentous year Sunderland beat Preston North End for the cup. 3-1 it was, and the year was 1937, and my dad was just seventeen. And I tell you they're so alive, all still so alive. Uncle Dick was at Wembley that glory day and I wish you could have seen him stood there in front of that magic picture telling all over again how we were a goal down at half-time and just minutes into the second half Bobby Gurney turns the game round, gets the equaliser with a brilliant back-header, and Raich Carter and the great Eddie Burbanks knock in the other two. All still famous names where I come from, and in the picture each gets his special star.

You'll say I'm biased, but to my eyes that picture's not just perfect, it is perfectly perfect, right down to their different sorts of hair or just the way a shirt tucks in, the woolliness of a stocking, every detail. But best of all is the way his pencil somehow gets right into the separate nature of all eleven faces, smiling or solemn, and that I'm certain can only come from not just unbelievable skill, and not just following them and revering them but loving them, living them, almost breathing them. And that is why I promise you I too can sort of go inside each face I know so well until it's like we're all thinking and speaking together, them in their picture, me in my bed! Now that's artistry, surely.

I know, surprising such delicacy from a big hand. Intellect too, in my opinion. I don't know how many hours I must have spent trying to make faithful copies of only even little parts of that picture, hoping to learn something useful off him, and I'd have a go at modern teams too, but none of my efforts ever seemed worth preserving, nearly all ended in the bin. I mean to say, just how did he get the same light to shine over all of them? Almost out of them, Uncle Dick said, because on that day they knew they were winners.

All right, some satisfaction was had while actually working, I grant you. But I'd only have to step back and compare results to see it's another gift he didn't pass on. Not only the aptitude, it seems I wasn't born with the kind of mind for what she calls free discipline, sticking with a thing you enjoy, even one you know you're not specially good at, sticking at it quiet and patient until it comes out the very best you can. That's what she's all about.

Not for one moment am I claiming he was some sort of genius, even unique, I know that now. Still, special. Not just Mr Jackson, it seems everyone he ever had dealings with thought the world of him. I'll give you just one more instance. Colin, one of the Church Lads I used to work the organ bellows with, his old man acquired his nose, his wonky nose, courtesy of Robbie Rowan. And what's incredible is how that man bears no grudge, no grudge at all. He'll wink when he sees us, curling a finger down over the broken ridge of it where my dad fetched him one behind the chip shop all them years back in ancient history. As much as to say, with admiration, affection really: Left his mark, your dad! Disfigured for life, yet not one drop of ill will does he bear.

Special. Very. And I know if any lad ever heard only half the stories I grew up with, how once upon a time there lived a perfect son who was also a rare husband and a golden dad, he'd similarly come to believe there never was his like. The one hitch being, with an example like that, how do you fit in, where is left for his own son to go?

FIRST HALF

1

Down at the docks everything looked as dull as Sunday. Not a soul about. The cranes stood idle. Gulls stood idle on the cranes. They all took off when a hawser round a bollard tightened creaking as though ships can tell when something is about to hit them. I was alone in the back row of an otherwise empty Essoldo half asleep under the projector's searchlight beams vaguely wondering why the subtitles made no sense, but when the hawser tightened and someone's mouth shrieked a monster tidal wave was due in just four minutes' time I was right in the picture, hands that were also mine yanked open a door. Outside, people and traffic were racing past and it was almost soothing to be part of the general panic, a whole population fleeing for dear life, helpless as shingle in the undertow. This time the black cliff of water didn't frighten me. What frightened me this time was the thrill I felt at the prospect of being crushed and swallowed and lifted and spun in a twirling arc out of this world into whatever comes. Scared stiff, I woke before it could happen, safe to imagine it ever since ...

Fifteen years have passed since I had that version of my old drowning dream: November 3rd 1962 on the train to Rome, just one week after all humanity risked going under. The long journey was nothing like my notion of crossing Europe together – sat right next to her but keeping my main thoughts to myself, mostly staring out the window, her nose never out of her book, and rain practically non-stop since Dover, even when we pulled into this city where I've managed to make something of my life it was coming down cats and dogs. We got a taxi to a cheap hotel she knew near the Colosseum, planning to take the very cheapest room and dump the luggage and then head back out to treat ourselves to something to eat and drink before braving the confrontation with her family. Instead, not very long after a terrible episode in that room, I might almost have been inside the same drowning dream again: running along a foreign pavement weirdly elated with despair, fists pounding air, and water everywhere. It sizzled under tyres, drum-danced over the tops of cars and buses, and jetted cold and accurate from overflowing gutter-ends as though fire-fighters posted on the rooftops took me for a bundle of moving flame. Through teeth grinding the sour red lining of my parka zipped tight to my chin I panted her name, pounded her name, the only word for the long tangled fuses of love and hatred fizzing inside me. Then came the wave.

It hit me head-on, an almighty rush of wind and rain that inflated my coat to an outsize life jacket, nearly floating me off the ground. Ten paces at least I drifted backwards helpless on tiptoe inside a big khaki balloon, before colliding with a stone doorway. For all I owe this city – a partner for life who shares this labour of love, two bright kids, work I enjoy – I bless that wave of wind which chanced to cast me up on a friendly shore. Above my drenched head a blue awning black with rain slapped and strained on its metal frame like a sail eager to go with the gale.

Bent double and heaving for breath, shaking the wet out of my hair, I looked back along the road I'd come – two crowded bars, two bottles of freezing *BEER-rah,* two failures to use a phone. From the shelter of other doorways a few heads craned to watch my next move, the nearest grinning. Seen through pelting rain their suntans looked painted on. No sign yet of the big postcard pedlar who'd chased me from the first bar to the second after flogging me a ten-card set of the Vatican when I asked for the Colosseum. 'Hello friend, you go schnell, whadyawan'? Your beautiful guide to Rome?' He was unfolding a maze of streets and ruins when I turned and ran again ...

The heads looked away, further up the street, over the other side where horns were honking insults at a little white car holding up two lanes of traffic to let someone out, someone who made my heart flip right over. She had the same shade of green silk headscarf the lass used to wear to church, if it's where she went. But an unknown face looked round to wave after the departing Cinquecento, fair hair blowing across her open mouth like that famous nude they put on the stamps. When I turned to push open the glass door behind me, heart still pitching, a pavement-coloured pregnant cat hardly bigger than a rat flew out from between my ankles and dived under the nearest parked car dipping her hard bellyful of kittens in the wet.

Even in my condition, I'm pleased to recall, I sensed something special about the place. It was not a big room, but bright and tall and lined with coffee-coloured panelling and wall-high mirrors, classy Roman version of the likes of the New Era espresso bar in my home town. The thirtyish-looking man behind the bar in a starched white jacket with twists of braid at the cuffs and epaulettes was more than just a nattier version of Daniel Dimambro who ran the Era before it became the Light of Kashmir, he'd have even raised the tone of the first-class passenger saloon we were shown the way out of on the Channel ferry. '*Buona sera*', he said quietly, so in control he had no need to raise his voice or even look up. He was pumping one of the long skittle-shape handles on a big shiny coffee machine as flash as the front of a Buick next to which the Era's sweating puffing copper boiler, old Danny's pride and joy, would have seemed a relic from the earliest days of the Age of Steam. The other bars had both been packed to capacity but his was nearly empty and even provided somewhere to sit. There was just one other customer, a little old lady dressed in black. She stood at the bar with her back to me, seemingly intent on not missing a throw in the fine art of good coffee-making.

'*Buona sera*', I tried. *Boo-AW-nah SAY-rah*, according to the first page of her dad's phrase book which I'd gone and forgotten in the shitty hotel (*Pensione Confort, 1°* piano). The old girl stole a quick beaky peek at me round the edge of her shawl, then shook her head at the man behind the machine. That made me more than ever the dumb alien intruder, further unnerved by a sudden queasy sensation I was back on the moving train. For a long lonely moment the pale marble floor went as saggy as a trampoline, bringing also memories of the heave-ho of the ferryboat a whole twenty-four hours before.

'Claudia ...' I moaned inside, only to steady the deck, making it 'Grappa' when I hit the bar. Strongest brew in Italy, the little book said.

'*Deutsch?*'

'*Grappa!*' from me again, and louder. Not even looking my way he selected a saucer from the stacks warming on top of the machine and wiped it with a dishcloth, as though he hadn't registered the order. At any rate in no hurry to oblige.

'*Ger-RAP-pah!*'

The tail of one eyebrow tipping a quarter-inch was all that showed he heard me almost scream. Setting the saucer on the counter for his other customer, not without an on-the-spot expert twirl, he turned back to attend to his flaming git coffee-maker. While me, still a bit short of breath and any notion what else to do, I looked long and hard at the shapes of my toes through the sodden dark tips of my hush puppies, and not until a dolly-size cup of steaming coffee black as slurry sat in the saucer in front of her nose-end did I deign to lift my eyes.

Well, I got the sweetest smile. True, her head was shaking, but with only the gentlest granny-scolding now. Inside warm nests of wrinkles her eyes were purest blue. For a moment of grace I was looking into my own beloved nana's eyes again, so keen they could pierce right to the back of your head and any thought you were hiding, even stir some you didn't suspect. Her hands were almost as knobbly as Nan's but wood-brown and smooth, one thumb polishing the back of the other. She had seen the distress in my eyes and expected an explanation, but even in my own language how could I make sense of what I'd been through these past hours, these last long weird weeks? Where to begin? Work at it backwards, like struggling to recover more and more of a dream?

After stowing a teaspoon and two sugar bags beside her cup the barman launched into some urgent tale of his own, and naturally a canny soul like her would want to attend to other people's concerns as well. 'Madonna' was all I could catch, the words rolled that fast off his tongue, but once it began to seem like nothing would stop the flow she straightened her narrow shoulders under her shawl and gave him her side of the picture in a surprisingly sharp voice, tearing him off a strip I thought, even glancing at me once or twice for support. I'd already had more than my fill of haggle and baggle so I just stood right there and let the two of them carry on parlaying away nineteen to the dozen across the high slab of chrome, her jabbering head swinging from side to side, he never modifying the machine-gun pace of his delivery even after shutting his eyes and clapping his hands over his lugs as though just the sound of her voice was enough to give a man a splitting headache.

This unfair tactic reduced her to no more than a few head-shaken mutterings, and when she peered at me with an angry tear in one eye I gave a little wobble of my own head too, for solidarity, though I was sure I was being inspected through the curtains of his eyelashes. Then, just as I was considering the option of heading back out into the rain to find some more neutral place of refreshment with a public phone, he opened his eyes as big as though he'd had a light-bulb revelation – all was suddenly so quiet you could hear the throb of his machine again – and placing both hands flat on the bar and bringing an astoundingly friendly face right down close to mine he gave the mildest rendition of the Swiss customs officer at Basle breaking into our compartment in the dead of night.

'British?'

Felix Rowan, British passport holder, born 2 January 1941, height 5' 4", eyes blue, hair sandy, no peculiarities recorded: 'Ah!'

'Good ears,' he said. 'Two very good years I lived in Great Britain.' Slowly he made himself tall again, grin widening further and further, arms straightening in a standing press-up, warm brown gaze fast thawing my icy blue. 'Ristorante Portofino. Dean Street. Soho.'

'I'm from up north.'

'Tottenham?'

'North England.' Blinking a bit at a neon strip-light overhead. 'Is there a phone here?'

'So why come to Rome?'

No fault of anyone present if at that moment I felt another wave of unsteadiness, followed by that sick abandoned feeling like all your insides are being removed by suction. Then in the long mirror behind his back Nana's good eyes found mine again and steadied me enough.

'It's the number I need.'

From my shaking fingers he had plucked a small folded paper serviette. As he opened it out on the bar top between us, bending to peer closer at the faint pencil marks in one corner, a small hairless patch showed near the crown of his head, and when I looked again his fingers twitched across it. Then they went feeling for a pen inside his jacket.

Carissimo Tonino mio, how horribly well I remember trying to feel nothing while I had to watch the blunt end of your red plastic biro tap down the curling edges of that precious scrap of tissue! Moisture on the counter turned tender paper to chrome as you went on to try to trace the faded figures she wrote for me when our train was marooned in Chiasso station, to demonstrate what she called their fortunate symmetry: 680086. But your ballpoint could not even mark the paper, the damp patch tore. 'Madonna!' Lifting a flap in the counter you stepped down, two feet shorter, my own height exactly.

'Go with me!'

'But ...'

No buts about it, kiddar. Next thing like a dumb dog I'm trotting on the end of an invisible string after a pair of smart two-tone shoes heading for an open doorway between an antiquated cash-till and a tall weight machine proclaiming *IL VOSTRO PESO! IL VOSTRO DESTINO!* Straight through that door gap we go and on down a dark passageway, our four heels resounding on bare wooden boards past the sudden stink of a toilet and out into a storeroom filled with boxes and bottle crates, lit only by a very small window. A clatter like hailstones overhead sounded like there was only a tin roof to keep out the rain. I don't know what he shouted over his shoulder but I got the message. The length of one white jacket arm was aimed at the biggest stack of crates. On top was a telephone, crouched there like a black cat cornered. A hand appeared behind his back, up from under his armpit, fingers waggling.

'*Numero!*'

I couldn't move, certain that just the strain of trying to get out her name would make me crack up... But then the fingers relaxed, the hand retreated, and a long cool trickle of rainwater ran out of my hair and sweetened a corner of my mouth. Things were slowing down enough for a person to think. Fiddling with all the buttons and zips on my sopping parka for the paper I knew wasn't there, I hit on a simple escape plan. He guards the phone, I go back for the number and just walk straight out to find somewhere they let you make calls unsupervised, and on the way I'll calm down enough to think up the one redeeming word that will stop her slamming down the phone the moment –

I'm staring at the serviette, it's fluttering in front of my eyes. Big joke apparently.

'*Grazia,*' I manage, heart sinking. Panic, Feelie, and you go right under, never come up after three.

It was the dippy look on my face that set him off, if I know Tony. His shoulders shook with laughter, silent helpless laughter, and the hand with my only lifeline crushed inside it rubbed that bald patch like it itched and itched. Only after he saw nothing he tried could make me even attempt a smile did he land me a good-natured punch just above the elbow, where even the lightest thump will give you a dead arm. But pain can help. It made me suck in much-needed anger as well as air, and I stepped back clear of his swing and left the bugger to it.

Knuckling a last laughter-tear from an eye corner he consulted the crumple of tissue I'd first seen wrapped round her Italian State Railways doughnut in the early hours of the morning while through the window we watched grey drizzle drip into a lake of fog. His forefinger stabbed a dial hole.

'Sick.'

'Hate.'

'Nothing …'

I went deaf. His mouth carried on shaping the only sequence of numbers to summon her up in the flesh, the dial spun round and back and round again, rain coursed down the windowpane like a dirty curtain blowing to and fro, and nothing could I hear. The soundtrack had failed but the pictures ran on and this well-meaning clown intent on connecting me to an impossible reality had no notion how far he had overplayed the part. Frowning at the roof with the receiver over one ear and a finger plugging the other he now had sole responsibility for whatever might happen. Let him find the words, and the right language too …

Mouthing something he pushed the phone at me. Life was in the flex, a trapped voice buzzed behind the holes. The professor, I knew that even before my hearing fully returned.

'I came with your daughter, Sir. It's –.'

I never thought her language could sound so harsh.

'It's the landlady's son. Is she there? I know I can speak English.'

'Mister, I afraid …' In a sort of English, but quieter and fading to a sigh.

'If she's hurt, Professor, hurt about anything, I can come round and explain, no trouble. Tell her, please.'

'No trouble.'

'Definitely not, definitely not. Only I've no address, see. So if it's not too much trouble could you please kindly explain where you're at, Professor like, where you live right now. If it's not too -'

'No.'

'Thank you, thank you, I knew you'd say that. She told us loads about you. And your wife. And I've got your book. Your very good book.'

'No, no!'

'I mean it, very good. You could sign it if I come round. Just to talk. And help you understand. And meet you after all this. And your wife. All this time. And help us too.'

'No come round.'

'But someone has to listen.'

'No come round, understand, no come round! Understand? No come round again, mister!'

'I don't know other people here,' I pleaded so quiet I don't suppose he heard. In any case now the line was purring. I'd been hung up on without so much as '*arrivederci*'.

The barman, after relieving me of the phone like easing a glass out of the fingers of someone asleep, gently pushed me between the crates toward the exit.

'Who is professor?'

Yes, who? Her dad was meant to be ace at our language, the only male in the family she ever talked of. Claudia had no brothers, only lovers. The brilliant pianist too sensitive to play in public? That voice still growling in my ear didn't fit her soppy talk of long pale fingers, it would better match the horn-rim specs and curly white chest hair of the man she called the lecherous goat, at least as old as her dad, who drew the loopy diagram on the back of his little photo which lived in her handbag along with other choice mementos. 'My life chart. In crisis I go to him.' Call back now and say if she's not there I know where and if she doesn't come to the phone I'm walking under a bus.

Only right now, leg dragging past leg, I was a good way down the dark passage with the barman still propelling me from behind, leaving at the most just five more steps in which to prove how much she mattered to me, for all her treachery. Not three, when I heard her say again in the usual hushed tones of reverence, 'His wisest advice was always to brush my teeth, no matter how bad things get. Understand?' Understand, understand – is that all you say in your family? Sure I understand all about the randy owd bugger, and this is a country where they shoot lovers' lovers …

Extra pressure in the small of my back made me realise I'd come to a halt, and the barman was likely repeating himself.

'Have a drink, mite. Then try again.'

Now that's what I call wisdom, and stepping out once more under his long bright tube-lights savouring a mental picture of the horny old goat bleating for mercy then butting air as bullet after bullet punched red holes in his fleece – I got a nasty surprise. Propping up the bar with one broad knee and a slab of forearm for extra leverage, beaming at me like a long-lost friend, was my relentless pursuer, the giant postcard tout. The last bullet got him smack between the eyes.

'Felix, whadyawan'? More postkarts?' he called, turning the volume up even higher when I skirted his beckoning hand and kept on walking: 'Father Adam? Curse of Jesus Apollo?'

The last of this earful was equally for the benefit of two newcomers who were sitting at the only table in the place. He looked fairly nondescript, she definitely belonged to the opposite sex to the one I'm lumbered with.

'Madame, Monsieur, regard! Wunderbar Postkarts. Ask my friend. All wonders of Rome right here!' And slapping the bulging satchel at his side he started unbuckling the straps. 'Bankrupt me now!'

The pair at the table didn't bat an eye between them, I thought to show they'd seen enough Roman wonders for a day. No show, both were sizing me up with blatant curiosity. 'Claudia …' I breathed.

I'd spoken the spell but it was the barman who saved me. In all my confusion I'd seemed to hear the conniving little chuckle of a drink being poured, the perfect excuse to turn my back – my good strong back, she used to say – and sure enough, waiting on the long flat of the bar like a thoughtful present from hell stood a small stemmed glass brim full of something colourless and smelling sufficiently lethal.

'Mind your head,' he cautioned under his breath, corking a squat brown bottle labelled GRAPPA JULIA and parking it right next to the glass. 'This country is beautiful but the people all bloomin' crazy. Crackers like him. You all prefer Rome, I prefer London. I lived right by White Hart Lane.'

'I'm not from London. Lived there a bit like. But not' – oblivion was in my grasp – 'not from it. That's what I was getting at –' whiff of surgery about it, dentist's fingers – 'at the time you asked before.'

Julia was at my lips when I heard a tongue cluck, followed by a low whistle like some use to call a dog. It was Postkarts of course, posting me a knowing wink as he tipped a phantom glass down a mock-greedy gob: Watch how you go, foreigner, here a real man sinks his liquor in one.

Right you sod, and in one gulp I'm sinking it like – *Madonna!* – kill-or-cure medicine, molten glass... Weak-kneed feeling again, but only for a second or two. Next moment it's uplifting, like being told to step over the side and walk the waves and finding you can do it. It earns me a thumbs-up from my self-appointed watchdog before he launches himself off the bar toward the two at the table, head down with that big mouth of his working like on a gumshield. Leaving me alone with Julia and her keeper.

'First day in Italy,' I pitch across the counter, feeling more buoyant than for a long while and not too bothered if the thread is lost. 'First and last. Oh aye, tomorrow you'll see us on a train to England!' Big decision that was, finally. Chuffed with myself, puffed with my new freedom, I looked triumphantly into his baffled eyes. Then at Julia.

'So maybe I should be fitting in some of the sights before I go, wouldn't you reckon? The old Colosseum and that. Always wanted to see this city of yours, Signor, more than any other. Talking of which, same as you I found a job down London. Right up until the fatal day I upped and joined the Army.' At the same moment both of us noticed I couldn't seem to keep my eyes off Julia. 'Funny, and there was I again but yesterday.'

'But yesterday?'

'A different day.'

'Yes?'

'Yes.' Because he's pouring me another painkiller.

'*Grazia mucho.* Caught us on the hop you did, starting straight in with the Deutsch. Dean Street? Sorry if I shouted. Just off Shaftesbury Avenue, right? So chances are we've likely even seen each other before, providing we were there the same time. Aye, must have walked right past your door any amount of times, my own place of work being only just over in Oxford Street.'

'Evening Sir, welcome Madame. A nice corner table for two? My first lesson off the gaffer.'

'Me and this pal from home, we made straight for Soho our first night.'

'And how are we today, Sir? And the lady? But my second lesson fetch me a whopping headache. A quid is a pound, twenty bob. A bob is a shilling, twelve coppers. Two shilling, one florin. A crown does not exist. A half-crown is …'

As he slowed up, dredging his memory, I scratched my chin with my shoulder to check out what was happening behind. All seemed peaceful enough. Postkarts was dealing his wares onto the table between the bowed heads of his latest victims, every card a winner. 'Holy Father. Mouth of Truth …' Captive audience as they say, which was more than could be said for my efforts to earn this extra grappa.

'Lack of the necessary will be the main reason I never tried what did you say they call your restaurant, that first night or any other. Hot dog and onions off of one of them stalls on wheels was generally the best I could run to, I'm afraid …' Just tell her I rang to say I don't want her. 'Which is a shame.' If she doesn't want me. 'Want to hear my first experience of the fleshpots of Soho? Losing thirty bob at the three-card game in Old Compton Street in fifteen seconds flat! And me and my pal were keeping it for a peep-show. Round King's Cross has a similar sort of feel, wouldn't you say? Seedy but fascinating. In its way. Anyhow – *grazia mucho* again. No, hang on, how's it go in Italian? Cheers, in English. Some say cheerio. A person from here learned us some Italian ways, only they don't seem to want to come back to us right now.'

'*Cin-cin!*'

Aye, chin up, bonny lad – and next instant that second grappa is blazing like lighted petrol in my mouth, and on down the hatch to stoke the dying glow of the first. Likely she purposely wrote a wrong number. Or it truly was the professor I spoke to. Or some sort of family friend, not a lover.

'Where is she now?' the barman starts in of a sudden with no prompting from me, spreading his arms as wide as they go. 'My London woman, mite, my sweet Suzie. We have a good relation, smashing, then all finish when she call me infidel. Why?' he demanded of each open palm as though comparing fate lines. 'Suzanne, how can you say all these bad things? The one I love is you, only you. You are my total existence. I repeat and repeat it, I cannot exist without you. I telephone many times but she is not very comprehensive. Many, many times, like you. Then my poor mother report sick so I come home to assist my dad here. And Suzie she no come to the station ...' By now he was bent half across the counter, chin almost touching my shoulder, gloomy gaze fixed on the wet street outside. So I turned to consider the state of the weather too.

'I know what you mean.' I twitter, hardly caring what comes out as the brief good spirits drain away at thoughts of the pair of us at Victoria Station only yesterday morning. 'And that same person I mentioned gave out it might still be red-hot here. And then look at ...' A burst of rain struck the glass door sounding hard as peas. Postkarts glanced up and then dealt another round: 'Hand of God,' he crooned, 'The Pity of Michelangelo ...' I know that I should have shown more interest in the barman's own lost love, but his gaze had strayed so very far from the here and now, and for me a glazed look is as infectious as a yawn, next moment I was miles away myself. 'The prevision is no more depression,' were I think the last of his words I registered, though I didn't stop looking into the mournful circles of his eyes.

I saw a duck pond with half-a-dozen ducks standing round it in teeming rain, all with tails turned to the water save one at the edge sipping liquid mud. That was one of the many times our train slowed far from any station and she used the spine of her Russian novel in Italian to wipe the steam from the window, and past the dripping hole she made drifted a red-walled farmhouse and that ring of ducks and a wire fence beside a long dirt road with a cyclist in a yellow cape pedalling past through long puddles. The middle of nowhere shrank from sight as his lids narrowed a fraction more to fix on something somewhere behind me.

'Not long before Dover,' I said reviving enough to let him in again on my wandering thoughts, 'our train went through a not long tunnel and out we came in solid rain.'

'One-a-minute!'

He had suddenly exited through the flap, taking Julia with him.

Now nothing came between me and the reality of my depression. It faced me in the mirror, framed by foreign bottles, sore-eyed and badly in need of a shave.

No come round again, mister. I knew you'd say that, and you can tell her if she's nowt better to do she can come to the station to see me off. See me off! Get it? I love her, Professor, she is my only existence – understand, understand? – tell her I love her, tell your crazy daughter I never loved her so much as this minute now, tell her I deserve one last chance, tell her I'll kill myself! *Mister, I afraid ...* My insides were swimming again, stomach walls tightening to fight a sucking sense of vertigo, that sinking feeling, all thinking shrinking to a sick gap that hadn't contained a scrap of food since a continental apology for breakfast on the Italia Express who knows how many hours gone. Faint for lack of solids, awash with bitter alcohol, I beat off the last waves of nausea by leaning harder up against the bar, eyed by that spitting image of a heartbroken lover who never more shall have what he cannot exist without.

RUTA. STOCK. ZUCCA. VOV ... My dazed gaze circled among the bottles, all stocked with different shades of liquor for suicidal customers' release. *STREGA. DIESUS.* Which one downed fast enough stuns instantly? A flutter of movement drew my eye. Blinked into focus it became the kind old lady, black shawl drawn tight over her white hair now. She was standing on the weight machine, terribly small under the big brass lettering, shaking her head over and over at something unpalatable about her weight or destiny. Yet when she stepped down I saw the same sweet smile that had made me yearn to share all my troubles.

In the glass I watched her cross the room. Passing between my position and the group at the table she muttered something. She was at the door before I nodded, possibly she'd wished me luck. Fanned by the sudden draught all heads in the room looked up to watch her back out through the windy gap fingering the flying ends of her shawl. There was so much thought for others in the way she dragged that difficult door shut after her. What was her destiny?

'All stand!'

I must have been deeper in my own world than I realised, for those two commanding words in authentic English gave me quite a turn. The young bloke at the table was on his feet now and facing me, holding a glass level with his pale gingery moustache. Same glass as mine only his was full. He looked authentic English too, a real live upper-class twit, snub nose dotted with pimples above the regulation sub-lieutenant's tash, his wisp of manhood to fortify the plummy voice.

'Pure rot-gut,' he intones.

'Not got ... ' I stammer. Smart-alec officer types have a bad effect on me until I can figure out their game.

But then, as if at a secret signal, my mate the barman pops up behind the counter again, Julia to the rescue. Refuelled, rearmed, straightening to my full short height I take careful aim at the stranger's glass over a big silver bubble still skating on top of mine. Let the bugger run on his line like any big fish, sooner or later he'll wear himself out. His bird keeps her seat but crosses her long legs and raises a glass of something too.

'The Queen!' he chants solemn as a toastmaster. It makes her snicker into her drink, teeth tinkling the glass. But since he keeps a straight face so do I. And down the hatch with *numero* three.

'Lovely lady!' he snorts, planking his emptied glass down on the table hard enough to crack it, and sitting abruptly.

'Attention, Felix!' yells Postkarts, one finger aimed over her shoulder like a revolver at all his cards spread on the table. *'Whadyawan?'* Some folk cannot stand being ignored an instant.

Her man, plainly another who hates anyone else getting a crack at the ball, spares me having to answer: 'Guessed you were a kindred spirit, old chap. You passed the acid test.'

‘Good on you,’ I go, not quite not stammering even yet.

‘We had a bet,’ his lady-friend starts explaining in that soft panting breath they keep for divulging secrets. ‘Kenneth bet you were English, I bet something else. The loser buys the postcards.’

‘Postkarts!’

‘My dad was a Jock, if that’s a help. Born and bred in Scotland but came down to England at thirteen years of age.’

‘Oh Scotland, bonny Scotland!’ she almost sings. ‘And are you equally knowledgeable about Rome too?’

‘Not exactly. Not that – ’ the tiny metal crucifix in the pit of her throat recalls Claudia – ‘that’s surprising. Only arrived today around three. What they said the delay was –’ poor plucky Nana out there still, hunched black sponge under teeming rain – ‘was all the flooding. I don’t suppose anyone can tell us where to find the Colosseum?’

‘Negative thinker!’ crows her bloke, fitting a pink freckled hand over her naked knee.

‘Kenneth favours a whole set of the Sistine Chapel, which is seemingly this guy’s favourite. Only I don’t get such a big charge out of Michaelangelo. Do you?’ Instead of me she grins up at the hulk in the check coat who flashes her the kind of smile I’m in no shape to deliver. Next, leaning back in his chair and putting on an American accent much heavier than hers, her hoity-toity Englishman levels at me: ‘Say pal, how come you get jumpy every time she opens her mouth? Mother Nature?’

‘Now Ken!’

‘Baby?’

Somehow my eyes still won’t stop jumping between the

little dancing cross and his leering fluffy upper lip, when they take a dive down a hole opening in Postkart's face.

'*Achtung Felix!*'

'What's eating the little fucker now?'

I'm on the weight-machine, the first stage of a panic escape bid. The platform is rocking under me like a first pair of roller skates, and when I glance over my shoulder I see Postkarts making straight for me. Clasping the solidest part of the machine I try to fit a coin into a slot which is just a fraction too small. But he walks past, I hear his boots banging down the passageway. And I've guessed the right coin after all, it slipped out of my fingers into the intricacies of the machine. A metal disk opens like a big eyelid to reveal a firm red arrow pointing at a whirling dial of numbers. My weight won't keep still but my destiny is clear enough, printed on a strip of nickel in the lower half of the window.

SOLO TU
PUOI ESSERE
L'ARCHITETTO
DEL TUO DESTINO

I'm nearly at the door when he stops me with an outstretched hand. 'Free up, man! Kenneth from Manitoba, Else from elsewhere. And you be Felix. Funny ole name. I'm no great archaeologist but if you want my advice forget the Colosseum. Go for the Pantheon, there you're straight under all the marble garbage and you'll see for yourself those old Romans had nothing to learn about engineering.'

'We popped in when the Victory parade was a wash-out. And now I've totally fallen for Roman bricks, they're so much thinner and flatter than ours.'

'They could pump the Colosseum full of water then hold sea battles. Did you ever hear that?'

'My husband calculates Ancient Rome lies exactly four metres under the modern city. It's kind of his job.'

'I have to be going.'

'Take care.'

'Be good.'

I didn't stop running until the very top of that street. There I ducked into the last doorway and looked back, panting. If anyone chose to come after me now I had a fair start. Half the length of a football pitch by the looks and uphill every step of the way. I'd reached a crossroads on the crest of a hill somewhere in the heart of Rome but there was no view – no white Colosseum – among all those buildings, in all that rain. Four ways to go, or in my case just three since I didn't much care for any stretch of the road I'd come. From now on I intended to suit nobody's schemes, Felix Rowan was travelling solo, taking any unlikely turn, the first gap in the wall.

All the streetlights came on. The shining empty pavements and the fact it wasn't yet quite dark made it seem a rehearsal.

Somewhere out of sight a man checks the wall clock one last time, an ordinary bloke like any other, and then he pushes the big button which gives a whole world-famous city light. Now there's a job which would have been up my street had destiny chosen to treat me different. People look up and wonder who did it and how he feels. Next moment they've forgotten they even asked themselves a question.

Someone was outside the bar. The barman, as I could see by his white jacket when he stepped from under cover of the awning. Either he spotted me or guessed I was the sort to head uphill, for he began flapping his arms in my direction as frenzied as a ref trying to settle the human wall before a kick at goal.

I slipped from shelter into slanting lamp-lit rain, and turning left set off at a trot.

2

Funny how things go. It's the mother who's half-English yet her big crush on England comes from the hundred-per-cent Italian, her precious dad. Nobbut best British baccy for him, all top pipe varieties, and I'm told he's the proud owner of a prize collection of old briars and such, which I will say does make him sound a right schoolteacher. Daft about Harris tweed and all, she posted him half a roll before we left, and I hear in their living-room stands a fancy cabinet chock full of choice Scotch whiskies, the little brass key to which lives on the end of a gold chain tucked in the professorial waistcoat pocket. What we're missing, eh Signor, what we're missing!

Still, I must say in some ways I was quite looking forward to my first chancy meeting with the prof and his missus, feeding them a load of cobblers about our interesting family connections, lah-dee-dahing the pair of them all the way up the garden path with me gob full of marbles. Because you can bet she never let on what a commoner I am. Not to the full extent at least, not till now. Aye, odds are she sat up half the night with the two of them getting it off her chest, spreading the muck. If home is even where she went. Though I'm not going down that road again, oh no. So.

So anyhow all her dad's talk about ye olde merrie England apparently gave her the notion that life for us natives is some sort of permanent garden party, the kind of England we only get to see on the news. All the time she was little, and not even so little I reckon, she says she pictured Great Britain like this big round green island full of mansions where seeing they rule half the world and don't need the rest there's nothing left for all the people to do but go out visiting each other to talk about when the rain is ever likely to stop. Thought it worth mentioning, these old delusions, so you'd find it easier to believe when I reveal what she was studying. That famous first day I brought her home she told us she was in England to write up a university thingummy on historical perspectives about social relations in our area or some other such grand title, never mind precisely what, for that too was forever changing. Apart from this causing Mam to crook her pinkie next time she lifted the teapot we hadn't the foggiest what she meant. Because, see, it wasn't what anyone would ever think, not the social whirl in pubs and clubs or the dog's life most have in the collieries, or how they make out down on the farm or shepherding up in Indian territory – no, she was in our good old working-class neck of the woods to study up the high society! Which rules pertain and when, who married who for what, in other words social relations of the toffs in castles and country houses who owned the pits before nationalisation and never went down them. Types like her own mysterious blue-blood granddad. Types such as definitely we're not. Man alive, I'd give a lot to have been a fly on the wall last night to hear all the garbage she was spilling them! Likely getting another instalment right now.

3

On main streets it was a rain-swept pavement, in the winding death-trap cobbly lanes where cars and scooters shot past winged with spray like motor launches or water-skiers it was no more than a man-wide gap between the old house walls and anything on wheels. Still it was my beat. There were others on foot, but if a pedestrian is someone with more time for a road than a wet space to sprint across in emergency with his coat hitched over his head then it looked like I was possibly the only one to qualify.

I don't mean there was a shortage of Romans, only that the foul weather kept them off my beat. At times, if they reckoned I'd strayed so much as an inch out of mine, a wave-winged four- or three- or two-wheeler would head straight for me with honks and shouts and all hands going like at a jugglers' reunion. The shops were shut being Sunday, but drinking-holes and eateries were filling up fast (hard for an outsider to tell apart, for nearly all contained millstone cheeses and dangling ham haunches and big old spiled casks, and in one window a tank of live eels, in another a boar's head with a heap of sausages filling in for the rest of it). From the other side of steamed-up plate glass or a big iron grille over a ground-floor window the smudge of a face could sometimes be seen marvelling at the endless flood and anyone mad enough to be out in it, and at times I passed (fearing-hoping for her) some solitary figure waiting for a bus or a friend in the shelter of a shop doorway or a house entry as big as a tunnel leading to an underground city. But the wet gap apparently remained the undisputed territory of one lone out-of-season visitor with no guidebook to help him find the Colosseum, let alone his lost hotel and the claustrophobic sixth-floor bedroom that had witnessed the sort of ordeal that has driven better men to tramp the gap for life. How I longed to make her suffer to see what misery she caused, though equally I knew I was in no state to confront her. Reducing that risk might have been easier if I'd managed to get her address, instead all I knew was that the parents had recently decamped to what she said sounded like another soulless modern flat, so any new-looking street might be hers. I felt safest in the old dark lanes.

Not all living things spurned my beat. For a start there were enough cats about, no end the more you looked, poor skinny starving strays barely half the size of ours. Up one dead-end alley at the back of a noisy restaurant I startled upwards of a dozen picking through an open sack of garbage, though all I remember in detail now is a mini off-ginger tom with flashing eyes and the last joint of his tail apparently his only living parts guarding pale worm-coils of spaghetti. Retreating the way I'd come, I almost fell over a three-legged soggy bag of fur and bone squirming out of a drain hole she likely lived in, and she hopped pretty trustingly beside me for a while along the gap. Later, rounding another corner in the dark, out of an upturned muck-bin whizzed a grey blur, legs whirring, straight between the wheels of a passing truck. That gave me a horrible homesick wrench on our Smoky's behalf, her old pal Scratcher came to grief like that, and when I saw no mess in the road I looked all over to see what shape she was in. Under a parked car I thought I spied a tight ball of fear then saw it was the differential. A nearby van on four flat tyres turned out to be home to an entire family of spitting adults and shivering kittens, all looking fit enough in the circumstances: seven pairs of glass eyes giving me an alley-cats' picture of myself, upturned head of Enemy Man peering between hard toecaps.

Needing a slash, I ducked into one of the gloomiest brick holes I'd seen during all my wanderings since the weight-machine told me to work out my destiny alone. The high stench of rotting cabbage and seaweed in there was proof enough I might well not be the only dweller-in-the-gap circulating in these parts, and in fact just as I was set to go I heard then sighted a shrouded figure in a high hat racing straight for my hideaway, splashing knees-up through the torrent coursing down the alley. It dived inside at such a lick we all but collided.

Panting with the effort and the relief he parted a rustling rain cape, releasing among the other stinks in that blind grotto the all-too-familiar whiff of damp uniform cloth, the human equivalent of a sodden sheepdog. Police! Stealthy as a Roman cat I inched deeper into the gloom praying he'd be done quick, only to be scared nearly witless when he launched into a pitch-perfect rendition of *La donna è mobile,* fast gaining in power as he savoured the booming acoustics of the place. I carried on aiming sweeping x – y – z's at the wall to sound like rain, trusting that so long as he didn't fluff a high note he'd have no notion his audience wasn't only imagined. It may sound hard to credit, still I swear that even in that tight spot it crossed my mind that if only in these last days I could have released a fraction of my true feelings in strains like that she might have modified at least some opinions. She's nuts on opera, whereas even after all these years in the land of music I still don't get what they have to shout about. But that's just another of life's little ironies, stick around in the same relationship long enough and you find not everything has to change. The first time we made love she announced we had nothing in common apart from needing someone, now I catch her agreeing with friends we're a perfect example of the true meeting of opposites.

Buttoning up, the singing policeman turned back to face the flood, only whistling now. On his head was a helmet similar to a London bobby's though squatter and in place of a truncheon at his belt I spotted a shiny leather gun holster. Armed patroller of the gap! And then, just as I thought all danger was past, I came within a whisker of exposure. He had started doubling on the spot, slapping his sides like a substitute warming up on the touchline, when fetching an extra-deep breath for one hair-raising moment he turned right round to face me, beaming like the man to save the match. Then he dissolved in rain.

During that anxious minute or two my eyes had adjusted to the dark and what they saw was that I hadn't retreated to the back of some kind of brick cave, I was already a good way down a narrow vaulted tunnel which must be leading somewhere. Was this the way the lions entered? An opening showed ahead, then my feet took me into a waterlogged courtyard.

Courtyard is too grand a word. It was no more than a square pond at the bottom of a brick shaft with a few unlit windows cut here and there in its tall sides, and the open sulphurous sky so high and small and flat above it might have been a leaky roof. One half of a broken porcelain sink shivered dirty grey under the rain-pelted water, and fixed to the wall beside me on a level with my drowned shoes a blocked downpipe bubbled frothy scum.

So lonely and forlorn was that sad hole that it felt like no accident to have finally fetched up here, uppers-over in water black as hate with only the sorrowful sounds of rain and a strangled downpipe for company, and my sick-drunk head tormented by a storm of humiliating memories and voices. Tormented, but then miraculously part-comforted, for as they settled into some sort of order it was plain all were combining to spell out nothing less than a revelation. And since it's not unrelated to the genuine miracle of my present occupation I'll give the drift.

It's true I've a bit of a punch-drunk boxer's gait even when sober, all the same one cold quip of hers was much too close to the mark not to set me off: I'm fond of him too, she goes, of course I am Mrs Rowan, but sometimes I do think just from the way he walks anyone can see he has no sense of direction. At that, far from springing to my defence, in jumps the woman who put this zigzagging ape upon the earth: She's right, son, you're all talk, all talk and no action, time you got off your bum. To which Miss Smug-as-they-come: It's dreadful what the Army did to him, I know it is, but I do agree with you that what would save him from becoming a permanent failure is to acquire some sense of discipline by applying himself – to something, anything. Fair enough, I eventually conceded (since there was no denying I'd been longer than usual between jobs), fair enough everybody, just so long as no one in this kitchen is talking about Army-type discipline drilled into your head by grown men who never learned to count past three, that got us nowhere, or the civvy street equivalent which is clocking on and off at a plastics factory in unsociable hours. Need I say, my words did nothing to advance my cause, in fact as usual I realised too late I'd have done better to hold my tongue, because for the rest of that night goodness only knows how many honest livelihoods those two workhorses proceeded to dream up for me, all to their ways of thinking a sight more appealing and no worse paid than eight hours at a stretch minding a machine which without human aid can turn plastic tubes into plastic cups at the rate of thirty-two a minute, or my other dead-end pre-Army job as dogsbody in a London department store. Ah, but never this. I had reason to ring back after all. Still sure I've no notion where I'm heading? Same place as your dear friend Charlotte. Archaeology, baby. Manual labour as intellectual as the way it's spelled. And tell the prof.

At that time Charlotte Robson was doing archaeology in Leeds but in the college holidays was generally to be found on the Saturday night and weekday dinnertime shifts behind the bar at the Two Hearts of Gold, and once I finally accepted I was never going to get off with her we became real mates. She opened me up, she was a good listener. My soul-mate I called her, though Claudia could never stand the word or her. Anyhow, way back in my first Charlotte-besotted days, one rainy out-of-work morning in the hope of improving my repartee I went so far as to delve into some deep-looking tomes in the archaeology corner of our town library which happens to be just a few doors down from the Labour Exchange and a cosy place to sit and peruse the sport pages while waiting for the pubs to open, even maybe get out of your skin a while by scouting for a bit of sex and adventure along its dusty shelves, and anyway the daft thing about it is I might have saved myself the effort because when it came to the crunch not one obscure fact that I'd laboured to unearth and memorise from the weightiest of all those tombs of words and engravings came to sound in my mouth like anything more than uneducated ignorance. She laughed so helplessly it just made her even more unattainable, and after that all I could find to say was I'd only done it for a laugh anyroad, joking that now at least I knew I didn't dig archaeology. My sole other early brush with my possible new career was long years before that non-event, back before Mam finally let me quit the Church Lads, one long winter's evening when before letting us loose on the squash and biscuits they had us all fill the two front rows of chairs at the Institute and sit still in the dark and harken to endless long-fangled words spilling from the mouth of an ancient gadgie with thick specs who kept the other rows spellbound for what seemed like hours about how he dug up and pieced together every pot after pot which Mr Pattison from the corner shop's magic lantern threw up for him on the screen, and having finally got through the lot he ups and says unless it's stretching his esteemed audience's patience too far we would now proceed to view every pot just once more extra-closely in the certain conviction that no one could fail to share his delight in the hitherto inexplicably overlooked hypothesis that for the very reason no two pots were exactly alike, that each in the subtlest of ways differed ever so slightly, in all probability the entire priceless collection was the product of no more than two, at most three, exceptionally skilled pairs of hands from the very same ancient workshop. And now, but only now, hallucinating in a flooded backyard somewhere deep within the actual ruins of Ancient Rome, the passion for their unusual profession shared by that droning shadow-man and my Two Hearts soul-mate at last began to make some sense to me.

Up to that time I'd had no more use for past history than my dad's brief experience of life and our combined collection of *Sunderland Echo* match specials, but now that I'm settled in this historic city with a dream job and a family of my own, and even more as between us we dig deeper into this big turning point in our lives, I've come to appreciate how a backward glance can throw quite a lot of light on what the future brings. It's only natural, Charlotte explained that same put-down afternoon, to want to preserve any little item from the past no matter how trivial if only for the comfort of knowing that people who died so long ago shared our same basic needs and desires. Think of it this way, Feelie, she says, looking that deep in my eyes she aroused my most basic needs and desires all over again, nothing else of them has survived yet the human race has. Are you with me, or are you just pondering another bad joke? With you all the way, Charlie, says I. Only instead of going out with me that weekend she went off to London with busloads of college-scarf types to march against the Bomb, like a lot of them do, and the following Monday dinnertime when I thought just a little bit guiltily she started to pull my first pint I could tell it knocked her back a bit to hear me say I was pleased she didn't have her priorities wrong. And I wasn't taking the Michael this time either, or not only. The wall was already up in Berlin and it wasn't to be very long before the great Cuba scare, and in any case my eyes had been opened for me during my soldiering days regarding what could be in store for all life on earth – and who in honesty can say anything has since transpired to free us of the weird thought that unless both sides in this Cold War find more use for the hot line we look dead on course for a man-made version of the big bang they now say brought everything into existence? They can bury their heads in the sand as much as they want, I can hear Nana chip in, but a brain like Bertrand Russell surely has a point. But enough talk for now, time to get back to the action.

Archaeology is everywhere, starting right beneath your feet, and to me most of the wall bricks did look unusually thin and flat. Bending down, I graffled about in the freezing soup of leaves and scum to test the hunch, leastways go through the motions. Relics of the recent past were everywhere, and trivial enough to break all but the hardest heart. A broken match. An old screw. A hairpin with some of the original hair attached, colour uncertain. But we are men of discipline. I chucked them back and looked about for more sensational discoveries.

A ruin of a motorbike, minus engine and one tyre, stood propped against a barred cellar window on the other side of the pool. Drawn to any black hole, I plodged across to it, ploughing through a brain-shape oil slick at one point I now suddenly recall, splitting it in two silvery eels. The unsteadied water lapped at the bike's exhaust. I had to squat right down to peek through the bars into the depths beyond the grating.

Four metres? Eyes met only black but other senses registered the steady ping-pong of water dripping into water, plus a foisty whiff of creepie-crawlies. On my hunkers there, up to my neck in metal skeleton, seemed a suitable moment to offer my little audience some random thoughts on *no-come-round-again-mister*. Human remains, I dictated just a shade too fast for that round kiddies' writing of hers, may upset the odd superstitious egghead – or gullible numbskull, I cackled mirthlessly doubled up before the blackboard – but to more level-headed freethinkers such as your speaker tonight they are rich food for thought, proof that Mother Nature has nothing to learn about engineering. Time strips even the most perfect body to the bone, and if anyone present thinks it's a shame then they haven't yet seen the beauties I keep in my specimen cabinet, even put one or two in the acid bath myself. With the skill, the exceptionally sensitive skill, of a world-class lover I carefully scrape away layer after layer of surrounding mud from what a common laywoman like you would take for a lump of dirt, carefully recording every millimetre scraped away, each being a century, until I am left with just a speck of something no bigger than this chip of rust or is it old paint lodged in my thumbnail. Instantly identifying it as a minute spelk of human thigh-bone from some long deceased forgotten female, to general amazement Prof Rowan declares that given the necessary funds he'll happily architect you a life-size working model complete with real red monkey hair of – next slide please, Mr P! – Neanderthal Woman crouching in a putrid swamp and …

It struck me (cramp was stiffening my neck and the need to change position likely brought the change of thought), it struck me that any normal female remotely in touch with man's basic needs and desires would straight off twig there was actually a subtle connection between my new choice of profession and the jolly workers Nana loved to relate her wee Robbie found far more entertaining than the clowns the first time she took him to the circus, those glorified binmen as nimble as acrobats who skip round the ring to sprightly music raking over the tracks of vanished horses or shovelling up the steaming leavings after the elephants have shambled out holding tails. For years after I first heard how her adored toddler clapped and laughed at the sight and finally set the whole tent going my day dreams regularly featured me running away with a travelling circus, though my sights were set on making it to lion tamer. My brilliant father may have died before my memories properly begin, yet no one meant more to me when I was growing. But we're getting a bit too far before our story.

Just above the cellar window was a horseshoe nailed

wrong way up. I tried to work my fingers under it to pull it free, leastways twist it round, but though the old brick crumbled like salt the thing was too deeply embedded. All the luck was slipping out.

Someone coughed.

My heart leapt into my mouth, I almost choked. My head swivelled round at once but my eyes found nothing to fasten on until near the tunnel exit they settled on a second opening. It resembled another tunnel save that now I could just make out a ghostly progression of stairs. In there, in there had to be something living and breathing. It took a very long silence to settle my jitters and convince myself that what had given me such a fright was only some poor little Roman cat retching. I started making my way back toward the stairs, miaowing softly and sending big ripples across the pond. I heard them slap the brickwork.

A disembodied skull with bony hands cradled beneath weirdly lit eye-holes materialised on the stairs, swiftly assembling into an old man sitting about a quarter the way up holding a lighted match to a fag-butt nipped between his lips. When the butt failed to respond to the kiss of life he spat it out into a cellophane bag filled with other dog-ends. The bag lay between his boots.

Since he didn't look up I knew he had been watching all the time. Wading closer, I thought if this were only England I might have explained that as an angler I was well used to standing about in water half the day. He was sat on a thin cushion of newspapers.

'Sigaretta?'

That one word, the fact it was just one, told me he

surmised I was probably not native to these parts. Such be the instincts of those who dwell in the gap.

'*Scusi*' came from me after a bit of a think, simultaneously shaking my head and patting a side pocket of my parka bulging with Rome's wonders, since they might have been taken for a crushed pack of twenty. *SCOO-zee.* When he lifted his eyes nothing showed in them, nothing at all. His voice was a low sing-song.

'*Joe?*'

'*Felice,*' I go, having reached the bottom of the stairs now, first tapping the chest of *Fay-LEE-chay,* then the air between us two.

'*Tu?*'

'*Bruno.*' A long curving thumb tapped the top button of his coat then tilted my way:

'*Embriago?*' The blank eyes did now seem to be directed at mine.

'*Londra,*' I tried after a moment or two, noting a slight quaver in my voice. I'd had to tell a downright lie on account of the fact that London was the only English town I knew how to say in Italian. Still, if *LAWN-drah* could be taken to indicate which division of Britain I hailed from then it was nearer the truth than what might be their twisted version of Edinburgh. But no matter, for with that our overtures seemed to be ended, leastways so far as he was bothered. His mouth had clamped tight as a padlock, nose-tip almost meeting chin-end, like Nana with her teeth out after a story she realised too late she should never have told, to show you'd not prise another from her. Spreading his hands in his lap, he settled his skull against the wall.

The strange eyes stayed open, but in other respects

he might have nodded off. His breath came so regular and from so deep inside, a steady wheeze and sigh, his whole upper frame rising and falling powerfully under the buttoned topcoat. It was very dark on the steps but after climbing a couple more and leaning in close I could make out every feature of his face. Through yellowish papery skin stuck occasional bristles like fine splinters of bone. But it was the pupils that were the queerest thing, milky drops centred roughly on the eyeballs.

Some feelings cannot be faked. Unfussed acceptance of your lousy destiny, the old fellow's bitter-proud sense of leave-me-to-my-fate, are qualities we could all do with at the worst of times. I too was an unloved reject, given the push by a demented disciplinarian who knew fine well how my life was already a long catalogue of disasters: half-orphaned before the age of two, bossed about at home and school and work, escaping south only to be reduced to volunteering to serve my country, thrown in the guardhouse for nothing – why, I could even have told him how it feels to tramp the streets of another stony-hearted metropolis strapped between two heavy boards – in short I felt so sick at the injustices meted out to all life's permanent failures that I came perilously close to placing in that vacant-eyed derelict's filthy palms one of the hanky-size Italian notes which for her useless sake I'd foregone untold pints of good mind-dulling ale to amass. Truthfully I didn't wake up to the full effect he was having until I felt something going for my purse. It was my own right hand attempting to break into the button-up pocket Mam sewed inside the front of my jeans as a precaution against Italian thievery. That sharp brought me down from the clouds.

I told my fingers to halt and wait for further instructions which soon followed in the shape of a silent order to scratch where there was no itch, just in case old Bruno's gap-instinct had got him supposing his silent appeal was about to be answered. No amount of fellow feeling could allow me to forget for a moment that what little cash I'd put by had either to see me back to England or subsidize a spectacular liquid suicide.

Disappointed, likely downright disgusted, he bent to rummage for a more smokeable dog-end in the bag of dumps between his boots, breaking into a long spasm of coughing but managing to sit upright again by the last high hack. Again he tried to light up, coaxing and wheedling behind sheltering hands, and again it was as useless as hoping to suck a tune from a broken mouth-organ. Then shyly he showed me a little book of matches tucked inside one wrinkled palm. Empty. Now I realised the double row of torn stubs was putting a question for him.

'No,' I said trying to make it sound as Italian as I could (*'NOH'*) but his blank unblinking stare soon had me repeating it again and louder, shaking my head for extra clarification. What more could I pull out of the bag other than *'Scusi, Signor'*? We've had it before (*SCOO-zee, See-NIOR*), now doing service as polite back-up for those two over-blunt negatives and for the fact I'd seen no call to memorize the finer details of Sig. Smythe-Johnson's visit to the tobacconist. Forgetting a slight hiatus in the Army, my mother's second-most odious lover turned me into a non-smoker from the age of eleven, anyhow I reckoned an Italian-speaking chain smoker could safely negotiate her own.

What possible interest was any of this to Bruno? He shrugged it off easily enough. Me too, settling down on the same step as his boots and tab bag. Finding nothing to say, I looked at the rain.

Same for him, so did he. Just an ill-assorted pair of lone gap-dwellers sitting together on a flight of cold stone steps gazing at a black square of water which from this angle looked deep enough to drown in. It was so uncannily quiet in that lightless place, with only the many little noises of water and our two pairs of lungs. Like being lost at sea, from all sides came swallowing sounds. The broken sink had sunk almost right under. The bike lay tipped on its side, one handlebar raised clear of the drink like a stiff dead arm. One rainy morning just four weeks back I'd told her I loved her to distraction, and now I was considering how many ways there are to end life and most cost nothing.

Bruno was the first to concede that having nothing to say did not minimise the urge to speak. Strong bony fingers felt my shoulder.

'Eem-bree-AH-go?'

'LAWN-drah,' I go again, seeing it more or less passed before. But it was not what he was after. To get my full attention he nipped my right ear between two fingernails, a favourite habit of Bill Hakes, my least favourite uncle who we've no space to take revenge on right here. It seemed he wanted me to turn round and watch carefully as he pressed his bare skull against the wall and bounced a hard pellet of phlegm round his stringy throat like a pea in a whistle. The faded pupils slid up and out of sight behind fluttering lids, and popping one thumb in his mouth he sucked on it so

long and hard I was beginning to think he'd given up on me again. When out jerks thumb aimed straight in my face.

'Eem-bree-AH-KOH?!'

'SCOO-zee?'

He rocked his old head from side to side in a grand pantomime of despair and then took me through the whole routine again, eye whites rolling skywards as he sucked on both thumbs now, guzzling like a babe at the teat long enough for me finally to see he was draining an imaginary bottle, possibly two, Adam's apple core yo-yoing away as if good gut-warming vino really did flow past it.

Who me?

Willingly would I have provided a full and proper account of my every act and aspect, only that what little I'd so far imbibed of *Vacanza in Italia* was not up to explaining that appearances can be deceptive and in my case the object was not to get dead drunk but to die a death of drink. For good measure I might have added: And if you think I look anything like you do, amigo, I'm nearly there.

I'd had a few, more than you yet know. But I was still in control of my actions, perfect control, and I wanted no wrong conclusions drawn on that point. To sharpen it, that point, I tried to get to my feet. I say tried, because on the way up I had to sit down again quick when Bruno grabbed the soaking tail of my parka, making frail efforts to rise as well. Fly owd bugger, mean enough to mock another broken soul yet not so happy to be left behind to your fate ...

Gripping him by both sleeves of his ancient coat, that big ungainly coat favoured by all dwellers-in-the-gap, I hoisted him to his feet. No feat in itself, Bruno being three steps higher. Immediately he pushed proudly free and hockling loud and long to dislodge that tiny pellet of mucus sent it skimming past my head into the hungry deep. Next, using the wall for a prop he came down to the foot of the steps, one at a time, then turned and stooped to gather up his property. The newspapers got painstakingly folded double and in long wads shoved under a string belt round his waist after he'd slackened it off, and the cellophane bag he sealed with a thick rubber band which he kept rolled round his wrist. Ready now, bag lifted high, he straightened to face the climb. With one boot in the air and both hands high (yes *amore*, I'm thinking of the twins when they were small enough to gather under each arm!) he resembled nothing so much as an overgrown bairn expecting to be helped upstairs.

I'm none too big, and even though Bruno was no heavyweight he had a good half-head on me. Still, by wrapping my arms round him from behind and locking all my fingers tight together under his ribs and wedging my chin in deep between his sharp shoulder blades, I managed to lift him clear of the ground. Seemed I'd taken on even more work than I thought, there was not just newspaper round his waist. And what a queer daft back-to-front embrace it was, hugging an elderly stranger on a steep stairway so dark that I had to feel my way upwards step by step perching his rear on alternate knees with most of the rest of him crushing my chest and half my face. I was in the identical fix to the sucker on the lower end of an upright piano being humped upstairs, with each step the weight seems to double yet for the life of him he cannot let go. Snatching a swift time-out before the last few steps I told my brain to catch another train of thought. Uncle

Harry gave me that tip, one-arm veteran pitman-cum-mariner Henry Crosthwaite the winter he moved in with us, some wet cold night before posting me out to fetch another scuttleful from the coalhouse. Whilst engaged in heavy manual labour, says he wiggling his toes inside his fender-warmed slippers and his comfy backside deeper into our settee, set tha mind to wander, young 'un, so 't body can get on wit' job in hand wi' nowt to tell it's tired. Harry originated down Selby way, as you can hear.

Well now, to render the idea, here's me posting my brain off on a forced hike which runs something like this: If I live we two will hide out together in the ruins scavenging for recyclable smokes and fighting the cats for scraps and digging away side by side we'll turn up all sorts with trivial bits going to museums and the rest sold on the side for decent wages and better tools for us poor buggers-in-the – - When my floating right foot, having toiled in careful tandem with its left twin all the way up eleven steps in blind faith there's a twelfth to come, treads thin air and finding no support for its sole plummets what seems like not one but the first of a thousand-and-one missing steps, in the split of a second landing flat hard smack down on solid stone which feels like it's come slamming up out of the bottomless pit to save it. As you'll appreciate, with the shock of that and all the extra weight on board I could hardly stop myself departing from the vertical, and the pair of us I don't doubt would have keeled right over but for the old chap's arms, my spare set of emergency arms, connecting with solid wall and suspending the pair of us more or less off the horizontal.

At times like that I've noticed your thoughts don't fall

as fast as the rest of you, as though taking flight in the belief this is your last fall. When most were more or less back in place I found they'd fetched a weird conundrum from wherever they go: I'd not be in this daft pickle, Claudia, if God existed.

Never mind, that was no moment for philosophising, for no way was old Bruno going to be dislodged just yet. First he tried walking his hands up the wall, and when that failed to shift his donkey he started hacking with both heels to convey he needed to be carried up still higher, further away from the slightest danger of drowning in his sleep.

We were on a narrow landing at the start of a second flight of stone stairs, though not quite so many this time, thank the Lord. Craning to peer round his skinny neck and filthy collar I made a careful count and study of those eight steps and before he could cripple me for good and all I was staggering up them two at a time shrilling through mouthfuls of gritty coat as though our English numbers are blood-curdling curses:

'Two, four, six – done!'

This time he was no trouble to unsaddle. Panting as though he'd done all the work he shuffled off and started acting like he needed to kick a hole through the wall ahead.

Myself, I leaned against cool brick, wanting home, wanting quiet, wanting my unfathomable bird. From deep inside the wall some kind of hidden water activity reached my bursting head. Accelerating, dragging, skipping, never a moment steady. 'Feel, again it missed a beat,' she said against my throat, and the memory should have made me weep. 'Go back to that doctor.' 'It never happens when he examines me.' 'See a handsomer doctor. God, pet, it truly does have a life of its own ...'

'*Arrivederci*,' I'm muttering aloud now, for the old fellow has suddenly grabbed my hand, toothless mouth stretched in a grin running almost from ear to ear. Only this isn't goodbye. With a wild welcoming look he's tugging me toward the wall against which he was denting his boots.

I can have taken at most two paces forward when a big section of wall fell inward creating a blinding door-shape burst of light. In the light stood a ranting woman of a fair height and nearly as bald as Bruno draped in black from head to toe and shrilling fit to wake the dead. Bruno's old lady, bawling him out for toddling off down stairs he couldn't climb?

The old fellow dropped to his knees before her, eyes white as eggs in the strong fall of light as he reached out for her flying hands. When he caught one he pulled it to his lips and kissed and kissed. She tried to snatch it back, but cunningly he clung on tight and so got hauled to his feet.

What followed looked to me like a reconciliation. She bent her head, nodding attentively with tight-pursed lips while he whispered in the knot of her ear. Only when her head lifted did I see we were not dealing with a woman at all. Over Bruno's sad scrag-end of neck the startling face of a middle-aged priest clad in ankle-length black lobbed a surprise question at me in a language only a few less miles from home:

'*Sprechen Sie deutsch?*'

'*Ja!*' A reflex response, so true only up to a point. Up to the miniscule point a soldier can reach in twenty days of manoeuvres with the British Army of the Rhine, not excluding twenty anxious minutes struggling to manoeuvre his way out of a well-defended brothel in Lüneburg. I tried to think up a more non-committal answer to the next question whenever it came, but all his sentences ran together at the same breakneck speed without ever sounding as though when printed in their weird Dracula script a question mark was wanted somewhere along the line.

But Bruno was soon in a far worse fix. In his unsteady grip he held up high his precious bag of smokes, swinging it to and fro to catch the priest's eyes while they went on drilling holes in me. A flat hat I hadn't seen before, possibly to impress the padre, was crushed on the back of his head. In the powerful electric light those soggy dumps inside their bulging cellophane looked as unsmokeable as cockles in brine. Pitiful were his efforts to please, he strained to smile right to the very back of his gums, when all of a sudden his tongue stood out rigid and then trilled an ear-splitting scream.

The bag had slipped from his fingers and burst open on the stone floor.

We all looked down. A soggy mush of tobacco and tissue was slowly sliding out of the split bag like something half-digested. A lot had already settled on one toecap of the priest's well-polished shoes. The shoe's owner sounded short of wind. Bruno was panting too. As for me, I listened hard for the water clock but all I heard was the priest's breath coming shorter and shorter as he screwed his voice right back up to its topmost pitch. Then, firing as fast as a Ferrari, he reeled off what can only have been something to the effect that poor old Bruno was a walking disgrace to the human race, anathema to the Holy Church of Rome and an abomination to his maker in heaven, amen.

It took about three seconds. Choking like a cat on a bone, shaking his head and his hat, the nearest I had to the makings of a friend in Rome retreated to the top of the stairs and began to feel his way back down, back to the cellars and the rising flood.

4

Listen hinny, my so badly missed Nana would go, listen hinny, whatever they say at school you have a good brain in your head, a good common-sense brain, and a common-sense brain is like a well-tuned wireless for your personal education and enjoyment, so don't ever stand for other folk finding you nonsense stations like Etheria or Jerusalem. Yet when my mother took up with the Spiritualists you'd think Nana too might have had thoughts about joining the club. See, she always upheld that the same night my father went missing she woke with his voice in her ears, a cry to tear the heart from her breast she always said, though straight after she was comforted by the feeling of a warm presence in the room. Warm as though the coal fire was glowing, she'd say, and she went back to sleep. The point being there was no fire, and next morning when she opened her eyes she knew he was gone, it was that instant in the night. She kept it to herself, hoping against hope it was only some dream thing set off by all her worries on his account, and then of course the awful telegram came. Well, freethinker or not, that episode in the night was too powerful to put down to simple coincidence, and too unsettling to keep quiet about for ever. In her book of the universe there was no such thing as a spirit body, which was of course Mr Telfer's explanation, yet she knew she had to face people with something. So she settled for calling it a mother's instinct. Made her feel a bit more in control, I suppose. Even so, you can imagine how the whole story gave Mam an inch or two of rope if ever their talk came round to what she herself swore happened to her at Marsden.

Nan always made sure to say that no matter what that soft-head woman thought she sighted near Marsden Rock it was no proof of survival after death – we all see things which aren't there but only simpletons think they exist outside their own brains. As for her own queer experience, she'd just say what in the end was so surprising? In his last moments he longed for her, cried out for her, for her and her alone, who hushed his first cries when she brought him into this world. That's how she was made, my fabulous Nana Winnie, none too bothered about others' feelings, and a little bit prouder than needs be.

Oh aye, a mother's instinct! No use asking by what actual mechanism his last shout before going under could travel so many miles. I for one never dared. Because I'm sorry to report she grew more bitter with time, more inflexible like, whereas I'd say Mam has mellowed more. And yet one of all the many things I loved about her, my old *nonna*, was how she could never stay very long out of laughing. And it was laugh till the tears come. Equally, mind, she could be a terror when she took the huff, though even for that I could not help loving her almost as much. All the same, thinking back, with them two in the same room I don't recall too many laughs. The proverbial hammer and tongs, Mam and Nan. Half my earliest memories feature their two heads haggling on.

Both had the fighting spirit, see, in itself no bad thing, only the shame was seeing it so wasted fighting each other. Had my dad lived longer I'm certain he'd have known how to mediate, seeing that in their different ways both worshipped him. Instead for that hard task they used me. Now of course I'm not saying there weren't good reasons for their flare-ups, there were, a lot of good reasons, for each had to take some very hard knocks over the years. But then again they weren't above rowing even over that, who was hardest done by and all! Never did it come to blows, mind. I'd have heard about that soon enough, seeing I had to hear about everything else. No, their tongues were their chosen weapons, and lethal enough.

Except Mam had to watch hers more. See, for all their warring she could never allow herself to forget that at the end of the day that interfering busybody Winnie Rowan was the one person in all the world she had to be certain she could always count on. I mean where I was concerned, and my sister too of course before she changed and was taken away. Mam needed to know she could dump us on Nan when things got on top of her. Until such time as she was back on a more even keel, if you see what I mean. But so what, I was well used to that too, all part of the scenery. Because when you're little everything's okay so long as all goes as you expect, and you know no different. Plus you know you're loved. I was just so very lucky to have the both of them, whatever they made of each other. Right up until Nan was hospitalised round about this time last year I tell you I could flit between their two separate houses as easy as cats seem to pass through walls, to cite her very own words.

5

'Bitte!'

'Ach ...'

'Bitte sehr!'

'Ach sehr!'

In a tight spot in a language you hardly know you're at the mercy of the very few words stocked in your head. My instinct was to stay with Bruno, keep him company in the gap a while more, but my limited German propelled me in the opposite direction. Also, that man in the frock was so sort of rudely polite, so dead certain anyone would jump at a chance to visit his shrine. And that is how, without a pull or a push, I found myself walking down a long white corridor with the rainy night and my companion in misery firmly locked out behind a receding procession of shuttered windows. I was even leading the way, one nod of his head gave me no option but to step out in front of him toward a far-off model of the Madonna holding out her arms to us from inside a bright loop of fairy lights.

Religious conversion, like treatment for people off their rockers, is known to work by administering shocks. And the loud reverend at my heels had straight off steered me into a shock situation: collision course with the Mother of God. Not many would put a foot wrong if the police only had the grace to step outside when a man drunk-in-charge sets out to prove he can tread the thin white line, just as walking a parapet would be a doddle if you could forget you're ninety-nine floors above the street. Which is all another way of saying that walking that unrolling length of white linoleum which even when I was way past halfway still looked another ninety-nine feet long would have been as easy as standing on my head if I hadn't been put off my stride by the fact I was being very closely stalked from behind, and growing qualms about how to handle the emotional meeting ahead. To avoid the tearful gaze of the pale lady whose heart goes out to all who stray from the straight and narrow, and impress him, I was working too hard on where my feet were going, which soon made that white lino a line so wide more or less any part of it could be the middle.

When I glanced round his fixed grin was scant comfort. There was nothing for it but to trust in my own god, the one who makes everything turn out okay in the end, and looking up from my footwork I hurried on the sooner to be done, steering a steadier course by keeping the whitewashed walls at equal eye-distance on either side, though still without a blind notion what to do once I'd have to pull up somewhere just outside toe-kissing range of Mrs Christ looming ahead of us now almost twice as large as life – when only a few paces short of the point I was rescued by Nana's good sense working in me yet: Pretend you're Catholic, goose! One glimpse of the vicar's white locks bobbing past the privet outside her window was like a red rag to a bull to Winnie Rowan, but that didn't stop her having an equally blind spot about popery and a long list of their crafty ways of recruiting. Hang your head, hinny, prayer looks the same in any language.

Just an instant before having to put that theory to the test the sound of a sudden hiss shocked me to a standstill. A couple of yards to my left I could see it still escaping through pursed lips shrilling like a puncture in a terribly old man's face. He was lying in bed just inside an open doorway which I'd been too otherwise engaged to notice. One watery eye held mine, the other was squeezed out of sight behind a mass of wrinkles.

That dormitory was massive. Under a high roof arched like a chapel ceiling stretched rows of beds down each long side, the same layout you find in an army billet or a hospital ward, with a metal locker between each bed. And each bed housed an old man. Some lay buried under covers but most sat up propped on pillows. All wore white pyjamas, and every eye that was open was trained on me.

Not a whisper. Maybe they needed permission to speak, or had expected Bruno to show up and I'd surprised them. The whistler seemed to find it harder to focus now I stood so near. On his locker was a stack of yellow paperbacks tied round with string.

'Andrea!' the priest cried drily. 'Andrea!'

A monk I hadn't noticed before since he was kneeling by a bed administering nose drops suddenly stood up straight and hurried across. A monk, because his robe was not black but brown, he had a white cord for a belt, and his toes were bare inside his sandals.

'English!' he announced as though he found it written on me somewhere, after a quick inspection through the thick bottle-lenses of his glasses. 'Come!'

Obediently I set out after his flowing skirts, on balance more relieved than not to discover an English speaker among that crowd of gaping ancient Romans. He set a fair pace and all, bare round heels bounding down the long aisle between the beds as though he had tennis balls for feet, though this time I had less bother steering an even course being the man behind. In fact I was swinging along right in step long before we reached the far end of the room, where he veered aside at the very last bed and without a word yanked the covers off a small shape in very faded white pyjamas. It lay flat on its tummy like a new-born baby, and when the fluffy head lifted off the mattress you could almost hear the weary brain: What in God's name? But one look at the brother's face set the wee man inching to the side of his bed to peer over the edge as though he'd woken on Beachy Head. He rolled out in a slow motion of agony.

Stooped but standing, barely shoulder-high to the bed and trailing a grey towel, he slid slow pained curled feet in the direction of a nearby doorway. The priest arrived in time to help him through.

Meantime Andrea was dragging out a big sacking screen which lay propped against the wall, and which he quickly unfolded round the bed and me to form a flimsy room. Squeezing back in between the screen and the wall he straightened the sheets and pulled the blankets up to the pillow again.

'My son, if you do divest and sleep...' Leaving the consequences unspecified and my side of the bed untucked, he backed from my presence with head tipped against praying hands and those giant eyes closing behind their magnifying lenses. '*Buona notte.*'

'*Grazia,*' I muttered, feeling no more gratitude than Rome's most senior citizen at being evicted from his own warm bed. The whole weird turn of events had me so rattled that I was beginning to fear I'd been lured into some long-rehearsed routine these religious fanatics had hatched up for the next heathen to happen into their trap. Something along the lines of that latest torture method of inculcating a foreign language by setting a tape recorder to repeat the same phrases under your pillow all night: sleep a lapsed Protestant in the warm imprint of a lifelong Catholic and ...

In strides the creepy priest with a pair of white pyjamas over one arm.

'*Nein!*' – Felix backing away nearly knocking over the screen.

'Attention!' – Brother Andrea raising an anxious shout from the other side.

'*Bitte!*' – childless padre compelling his terrified guest to attend to the fact that the institution pyjama is a single convenient sleep-suit with only four easy-to-do-up buttons.

'*Nein nein nein danke sehr mein Vater ich bin das Englisch Tourist!*' – ex-church parades defaulter Pte Rowan stammering out his longest-ever sentence in German.

'Andrea!'

Enter interpreter, glasses flashing. 'How do you do?'

'I've only this one night in Rome, tell him, and yet to see the Colosseum.'

'Wet to see Colosseum.'

'It's to help me find my hotel and catch a train to England.'

'Abraham got us a villain ...' sputters the priest before revving off on another lap of breakneck German, possibly Italian, with co-driver Andrea frantically trying to cut his speed by tugging and spinning levers and dials on an invisible control panel in the air between them.

Keep your head, hinny. Remember you don't use a French letter as often as non-Catholics reckon you should, and if you haven't the immaculatest conception how to spout a Latin prayer just remind them it's been a dead language since we kicked the Romans out ... But instead of having to face the full fury of the Inquisition right there and then it seemed I was to be put through my paces elsewhere. With no explanation I was directed to follow the course of the tennis ball feet once more, bouncing through the doorway through which the little sleeper had been propelled.

On a bare mattress next to a row of washbasins, curled up under the towel he'd brought along, he looked lost once more in the world of dreams. The monk was attending to something else. Down at the far end of the washroom he was unlocking a massive door with a big key he'd unhooked from the wall. The size of that door, the long creaking yawn as he eased it open, already told me what was on the other side.

Very dark, even for a church.

'Old,' he whispered deep in my ear as though any noise might waken demons in the eerie place. Past our two long dim shadows all I could make out was a potted palm set on shiny marble paving, and a holy water font wrapped round half the side of a pillar.

'Come,' he whispered, 'Come, you tourist of history.' His goggle eyes wheeled like they followed black bats circling the night in there.

When he padded into the dark I kept close to his side, thankful for any company. Dipping fingertips in the font he tapped the bridge of his glasses and crossed his heart, lips working fast and silent as though cussing himself for forgetting something important. No way could I perform what I'd just witnessed, paddle two fingers in magic water and cross myself, though I will never forget the formula the Major used to chant when bestowing drunken blessings on me and Smoky prior to retiring to my mother's bed: spectacles, testicles, wallet, watch. This was Claudia's scene, not mine.

We were not in total darkness after all. Night had thinned to gloom, I could make out stone ribbing high overhead balanced on giant pillars like monster bones. I touched a leaf of the palm, the spiky blade was as dry as straw.

Side by side we set out toward a faint glow ahead, the only apparent source of light, skirting the long chill glint of a marble side-wall. More disturbing than the vague whiff of incense was the graveyard smell of cold stone, everywhere. When the wall finished we turned to face a gilded ironwork gate beyond which burned a single candle set on an altar made of a big slab of stone laid on spiral legs. The flame was knife-thin, tapering to nothing under a massive altarpiece which was just a gold-framed black hole. In the unwavering light the winged babies' heads and botties modelled up and down the walls looked as dead as rock.

Some hope, Nana, if they expect a pagan like you made me to bend a knee and pray for souls in purgatory, grovelling to no God on the hard floor till …

My eyes had taken a moment or two to adjust to what they were ever more intently exploring inside a long glass case positioned between the altar legs. Stretched out on silvery satin and dressed in see-through lace was the first dead person I ever saw. Her stick-thin arms were crossed over her high rib cage, and on each withered finger black as pipe stems, even every toe, were gold rings set with precious stones. A rope of pearls coiled up her neck column. What was left of her face inside a lace bonnet fringed with flower-shaped jewels looked made of tough gristle and leather. Tense and fanged it lay on a velvet cushion, tipped to watch the worshipper through big eye sockets like dark glasses without the glass. And deep inside each brainless hole a twinkling diamond looked straight at me.

Mouth gaping, gagging, I tried to turn away, but wherever my eyes went they found Claudia's last vacant stare floating inside the skull of the skeleton bride. Two cold gems willing my extinction were the only constant points as everything else swirled around me so convincingly that I knew for certain the entire hollow mountain of stone and plaster was hovering in air the very last seconds before caving in – unless by turning the other way I could twist it out of its top-heavy spin. Reeling into the open space of the nave, gulping for air against the suffocating terror of burial alive, I tried to beat off the sickening sensation of old mortar loosening and slipping everywhere by shutting my eyes as tight as they go. One hand banged something that was not cold, moving too but it was all I had so I clung on tight, hugging it as if it was alive.

My other hand closed on something almost human.

Cloth.

A hot clot of vomit shot up my throat, filling my mouth like salty barracks porridge, gritty and gelatinous. The cloth I clutched in my fingers steadied. High in my chest my heart was thrashing wild as a budgie when a hand reaches in its cage, small and unimportant but with such a bold fear of death. Somehow I swallowed the entire foul mouthful and managed to breathe deep and fast again, and, strange, I could smell the bitter sweetness of Claudia's cigarettes.

Gently the priest removed my hand from his arm. We were embraced by a column in the nave beneath a high half-circle of gold. All I saw at first was gold, then other colours forming shapes inside the gold.

Tall men in white togas with white faces and black beards and big sad dark-ringed eyes stared steadily past our heads as though they saw straight into heaven. The toes of their sandals were all in line, and shoulder to shoulder they stood on green and gold grass on either side of a blue band of water. Like twin lines of chorus girls all pointed sideways at the miracle in the centre. It was Jesus standing on the water. He had the blackest beard and the biggest and kindest eyes of all. Two long feet resembling thick pinewood chocks with carved toes floated him on the rippling waves. Curious fish swam up to look. One palm was raised to show a round nail hole and his other hand held a white scroll: EGO SUM. At

Marsden Rock my mother saw my father rise naked from the sea and longed for him to tell her how to live.

'Son of Man,' whispered the monk, glasses glittering like big gold tears. 'So beautiful.'

I couldn't tell if it was very old or just newly done.

I've been back several times since, and I'm still not sure of the answer. The guidebook says it's restored almost out of recognition yet it never fails to move me, in part on account of this first time I saw it. I took our fourteen-year-old Roberta there not long ago, after she said a poet they have to read at school made her feel so low she almost wished like him she'd never been born. I don't have her mother's faith but I thought the outing might help. Holding hands beneath that wondrous picture I gave her a fairly accurate version of the events recounted here, and long before the end I hadn't seen a smile light her face like that for days. I found I wanted her to know that in some sense this is where she originated, and possibly the only virtue I have worth passing on is the knack of floating.

'Electricity cost more than bread,' was the monk's sole other comment, uttered as he reached behind the column to switch off the lights.

As they walked me back up the darkened nave I was almost sure I heard a grumble of thunder along with all the rain blattering the roof, and despite the holy mood was reminded of how I first learned the easy German word for rain from the red lips of my very own fifty-year-old Fraulein while fumbling for any excuse for why I felt off form. With foreign languages it's as well to use a word before it goes again.

'*Regen*,' I said looking up at the shadowy ceiling arcs

and seeing her motherly body again. But the two men for all they were moving might have been posing for the part of saint in a mosaic. One by one we wheeled aside to enter a low alcove enclosing a small side-door with a handle in the shape of a big iron ring. The priest gave the ring a half-turn and beckoned to me to take a look outside.

All I saw was a black puddle boiling with rain. I wasn't wrong about the thunder though, it was rumbling on all sides now as though a battle for the city had just got under way under cover of night. Tanks toppling the outer walls, artillery bumping like quarries in the hills. 'O duly begot …' The two men of God, heads bowed as they exchanged anxious words, glances meeting, might have been praying together for a favourable outcome.

A blue-white flash of lightning lit up the mud of some sort of garden out there. I glimpsed stone benches, weird statuary, and beyond a long low parapet the domes and roofs of a fabulous city.

'Can you see the Colosseum from here?'

If a reply was ever uttered it was never heard. A thunderbolt broke directly overhead in two sharp bangs loud enough to lift the roof, and well before the echoes died we were shaken rigid again by a long splintering racket which seemed to set the old building rocking right down to its foundations, rattling the iron ring in the priest's grip. We'd have had no more warning if a jet fighter had flown in low behind its twin rockets detonating split-seconds before its deafening arrival and angry acceleration in pursuit of a distant hum. Gunfire crackled in the mountains of the sky. Then came the peace of rain on leaves.

When the priest tried to close the door he found a foot

in the gap. They made no effort to stop me, one even shook my hand. The door stood wide open again, the night was as black as before.

'The love of God go with you, my son.'

This time when forked lightning cracked open the sky I saw the statues seemed to stand on tombs. Through driving rain I scampered straight as a frantic duck for a hut-size chapel or chapel-shape tomb, not sure which, clearing a long shadow that I took for an open grave just before I reached the place. I was soaked right through again and the porch gave a bit of shelter.

Looking back I saw no trace of light. Would she not be shocked to the core to know my last night on earth was spent in this inhuman place? Claudia, I think so much of you. Do you?

I shivered. Water was seeping into my shoes again and I remembered she was heartless. There was a favourite story of hers she got I'm sure from that frigging astrologer about an Irishman laid out for dead who when the wake gets out of hand sits up and swears at all the mourners for disturbing his rest, and it was easy to imagine nobody this side of the bricked-up door behind me would have been any the wiser had some poor soul boxed by mistake spent his last hours beating bleeding fists on the unforgiving lid screaming for help. Bugger her. Nothing I endured would alter her mentality, not even if she heard I'd perished by lightning in a flooded foreign graveyard, face-up like a drowned rat. Peering into the darkest corner I kicked out for rats, then scarpered like greased lightning when another flash showed a gap in the parapet and through the gap gleaming cobblestones set close as teeth.

Now down steep slippery steps see me go skidding two at a time and on over hard-backed black cobbles toward a solitary street light swinging on a loop of cable in the wind. It swung my shadow up and down an uneven wall as I trotted past. Turning into an inhabited street I slowed to a fast walk.

High up ahead a single lighted window flickered silvery blue amid the black bulk of the rest of the buildings and it gave me a quick consoling picture of her sobbing her heart out with only a shorting night lamp for company, face pressed into a tear-soaked pillow howling for her indifferent lover. Rain thick as teardrops whirled round the inaccessible room, but once I drew level and looked up again I saw human shadows coupling on the roof beams. Pressing on, glad I was drenched, a blood-curdling shriek split the night, then a single pistol shot from down a side-alley answered at once by a long shuddering burst from some automatic weapon, Tommy gun or Sten, repeated again and again behind more windows filled with the same nervous light. The shooting became shouting, then loud catchy music, brisk follow-my-leader stuff like a military band heading a march-past as I neared a small darkened bar where a big TV screen packed with ecstatic faces cheering a man and a woman in the back of an open limousine lit up the otherwise empty room. On every side and on every level now window after window glowed as white as washing strung across the lane, all dimming together as the crowd effects faded. For a couple more seconds the silence was electric, broken only by the patter of rain and my footsteps. Then along the curving lane behind me gathering swirls of rubbish as it came swept a great gust of wind and applause that whisked me round a corner and down stone steps to be greeted by claxons and lightning exploding like flashbulbs as I emerged, alone, on the kerb of a main street along which bumper-to-bumper traffic including a long lighted bus was moving at not much more than walking pace under the relentless rain.

In the headlamp beams it fell grey as sleet. Two deep, all rolled in the same direction, the wet street hissing under the slow-turning tyres like boiling fat. Behind streaming glass and the half-circles scooped by wipers, stark white and black in the glare of lights, the drivers sat expressionless, even those leaning on their horns. One bent across the passenger seat for a good squint at me, and when I turned away I saw in a shop window a red wig made from all her hair.

The sore, soft, yearning hole she left in me expanded so fast all my innards melted and rushed to fill the void, generating intense heat. To preserve that precious warmth I spoke her beautiful name to the mud-splashed side of the bus, searching for some reflection there, yet this time what seemed also to up the heat was the sight, or sense, of a sleepy-eyed plump lass slumped against the window glass suddenly jerking her head out of the warm crook of her arm as from a fierce embrace. What made her look out? Startled by strange eyes in hers she swallowed, tightening her lips. Are pangs of loss and lust no different?

The bus groaned and pulled away. The ticket collector in the seat behind leaned forward and patted her shoulder.

SNAK BAR.

The double doors were locked and chained, but when I pressed my nose against the glass I could make out sections of the menu on a board beside the bar. *Caffe Hag. Birra. Ponce. Hot Dog. Sandwic.* One or two hot dogs on an empty stomach would provide a good lagging of pork and bread to soak up the fatal dose required, reduce the danger of it coming back up fast …

I nearly jumped out of my skin. Honking the first six notes of *Colonel Bogey* a long white Maserati or some such show-off crock had ridden two tyres right up onto the pavement behind me, all lights flashing, scaring me even tighter against the door. The smart-arse behind the wheel barked out something which set the blonde beside him shrilling with amusement. Mindless Wop thought he scared a thief or something.

My last meal wouldn't be anything to enjoy. Spaghetti in beer, say, slops so sick only a death wish could force them down.

HELL UND DUNKEL

It was a German beer house plum in the middle of Rome of all the places, done up in Alpine style with heart-shaped holes in its wooden shutters, which were all shut. But light showed behind the door. Through a heart-hole I spied stools upturned on long pinewood tables, and a black Alsatian with ears pressed back and hackles rising. I stopped rattling the door. I don't like dogs and dogs don't like me.

So who puts out the big lie that on the Continent you can get a drink and a bite to eat at almost any hour? Worse than bloody Blighty, everything shuts down early, leastways Sundays. And for the matter of that, what time of night is it? The street was emptying fast. The bus, last in the line of traffic with its only two occupants sharing the same seat now, rounded a bend trailing the sound of deep frying under its wheels and the twin ketchup stains of its tail lights.

I never reached that bend myself. Up a side alley I sighted neon lighting, a blue scribble above an arched entrance to what might well be a restaurant. *Grotta di Nettuno* I deciphered as I drew nearer, amid further signs that it was quite a posh place, and posh places generally keep their own hours. A fancy brass lantern illuminated what looked like a well-packed menu in an elaborate gold frame. Stronger, warmer light fanned from the door as a hand in a white cotton glove emerged to test the strength of the rain.

Hearing steps, the doorman opened wider to see what was coming, and before he could change his mind I was inside.

6

Whoever knows what will happen? Maybe it was no more being so very used to each other without a break and that gives moods more time to come out, then the endless rain, and in any case I think it's fair to say the journey felt not quite right for either of us. An entire day and night of drizzle and dark, and when in the morning it was wet even in Italy she seemed only to want to finish her book, when not fretting we were running late, saying this is Bologna when it should be wherever.

I held my tongue and told myself getting here was the thing, reaching Rome intact. And when at last we pulled in to that colossal station anyone could see at least one of us looked chuffed enough about it, heaving our things out front through the crowd into a jumble of cars and yellow trolley-buses and green taxis and every detail fresh, fascinating, and the air twice as warm as England for all the wet blowing. And I daresay they'd have read it in her face too, if for other reasons: Rome at last. Myself, I truly did feel things were due to change, the worst was behind. New lease of life, same feeling I had the only other time I got out of England, three weeks soldiering in Germany, though we saw more tents and tanks than Germans and only got one real night of freedom.

Her feelings? How should I know, she took good care to hide them until she blew up in the hotel. You could see she was back on home ground though, the way she stepped off that train and straightway went as Italian as all the rest of them. Jumped the entire taxi queue ignoring the stir! I had set down my bit of gear at the back behind the last in line, and this almighty case of hers filled to bursting with all her books and papers, and when I look round, no Claudia. Queer moment, close to panic. And next thing I see her waving from out the front cab! Some acted like they wanted to lynch us, understandably, and I thought the driver was creating as well, instead it was his wild welcome aboard like we're all old friends, and she's going something like, *presto, presto,* pile them in! Using the Italian even on me. I had like a little tug-of-war with one old thing, she kicked my shin. Some change, I'll say. Barely a word out of her for umpteen hours stuck in that Turgenev affair or doodling in the steam on the window, and now here she is delivering a git big long streaming mouthful round my head to the effect I think that if anyone objecting's clocked more kilometres and two hours late into the bargain we'd be only too pleased to swap places and stand an extra hour in the wet. Suddenly I saw she belonged, how she blended with all them unknown faces laughing and shouting and looking in to see the kind of man a blazing woman like that would choose, before we're scooting off into the storm chucking it down like sacks of coal on the roof. I did feel sort of proud, I must say. Of having her like. And her having me. And definitely he seemed to think we were something special, the driver, asking if we're just married and stuff. To shut him up she gives the hotel's name and address, which unfortunately I didn't quite catch it all, and away we go.

To me in the back there with our legs spread over the luggage we were indivisible again, Felix and Claudia, easy as kids. Which is really why I suppose I started acting crazy-happy shouting Roma! Roma! and what's this what's that as things flash past she probably told us all about in England, and she's yelling back at me every name she knows. Then he skids round another bend or maybe it was a truck which anyhow chucks us more or less on top of her, face to face. From where naturally it gets to what you'd have to call a clinch. There was rain on her skin, tobacco on her tongue, and I didn't feel any need to wonder if she particularly minded. Alright, it was dark on account of the storm, a bit too dim and dark in there to see expressions so well every moment, but at such close quarters you'd think I'd be bound to notice if anything abnormal was in her head. I mean, if she was having second thoughts or anything.

And while on that, an episode on the train just occurs to me, and seeing it springs to mind I'd better deal with it. An episode involving a soldier, an opera-lover in uniform, who for reasons best known to himself happened to be hanging round our corridor in the dead of night. I never asked his nationality but she spoke his language, and anyhow I saw her, I heard them both, so how could I not do something? Yet the worst I did only amounts to asking whether it was showing consideration for other passengers, singing away like that while everyone was sleeping with the unknown soldier. The look I got! Yet not two minutes after telling them to break it up she dumps that queer red head of hers back on my shoulder again and out she goes like a light, leaving me to trouble over it for hours. Still, in the end I had to reason she'd never do a thing like that unless she rated it only a harmless episode, over and forgotten in them same two minutes. So, no, all the strange confused time after her bombshell in the hotel, hard though I tried I just could not find any one particular thing I could put my finger on and say for certain, that's it, that's what it must all go back to.

7

Blue-carpeted stairs plunge steeply, and so do I, after side-stepping the doorman before he can finish inflating himself to bouncer size. At the bottom I butt into deep smothering velvet curtain thick with fag smoke, and push on blind.

Nae outdoor habits wanted here ... From behind the curtain and out of a big mirror on the opposite wall another stuffed uniform levels with me in one long stride and grabs the back of my parka collar. My cold-fingered efforts, all thumbs, tug big leathery knuckles deep into my nape. Every buttonhole has shrunk with wet. From an alcove packed to the ceiling with fancy coats and furs a handsome signorina with a very Roman nose is also watching me undress.

Finally I had to let it go, my twenty-first birthday present from Mam, black and stiff with rain, transferred as fondly as a flattened alley-cat from his fist to her mother-of-pearled fingernails, dripping a trail as dark as bloodstains across the sandy-coloured parquet. Without my last protection against their alien world I felt stripped and shivering, and all the top half of my old army jumper was dark with rain. That khaki souvenir had also seen better days, like the ex-squaddie in a cold sweat inside it multiplied everywhere in mirrors shaking a leg inside clinging soaked jeans like he just wet himself. Turning from all those replicas of my misery I work my arms in their soggy sockets, jittery as a boxer after the seconds have whipped the silk gown off his back. Just point us in the right direction someone.

'Prego!' It's the wardrobe miss and she wants my hand. Into my palm she presses a slip of paper, the chitty for my lost coat. *'Prego'* again, long eyelashes quivering like fins over very beautiful eyes. And *'prego'* from me, blinking a bit too. My lucky number, and I'm storing it down here in my special ...

Only now the mute in uniform is twisting my wrist to draw my attention to the fact that on the back of the little yellow ticket is printed in several languages including mine *CONSUMMATION OBLIGATORY,* which has me posting a mute appeal round his elbow to tell her to tell him *PRAY-go* so we two can put our heads together to sort out something cheap and filling under the 'Farinaceous' section of the menu part-memorised from *Vacanza in Italia* – Festuccini? Canaletto? – when to break up the party out of nowhere pops an excitable character in a silver sharkskin suit snapping his fingers to demand what looks like a white zip-up seal pup, and now she's freezing me off with a none-of-your-sauce look and the surly attendant is clicking his own baccy-stained fingers very close under my nose, and accordingly off I go after two brass buttons on his tail along a passage no wider than a train corridor which all at once opens out into a big uncertain space filled with jerky music and shafts of colour lighting revolving like in undersea films. In emerald ripples an ancient crooner with an Elvis haircut is inhaling oxygen from a mike while his equally decrepit accompanist doggy-paddles up and down an electric keyboard, smart couples and smoke trails everywhere linking and parting to his fingering.

A sudden commotion causes me to lose sight of the buttons. Two waiters have started a scrap right in front of me, fists and elbows going like nobody's business, so near I have to back off quick. They break up when a new contestant pitches in just a bit too fast for his own feet, a commanding-looking heavyweight dusting off a knee as he pulls out a chair for me at a nearby empty table.

As I take my seat he hands me a gilt-edged menu which at first I can make nothing of since he elbows a big red sculpted candle into the middle of the table and strikes a magnesium match, and the white dazzle of it makes me screw up my eyes. I don't much like the feeling the bright light is intended to make a new arrival the centre of attention.

The menu lists only the drinks, a lot with English names, alongside four-figure prices in Italian. While awaiting my order his head bends so close I can smell the quality of his haircream, unless he is pointedly putting his eye to a hole where my tie-knot should be.

'Gin fizz,' I say into the little hole in his ear, raising my voice to impart the finer details since the singer has just launched full-blast into *Ciao Ciao Bambina,* a number which even made it to the Era's jukebox that year. '*Grande* gin, *piccolo* fizz.' And away speeds my own personal *cameriere* nodding mental notes to himself.

No bother finding the words, and a fairish Ay-Tie accent and all. Any skill needs practice and none more than a foreign language, but with more exercise like this my command of the lingo should sharp improve by leaps and – *Mamma mia!* Across the floor, solitary and sinister in a blood-red gap opening between knotted dancers, sits a heavily built man alone at a table, dark glasses trained on me as steady as a pair of binoculars. I try to retaliate with a hard glare of my own, but after a second or two those unnerving shades send my eyes elsewhere. And just behind my back they meet a very different sight. So near ...

Eyes-fronting fast, heart bumping like crazy, I stare with mounting excitement at the burning candle, Neptune nude gripping his trident. The hot flame makes all his head glow luminous pink.

To rise to the challenge (incomprehensible words for her man, coral lips moving for me) will take a lot more nerve than I can summon on the spur of the moment, so just for now I intend to carry on making out I have my own pressing private thoughts to attend to. Then all in good time she might just get to view my interesting profile again, casually looking round to see if my order's coming. Not too soon, mind, since I've just done that very thing, and more or less in all innocence.

Waiting, hopefully not too much seeming like waiting, I tap the backs of my knuckles against the under-edge of the table in time to the rolling opening beats of a familiar English number, who knows played specially for me. *Oo-bah oo-bah oo* ...Neptune's curly locks are melting fast, gathering drop by drop inside a deep groove between the muscles of his back.

Oo-bah, oo-oo-bah,
Why does the rain fall from up above,
Why do foo-ools ...

The flame dips and wobbles dangerously as a silver tray carrying a little bottle of tonic, a bowl of ice cubes and about half a tumblerful of gin glides across the table toward my hovering hand.

Why do they fall in lo-ove?

I grip the glass, I out-glare the flame. *Ciao bambina.* Bye-bye Claudia ... And with one toss of the head I down that giant tot in a single shot – like flipping a neat back-header into the net – then tip my chair forward again almost as quick to face the soaring flame, eyes filled with the dazzling snapshot they've just taken. What a doll! Sexiest I've ever seen outside a magazine, brazen centre spread, tanned skin glistening like scales through the flimsiest gold-mesh affair, and oh the power of her eyes!

Tell me why-y-y ...

More is coming out than I thought, the snap's a double exposure. Under the smouldering image of my neighbour I can just make out a faint impression of Claudia. And it gives me a very satisfying jolt, she's burning with jealousy.

Naturally I'm affected, pet. But so what? Only a reflex action, not a bookable offence, just one extra thing we men have to put up with. Unless, well unless it's my luck to excite a local dish who – 'Pardon me!' – not content with one good-looking bloke for company means to go right out of her way to try every trick in the book to turn the head of a perfect stranger, such as hot-breathed words tuned so low now I cannot guess even the language, only that I'm sending her wild. Tell me why, tell me why! How do I know, baby, never thought I attracted that level of man-eater. And don't you start on about it all going to show I don't care a fuck about your feelings, no, because you just watch this now, aye just see if I don't turn round this minute and eye that bit of fluff like she means no more to me than you. Next chance we go, and judge for yourself if it doesn't look like I'm only doing it on account of the little bit of fuss... Okay, okay, you might even be right, only asking for trouble when it sounds like her man's going right through the roof on account of how she's openly carrying on about your ex-fool or whatever I count as now. And I hear scraping of chairs and all so maybe – 'Pardon again!' – maybe the one we should really be sizing up right now is not the man-eater herself but the muscle-bound fancy man she has in tow tonight, just to check he's not one more of them smooth-as-candle-grease pasta pricks you stuck-up slags at the lift of a finger part your legs for every time, deny it, like that slimy son of a cardinal or whatever he lied he was – you asked for the truth – no more interested in a woman's own actual feelings than that pervert Pocus or this fat old Wop here smirking so full of himself he just cannot get the message he's not wanted, and doubtless same as all the rest of them under the tinted glasses and expensive suntans – you asked for it – every last one bent as ...

'Crisis over. The lady has vanished, and her Mister Universe too. No objections if I take a pew?'

'Yes.'

'Much obliged. Still hissing down like the second flood up there, I divine by the state of you. Never could stomach the bitch, on screen or off, yet I solemnly swear I have this moment witnessed her one and only memorable performance to date. Put the repellent thing out – her whole body said it, her whole face, wrinkling up her nose, that pretty new nose – out like the cat! Up goes one bare arm, straight as this – feel yourself dangling on the end pinched between the stick-on talons as she swings you exit-wards? Talons part a fraction, only a fraction, and out you go, down you drop. Down, down, down, boyo! And not once do those mean eyes leave the back of your – *hic!* – nick. And you with your mouth going all the while, chewing motion – you're at it again! – camelwise yes, masticating the two of them into little bits. On and on and on, even as they're beating a retreat! God above, it is about the funniest ... Alright, from anger to laughter takes time, the comedy always hits later. Distinct suspicion he's outstayed his welcome.'

'English?'

'Nice one. Bless all us dear ex-pats, how cordially we loathe one another's guts. Didn't take you very long either, did it, to sniff me out in my lonely corner?'

'They do food here?'

'Do the dead eat? Order more drink, and while we're waiting help me solve the mystery of why Whale took up the cudgels on your behalf, the entire morgue is dying to know. No, no interruptions yet, please! We'll have the King James version first, let the old boy have his say. Enter diminutive youth in clapped-out jeans and army-surplus sweater with much elbow visible through a hole in one arm, wet as a river, not shaved since he last remembers, and with traces I detect at this close range of what might be mud or so help me paint in the fuzz on his chin. Half-inch more this way – rub – and all across the back of your hand too! When up sprints the chief lackey of authority in this godforsaken dive, and I mean sprint – only for his audience to be treated to – what? Sensation. Whale falls under the offending scruff's spell. Falls, literally. Yes, shoving his protesting penguins aside Balena actually skids over on his bum in his eagerness to please. Well now, boyo, this turn of events may all be in the order of the day to you, but we ordinary mortals were just a trifle nonplussed. You do not lack a certain style, I appreciate that, take the way you sat down ignoring the scandal you caused. Sure, such cool-headedness takes style, uncommon style, and no doubt some obtuseness too. But what else did you work on him? Almost beseeching the way he held your chair, humbly awaiting the command. Only when we saw the size of the drink he produced in such record time – pure beguiling unadulterated gin, his twitching nostrils tell him

– the sheer size of the marvellous thing, only then did it click that what impressed Balena is a certain indispensable attribute of your somewhat unconventional style. The fact that such a hobo look these days may well conceal a silvery lining, and trust his fine antennae to detect its glint beneath the modish rags. Only the rich can afford to dress poor, as folk were wont to say where I come from. Money's no object, right? Though of course I stand corrected if I'm wrong.'

'Wrong.'

'Dirty subject, I agree. Poor taste, slaps wrist. God almighty, you know you're well and truly doomed when you're reduced to sipping another man's tepid tonic! Once met a Swede in here, twice your height but dressed as bad, and he turned out to be the only son of a millionaire in paper. Something big in wool himself. And guess who fleeced him! Ha! Anyhow, admit it, you've enough not to worry.'

'Good joke.'

'Thanks. Rome not a patch on Stockholm was just about the sum of his conversation. Man of few words, such as your good self. Your kind take offence too easily. Remember the fraternal greetings you sent my way? Up go the true-blue eyes and what do they espy seated somewhere in the murky depths if not another exile son of Albion? Well, I'm afraid that's where you slipped up, as the actress said to the bishop, for although his birth certificate incontrovertibly testifies he was born in South Croydon an unconscionable number of years ago the sclerotic arteries of James O'Cain still course with blood as pure-bred Irish as his name. Pure one hundred per cent Gallic gold, me boy. Bejaysus, it was written all over your face: Another effing Englishman, shut the bastard out of my mind! And now I'd appreciate your opinion of a little theory I'm working on.'

'You've the wrong end of the stick.'

'*Hic?*'

'You have hold of the wrong end of the stick, mate.'

'Premature verdict, surely. Like it or not, the erroneous old bore addressing you over the rampant god of the sea has something of a reputation as the local guru. Living in this city is so original-seeming, is it not, so flattering to one's abject need to feel out of the ordinary run – painter in Rome, poet in Rome, whatever your act is. So original in fact we need do nothing else about it. For if this city of eternal decay still has anything going for it, old son, it has its name, the most resonant of all. Roma! Ah, I hear you say, how right he is, the truly talented soon go, soon turn tail and head off somewhere more conducive to achievement, while the likes of us linger on more and more detesting the sight of each other. Paranoia being the other side of the coin, the last feeble stimulus there is. So what do you say to that now? Awful thought flashes through the addle brain: this is where the affluent young so-and-so discloses that his every waking moment at home is dedicated to the sedulous application of paint to a load of thirsty canvasses. Whereas all this lost soul confesses he has to justify himself before posterity are some not unworthy aquatints done in an earlier incarnation. Or does his artist's intuition fail him again?'

'Load of walls, more like.'

'Balls? Prods deep for earwax, momentarily befuddled as to how to take this thoughtful dismissal of his finest creative endeavours. Though of course it proves my theory.'

'That table.'

'Paranoia again. My name is legion, hate you for being me. And vice versa, I'm sure. You were saying?'

'That table's waving at you.'

'Aha, the women are back! And here was I supposing we were deserted for good and all. Never you worry, girls, bringing him over for close inspection! As though they can hear anything above this circus music. She's Mavis, she's a dear. When it was hot between us how she reeked of bed! Know what I mean? Sybil's the little mermaid tugging her forelock, favourite habit. And to think they missed your whole act!'

'I'll stop here.'

'The mother or the daughter? Take your pick. Spotted the family resemblance, chests apart? Are you in no state to stand?'

'I'm stopping here.'

'We need your influence to con another bottle out of Balena.'

'I've got things to think about, Legion.'

'They're both dying to talk, can't you see? Slept with both. Not simultaneously. Thought that might get you to your feet. What did you say was the name?'

'I'm not stopping, I said.'

'Here, how much have you put by? Slippery as a bloody ice rink, and band's no better ...'

'So who's the fresh new face, James?'

'Well well well, and how are our two lost ladies? We're in booze again. And all by courtesy of – of ?'

'Felix.'

‘Whose poison is gin. Youth of many parts, don’t let the sodden rags mislead. Exudes a certain brusque charm. And what is more the fresh new face wields uncommon influence with the management. Oh yes, you watch the magic he’ll perform. Nothing less than a full bottle, plus regulation tonics for more delicate palates. Right, Felix?’

‘Not fussy like.’

‘Lancashire man?’

‘North East.’

‘Geordie boy?’

‘Thereabouts’

‘Well fancy that. First well-lined Geordie I’m sure I ever had the pleasure of. Coal or shipping? Shipping coal? Sit down and make yourself at home next to our delectable Sybil and at least attempt to etch a smile. No, she’s Sybil, she’s more your age, laddie. The lassie has hidden depths, even if she is promoting a hairstyle called the lunatic fringe. Mavis here’s her doting mamma. At which juncture J. O’C, egregious painter of a load of balls, eases his ageing carcass into the fairest bosom in Neptune’s grotto. Eeh by gum, woman, yon lass of thine doth gawp most rudely! Never seen a Felix before, Sibs?’

‘He’s wet right through.’

‘I got caught out in it like.’

‘Caught out like! You’ll not win her that way, me lad. Ladies, shall I reveal all? Meet Felix, the spirit of the storm, nine parts water like the jellyfish and the rest is all neat gin. Nautical man, something in shipping, out there in the hurricane, in peril on the sea, best sou’wester and the rest of the crew gone off drinking with Davy Jones. Forty-eight hours lashed to the wheel glaring into flying spray, doing a grand job for the owners. But as fate will have it the old girl goes down in the end, has to, fifty-foot towering waves and the flood rising all the time. Suddenly she strikes a submerged object which turns out to be the dome of St Peter's and with one last orgasmic shudder sinks like a stone. Ah but stay those salt tears, ye sea-nymphs. Our hero at the helm cuts himself free and friendly dolphins waft the hapless youth to our grotty sea cavern, soaked to the bone and calling for birds and booze. Thus is it his dubious destiny to wind up here of all places, at catacomb level, full fathom five, cheerfully shelling out three thousand for two fingers of gin. But the birds, where are all the birds?'

'Tweet-tweet!'

'Yes, laddie, they're your lovely dicky-birds. Well aren't we on form tonight! *La madre o la figlia,* boyo? The little chappie and I had a most interesting talk, Mavis. Balena! Had me splitting my sides while you two were off powdering noses. Uproarious. Balena, Balena! Holy mamma upon thine altar in the sky, is Whale still studiously ignoring us?'

'Darling, I've a shrewd suspicion we've been auctioned off.'

'Worse sins have been committed for a bottle of gin, Mave. Ever been drunk with words, me boy? I fear not. You'd settle for being plain drunk without. No gift of the gab, lad? Preferred to stop and think, eh?'

'Aye.'

'Spoken like a true mariner. Man of action, Sibs. Aye aye sir, needle steady. Few words and simple, and in that irresistible out-of-the-side-of-the-mouth style.'

'Excuse me everyone, aren't I up for grabs as well?'

'Mrs Mavis Batey wishes it to be known she is now finally a very edible divorcee. Take a good look, Felix, and above all take your time. A drink might aid you in your difficult decision. Ahoy there, Balena! Why I do believe we are about to enjoy the privilege of his attention at last. This is your big moment, laddie, your finest hour. As I scarce need apprise a gentleman of your resources, even in such chic establishments it's not strictly permitted to purchase spirits by the bottle. But money opens all Bluebeard's doors. Balena! Fit the cretin a deaf-aid. Jesus wept, I'll have the microphone off that lousy fairy castrato.'

'Jim listen, who's paying?'

'Yes James, who?'

'Roman style. All chip in. Have you noticed what this light can do to people's teeth?'

'All?'

'Ssh! Salvation approaches, wreathed in wary smiles to the gills. Fix him, Felix. Down on your knees and grovel, slave girls. This had better work ...'

'So how did you meet Jim?'

'He met me.'

'Picked you up, you mean. Mother's halved his allowance to make him quit drinking like a fish and get back to painting. He's one of those people you can never quite decide whether to love or hate. I mean, without being asked he took me to the airport to see President Kennedy's arrival, which was so thoughtful. But what was he holding forth so conspiratorially about over there? Not me, I trust.'

'Rome, I think.'

'Which doesn't not mean me. Or my mother. Have

you seen the river? On the island we got out to look and it was right up under both bridges, I wouldn't feel safe in the Jewish Hospital tonight. A man claimed he saw bats flying around at midday, the water had risen so fast. Don't look now, but I suspect poor Jim's getting nowhere in his negotiations. Don't. He mustn't always be allowed to get away with this kind of thing. Just keep looking in my eyes. More than once he's told me he expects people to stand up to him in this state. Which they should, seeing he's not exactly one for beating about the bush.'

'I told him he had the wrong -'

'God above, boyo! Why leave it to the man with the worst reputation in the place? Where were you skulking when duty called?'

'Having a private conversation with little me, Jim.'

'Lost interest in our scheme, has he? Usual colonial policy, sit tight and look the other way, let the aliens do the dirty work. Whale's not playing. Gave me the customary crap about his job being on the line if he concedes even a half-bottle. In plain man's language that means grease-my-palm. You only had to let him see the colour of your money.'

'Dear me, how low some do sink!'

'Now hark at you, Mavis. Are you taking his side as well? You saw them confabulating together, the way your daughter's taken her cue from the little runt's we-are-not-amused expression already. Well, grovelling apologies, Lord Muck, for being a lowdown Mick and poteen-swilling ignorant son of the peat bog. Me Felix, me so happy, serene as the Rock of Gibraltar!'

'Ignore him.'

'Gibraltar's English because we're the last lot here. We'll

build our very own Clackton-on-Sea in the Med, sunny last bastion of dreariness and our good old class democracy. Fish and chips forever, muchachos, and bingo under blue skies!'

'Me dad came from Scotland, I'll have you know.'

'Rabid racist into the bargain! I'm pure Irish, boyo, born in South Croydon, but at least I can accept the –'

'Mother, Benito's trying to catch your eye again.'

'Shut your mouth, Sybil. Shut that prim little twat. Don't either of you care what he thinks of us, sitting here at our table rubbing his hands like the ghost of a flea? Hey, sailor-boy, who said you were wanted? Say something for once. Speak!'

'I wasn't Navy, I was ... '

'Ignore him, I said. Which bit of the city do you live in?'

'This kind of hotel somewhere. I only got here today.'

'Straight from England, you mean?'

'Aye.'

'Alone?'

'Not when I arrived.'

'Female?'

'Maybes.'

'And she travelled on?'

'That about sums it up.'

'You look sorry.'

'Me? She's Roman and her people live here. So she went back to her people. Far as I'm given to understand.'

'And what if she knew you were down here with us?'

'She'd lose no sleep.'

'Oh you do sound bitter! Would it help to talk about it a bit?'

'Whites-only club, push off you picturesque coolies! Talk into your gin glass, don't talk to the natives!'

'You're doing very well. Attention's all he's after. She calls him her pet angry old man. Anyhow, with drink real Irishmen wax lyrical.'

'You're whispering again, Sibs, catching his diseases already.'

'I merely said drink makes most Irish poetic. And if it's of any interest, look what's coming!'

'Bravo, Balena, *bravissimo!* Gordon's London. And bravo Geordie, bravo indeed, you performed your magic after all. Wine's kinder to the liver but I stipulated the old green bottle in your honour. I take it all back, every ill-considered word. Infantile tendency to cyclothemia, the common or garden desire to kick when thwarted. Your hand, good sir. Nice to have you with us on the show. I like that fresh open face of yours, and I sure do appreciate the wonders your money can perform.'

'Is that the best you can do, James? I'd say you owe this exceptionally generous young man a proper apology.'

'Heaps sackcloth and ashes on few remaining grey hairs, beats collapsed lung. Call me an Irish joke, forget I spoke. Okay? You know how it goes, my well-lined friend from the land of George, not to mention George and the Dragon, one misunderstanding leads to another. But happily sanity and prayer have in the end prevailed, as the Holy Father declared from the balcony this morning. And now be a good fellow would you, and reach me a glass from that table. Here, where's yours? You don't appear to have one either, as the actress said to the actress. So Whale expects us to share germs, Mavis. How's that for comradeship?'

'Well dears, now everyone seems to be friends again perhaps our much-maligned new acquaintance might be permitted to make his choice.'

'Choice?'

'You get your poison, he gets one of us. Wasn't that the very male agreement? There's something so absolutely disarming about his gappy grin, Sybil darling. Not unlike a quieter version of poor Massimo.'

'They'll tear you apart, boyo, and much good may it do. On your left is Sibyl Batey, dreamy little backfisch fresh out of nappies, and in the right-hand corner – tonight's contender, *la bella mamma,* Mrs Mavis B, self-styled Ideas Woman, Einstein's perfect partner. And the conniving little cat among the pigeons, gappy grin flashing both ways at once, is the one and only – '

'You're getting obnoxious again, Jim.'

'Realistic, duckie. Here he sits next to unkissed you, and it's only filthy human nature he's having trouble recalling his late woman of Rome. I trust you've noted your expensively brought-up offspring's technique too, Mave. Knee warming his, and always so quick to leap to his defence.'

'Not missed a thing. Green with envy, and dying to hear the story of that chipped front fang. Darling, I do declare you're taking unfair advantage, just because James chose to plant himself between me and his latest victim. In fact I'm of the opinion it would only be fair to have first go with him on the floor, on grounds of seniority at least. So, young man, what say we two trip the light fantastic?'

'Here comes Benito, Mother, and you can't refuse him again.'

‘Crafty so-and-so, is she not? Till later. And remember when the time comes I want you all to myself. Remember.’

‘Now boyo, how’s the score?’

‘Score?’

‘The maid or the mother? Permission to let him in on a little secret, Sibby?’

‘As though we hadn’t been treated to enough of those in recent times.’

‘Tut-tut, no respect for her elders and betters. Silly old fool musing to himself. I was merely pondering, old son, pondering on the way she dances with one hand free on that bald young thug’s shoulder, same side as her chin, that ever so slightly receding chin. Keep watching, because I’m ready to bet any moment now, with that same hand, we’ll see her rub her fingers along here, forefinger and thumb, down the bridge of that fine straight nose and back again, smoothing the skin in the dark mysterious hollows at the corners of her eyes. I suspect no one’s yet told her she does it, and doubtless she’d be mortified. In point of fact at that moment Mavis Bates scores more with me than any other woman. Diana bathing, one of those rare moments they’re not watching themselves. See, told you, gently smoothing the nose-side of those warm and weary grey eyes. There, right in there, is the softest part of her body, and each and every time it gives me a rare sensation that can only be described as arising from the deepest tenderness. Here endeth the lesson. Only one place as tender, boyo. That salty pink oyster they keep locked away for our delight. Luscious as the hot inside of this one’s elbow.’

‘Hands off! Come on, you. He’s got sex on the brain because he’s got it nowhere else!’

'One more word before you get your paws on her, my son. Whale likes his debts settled straight off. So yes, if you could see your way to ...'

'Here!'

'God above, look where he keeps it! Thanks a million. Now listen to me. Push off, Sibs, this is not for your pretty ears. Made a study, made rather a careful study of the resemblance between mouth and twat. And after much consideration and some not inappropriate experiment I think it may interest you to learn that my researches on these two specimens lead me to the conclusion that the hypothesis has much to commend it. The mother's mouth is firm and strong, you will have noticed. Little Sybil's lips are soft and fat and full of blood.'

8

Maybe I sound simple, I suppose I do. But what's true all the same, I believe, is that before all this carry-on I took love to be nothing much more than a necessary sort of relaxation. Necessary and enjoyable, mind, like fishing, if that makes better sense. Some like to call fishing a sport, but fishing to my way of thinking is not a sport, or not a competitive sport, same as the best kind of love is not a sport. In other words love and fishing are the opposite of football, if I explain myself. I tried to explain it to her too because I thought it was the type of thing she'd like to hear, though no less true for that. Flower, I said this particular day we were in the long grass, is it not the case that if nobody cared who wins or who loses soccer would have scant appeal, probably wouldn't even work? Whereas fishing, my kind of fishing, is a whole other way of going about things, with no winners and no losers. With not so much depending on it, not so much agonising. No lack of excitement but not that many anxious moments, and above all time to ponder, time to dream. I don't know what she made of it because just then she decides to roll over and pull her knickers up and hunt in her bag for her ciggies and matches, then her bloody notebook. Must have had another brainwave for the thesis.

Yeah, of course I know fishing has scant appeal for women, and not too many are mad about soccer either. But the thing I was endeavouring to explain is that although they might not be interested in fishing that doesn't stop it coming close to what most of them seem to want from love. Listen, I said, listen, though from the way she bit her lip as she scribbled I'd well and truly lost her by now, I'm still talking about love here and I'm saying that at least from that point of view I think fishing has more to teach than football. I'd been working all this out when I was on my own down by the river, trying to get it clear in my head how to explain my twin obsessions, see, wanting them to mean something to her as well.

Maybe I still sound too simple. But her tendency quite honestly is to make things so much less simple than I reckon they mostly are. Or should be. For her even love has to bring in religion and philosophy and that, not to mention the entire medical side. She claims her Indian wise men shaft seldom and then exclusively for high-minded reasons, for them a good shag if you'll pardon the expression is a sacred act of worship. One night from somewhere among all her books she produced this little one with pictures far plainer than anything under my mattress, old temple carvings where everyone's at it all ways together, back-to-front, upside-down, practically inside-out, and of course I presumed it was only for a bit more inspiration like, and it worked too, until she goes and says they train themselves to hold them identical impossible positions for hours on end and by the look on their faces couldn't I see they were all on their way to heaven. Expecting too much again, see. Try your beloved Father Brendan on that theory next time, I should have said!

You and me, we know how it is. It's not stored in your pocket but on your person, needy but touchy like the rest of you, an extension of everything else we happen to be. A man, she didn't always seem to appreciate, can still seem to show willing but does suffer, particularly if operating under pressure or when a bit too over-anxious to please. Bed with a brainbox like that can get you so wound up that either before even you properly know where you are you've shot your bolt, or else after minutes and minutes of toiling you catch yourself wondering if ever you'll be able to summon the extra burst of enthusiasm to finish what from that moment on you heartily wish you'd never begun, this little voice in your head keeps saying never ever will there be sufficient elastic in the catapult, mate, not if you carry on like that till you're blue in the face. All the sex manual maniacs agree that form slips if you start to think overmuch about it, leastways once you're past about fifteen when you'll fire off at just about anything that moves. But does it have to be so? I mean to say, I'd be at it with her ten times a day in my head, even ten impossible Indian ways, but then of course when ... Ah never mind, I've said plenty enough now for you to see what seems to have been going on with me. And not even really so much between me legs, more between me ears. In the end she made us feel not even remotely connected to the fairly happy-go-lucky person I used to be, to the point of having to boost my sinking opinion of myself with lurid memories of earlier adventures, like even the earliest of all with this semi-bedridden warder's wife living only three doors down who Mam had us run messages for. Mrs Perkins liked to joke on I was the same as our Scratcher, she only had to run a hand down my back and up went my stub of a tail. She was from down London and she called us Poppet.

Oh man, how did we ever get on to this? Frustration, sheer frustration. Though most of all now I think it's the frustration that she's not here to hear me dealing fairly openly with all these things I didn't always feel would be to my advantage to debate too fully with her. Again and again, as I hear myself struggling too late but so hard to be sincere and in free speech like this finally begin to sort out the tangle we got ourselves in I find myself dreaming the same impossible thing – if only she was listening as well as you!

9

'I always think thunder and lightning are more than just thunder and lightning, so I was already expecting something. Then outside my window, right outside, I saw two Orientals, Chinese or Japanese, at any rate a long-time couple because so at-one seeming. Don't you too long to be old and wise? He was holding an umbrella over her, a beautiful big yellow umbrella, and she was bending down to look at something in the gutter. With a twig she hooked it up. A worm, a drowned worm, long and thin and all pink and grey and drooping, and very carefully she carried it to the base of the pine tree to revive, not be trampled on. I thought if I were a drowning worm I'd believe that couple came all the way to Rome to perform that solemn act of charity. You smell like a good person but the way you breathe is rather anxious-making. Why is that? The female who travelled on?'

Oh Claudia, Claudia, what am I doing, wrapped in the tentacles of a lass with soft fat lips I don't know and don't want to know? In the corner of the one eye I can see through floats a bald head as round as a prize gold football, cupped in a woman's hand.

'Watching, is she not?'

The head, turning Cheddar orange now, belongs to the Italian partnering her mother.

'Yes.'

'And with that smile that lifts only the top half of her face?'

'Yes.'

My right thumb, bent backwards, is being pushed up inside a tight buttoned cuff round her wrist. Strong fingers press it against skin and bone in there, a supple bone crossed by a tiny vein as slippery as spaghetti.

'Better?'

'Bit – ' to spit out a long lacquered hair without making a sound is not easy – 'better than before.'

'Before?' Like a hot rush of ear-wash.

'This church with a dead corpse dressed in jewels.'

'Kiss me.'

'And Jesus on the water.'

'You're in such a mess. What did that Italian do to you? Just kiss me!'

'Wazzanideasooman?' Desperate as mouth-to-mouth resuscitation, only a ventriloquist would know how not to offend. But it gets her off.

'After she's spent all Daddy sends for my education she writes round to about fifty firms saying she has this brilliant idea she'll part with to the highest bidder. The latest is her famous home scalp invigorator, her darling Benito's last desperate hope. Jim says she really only likes him because he bites.'

'My dad was an inventor.'

'He retired?' Those lips are sucking the curly hairs at the neck of my jumper now.

'He died in the war, before they reached Rome.'

'Mine left us and went back to England. One night this summer she made me come to the then boyfriend's roof party and got so impossible I slipped out and walked all the way –' right up my bristly throat – 'along the river to my favourite private place – ' under my left earlobe –

'where the plane trees whisper like ghosts. Ghosts inside the leaves everywhere, crowding the parapet where the old river flows. And it just might interest you to know who I think they all were.'

'Shouldn't we be moving?'

'The souls of every person who ever wished they'd seen Rome before they died!'

Her mouth is are after mine again, so I move my face. 'Can a man be Andrea here?'

'Benito, Benito. After guess who. He lost his hair when he was just five, when we bombed his home in Sicily. You don't like me, do you?'

'That's where he was stationed.'

'Why?'

Out of pity, pity for us both, I make the mistake of licking some sweet-tasting dry powder off her cheek. Next moment my mouth is filled with an extra tongue as long as a finger poking about. My own tongue works to chase it out, but the more mine fights the more hers burrows as though it only lives to get at that little flap at the back of the throat. I have to pull free, scared I'll throw up. Her gasp of shock is heard only by me, but the squeal of her hurt is piecing.

The nearest couples stop to watch, mouthing comments. Her mother pushes past, trailing the burly Sicilian by the hand.

'And to what, pray, do we owe this latest scene?' Looking everywhere but at us.

'Just get that stinking oik away from me!'

'And you just stop this nonsense or you go straight home.'

'I hate him, hate him!'

'Then I'll borrow the boy, till tempers cool. One dance, no more. Benny'd be happy to swap, I'm sure.'

'Deaf old bag, I never want to see him again!'

'Dearie me!'

'I need to sit.'

'Her father's a normally mild man with the same sudden foul temper.'

'Lady, I have to sit down.'

'Very well, conduct me back to our corner then. One was once a know-all seventeen too, I suppose I should remember. Now where in hell are you going? This way! Your table's taken, that makes you one of us. She regularly stages these scenes in the hope of being sent back to her father. No, no, move round here next to me! How can we have a heart-to-heart over such vast empty spaces? It's not you Benito's wary of. I see James also had to go and order his favourite red the moment your back was turned, in these moods he never knows where to stop. Benny's not the most observant young man, but he did manage to remark you look like a soul in distress. Privately I agreed, though I told him you were indulging in a bout of sulks after not seeing eye-to-eye with the obstreperous family mascot. Do the honours, dear.'

'There'll only ever be one woman for me.'

'That's nice.'

'You don't know what I'm talking about.'

'Second time I've heard that today. The Woman of Rome, as James put it? You parted amicably and now you're saying it was all a mistake?'

'It's these gut reactions. She comes so alive inside me.

I try to numb up, try and feel nothing, next minute every chewed nail is digging right in. In the weak spot here, the gut strings or whatever they are.'

'Here?'

'Same place when I lost my nan.'

'Something's definitely churning away, like the first stage of labour almost.'

'Same place, same feeling.'

'Take deep breaths.'

'Now I know how he feels, this friend of mine's husband, a face-worker who's not been right since the cage went out of control at the pit and grown men were grabbing each other round the neck. By fits numb or in turmoil, she says. It comes in waves, she says, shock waves left over from this terrible thing that happened.'

'Breathe in and hold it as long as you can. We all have to numb up, how else would we endure? When they removed the poor child to that appalling school in England I had to learn the meaning of that all over again.'

'She's right, your daughter, I'm in a mess.'

'Are nurse's hands no help?'

'It's going, thanks, it's passing. You can take them off now. And she had the gall to say I'm insensitive.'

'It's been quite a day for me too, if it's any consolation.'

'Take them off.'

'I was all set to go out to what promised to be yet another nerve-racking showdown, when in the hall mirror I faced the ghastly truth. I can't tell you how it felt, I even said it out loud. Mavis, you look as silly as your shoes, don't seem secure. You'll think I was mad to be talking to myself, it was the crocodiles I had on, I knew they weren't really me even before I left the shop. But guess what. I kicked them off on impulse and stood there wiggling my toes inside the school-girlish black stockings the child actually permitted me to borrow and never stepped outside my own front door. And all because of that ridiculous lost woman in the mirror. I unpinned my hair and marched straight back into the kitchen to consume another mortadella sandwich with the little man who comes to clip the poodle and did a solid hour's housework in my liberated feet, being the maid's weekend in the mountains. Which deserves more respect, say I hovering George's dumb tiger, your tender tootsies or this world of crocodiles? Only when I had Sibby out of her wet things back from school and ensconced in the shower after removing James's repellent drip-dries, only then did I plug in and dial his number, coolly giving my own fair name.'

'You live here, you know people. Me, I'm a thousand miles from anything I know.'

'She kept her hand over the receiver while they jabbered away, but at least that gave me time to think up something suitable before she put him on. I said it seems to me quite extraordinary how much two people I'm told have nothing to say to each other have to say to each other.'

'I tried phoning.'

'Such a fool one feels, such a begging fool. That ring-ring soon starts to sound like the most humiliating pleading. She gets far more time with him, and what harm have I done that wasn't done long ago? About time she accepted the finality of it. Here, where do you put the stuff? You've hardly swigged one before another's on its way down.'

'She wants me to disappear off the face of the earth and

I intend to oblige. And when I'm gone, lady, tell her I could never love anyone but her.'

'A noble epitaph. But love is not for ever, dear, love is for now. I think the sanest thing a man ever said to me – he called it his recipe for living, and I remember he put a finger to my lips – is to give all things the very same importance, even the most trivial. You'd think it would have made him frightfully self-absorbed, yet not one bit. Not a day older than you, and quite mad about me and I thought he was divine. Truth is plural, that was another of his sayings. And how clever, how true. For instance I look at the prickles all over your face, this glittering mass of stubble, and I wonder to myself: is he growing a beard or has he simply forgotten to shave? Sprouting his first fiery burning bush of a beard, not sprouting? Churning with yearning, or just fooling himself? There's evidence aplenty but who knows what I am to believe? Only you, my dear.'

'Sorry, lady, I forgot my shaver when we almost missed the train. In the first flush she was all on about us growing one, then I got wind the last boyfriend but one he had one, so was I going to oblige by stirring up old memories and daft comparisons?'

'Dearie me, just look at that – so much for moralising teenagers! And now she says she hates even her name. Can we never get back to when we both so needed each other? She'd be inconsolable one minute then so gloriously happy through the tears. Now it's this infuriating mix of profoundly childish and much too impatient to be adult. And I should say we have ample proof of that before our eyes.'

'You were watching before, same as now. And you saw

how she acted. And you know how that sort of attention affects you normally speaking, if you're a man?'

'I'm not, but I think I do.'

'It wasn't normal.'

'Do I really need to hear this?'

'So you see what I'm saying?'

'I have a very clear picture indeed, thank you. Is it to be measured in inches or feet?'

'No, man, no! This is about how I feel for her, how much I truly care, whatever she thinks. So imagine something about me with your daughter that's tantamount to living proof only she can have the type of affect you think.'

'Heavens!'

'And isn't it like extra proof I'm not ashamed to admit it?'

'What kind of monstrous innocent are you? As proof of some sudden all-consuming passion, if that's what I'm expected to concede, I tell you it holds no water.'

'Women never understand.'

'Understand? It's enough to have to endure that pained smirk. We understand only too well. When you reach my age the male anatomy has no great mysteries, I assure you. No, the little matter I'm afraid I failed to understand is *who* the weak spot keeps churning for. So let me put it in plain words even the simplest oaf can follow. In your roundabout yet obscenely boastful fashion you actually want her own mother to agree that after the failure of one attachment your grubby little affections have switched to her wayward daughter, and all because a little teenage lovey-dovey furnished you with a record-breaking erection with attendant ejaculation, excuse my French!'

'Where do you get that from? I felt no feelings, none. Without her I'm good as dead. Dead. And it's nothing to laugh at either, I tell you.'

'Dead! And abusing my poor lamb to prove it. Now that really is sick.'

'Only the way they pull their hair's the same. Here, at the front.'

'Well that's quite a weight off, I must say. James says she's lonely, I suspect she's plain immoral. Here, steady on with the hooch – and how about attending to little me? Surely I qualify for a pick-me-up after that ordeal. So it's the Woman of Rome who unmanned you, is that the story?'

'I just need someone who'll listen to me.'

'I'm all ears, dear, all curious to hear the whole sorry saga, but do please call a spade a spade. And do also keep it reasonably short because soon I fear we're going to have to mount a search party for James. A lot of your gin found its way into his hip flask, and then I daresay on his way up for air he couldn't get past Sirena. She's our tempting new cloakroom attendant. You look distinctly odd. Is there something still more shaming to confess?'

'It's that gut feeling again.'

'Well, no doubt it proves it's genuine.'

'I was plain-spoken enough just now, wasn't I? Don't go thinking I'd discuss such things with any old woman.'

'Any old! That's the kind of thing I have to put up with almost every hour from the child. Barely forty years I've had this body. Does it look so bad? Tell me the truth.'

10

Missing believed drowned. Out of the blue it came, the official telegram. Weeks later arrived a letter from the pilot himself, a Flight-Lieutenant Leonards, saying it happened here in Italy near a place called Augusta, a dot in my school atlas of the world midway along one edge of the island of Sicily. A most regrettable accident, it states, such as could equally have occurred in peacetime. Yet reading between the lines it's plain they should never have lost a man.

It hit something heavy in the sea at take-off, their flying boat, and on bringing the aircraft down it became evident they were shipping water. Evacuation procedure was at once implemented, it says, and rigorously observed. The state of the sea was nothing alarming, the night was clear and full of stars, there were two inflatable rafts and time to inflate them and time to get in. On proceeding to harbour a patrol vessel intercepted the rafts which had briefly become separated, and it was therefore only when the eight-man crew was assembled on deck that their sole passenger was found to be missing. The vessel of course revisited the scene but detected no sign of life. The Catalina had sunk without trace.

True, I have it all by heart. Nothing of him remains to return via normal channels, his unit was at once contacted and it must therefore be presumed any personal effects went with him. Do they copy it out of a manual? Not a word to say what a soldier was doing on a seaplane. Or how he could ever go missing. He was a strong swimmer, as a little lad he could already dive off the middle arch of the stone bridge over our river. Dive, not jump. Was he taken bad, did he slip getting into a raft? Mam says she used to see a massive wave suddenly pick up from that nothing-alarming sea, so real she'd hear herself shriek a warning. Nan never got over it.

Myself? Signor, can I first add another side, then tell something I never told before? After the war, a good four or five years after, Mam and Nelly our neighbour went through to Newcastle on the train to look round the winter sales, like they still generally do, and there was a man in the same compartment who seemed to know all about it. Barely a half-hour ride, yet it came up in the course of conversation, Mam happening to mention his fate after she heard the man say Sicily was the most beautiful place he'd ever seen, courtesy of the war. That's all it took, her mentioning my dad, and next thing he's telling a tale which sounded terribly familiar. A long-range seaplane in coastal command sinking off the island of Sicily one night in 1943. Yes, he said, it was just off Augusta harbour, and yes, it may well have been early November. Almost unbelievable, particularly when you think that to anyone not involved it's not really a particularly memorable story, considering everything else that happened in the war. But this man, this total stranger, was seemingly on the very boat, an MTB, the actual patrol vessel which spotted the rafts and took the crew on board and then went back over the scene. Every detail tallied, Mam and Nelly decided, save one important thing that got no mention in the letter. The man said he remembered, very definitely remembered, at a certain moment they sighted something in the sea, something that seemed worth investigating. There was even debate about throwing a lifebelt, he said, though that got no further, because when they raised the alarm there was nothing more to be seen, nothing at all. Which brings us on to the thing I was wanting to tell, when you asked how the fact of my missing father worked on me.

Before ever those fatal words were spoken on the train, long, long before, I made it all happen. All of it, all of it and more. Not just the patrol vessel and the sighting, even the lifebelt. All the same I could never reverse history, never do the job. A hand would come out of the water, his, only for the next wave to flip the belt just out of reach at that very moment. Then if I got it drifting back, right over the right place, another wave had buried him. Things like that, lots and lots like that, when trying to rescue my dad. And the boat, the rescue boat I called it. White, very big and white it was, so that a man overboard would see it even far off in the night, not grey, crossing and re-crossing Augusta Bay trailing lifebelts in all directions, some even under the sea. I'd add more and more, more lifebelts and more ropes to reach even further, and still they could not go far enough, or far down enough. Or just didn't have the strength. Rope rotted through, like old fishing line. Or I'd watch some vital knot undo, like in the films when people have to cross water on rope bridges. So then I got ropes of metal, cables thick as this, reaching everywhere possible into the sea and the night to find him. And dragnets, after I heard about them. But even when I had him on he could not keep hold. Fingers numb with cold, wires slimy, or I'd haul and haul and the weight of him was too much. Nothing I invented could do the trick when trying to fish out my dad.

11

'Our room was down the far end of a long twisty corridor, and when she got the door unlocked and we both went graffling round the walls to find a light switch, for one queer moment I saw us like under glass, our two shadows moving in something deep as a mirror. She found it outside the door, the switch, so then we could see it was not a mirror but a window, and the only one and what a one – for inspecting the flaming lift shaft! And this, lady, was where we had to start the new life. Two fish in a bowl, she says, and the cables made her think of weeds, she said, black oozy weeds. I tried to mollify her, pointed out rigging a blanket over the glass would make a reasonably cosy first hidey-hole, and after all we'd barely arrived and we had each other, and seeing it was likely only for a short while we shouldn't let our surroundings get to us. Besides, the lift was out of action, or so we thought, because after taking her money and our passports the joker on the desk wagged a big finger at the lift sitting there and says something in Italian to her and points at the stairs, so making us hump our stuff up literally flights and flights. When it came to our attention it was really live it cut her off in the middle of whatever she was shrilling at that particular moment in time, clamouring like it intended coming through the floor. Then what? She claims it's my fault and throws another fit! Because blowed if ever they'll give ear to our two pennies' worth. Start explaining how it feels to be you and they stop listening, they never want to put themselves in our skins for a change. Like talking to a wall. Here, are you another? I thought you were all curious.'

'Aquarius yes!'

'What?'

'Aquarius. Clever guess.'

'Guess be buggered! So you swallow all that effing gobbledegook too?'

'Glory be, everyone goes deaf in the course of even the tiniest yawn. Besides, you can be rather hard to follow.'

'I didn't mean to get at you. She makes me say these things.'

'Blame everyone but yourself, we're all of us guilty there. Not so many moons ago I found myself in a dreadful entanglement. The creature in question was a thoroughly nasty piece of work, quite a power at the Forty Martyrs, acting as though his mere presence makes this city the centre of the universe. Yet he had me crawling. Oh yes at the drop of a hat I was right down on all fours before the master, content to let him twist me round his little finger, I do not exaggerate – until the momentous night I opened my eyes and took a good look round me and saw the unacceptable, everything asking to be rectified. Dear me, when it sank in what I was letting him get away with I was utterly taken aback, it was so debasing. I'm gazing up at his ghoulish painting of Saint Sebastian as in a trance, next moment I'm thinking, Mavis that's you, shot through and still smiling, don't you even realise the onus is on you, you've let a self-inflated little bugger get on top of you and if you hope to preserve one last shred of self-respect he's going to have to be made to snap out of it and fast! Don't ask what came over me but hey presto he faded very quickly from the picture. Not without his little revenge, of course. An appallingly graphic anonymous missive to my poor innocent daughter. Apart from anything else it would make your hair stand on end to think a young man in a dog collar can have such a twisted imagination.'

'I know what you're saying but -'

'I was in need of spiritual guidance after the Dragon appeared on the scene and he was recommended to me as a promising theologian with a first-class brain.'

'I know what you're saying but it's not that I blame only her, I blame myself for being so blind. Because you know the first thing I'd ask if some time in the far future we could put this whole mess under the microscope? I'd ask if every second of the journey she wasn't figuring out how to dump us. Dump, lady, like unwanted baggage. Even holding my hand when I was near sick at the rail. And all this morning, all this long morning on the train her eyes were sort of pensive-looking. If I said something or pointed out the window anyone could see she wasn't there.'

'The little show-off, it's a wonder she can breathe!'

'In the Army we slept thirty to a hut, down London I shared a mattress in a cellar surviving on bread and Marmite, so was I going to descend into an argument about the place not being quite up to standard? Who negotiated it, who paid a full week's rent no questions asked? And I still reckon it wasn't such a daft notion to get us a couple of rings. And if she said she needed a better light for her bookwork what was so wrong with rigging up a lamp from her mother run off the socket in the ceiling?'

'Dearie me, maybe after all her father... Rings? Was it that close?'

'Electric. For her to cook on. Instead when I appear with her bookcase she just takes leave of her senses, all in a moment going off the deep end screaming I don't just not love her I loathe her, for Jesus Christ's sake!'

'My word!'

'Ah now you're listening. While me, I couldn't get one word in edgeways. Any pause in that barrage was only for time to reload and pelt us with more. And all of it shite, at any rate way out of proportion. For one, how can she claim I never ever cared for her when twice she nearly got herself pregnant? Fucking two times, lady! But apparently I'm only selfish, apparently I never spare a thought for her needs. You say us, she shrieks, and you mean me, me, me! Just picking on the way I talk, all of us talk, and then only when not thinking. No wonder I went mental. To uproot for another person, I says, entirely uproot, are you telling us that's a selfish decision? Fine man of decision, she says, ignoring the issue, a bloody fine man of decision I got myself! I should have warned you about her mouth, it's because she's not English. She was sitting there, maybe kneeling, anyhow up she jumps, stubbing out her cigarette like this –'

'On your knee!'

'In the tin ashtray. What do I need him for? Real triumphant-like, puffing it all out along with the last of her smoke. What do I need him for, what bloody for? I've made my decision, she goes next more or less under her breath, leastways quieter than I can say it here and you still hear. So she'd left off screaming, left off for good, though maybe this sort of muffling thing was worse, like I wasn't there. Don't I, muffle, don't I have another life to live for?

And how, muffle-muffle, how could I ever share it with a man who doesn't know what he wants or where he's going, probably even who he is? And that, lady, was the flaming fucking bastard limit, twisting my whole philosophy. And I have to take it from a woman almost fully three years older who cannot make the simplest decision without calling a phoney stargazer she keeps on the line here for the slightest emergency. Likely on to him this moment now, her wise Signor Hocus Pocus, if not already summoned to a private consultation, because I happen to know he's after her tail as well as her pocket.'

'Ah the music's jazzing up at last!'

'It was the finality of it. It was just so painful – and all so –'

'Final. I know, it must have been wretched for you. You'll have to partner me I'm afraid if James can't tear himself away from that coat-cow.'

'Final, yes. But also so – '

'Painful.'

'Yes. And empty.'

'Yes, yes, but how did it all end in the end? Seems we'll never get there, and certain looks I'm getting are plainly asking if I need rescuing. And frankly poor Benny really might have grounds for feeling you've monopolised me enough. Just round it all off in a sentence or two and we'd better be on our feet.'

'She started it, remember. After that anything I may have done was only to stop what I could see was coming. And like I say, I've not felt in the land of the living ever since.'

'So welcome to the land of the dead! Sounds like both

parties were being very Italian about the whole thing. When love or need or whatever it truly is gets to the point of no return the nearest thing to drama is someone forgets to phone. Sad and simple as that.'

'I did phone, I told you.'

'To declare you were drinking yourself to death?'

'Think that's funny? To hear if she'd come to her senses.'

'A label like that deserves more respect. And so perhaps do I.'

'This man there wouldn't let her speak, if you want to know.'

'Oh you do go on so! Put that glass down, just put it down. Time we danced. I'm sure I'm the last person to object to anyone drowning their sorrows, but at this rate you truly might achieve a more permanent oblivion.'

'One more thing she'll have to answer for. I sank most of the half-bottle of whiskey Muggins bought on the boat as a grovel present for her dad. How else could I take a step outside that room? And I've sorrows enough to drown today, lady. This is the night my father drank himself to death. Oh aye, swallowed too much sea water! So think on that, think of a good man all of twenty-two on his way to the bottom of the Mediterranean Sea one starry night of the last war, nineteen years gone possibly this very moment now. Then ask if it's not going to affect his bairn!'

'You're raising your voice again – didn't the Army teach you how to behave? I'm sure we all have our various very private sorrows but this way I fear you're going to have to contend with Benito. And I'm warning you, he can be rather bloody-minded when he has my interests at heart.

So I do respectfully suggest, if you wish to prolong the true confessions, your best plan is to take the lady for a twirl round the floor. So ups-a-daisy!'

'Last time I crossed the sea before this daft waste of a trip was a troopship taking us to Holland for Germany, and looking over the side what did I see? A drowned man, a drowned man way down deep. But clear as I can see across this room. Clearer. So now maybe you can guess what was going through my head when it was blowing a gale over the Channel, clinging to the rail with her and watching each cold wave heave up. The sea is cold, I kept thinking, so cold, thinking how it would be to be full to the tongue and your mouth still going like you can never get enough. Because so long as we're still alive we keep on fighting to get air inside, I believe, to bring everything up.'

'How much longer do I have to stand here holding your hand?'

'A man on a train saw him.'

'On your feet!'

'My leg's asleep.'

'It's the stupid way you were sitting. Get up!'

'I only came down here for something to eat.'

'Hold me as if I'm a woman.'

'I wanted to talk.'

'And you dance like you talk. That was my foot. Your unwashed state doesn't scare me, or your awful breath. Or the sandpaper on your chin. Now that's better. I was wanting to say, if you can't find your hotel you can always stay with us. We're the same height.'

'I'm only five-foot-five.'

'So was Lawrence of Arabia, I was reading. Instead

George was far too tall to stretch himself, as James once rather memorably put it. He'd nod off straight after his dinner like a baby after its feed. Making up for it now though. I'm informed the Dragon has him well trained.'

'I'm not violent, she knows that. Before, when she was changing her outfit, I thought it was to get a bite to eat before facing her people, we agreed we were starving. Then when I saw it was to leave it seemed wrong for her not to be in the same state I was. That's the reason I went to get the jumper off her, the only reason. Over her head, pulling this way and that. But she kept her arms down, tight down, and her head with her neck so I'd never get it off. And every finger was stretching from her wrists to show she meant to get her rain-cloak affair off the hook the moment I let her. Other parts are gaps. Though I remember I started saying things, weak pleading things. Which is why I got her by the hair, her new red hair. Behind the ear, here, this ear ... Claudia, if you knew how I feel now!'

'I was wondering when you'd ever reveal the sacred name. But just what on earth were you proposing to do to the girl?'

'She chose to move her head. That's all I've been wanting to tell her ever since, she chose the wrong moment to move her head, and that fucker wouldn't even let her come to the bleeding phone!'

'Whatever next!'

'I'm standing bollock-naked in an ice-cold cell staring at the door she banged, that's what. I got the bottle off the floor. What else do you expect? Every sound was her, or something to do with her. The lift went all the way down, and then it started up again. I heard the cables crack, saw them stretch. Slowly all the way back up it came. Till it filled the window, lady, knocking on the glass. Imagine waiting. Imagine listening for the person inside. Then it goes clanking back down. What could I do? Never would I knowingly harm her. Who pressed the button? My teeth were chattering, what could I do?'

'Tell me, dear.'

'I slept. Was it wrong? It was that cold. I got into bed, our bed, to stop my teeth. Stop thinking too. But then naturally I had to wake, not sure how long after. A minute, an hour. Wheels. Wheels were going round and my heart was going round and I didn't know where I was and my eyes came open and we were safe on the train. The bulb in the ceiling was the bulb in the ceiling on the train. Then the wheels were saying we're a lift, and the bulb, the bulb ...'

'Felix and Claudia. Names that sort of go together, but do somehow sound incompatible too. Dear oh dear, what makes one say these things! They just pop out, and I don't even know the creature. And that frankly is something I do feel a bit of an absence of, despite all the words. Yes, some solid physical impression, please. Appearances do count, you know. I see fingers stretching, and that poor ear, and red hair which is rare in these parts. But still I wonder what sort of beauty I'm meant to conceive of. Easy on the eye? Very easy on?'

'Easy on.'

'Not very forthcoming. At least you might reveal what sort of red to picture.'

'Yellowy. Yellowy-goldy red. Leastways last time I set eyes on it.'

'It changes colour?'

'Only since I started going out with her she's had it well-nigh every colour in the rainbow.'

'Haircare's my special province, you know. And what length would it be?'

'Lady, I'm going to have to pack it in, I'm afraid.'

'Oh no you don't, young man, I'm not having you going off and wetting your whistle again. Over my dead body!'

'Remember all I've been through. Also I'm starting to feel the effects, slightly. Aye, commencing to feel just a little bit tight and…'

'Stop taking backward steps all the time, you'll have me right off balance. And?'

'And on an empty stomach, I might point out.'

'Slow down. Go with the music. Relax.'

Claudia …

'Ah, that's it.'

'Claudia!'

'M'mm?'

'Nothing.'

'What word did I hear?'

'No word. My nan was a hairdresser.'

'It was a word. Nearly got her pregnant twice? Doesn't sound like you set much store by safety precautions, either of you. I tell the child it's a woman's duty to protect herself. Cocks don't think, particularly in these benighted regions. We plough the fields and scatter, that's the male attitude round here.'

'Call it the centre of the universe but to my way of thinking it's a world-famous hole more like a cross between a garbage dump and a bombsite. Not noticed a single column yet. They go on about Kennedy but I think it's Khrushchev who saved the world.'

'Shush now, you're such a frightful chatterbox. Perhaps it's my turn for a confession. Between you and me and the gatepost I adore thick tangly hair like yours. Adore it, darling. Not a few women I know would pay the earth for a good mop like this.'

'Now I don't even know if we redeemed ourselves after last week's shock.'

'Really, is this the moment for politics? Yes, a good rich mop. You know, you've not allowed the poor thing a single saving grace. Does she have nothing going for her?'

'We're unbeatable at Roker, see, but we were away from home yesterday and that's always a worry. Because I'm thinking we don't want another Norwich if ever we're to get back to where we rightfully belong.'

'I asked a question.'

'Aye, I'd have been a lot more use at Grimsby – there's a thought!'

'I'm rather grander than hairdresser I'd have you know. Goldy red? Not too carroty, I trust? Unless it's a very unassuming carrot.'

'What?'

'Listen, if it's the two of them, if that's the trouble, dear, just stop thinking about it. They're only misbehaving to spite me.'

'It.'

'Yes?'

'It's that she.'

'Go on.'

'She dyed. '

'Died! Are you poking fun at me?'

'Dyed it what you might call a kind of carrot, now I think of it.'

'Alleluia! Not so dead to the world after all, eh lover boy!'

Throwing her head back for a full-throated gloat of glee, she twisted a whole clump of my hair so fiercely I heard the roots creak. And in despair I sank my teeth in perfumed neck meat, warm and slippery and tough.

12

Signor, often I used to imagine that train compartment. First some general chit-chat about the war, everyone chipping in with a favourite story, quite excited, as happens when people are glad a thing is over but now they're back to normal it's like they're missing something. And Mam will talk to anyone. Nelly too. Then, imagine, all of a sudden a stranger is giving an eye-witness account of what sounds like the accident which cost your man his life. Of course they had lots to ask, questions and questions, so when they're pulling in to Newcastle he said why not all go off for a sit-down in the buffet. More questions. Because of this new side to it, the thing never mentioned in Leonards's letter. Definitely, he says, very definitely we saw someone or something out there. But that's the most he'd commit himself. Someone or something. Probably thought it the kinder thing to say, leaving it in the air.

It was night, no moon but plenty of stars, which tallies, and he said he'd have remembered if the sea was bad. Then at one point he and one of his mates thought they sighted something and thought it worth a shout. He himself, the man on the train, he said he was the first to shout. What did they see, all of them? I'd like to know. When the spotlight swung round to their side nothing showed, he said, nothing at all. An officer called through a megaphone a while then ordered them back to their stations.

Nan used to say the pair of them must have been off their heads not to get his address, she'd have liked a proper talk with the man. Now I think it would have been better had Mam and Nelly never gone near that train, it would have saved a lot of heartache. The more they pressed the more he spoke of a wife at home waiting. Finally he said most likely it was not a living thing, seeing it neither shouted nor waved. And what are we supposed to make of that?

For as long as I was on top I'd keep trying to make contact. Do something. Anything. Call out. Shout like in Nan's dream. At the least put up a hand. You'd have done that, surely? Unless, I sometimes think, unless he saw the commotion and thought, Ah I've been sighted, and went back to trying to keep afloat, treading water waiting for his rescuers. But what I also fear is that when he saw the lights and people at the rail, all the reflections in the water, he'd maybe not recall what a black emptiness the sea at night looks to anyone on board.

A mystery makes you add bits and pieces of your own. Such as, what if after holding out so long, after all that time in the water, he had reached the end of his limit, knew he was done for, knew he had only one last very short space of time in which to cram all he ever saw, ever felt, all he had to leave, why even bother to signal before going down? Naturally I'd also wonder what some of those thoughts might be, and I don't have to tell you I hoped at least one was me. To get closer still, I'd make myself imagine past even that point, to the point where the end is so near there's no room left in your head for anything else. It could come almost as a relief, I found. In the Army, on night-guard duty trying to fight sleep, fighting hard, always the moment came when you forgot the fight, and at that moment you'd dropped off without another thought. When it's that close I think you might just stop caring.

Up at the hospital one night visiting Nan round about this same time last year after she became a permanent bed case, walking through the long ward to her bit territory in the corner, this is what she said, not even giving time to say hello. It was him, it was my ginger-hair Robbie out there, and why he neither shouted nor waved was to save himself a waste of agony. It's how the trawlermen go, she says shutting her eyes I thought to stop the tears, and he knew all about that because there was enough deep-sea fishermen in the family of that fusionless father of his, three Arran cousins for a start, all sailors and not one could swim. Your father could, he was good, but even he was no match for the open sea. You pull your arms to your side, tight, or stick them above your head, high in the air. Showing it where she lay, the knobby hands bumping about the white bars, and the blue eyes open and clear now, not shut against something she did not wish to see. Death's inevitable, she says when finally they come to rest in mine, but not our arrival. Remember that, hinny, remember that always.

13

She stiffens, still pulling my hair though now it's to force my teeth apart, and she succeeds just as something cracks me behind the ear so hard my knees give way and I'm in someone else's arms. The bald Sicilian, squid eyes spitting venom, twice my weight and strength. 'She wouldn't listen,' I try to say, though it's as useless as shouting under water. Our foreheads bang. His hands tighten round my neck as other faces show alongside. The daughter pale as death, looking frightened for me. The mother snarling, 'Guttersnipe, the gutter's where he belongs,' while I'm being dragged over the floor, fighting for air and close to puking.

He drops me on a chair beside a familiar figure who does nothing to intervene. More spitting and snarling, so I keep my head down, fingering my throat. When all the legs go away I look at my hand. 'No blood,' I say to O'Cain.

'Brother, you're in the Mediterranean now, and lucky your testicles are intact. Don't mess with others' property. Yet the first thing a husband tells you is he's two-timing his wife, just in case you won't think him a man. Should I refresh your glass?'

'Here how many numbers have phones?'

We're at the same table, drinks everywhere, but the

women have changed. Two pairs of big solemn mosaic eyes are inspecting my throbbing face.

'Adriana,' says one.

'Patrizia,' says the other.

'Majora and Minora, and both slobbering to meet the martyr. Fatty dabbles in English. Skinny does German, I'm informed. If you care who does what or what for whom.'

The large lass comes closer, her fingers touch my cheek. 'You are trembling.'

'No blood,' I repeat pathetically.

'Cry, cry, cry,' she murmurs kneeling right down beside me, big breasts suddenly like pillows for my thumping head. 'Only humans cry.' A voice so like Claudia's, but warmer, warmer.

'He must not float upon his water bier, tra-la, without the need of some melodious tear. Have a suck, Felicitous.'

'Mans must cry too,' she says, and her hair is tickling my cheek like a running teardrop. 'Each is same, mans and womans the same.'

'Yes.'

'Same? Twaddle. The Nyzam of Hyderabad has forty-two concubines and two hundred children. Claptrap, as the bishop …'

'Oh!' she gasps. And my comforter is gone, yanked backwards by her companion.

'Don't look so mortified,' gurgles O'Cain. 'Didn't want her rump fondled, or not by me. Tonight I could swallow and swallow and still die of thirst.'

'Her eyes went sort of blind, then loaded with luggage she went through the door and out of my life forever, slamming it with a foot. Eights and sixes it has, I think, and nothings. How many per – how many permutations is that?'

'Try VAT 69. Pray for me, Pop, for I have sinned.'

'But would she speak?'

'And all for a convulsion, my son, a tiny convulsion.'

'She had a green top just like that brown-hair lass there. Green silk. Looking this way now, smoking and dancing.'

'Yes, think of that mouth wrapped round your maulstick.'

'She learned me the twist.'

'Cat, sad lovesick cat, you're licking your stubbly whiskers over one of our all-night jitter-buggers. Irresistible the way they move, I know, but to interest one of them we must be exceptionally twinkle-toed, and you and I have drunk ourselves way past that capacity. Furthermore, that tasty-looking morsel is not in fact a good chew, I have it on good authority, too many bones. Why mess things up with Sibs? Our whimsical little shrimp was the one for you. And now I daresay she too could wring your neck.'

'They're in the book, only the entry's wrong. They've moved, see, they're on another line now. And I went and left it in a bar and now likely it's been thrown out.'

'So cry, cry, cry. Are humans sublimely ridiculous, or vice versa? Castro's man at Moscow airport – heard it? Let me through, let me through, I have an urgent appointment with Mr K! Niet, says Ivan at passport control. But this is a matter of life and death, compañero, the fate of mankind hangs by a thread! Cuba? asks Ivan, suspicious. How do I know you're not CIA? No beard, no cigar? Ssh, amigo, secret service ... Whereat he unzips! See what I'm getting at? Don't be mawkish, sonny, learn to laugh at yourself.

Plenty more fish in the sea. Get over one by getting over another. A man who has not a sort of affection for the whole sex is incapable of ever loving a single one as he ought. End of quote. Shall we drink to that?'

'You can.'

'Then I'll be priest and down it for you.' Lifting a glass of wine and another of gin he attempts to imbibe from both. Threads of pink run down his chin, splashing onto a silver salver floating in the air as though for the purpose. The hand gripping the salver belongs to the headwaiter, Whale, and in the centre sits a little drink-spattered card. O'Cain peers at very small writing on the card, then his eyebrows shoot above his polaroids.

'Have I been labouring under a misapprehension? The haruspex has his eye on you. Be upstanding now!' He's on his own feet already, pulling my arm. 'You're wanted, old son. Body-snatcher-in-chief requests your company.'

'I don't need company.'

'Captain's orders. *Il padrone,* the big power round the whole damned place. Bit reclusive, but very rich, and strange to relate as tight as a fish's backside. Still, not unknown to concede a few droppings, if we kowtow.'

'Where's the way out? I don't feel good.'

Arm in arm, we're progressing in an irregular path between tables and the legs at tables.

'Be your simple self, he'll like that. And put in a word for old J O'C. Unmentionable things were done to me in South Croydon, Felix. Grey things. Sibs was a trifle unfair, she knows I have no trouble in the implementation. Now salute His Irreverence. See, he's reserved a special place right next him on the famous couch.'

We have halted somewhere gloomy beyond reach of the gyrating coloured lights, before a ring of six or seven shadowy figures seated round a guttering candle. Perched at one end of an otherwise empty ink-blue divan is a small person with a very large head peering up at me out of eyes tight-squeezed between round cheeks.

'Welcome to our little circle,' he says in impeccable English. 'I am pleased you passed our way.'

Perplexed, I look round for O'Cain, but the know-all Irishman is fast back-finning out of view, stout bespectacled carp comically mouthing: A good word, a good word ...

'We noticed you were not happy with the English woman. And her present partner is the sort who makes one ashamed to be of the same race. Be seated, please. She is compelled to repeat herself ad infinitum, we name her the Squawker.' He translates for the circle and the circle smiles.

Now I am next to him on the divan, my right hand clasped in his, while a tiny slate-black dot of a pupil scrutinizes my face. The other eye remains out of sight behind a motionless lid. A familiar but unplaceable tangy smell comes off him. Leathery. 'I thought she'd help, I thought I could talk to a woman about a woman.'

'Between men there is often more understanding. Also we need fewer words. You are unwell?' His thumb is feeling my pulse.

'You're a doctor?'

'All are doctors in Italy. But I am more doctor than most.'

It must be another joke, because when he murmurs something in Italian the circle ripples again.

‘Tell us what is your deepest ambition, here in the Eternal City?’

‘All gone,’ I blurt, sensing somehow he will understand. ‘I lost my way looking for the Colosseum and drifted in. I arrived today.’

‘I mean your most personal aspiration. After all one travels to find what one cannot find in one’s own country.’

‘Archaeology’s a thing I thought of.’

‘Naturally. No other gratification, stimulation?’

‘A lass was going to show me all of Rome’

‘Lass?’

‘A girl.’

‘Good. Here one must not only be able to swim but to navigate. Our lasses are very appealing. No?’

The heavy smell intensifies when he opens his mouth. Something eaten. Garlic? Dog? The penetrating pupil does not quit my face.

‘No?’ he prompts again, finally releasing my hand.

And in a rush of relief my story is pouring out.

‘Signor, this has to be the worst day of my life. I know she was happy, she used to sing. Then she closed up, the spark went. Still I tried to be considerate. Now this. It’s not you she kept saying, not you, and I could tell she was thinking, leave us alone, leave us alone. To the point of inventing she was iller than she was. Then for no cause I can see and with her writing nowhere near finished she announces she’s leaving England. So to me it made more sense to come away too, better than moping round home without her. Which I told her eventually, how I was willing to try my luck out here, see if I couldn’t find work. And it was all agreed, all settled and agreed, eventually. In any case,

Nan, my gran, I always promised to come here for her sake. So after the journey and all my patience she rents a room, changes her outfit, and all at once we're having words. Or she is, terrible words. The upshot being she leaves, making us feel I'm nothing. She says she wants another life now. What's behind it?'

The pupil leaves my imploring two and travels round the silent circle. Their Neptune is a squat red dribbling stub.

'Did she only go with me because she had no one else? She liked her room, she liked my mam, she liked our town.'

'Never is there no reason.' He pauses, sucking his lips so they almost disappear, while the pin-point pupil seems to revolve inwards too. 'However not always is the reason agreeable to confront.' He only speaks after these thoughtful pauses, as though the one good eye deep in its folds of skin needs time to scan the contents of his mind as well as track my every reaction. 'What generally explains all is when you can see yourself as the other sees you.'

'All's fixed before it happens, that's her creed, so you'd think it was meant to be. Only a man here sent her life chart on the back of his photo and she decided to go into herself, in deep where no one can get. Locking herself in and writing things down. But then last week did come a change, I thought, a real change of heart, like all the world after these danger days. She was depressed, she said. Maybe she really is ill, mentally ill. In London she was sick on my arm just walking along.'

'If you wish, I will make these people go.'

'He told her it was never meant to be, that's my theory. Yet she wanted to resist, I think, in her heart. Otherwise why are we here? Yesterday morning she found a twin-yoked egg at breakfast and I thought she was going to break down and cry. What was that about? '

'They mean nothing to me.'

Only three remain in the circle now. On the distant floor the dancers are bobbing up and down to *Marina.* 'Everyone here smokes her cigarettes.' *Marina, Marina, Marina* ... 'What do I know about her life, Signor, the friends she has?'

Can he really be so rich and powerful? He has a gold watch, also a gold tie-pin on which I can make out the initials ES in white enamel. But apart from the size of his head everything else about him is so very small, hunched even smaller now, the collar of his jacket riding high behind his big round face, like a halter. The power is in the brilliant brain behind the all-comprehending eye, all his riches are no more concern to him than his comical head and his bad breath and his dwarfish other parts. Maybe my sister, if she'd lived, would have grown to be like this, a clever mind inside a massive head on top of a mini-body. He just seems so glad to be sitting here holding my hand again.

'I'm pleased I found you,' I hear myself saying. 'I was wanting someone to listen. The only person I felt might understand, we didn't have a word in common.'

He doesn't respond, still seems buried in thought. The sad-reeking breath exits and enters in little pops and sucks, alternately puffing and crumpling the little mouth and the folds of skin ringing the hole which houses his one good eye, now withdrawn in contemplation of some deep inner truth which in the course of time he may reveal.

'This is the place my father longed to see, I keep

remembering. So was she right, all's destined to be? Getting here, losing her? Is there some connection?'

'*Bene, bene!*' he murmurs, back from the depths, letting go my hand and tapping my knee. 'Let us consult our friend here. He is the specialist.'

All have slipped away, all but the specialist friend I seem to see for the first time. Perhaps it's my condition, all the effort it takes to focus on more than one thing at a time, but the ageless face across the table seems to advance and retreat in the candlelight. A shock of silver hair rises like a well-groomed wave over his forehead, sweeping back to neat curls behind his ears. Wide nostrils and the crest of the wave catch the glow, mouth and eyes lurk in shadow. Even the voice comes and goes. My gentle neighbour is interpreting for me.

'Think like the enemy, he counsels, then you see more clear. And never presume too much intelligence, he says, even higher intelligence, or the workings of their minds will always perplex.'

'At times I felt she was the enemy, yet I always knew she's worth ten times what I am. She speaks three languages perfect, she reads heavy books. If I tell you everything, all that happened, and all she said, then you…'

But the silver-haired man is murmuring again in his world-weary drone and my friend is attending very closely, or that is how I interpret the gobble motions of that mouth no larger than a barbel's. Or ruminating? For when they arrive it's not possible to tell which words are the specialist's and which his own.

'Why suffer, if nothing endures? We can only be acquaintances, this is the real curse of Adam. Learn to master yourself or you will never master others. For this reason the only great leader our nation ever had was right to despise his own people. Women are happy to see men suffer, he says, but what woman wants love with a man who suffers? If you want success it is not love you must love but the intrigue of love. And cheat, he says, faster than they cheat you. But why so much fuss about the ladies?'

His funny shrewd head is tilted, one-eyeing me quizzically, thickets of hair bunging each nostril.

'The female is a natural commodity, observes our friend. To fecundate, to perpetuate man. Of course he wishes me also to say he does not mean to offend your mother. Naturally not, every mother is sacred. A father has always been there before, but a mother never ceases to dream for her son.' The lone pupil revolves inward, the little lips purse in sorrowful acceptance of the way things are, and no doubt pity that I too have to suffer them. Then a finger taps my knee again.

'If you want work, it is best to know the right person.'

'Oh I couldn't stop here, not anywhere she is. After all this I'm going away, far away. A man in Australia keeps writing to my mother saying the boat costs just ten quid, so long as you've work waiting. If she didn't want love I still know she wanted something. Why could she not say?'

'My recommendation could help. I do not promise archaeology! But now our friend has what I believe you call a burning question. Which I think is also my question. Are you perhaps sacrificial?'

'I don't understand.'

'Are you a submissive boy, we wonder? But never

mind that now. He also asks, does the lass have headaches, complicated medical troubles?'

'How does he know?'

'He has had many women. How many? *Quante?*'

A bony hand rises in the candlelight, all fingers spread.

'Five?'

'Five hundred. It is perhaps better to acquiesce at times, to surrender, then one may be more surprised. It is a kind of freedom, to accept that we cannot control what may happen.'

'Almost her words. Also she claims everything comes round again, so next time we can get a better chance.'

'Standard classical thinking, of course. What does Virgil arrange for his hero to find in the underworld? A resentful lover claiming to be his conscience. A dead father who explains that in order to submit once more to life one must have no memory of the misery one lived before. And was your pretty informant also able to disclose how many lives each person has?'

Is he a professor? He talks like a book. It's not just all the things he knows, it's how he comes out with them. They emerge perfectly rounded and finished, in shapely pushes of those flexible lips, each one sounding so well chewed over and long digested. Think before you speak, Nan was partial to saying. But at times I find it's hard to think unless I speak, times like now. Claudia maybe thinks too much before she speaks, anyhow prefers things written down, though being a walking dictionary she has so much to choose from she can get almost lost in the choosing. Or choose not to speak. But in his head every word lies rich and deep as thought, and no gap between. And now I know what to say.

'On the train I dreamed a wave, a tidal wave big as a mountain. It's come before, many times. Always getting higher and higher and darker till there's no sky left. Only this time was different. Normally something holds it back, all that water hanging there, bubbling on top, like it meets glass.'

'Good,' he says, lips bunching in a tight knot, and I am surprised he is almost tittering. 'Being your creation, the monster waits before breaking the glass, and so you awake.'

'But this time, on the train last night, I wanted to go with it. I wished away the glass. I wanted to drown, Signor, I wanted to drown! I woke terrified and she was gone. And now she really is, unless I can reconstruct her number and speak. This person put us through and her dad said not to come. If it's who he was. No come round again, and the line went dead. She worships him. Her book's for him ...'

The little pupil is examining the wet inside of my mouth, so I shut my mouth.

'You are tired, my dear boy, I can see. And unhappy. And very lonely. Later it will be quiet here. All will go.'

Only he understands my feelings, only he can make me think, and only he can make me say it.

'Does love only go deep when you get none back?'

'*Solo tu,* it is a beautiful song. Listen with me.'

'She's right, Signor, I don't know what else in the world I want apart from her. What's *puoi essere* mean?'

'When I saw you enter I sent Balena. We have many very silly songs about the moon. This is a slow about two moons, two lonely moons so deep in love. The moon in the sky, the moon in the sea. A narcissistic fantasy, of course. Listen. Or dance if you prefer, I do not mind. I will watch again.' And I instead watch mesmerised as the tip of a little stubby finger probes his left eye, the lifeless one, tugging down the lower lid to reveal a dead moon inside a pink pouch of clouds. 'Two moons, dear boy, like lovers' faces.' The moon eye vanishes, and now I am intrigued by the movements of that tiny restless mouth. Trembling, swelling, the lips are clenched against something massive behind them pushing to get out, squeeze through, possibly an enormous yawn. Only when they expand to a round 'O' and a hot blast of sewer-foul air fans my face do I realise they are yearning for a kiss.

Next moment there is room for three between us on the couch.

But I still hear his voice. 'You have not understood, I own this place. I can make them play something you prefer. *Twist and Shout? Arrivederci Roma?* You all exist at my discretion...'

I stand up, very shaky, looking round for the exit. Trouble is I cannot see too well. Here it's almost as dark as though the lights have failed, unless his stinking breath has blown a thick sepia film of grease over my eyes. My stomach and the floor are heaving.

'Yes, go back to your friend the improviser. Originality at all costs is so futile.'

From where did O'Cain appear, swaying before me, in and out of focus?

'Spread those legs, Cat. Ride the rise, go with the fall.'

'Me head's like wheels turning. Who's that person?'

'Head shlike wheelsh ... Touch of seasickness, light blurring, speech slurring? Byron's cure was a good beefsteak. I'm so perfectly pickled too, Felicitous. The thing is to work at it steadily, stealthily, paint or page, and unveil only when you feel it was lodged in your head since the day you were born, because then it was obvious but you had no means, no damned means. And what it is, what this unutterably irretrievable wonder is –' he staggers – 'is – '

'How could you leave us with that bag of shite?'

'Love of mystification is contempt for the ordinary, I know, I have been told. But I presumed you were on the wanted list.'

'I thought I was wanted, but not like that.'

'Who wants a wanted man?'

'He's one of them – and you knew it!'

'A bit of a devil, even a bit of an old pig, but not unentertaining if you relish Hieronymous Bosch. And piles of money. But I'm forgetting you hail from a primitive corner of the old country where a man's a man and a poof's a poofter.'

'Dead right I do! And I'm going back to where from I hail. So out of me road now or I'll knock your teeth out!'

'I can remove them myself, thank you. I have nothing against you, boyo, far from it. Endearing muddlehead, you're the least moribund of us all. Just thought you could do with a little fatherly advice. But see here, is there nothing more in that ridiculous pocket?'

'Out of my road!'

'Don't get it, do you? Before departing for that drab man-in-the moon-shaped island there is the small matter of the bill to settle. Balena informs me we are still eight thousand short.'

'Where's ... My money, you have it all!'

'Wrong tense.'

'I demand it back! I need it!'

'Settle down.'

'Give me my wallet!'

'You're in deep shit, old son, and attracting an awful lot of attention now. Slip away, this is no place for you. Get back to Muggleswick. In case of default Balena will be pleased to see you off the premises.'

'Just who do you think you are?'

'Good question.'

What's happening? As I ready to take a swing at him everything changes with the dizzying speed of a dream. In his place is a hooded face of gristle and bone with empty eye-sockets. Is down up, up down? I need air, it's suffocating down here, like when the whole house filled with the stench of the major's shaving cream and pipe. Then I'm out of the trough, not upside down, back up on my own two feet readying for another swipe. Only now it's the Sicilian bruiser who faces me, huge fists up, wanting to finish the job though I never intended to offend. But I have to get straighter first, and breathe, breathe deep and strong to settle my floundering heart which missed whole beats down there and now bangs and bangs and bangs. Everyone is speaking their language which blocks my ears and waterwheels are churning and now I'm moving, independent of my legs, past the hairless Sicilian slow-clapping mockingly and the daughter looking truly frightened for me. Sorry, sorry, I may have called, though all are clapping too loud in time to Benito's beat or the beat of the music and we're piling single file through the narrow corridor on each other's heels, some dancing the conga, when Whale heaves me up by the armpits out into the vestibule of mirrors ...

'Die! Die! Die!' a voice calls from high above and I know it refers to me. I had a coat, I'm thinking, somehow upright at the foot of the long blue stairs. O'Cain's glasses have gone and his eyes look small. 'Trial by existence, Felix. Some turds float and others sink.'

How can I climb all that way?

'Good lad, up you go. You're a floater.'

Up, up! I'm on my knees and crawling, struggling to swim my arms into my parka, while far below me now the Irish soak still booms: 'Bye bye, Felicitous. Go forth and multiply!'

Nearing the top, in the door glass I see my own straining face trapped between the doorman's spread striped trousers, mouth like a dying fish's gagging on a black rubber ball too big for it, Bruno on his knees before the priest. Holy Father, Mouth of Truth, come for me now, bring her back ... He grasps my hand, helps me off my knees, and a stream of cool air rushes in.

'Pensione Confort?' I plead before the open door, glancing back down the long plunge of stairs to the lobby now void of people.

'Come in!' he grins, shoving me into the night.

14

I can swim, I can float, but water's not my element. I hate opening my eyes under it and I hate to have them shut. Yet

I love fishing, quite mad about it. So it's not rivers and lakes, it's the sea I'm wary of. One false breath and all down your throat you've a festering sore. I hear your Mediterranean is saltier even than our North Sea, but bears people up. And warmer too, a lot warmer. *Cazzo,* you'll never catch an Italian in that!

That's what she came out with another time we were by the sea, and I knew the word because in certain moods she liked to learn us all them sorts of things. Seaham Sands it was this time, not Marsden, and in my opinion plenty warm enough, though blowed if she'd oblige even to the extent of removing her top. Everyone else was stripped off, sunning themselves or splashing about, and she's after finding a dip in the dunes for herself and her notes. I asked if she was riled for some reason and she said, no, no, only she couldn't any longer bear sitting on my wet towel in a cold wind having to watch this little lad, the smallest and definitely the skinniest of the lot. It got to me too, the moment she said it, seeing him trailing round after the bigger lads like a keen kid brother, skin blotched all bluey-pink, a mix of fear and cold. That was my own self by the sea when I was small, and if I'm to be honest I'm not that much different right to this day. There was a jittery bairn hidden inside the he-man in tiger knickers doing one-arm press-ups and yelling at her to come and play in the waves, shouting it could do wonders for that dicky heart she has. But all summer was one long bid for attention, I see that now.

Man, it's like you were there too, you've got him to perfection! Rubbing his elbows, shoulders round his ears, yes, tight as a collar, the knobbly kneecaps bouncing away. Then, yes, slowly venturing in, stretching each leg to twice its length, tummy sucked right up to his chest as the breakers splash higher, arms out, dancing on his toes and giggling like water only makes him ticklish even when it's closing round his neck, that's it, that's exactly it, head swivelling about like a lost duck. You're a brilliant mime, I'll say. And I suspect an excellent swimmer.

Oh it's the biggest thing we'll ever know, and to me it says we belong on land. Which puts me in mind of something else about him I could find to tell.

One freezing morning they decided to ship the lot of us off to the coast. Truckloads and truckloads of raw recruits all shivering like jelly on a plate, and so cold hard slippy underfoot that when we had to pile out and fall in and stand to attention it was as much as anyone could do to keep upright on rutted slopes of solid ice. We had our greatcoats on, we had our battle gear strapped over the top, we had our little woolly gloves, but you still got screamed at for putting your hands over your ears, army berets not being designed to reach them. Orders were to patrol the foreshore and vicinity for what turned out to be miles on the look-out for an enemy they of course omitted to say was so well camouflaged in snow suits and white balaclavas that when my moment of reckoning came I took a bullet plum through the heart. Point blank, no more than from here to that little green bush. It had crossed his mind to hold fire and mock-bayonet me, he said after, since for all I was looking him full in the eyes I didn't seem to see him. And why I wasn't all there is the reason I started this story.

A while before, after rounding up our section and one or two more on the excuse we were dragging our feet, they made us climb back aboard this three-tonner waiting right there on the roadside for the purpose. Then after a mile, maybe a mile and a half, they got us to perform this sort of delayed drop-off, to get us up near the big ambush I realised after, and then all head back to the warm. Picture the sight. Every so many yards one more squaddie plops off the tailboard, all while cruising at fifteen, twenty, and of course with the ice and the speed a trail of lads is soon stretching behind that truck like it's run over them all. When my turn came for the tap on the shoulder I made sure to hit soft snow, and picking myself up in one piece and digging out my rifle I made my way along this very steep bank which was there, an earlier section of the same long stretch where that chalk-face devil likely had us in his sights already.

So here's me plodging along through this quite steep drift spilling down to a wider part of the beach, up to me knee-pits at times, in over my belt at one point and holding me bloody rifle high aloft like I'm already surrendering, and time and time again my eyes I noticed kept straying toward something way out by the water's edge. A shape where the full white of the beach finished and the grey sea began. It was supposed to be a manhunt and it did look like a man, but equally I told myself no one in their right mind would issue an order to adopt an exposed fire position like that, right out in the open and not even stirring with his boots in the water. So then I began to think a body had been washed up.

It was an arrangement of stones, nothing more, but to my eyes it looked not like stones but a human. I was by water, same as Mam at Marsden, so possibly he was already at the back of my mind, the sea after all being where he is. But the main reason my eyes could not fully accept what they were seeing was the fact it was held together with ice, the entire stone arrangement, ice so solid-packed in folds of frozen black such as never would you imagine even that level of cold could achieve. I mean, considering all the salt there is in the sea.

Signor, I swear it felt like I was looking at a man frozen under a black tarpaulin, or inside a shining sack. Even right up close, this close, so near in fact I could have touched it with the rifle, it was still more than ice and stones. And that is when I did remember – what else, Marsden Rock. I stood there a long time, staring through the ice.

15

Who wants a wanted man?

Whipped by wind and lashed by rain, I stumbled on down the unlit alley, head thrumming like the wheels of the train I rode day and night with my false woman, and in my gorge a sour knot of stomach juice and vinegary gin stuck not low enough to swallow or high enough to spew, sore as seawater, fetched up on a lone sob when I was pushed back out into the wet and cold.

No one wants a wanted man.

Weeks hoarding dole scraps, painting walls for peace with Mam, forsaking the pub, forsaking my favourite Era fry-ups and frothy coffees by sleeping away whole mornings after the women left for work, forsaking my beloved team – all for a ticket to a better life in another land, and instead of passing me up when I might have got a refund she'd had me tag her all the way to ruddy Roma to lose the lot. Rain spat, wind jeered. When they fished me out of the Tiber she'd maybe begin to see what she'd set in motion, finally start to appreciate that before clashing doors in faces some with more sensitivity might stop to think where the best of the Rowans go. In the drink. The first proper kiss I got off her was when I made her weep salt tears to hear how once I had a special dad, everyone said so, I licked them from her eye-corners, and yet that didn't spare him a watery grave, all of twenty-two. A good soldier, his colonel wrote, above all a good man, very resourceful too, clever in both hands and brain, a foot taller than his baby son would ever be. And just possibly even now, if she was commencing to start to have just some regrets, I'd have her filling buckets with the revelation that a little lad chucked out of school a second time and missing his dead dad so bad shinned down a cindery embankment blubbering like a baby and ran to lay the back of his neck on a big cold rail of the Newcastle-London track, so glad and sad he was a failure, a permanent failure, pleased to leave it to the engine driver whether he lived or died, fighting off the horrors running through his head – steel wheels speeding down the line like so many guillotines – by hunting for friendly cloud creatures in the sky. Wheels whirred, my legs went faster, the lane dropped steeper, I could barely see ... Lost in darkness I let the wind take over and do as it pleased, bully me the rest of the way downhill.

A wanted man is wanted dead.

Jerked out of that nightmare of a tsunami by my terror at longing to drown and a broken-neck feeling because my head was lolling in a hole where her head had been, I'd waited and waited for her and then clambered over sleeping strangers' legs into the empty corridor to search the whole length of the train through screaming draughty carriages lurching and rocking like this tunnel of a street, and back along them all in a growing panic, scared she might have got off at a station, jumped off, beginning to run – in Switzerland, to Italy, for England – only to find she'd got off with a soldier and was singing loud opera at the far end of our own carriage, last on the train, not letting up even when she looked up to see me racing down the long corridor. What's this situation? What situation, *amore*?

Ah-MORE-eh!

Hooking an ice-cold finger far down the collar of my parka and another up its tail, groaning, a sudden extra-strong blast of wind heaved me off the ground within sight of a bright main street – and dropped me flat on my face.

On no account move victim. Tell him to breathe out, out, and try to whistle. Same dodge under a thrashing, puff out for as long as you can haul up still more air to push away the pain, keep it spinning above the skin, not yet drilling hot holes of hurt ... But all too soon I needed another gulp of oxygen, and at once some section of the brain beyond my control, one of the many, started itemising the damage, each injury registered by the innocent victim with another twist of his head like a fresh insult, fate kicking a man when he's down: sore palms, a funny funny bone, a knackered knee.

The instant before take-off I'd glimpsed what lay ahead, a wide road with bright shop fronts and racing cars, no place for me. Behind, somewhere off to my left, still howled the powerful cross-current which had sent me flying. Opening one eye I sighted a tall dark alley slit between high walls just a moment before bouncing bright car beams swept across it to spotlight me sprawled right in the middle of the road – and now somehow I'm up on all fours, dazzled crippled street cat dithering between certain death and bolting for safety out of the path of a speeding enemy with headlamps trained on me like flame throwers. I hopped out of the light only in the nick of time. A long black Alfa splashed past without a hoot or a jeer, then braked in a red glow. Not to pull up and enquire after my health, mind, only to slow down before turning into the main road.

That gob of stomach curry had jogged into my mouth in the fall. Stepping back into the centre of the lane, feet planted on the spot where that lunatic driver might have killed me, I spat it ten yards on the wind after his disappearing tail lights, swinging up my good arm in a vicious English V-sign. Now crash!

Turning my back on him and all his kind I ducked into the side-alley and began to climb. It was like battling your way up a wind tunnel, the gale gusting down that steep vennel was wild enough to blow me out again. Only I was wild enough myself. Even so, what with my busted knee, and the gradient, and a force-ten in my face, making headway was painful slow, at times a classic case of one step forward and two steps back. But punishment can goad a good man into beating it, and returning it too. Bang goes the gong and – wham! – my bunched right halts the tubby Paddy twister smack in his tracks. Nothing more in that ridiculous pocket? Coming now, boyo! Two more drifting dancing steps uphill in the company of a pair of cracking left hooks are just the playful prelude to a sizzling sledgehammer of a finisher which slams fifteen stone of thieving ignorant son of the peat bog smack into some Roman's solid front door. I'll give you Felicitous, I'll give you Muggleswick, I'll give you floater! Torrents of cheers and catcalls greet the plucky wee northerner as he slicks back his rich thick tangly hair and squints up ahead for more trouble, ice-blue eyes narrowed to slits against another salvo of stinging rain pellets. And *cazzo,* what do they spy?

Solo tu, dear boy. The one-eyed midget poofter blowing fithy kisses from behind big Benito who's squaring up to do the heroic thing, jumped-up great leader daring mighty Inghilterra to take a poke at him. *Arrivederci*, he sneers, underlip jutting like for shaving his chin. Only the young Englishman's mouth has a nasty twist to it too. *Arrivederci,* he hums in perfect Italian, *Roma,* packing home a pair of steely knucklers that send the bullying bullet head and the stinking little arsehole spinning down the lane together in a last waltz with the wind. Dance with yourselves. I'll give you sacrificial, I'll give you anonymous bosh. That's for thinking circus football and dirty tackles can outclass England, falling over in the penalty area, play-acting mortally wounded, arguing any fair decision with the ref, every man a prima donna ... On I weave against the gale and gradient, staggering my punches more to save my sap and sending a black rat with scared little ball-bearing eyes back down its hole just as I near the top of the lane and find no more resistance in the wind. My dad fought all you worm-eaters to the death, and who won?

The gale is played out now, the pellets are falling as soft as petals. All that can be heard apart from my panting is the babble in my head. They threw everything at us, they thought they could hammer us into the ground, Dad, and we came back from the dead. And you just wait for the next World Cup! In the sudden eerie silence the sleepless slept at last, and the sleepers roused.

A wanted man wants.

By the law of averages over half the inhabitants of this city had to be female, thousands upon thousands of them, and by the law of nature hundreds must be dreaming of a man right this minute now, one or two surely not so very far away, passionate solitary signorinas. Which bell do you ring? No one should be as alone as this, even dogs have a better life. Call it evolution if after all the generations since we began not one specimen of the human race yet got round to evolving some instinct for putting sex-starved members of the species in touch, some sure-fire way of linking up through space, such as a fine nose for a single hot naked scouting molecule drifting by on the night air to set you weaving away upwind on its trail, scenting them more and more thickly swarming as you near the source, knowing it will be safe, knowing you're wanted? Woman of Rome, I'd be there now!

She wouldn't barricade herself in her room accusing you of having no more than a physical interest, wouldn't keep a secret diary of your crimes, straight off she'd know you were the real thing, real as only a real woman can make a man. I'd come these thousand miles to find her. But what was her name? In the Army I read the book right through twice, purloined from the brigadier's collection, certain bits umpteen times, and I knew there was only one *uomo* in all Italy with the power to stir her to the core, electrify that beautiful man-weary body. *Donna di Roma.* What was it, what is it? Adriana! Ah. Softly I call under tight-locked shutters – Adriana! In the warm woman-smelling dark she listens and dreams. *Ah-dree-AH-nah!* The salty pink oyster listens too. Glistens.

That mother and daughter were too upper-crust English, not really the hot numbers they tried to make themselves out to be, they'd never break into love-song for me. Too above it all. Claudia, three-quarters Italian, did at times hit top C but just as often when I was sure she must be nearly there I'd open my eyes to find her with teeth clenched staring past my head as though Father Brendan told her to memorise every crack in the ceiling before letting mortal sin be a pleasure, even with her head bouncing on the pillow like on a train, and as like as not I'd fall to wondering whether the radio was up high enough to drown the tell-tale squeal and sigh of springs and the thump-thump of four brass casters punching dents all over Mam's new blue linoleum. Too many ifs and buts. But oh my Adriana, with you one touch is enough, one wicked wink from *Fay-LEE-chay* and all your bells are ringing. You are trembling. Yes, Adriana. Each is the same, mans and womans the same, but never was eet like this with Italians mans. You too are trembling, Adriana. Trembling remembling. What, Adriana? This! Grabbing it, hauling on it in a frenzy, Claudia, the swollen red snout squeezed. Lie down please, *amore,* queek-queek, on your back. Is this another of your terrible tricks? *Amore, per favore ...*

O mio Felice! O mio Adriana!

Oh Ah-dree-AH-AH-AH-AH ...

Felix!

Was I hearing things?

'Felix!'

A man's voice, definitely it originated from outside my head.

I walked faster, too scared to run, running would reveal I'd heard. Another main street was not too far ahead, possibly a section of the one I'd sighted before, and the going was downhill again. Normal to walk faster. I risked a backward glance, casual-like, as though checking the nature of something trodden in.

Nothing.

Then the sound of heavy boots running ...I sprinted to the end of the lane and straight across the street through glaring honking shrieking traffic.

A bright-lit bar beckoned not too far up the pavement and I made for it as fast as my legs could carry me, dodgy knee playing up for all it was worth, not daring to think what I'd do if the door didn't open.

It did. Inside, breathing hard, I looked back through the rippling glass in time to see a burly figure appear in the alley exit, head jerking this way and that. Hit by wind, Postkarts hitched his bag back on to his shoulder and lumbered away downhill.

When I turned to face the room my head was thumping as though my heart was in my head.

16

Do you believe in fate? I don't, and one hundred per cent not where the future is concerned. When a thing is over and done, I says to her again, that's different, that's totally different. When something bad happens, after a tragedy say, anyone can look back and see something fatal if they wish to, that's easy. But what's happening now is what matters. Look at my father, I said, he didn't live like he thought he'd be dead at twenty-two. Or my sister Felicity. When she was born she weighed more than I did when I came out, a whole lot more, and if things had gone on the normal way it's a fair bet she'd have finished bigger than I ever have. Likely a lot bigger, our dad being on the tall side, six foot four and a bit to spare. But then when she was five she got a disease in the head, some ailment where the brain won't let the body develop, won't give the right instructions any longer. And she was the picture of health before, lively as a lop they all say, happy as her name. Then she just ailed. Alright, maybe Mam came to think it was fated to be. But Nan blamed the disease.

Ail? Ail is like waste away. Yes, my big sister just started wasting away, seemingly there was nothing anyone could do. The head develops at the expense of the rest, so the specialist at the isolation hospital said, who made his name on her. Being the first to detect that variety he gave it his, his own name, plus a travesty of hers. Pearson's Infelicity. So now my sister's a notoriety in medical circles, a one-off, while to the rest of the world she might never have existed.

The only photo we have after she was a baby is nominally a girl of seven but you see straight off something's not in proportion. She's on her back and her eyes are shut, which is a shame, seeing as I say it's the one and only record we have of her as a girl, torn out of a medical magazine and posted on by a nurse or something who sounded quite fond of her.

Sad, aye. Very. Yet truth to tell I feel far sorrier about it now than I ever did then. All I knew was I had a big sister getting special treatment in special homes where boys were not wanted as they wouldn't want no noise around. Even when they brought her back, or as Nan claimed when they'd finished their experiments and were ready to print them up in their wee magazine, little brother was nowhere to be seen. The morning the big ambulance came gliding up our street I was already installed far away in Glasgow to stay the first and last time at my grandad's, conveyed there by train under escort by Bill Hakes, though that will have to wait for another day.

Funny to think I could be jealous of a little creature with an outsize head. So brave, so good, that was it, always having to hear how brave and good my big sister was. Hakes made us join the Church Lads for her sake, Hakes plus Mam. I beat the side drum for her, and I was the smallest of the lot. The day they made me join we went first to see where they buried our Felicity in the graveyard behind our house, before the two of them went in to fix things with the vicar. I used the time to swing on his gate, and he comes suddenly like sort of flying through the air, a big red face with long white hair like wings. I thought I was in for a hiding instead I got a pat on the head. A whiff came off him like the cupboard where they kept the choir robes. Or was that another day? No, I hear his voice, still smell that smell. There, there, little man, no need to cry, think how happy your baby sister is now she's up in heaven with Daddy. Baby sister? Fourteen month our Felicity had on us. And how could I square her pile of mud with his sunny island in the mighty Mediterranean Sea?

Later I found the day they buried her was the day I was taken to Glasgow Zoo by the perfumed lady who'd moved in with my grandda along with her two kids, to see the new gorilla, and never would I have associated the two were it not for my old granny being so fond of going over past times, for her own sake as much as anyone's. And how ever would I? In one place is a maddened monkey hopping up and down like a little King Kong rattling the bars of the cage and crapping in his hands and hoying it at the cheering crowd, and on the identical sunny winter's day in another place they're shoving your big sister underground for keeps in a child-size box. No connection, that's what I was thinking to myself. But then Nan said life is made up of many separate bits, existence is on too grand a scale for it all to link up neat and tidy, but at least we always know that when one person dies somewhere else on earth another is born.

That's when it first hit me that it hadn't affected me so very much, the loss of our Felicity. Long before she died I think she was hardly alive for me, not really real anymore, though later I did generally manage to remember Nana said to say something to her patch of ground, if ever I was playing near the tip. It doesn't need to be a prayer, she said, just a thought. They prepared us well, I suppose, made it seem for the best. But knowing I once had a dad who was never seen again after a mystery plane accident, that made no sense to me, no sense at all. Not because it seemed unfair, as Mam said about my sister. Just senseless. So then I suppose I had to find ways to make some sense of it, I think that's what happened. Hard to reconstruct now. Suffice it to say that although he disappeared before my sister, long before, for all the years I was growing, all those vital years, deep under the sea he may have been and yet I tell you he was closer to me than anyone who ever lived. Ever.

17

A middle-aged man with not much hair on top but a very bushy moustache looked up from swabbing out the sink behind the bar, shirtsleeves pushed to his elbows. Across the barrier of the counter we eyed each other in silence, one recalling he had the Italian equivalent of about tuppence in his jeans, the other as though defying anyone to claim that bartenders have a good life.

Maybe he decided I was too out of breath to speak, anyhow without waiting any longer his slightly bulbous eyes shifted to the TV on the wall. I looked over my shoulder too, in my case to check a hulk with a satchel wasn't about to blow through the door. On the screen a woman with piled-up blonde hair was speaking *italiano* at an unbelievable lick.

'Water,' I wheezed. '*Acqua*.'

He squeezed out a sponge, didn't reach for a glass, and with no emotion yelled 'I told you!' On the TV reflected in the mirror behind his back a man with piled-up blonde hair was speaking unbelievably fast *italiano* as though it was a lot easier than smiling. Then, just above, right in the middle of a long packed shelf, I spotted a miniature bottle of tonic with the same yellow label they have in England – and funny, the little Schweppes propped a postcard of the Tottenham Hotspurs 1961 champions.

'The Cup-winners!' I was almost yelling too. 'Wembley last year. First ever team to get the double and they only stopped us in the replay!'

Not even lifting his round gaze to where I was pointing, he leaned over the cash register and brayed 'Antonio!' at an open door. It sounded the same as before only this time I heard it in the right language. By the door was a big brass weight machine. Nothing doing until through that gap comes someone answering to the name of Antonio.

A toilet flushed, a door unbolted with a snap.

IL VOSTRO PESO! IL VOSTRO DESTINO! Light paces on wooden boards are approaching, and the pace of my heart quickens from lollop to gallop again as it finally dawns this isn't my first time here and I owe that register the price of three mega grappas, and no prizes for guessing who Antonio will be.

He appeared as dapper as ever in his whiter-than-white barman's rig, shoving a comb into a back pocket so as to have both hands free for anything from a VIP to a spot of bother. But the only novelty is a fairly familiar customer who seems engrossed in the telly, at the present moment showing a steam engine chugging out of a big shadowy station with a long line of wagons in tow and soldiers waving from every window and more soldiers lining the platform.

'A good night, mite?' My right hand is being pumped up and down.

'Well …'

'Good. Where you been?'

'Where I been, where I been forgetting to … '

'What you fancy now?' Lifting the flap in the bar he beckoned to the older man to step down, looking happy enough to relinquish command. Then Antonio stepped up, two feet taller, back in business. 'The old geezer is my papa. The guvnor. Grappa?' A bottle spun like a top in his hands, halting for me to check the label. Our old friend Julia.

'But how much do I …?'

'How much nothing! You pay when I come to London. British people stand for democracy which is a good, if the good govern. But in this bloomin' lunar park, this state of Italy, we prefer a beautiful confusion. All singing in the rain with a smile on the face. A glorious feeling, all sing, with tangents and stealings. And all conduct to violins again. The old story, mite. Reach and pour. Rome is nicer to tourists, London is better for walkers. You love Rome?'

'Love Rome?'

Relieved to be freed of my debt, distracted by my own thoughts, mesmerised by his practised movements, I'd not paid too much attention to what he was actually saying. With a bunched dishcloth he had bulled up a circle as bright as a mirror on the chrome between us, then placing a saucer in the centre of the circle and balancing a rinsed glass on the saucer and collaring Julia and flipping her cork with his thumb and catching it in his free hand he'd filled the glass right to the rim without spilling a drop – and all the while I'd been thinking to myself how different everything might have been if instead of quitting this place in a blind panic I'd passed my one and only night in Rome in the congenial company of this big enthusiast for the British way of life, and no doubt keen Spurs supporter, who sounded pretty well up on his own country too, the two of us gabbing away in broken versions of each other's languages, me supping free shots of heart-warming grappa in exchange for a few tips on basic English, and maybe quizzing him why Joe Baker and Dennis Law and Jimmy Greaves all decided to get out of Italian football, and just maybe also how he'd rate my own chances over here someday, jobwise and local-talentwise.

'Love Rome? Snosh what you first spect. More where for cash and rats. One point mind I did find a monster church with fantashtic mosaic. Gold that bright hard tell sold or new. Think it was saying something. *Fantashtico mosaico, Shignor.*' Why was almost every word coming out wrong?

'Here, you remember that nice bit of crumpet sitting on my seat there? Bit flirty, remember, with the snob boy? She said come see us in America sometime. Listen, I says, listen, I am Italian communist and proud of it, you going to give me a visa?'

'Funny,' I enunciate carefully, fondling the glass and extra-careful about that too, seeing it's full to overflowing. 'Funny landing right back here. *La forza del destino*. I say it right? Maybe it was wanting to say miracles do happen.'

Weird how simple all suddenly seemed again, getting every word right, even citing my ex-lover without a twinge.

Might even trouble him for the use of his phone again, tell her in this very natural truthful voice I'd re-acquired not to fret on my account. 'I mean all the bother they went to, them two church people there, opening up for a blank stranger. And wanting us to stay the night, unasked, along with all their other charges. Well-meaning, good-hearted, like almost all the rest of you people. One old fellow, sort of a staircase dweller, we didn't need no language to speak. Wonder how he's doing. My one and only regret is I never did get to see the Colosseum. Still, I daresay it's not all it's cracked up to be.' A long speech and word-perfect.

'Tomorrow you see.'

'Tomorrow I'm hitching home.'

'Tomorrow the sun come back.'

'*O sole mio*, eh? Oh my sun!'

I nosed the grappa, too happy to hurry, too happy at the old magical unity of brain and tongue, and for reward I received a sudden nostril-stabbing chill whiff of pine and mist and mushrooms in autumn days of old stalking Merry Men-proof rabbits at the edge of the river and the woods with homemade bows and arrows.

'Magic!' I murmured, marvelling. And for my new Italian friend: 'As if by magic I saw the pond where we all fished and the shops are now, and the big field across our street, all like it used to be. You could climb the gate and go up that path and over the stile into woods we pretended went a hundred miles. We called it Sherwood Forest. And now I almost get the same feeling here. Better even. After all our little town's nothing next to this famous city of yours where half history happened.'

'Cheers!'

'No, have one too!' Hello, stranger, guess who. 'And your dad.' Just thought I'd call to say I found this flash nightspot where all the birds tumbled for your old pal in a big way. 'Come on, Signor, must be about closing time. What harm can it do now?'

'Cheerio!'

He raised an imaginary glass, I raised a real one.

Long before the last drop of that liquid ether was down my neck I knew I was dead drunk. Blitzed, legless, pallatic, mortalious. I couldn't have remained upright if I hadn't happened to be sprawled far enough across the bar for it to take all my weight. Legless is the word, the blood had drained so fast from my lower limbs I never even felt it go. And blitzed, my head was like split in two, one eye pirouetting around the room of its own accord, the other only interested in a brown mole on the back of my left thumb, never seen before nor since. When there wasn't enough variety for the roving eyeball and the other found the telly in the mirror both teamed up to view a loaded stretcher being passed to two nurses in the back of an open truck packed with other stretcher cases. Which black and white war are we in? But I wasn't going to be allowed to forget my own catastrophe by watching other people's, because now the bug-eyed guvnor with the big mustachio looked very keen to make my acquaintance properly, advancing on me steered by his son leaning right across the bar with one arm about his shoulders. Handshakes are the rule everywhere save home yet how could I spare even one finger when all ten were needed to keep me bolted to the bar? His son was my good mate and might have noticed my quandary but for bright TV screens like tiny strips of sticking plaster blinding each pupil. To meet the emergency, and resist the sickening pull of the all-settling floor, I hauled the last crushed end-slats of my ribcage up over the hard rim of the bar to take some of the strain off my two hands trembling white with effort on the ends of stretched forearms pressed down flat on slithery metal. There had to be some trick – mountaineers dangling over a ravine by just their fingertips must know it – some knack of securing yourself by the length of one arm as strong as a rope, so the rest of your body is free to swivel round and grab a saving …

He was no fuddy-duddy, his grip was as strong as his son's, and his mouth and eyes were shaped in a smile. Grappa was on both our breaths. He seemed to say 'Sink you' then his attention and a good portion of mine too drifted to a trench full of helmeted troops, not the ones who were singing unless they were singing through gas masks. The picture switched to a leafy tree shading an old-fashioned field-gun like the Waterloo relic on cartwheels outside the Officers' Mess that they used to set me to polish whenever they ran short of ideas. It banged out a cloud of smoke and recoiled, swaying the tree.

Strong fingers were massaging my neck. With now no more than my two elbows to stop me slipping to the floor, I needed to twist it, my neck, to make any sense of the son's lips moving almost in my eye.

'She calls you love, she calls you darling. Yes Suzie, and also the lady on the bus says four pence darling, and this signifies we are lovers?'

Each time I tried to make my legs take a bit of weight they buckled like when you get an unexpected tap behind the knees. 'I thought they agreed not to have a war ...' Weird in what shape we can still manage words, even if everyone effects not to hear.

'Help!' I may or may not have said, by now in a drunk's equivalent of one of those dreams where you're looking down from the ceiling at your body exposed on the operating table wondering why no one else seems remotely concerned. Shaking hands with his old man had got me into an impossible position, the exact reverse of the previous one but still more dicey since it put a strain on my shoulder sockets such as they haven't been expected to take since we came down from the trees, the only advantage being, I hoped, that it made me look a little less pallatic: bracketed backways onto the bar by the last inch of my elbows, legs flowing loose, hooded eyes circling the room. The saloon-bar slouch, obligatory if you've just ridden into town and need to look tough but casual to survive. Trouble is, I felt as feeble as though apart from a supersize slug of liquor inside me I had a few lead ones as well and was bleeding to death before their very eyes.

The father was shaking his head over and over at the telly as though he personally knew every casualty in that war, and I tried to sink myself into it too, summon Uncle Harry's mind-wandering theory to the rescue. In fact finally I was staring so hard at that bright square of glass that it scorched my eyeballs. Then I knew it was our own black dagger-shadow flitting over flat fields and fast up a long straight road where miniature humans scattered to either side as we planted explosions among them like little puffs of trees. To do more damage get yourself a Flying Fortress and get up high and open the hatch and out they spill like iron turds.

A telephone rang shrill as an alarm and a howling siren scooped to a pitch so high it set all the tubes buzzing and a line of terrified faces broke and rippled like water. When the set readjusted we were looking down at a mass of people fleeing toward the edges of a sunlit town square pursued by an expanding white circle at their centre. A dome popped like a balloon. Again the phone rang.

I made a move of sorts, toward or away from the sound I could not tell since my legs were still useless. Among the crates in the back room she was calling because soldiers were chasing a whole bunch of kids over rubble, calling for me to pick up the slowest and smallest and run it to safety. The camera wasn't steady anymore because now the bairns and the soldiers and the cameraman were all being machine-gunned. I was scared witless when she said she had my baby inside her.

The ring-ring stopped.

Stopped as sudden as it started, and no one in the room had done a thing about it. The older man, staring at me as though expecting the reply to a question of life and death importance, shook his head and turned away. His son's mouth was gnawing at my eye again.

'This is Italy,' I lip-read. 'Nothing functions. Coffee?' Invisible bullets whined back and forth in a shadowless street where an ancient black Ford was living the nightmare of not being able to run away.

Somehow I launched myself off the bar, top-heavy torso on quivering legs. A person's weight and destiny are secretly connected, all you have to do is activate the machine at the right moment in time. I only needed to know if I would ever see her again.

I'm on the wobbly platform now, pushing a coin into the slot marked *Novembre.* The weight dial spins far too fast, but it is not my weight I want, it's my destiny, each chipped black word of it on dented tin.

**UN PERSONAGGIO
IMPORTANTE
S'INTERESSA
DEL TUO CASO**

The floor is even rockier than the platform when I step down. Sawdust and flattened dog-ends and a maze of footprints – all mine? – tilt like a deck at sea. Ride the rise, Cat, go with the fall. Easier said than done when everything is not just tilting but turning and for the life of you you cannot make sense of your destiny. And your feet need attention too, you order them back under you, and instead the revolving floor heaves up and pitches you into the dead centre of a public room in a foreign land. Colours dip and flow as they gather speed, you're riding a merry-go-round. Yet what's to stop you being the fixed centre pole round which all revolves, too giddy fast at the extremes, so safe and stately near the centre? Stout pole, only apparently turning, it's the mirrors and the faces in mirrors which are on the move, and how they admire the bloke who takes the money, tramping round and round against the dizzy rotation.

A voice calls from a hiss of steam: 'Coffee!' And what a funny unlikely voice too, Mam's on a morning without a care in the world. The steam clouds part and there on the swaying length of the bar sits the cure for everything wrong with life, sanity pillowed in sugar bags. Drink me and all will be well. My heart goes out to it, soon followed by more practical parts of me, legs working a treat. I have destiny and the TV says all is FINE.

Arrived somehow, clinging on tight, I find the only aggravation is that this particular section of the bar wants to play up a bit, won't settle down and let me have what the man said was mine, forcing me to exaggerate the urgent need for hot healing black.

Aware of difficulty, from his height behind the machine the barman swoops to the rescue. A sun-browned hand presses firm on the counter and all returns to order. The world straightens out, my legs too, and one by one I watch two fat little sugar bags fly to his fingers and sigh out their white lives into the dark pool, which mounts. Then he flits back to his perch, too bright to see under the dazzling strip-lighting.

Left to my own devices, I line up two finger pads and pinch the nickel teaspoon by its flat end. Leaning my weight on my right elbow, not relaxing my clutch on the counter with my other hand, I dip and stir. Clockwise, since she says it's the good way of the world.

Her number!

To show I'm in control I first drain a slow brown dribble off the tip of the spoon down the cup's rim, its inside rim, and stow the tinkling spoon alongside without nearly knocking over the cup. Now I only have to get it to my lips.

'Where's that number?'

Hand shaking, head swimming, I've got the cup in the region of my mouth and the hot sweet stuff all comes lurching in, racing to calm my yearning insides. I set down the cup, not breaking the saucer, heart thumping so loud he'll never hear.

'Numb ...'

'Alright, mite?'

It's too hot and black to hold down and comes so quick to the boil. I even see it turn from black to red. The first scalding splashes make my gullet stretch painfully into a long taut tube greedy for more of the hot sour brew bubbling at the top of my chest. A filthy boiling frothing fistful punches up my throat and fills my mouth, spurts in a long jet through the gap in my teeth. After that I open like a sewer for gush after gush, and I let go and drown in it. The bright strip-lighting drowns in it, and father and son drown in it.

My last thought was strange. I could fly under water, and if I could get down deep enough I might find a place where I could breathe again.

HALF-TIME

I surfaced slowly, wary of meeting the fearful memory of some unforgivable crime, until I recalled that guilty feeling is only a sleep device to hold us in the land of dreams. A bad head was the reason for waking in a sweat, and Smoky lodged on my stomach, warm and heavy. During the long quiet of a Sunday morning she loved to steal upstairs to share body heat, patiently riding the waves of my breathing until she heard Mam getting ready to go downstairs to find her scraps from the fridge and batter the coal fire awake again with a handful of sugar and a clout of the poker. Sunday morning, all the time in the world to sleep off the usual Saturday night skinful. A bit of a sweat, a bit of a head, and a faithful puss in the wrong place, wrong time ... Smothered in blankets, warm in my smells, I rolled onto my side and pulling my knees up to my chest sank back down to the point in the dream where I was squatting out of sight behind the big veg rack in the Pattinsons' shop at our road-end. Then, too late, I recalled it was the dream that was worrying.

Humming numbers to herself, head bobbing to the dance of her pen, Mrs P was totting up our bill on the top sheet of the bundle of old newspapers she kept on the counter for parcelling up. So why, when I was invisible, why the uneasy feeling? That persistent tap-tap was only her red biro knocking the side of her big specs as she scribbled, so near-sighted her nose practically touched paper too. This was my best chance, Mrs P always happy money flowed her way, me too with such a feeling of relief, quietly undoing my fly. Only the buttons were stuck, also her hums and taps had stopped. Her head stayed down but not bobbing anymore, and I could see her nearest ear was thinking Ada's lad's abnormally quiet, as sure as I now knew her wiry grey hair grew through just a few holes in her scalp, like doll's hair. Her shop was like a second skin, forty years she'd lived in it, she could sense something was up just as though it was her own dress I was fiddling with. Yet all I'm doing is squatting down here for a better squint at what's on offer among the wrinkled parsnips and muddy spuds, grab the leek I want and never mind old Mrs ...

'Mucky robber!' That was Major Arthur's no-pocket-money voice, hoping to scare me out of my hidey-hole. 'Cave boy! Muck want to say shame?' What's he doing here, I'm the one Mam sent shopping, not him. I could hear his heavy-smoker's breathing, see the back of his trench coat ashy with dandruff almost close enough to touch, cut in sections by three slats of the rack. Mam's purse was in his hand, her special purse with the brass zip, I must have left it on the counter for anyone to pocket. He always said he had eyes in the back of his head, he knew I was up to no good, pulling the zip, thick fingers feeling inside ...

On all fours hoping I looked like I'd lost something, like maybe the purse, I squeezed myself on my stomach to wriggle under a long sagging shelf heavy with red tins oozing a smell of soup. I came out under the springs of Mr and Mrs P's double bed right next to the hot salty stink of a brimming chamber pot, and spied an open door and reached it still struggling to unbutton while I crawled on down a long corridor lined all the way like their shop window with ten-pound sweet jars packed to the lid. Dolly mixtures, farthing chews, gobstoppers, black bullets, soda balls, bull's eyes, jelly babies all colours, I'll wet myself before ...

Funny forgetting they had a bit yard out the back. In the open, under the stars again, I slithered down slippery stone steps free at last to – nipping behind stacked crates of fizz and pop – drain all the pain a bladder can contain. It poured and poured, I was over my ankles in no time. Only the pain was the same, I filled as fast as I emptied. In the bright light from the door stood Mrs P looking to check I was already over the wall. But the major was after my bones, snuffling like a hound on the leash to sniff out the human leak, fuming 'Okay spawn here!' while I trembled helpless knowing my only hope was to start in earnest, slow down, relax, go with the ...

No, no, it's a dream! A dream, a dream, keep on saying it's a dream, only a dream, a hole will open and you can float through. Say it, want it, and your wish comes true ... Gripping the root of all trouble and joy like a magic wand I soared over the wall into this one and only wonderful world where what happened never happened and never will.

Safe under bedclothes, panic subsiding as I remembered the major was long since dead and burned, I could tell it was bright day outside because the traffic was heavy on Windy Bank, almost as loud as my breath roaring against the sheet like inside a mask.

There were a couple of callers in the kitchen having a bit crack with Mam. Must be coming up to mid-morning for she had our Sunday dinner going, I could smell onions and a whiff of sage, imagined good roast chicken in the making. I clung on hard to that notion until a clatter like milk bottles kicked over in our entry had me punting my bed round in a 180-degree spin.

'Katie peel ya?'

'Chaos, pet.'

The voices somehow belonged with the terrors I'd left behind, though it was fun too, this sensation that my bed was a raft I could turn at will. As at the stroke of a paddle to and fro we swung between wall and window, back and forth between the puzzle of voices. One moment my head was under my dad's brilliant drawing of the 1937 Cup winners, ears tuned to another remark drifting up the stairwell ('Our cat's a boy'), but next time someone spoke I felt myself lying the other way about, under the photo of Signaller R. Rowan on the opposite wall, harking to two strangers having the weirdest natter on the pavement right under my window.

'Quell any man-painer, no?'

'Ah kissed a fish end!'

'Mauve hairdo.'

'Boo!'

Traffic honked in my brain like Bank Holiday now, and no way round could I make head or tail of their goon talk. Goodness only knows in what state I'd come home, or why ever I'd want to shift my bed. Straightening a leg would fix my position for good and all, according to whether toes met wallpaper or thin air ... They pressed the cold end-board of some wooden frame. Nightmare again, in a padded coffin with my living heart pounding in a special rubber bag, and then I knew the only way to find where I was and why my throat was as sore as when I first woke after having my tonsils out was to stick my head out of the covers and see something real, no matter how bad.

Black night, save for a tall thin upright L of light, the reverse angle of my bedroom door. That propelled me through the ceiling into her no-trespassers bed in the attic, pursued by hot terror we'd overslept and by now Mam ... God no, home's a thousand miles away, she's gone for ever, that door she kicked in my face. The nozzle of flesh awake in my fist fast shrank to nothing as I saw her mouth twist in disgust at her own tears then bite into the knot I tied in the kitbag cord, and even with her back turned I could see by the tremble in her neck how hard her teeth were working. Worse, between her gritted teeth she said something I couldn't quite catch, though every sound was still in my head from yesterday. You'll forget this all so quick. Was that it? Too late to know, because she had unbitten the knot and was filling the bag as fast as she could go, and the voices were right behind the door now, loud as police.

'O.K.F.I!'

'M.O.V.T!'

I curled in a ball, heart knocking. Oh let's just get it over quick! Something had toppled off the bed, smacked the floor.

Light shone red through my lids, someone was breathing very near. I made my own breath as regular as I could, before opening.

Two eyes with big irises speckled brown and gold were suspended over mine, so close they looked as big as mirrors in the ceiling. When they pulled back with a satisfied-sounding sigh I saw a big moustachioed face I first thought belonged in my dream world. He looked down at me, nodding. I nodded too, since now I remembered shaking his hand last night, that same large hand now holding a piece of paper. He was in shirtsleeves too, just like last night. Then did he not turn away and seem to grieve for TV soldiers?

'Good morning,' he said in very distinct English, eyes lowered to the paper.

'Rise and shine!' His son had popped up by his side, dressed in white shirt and dark trousers as though it really was Sunday after all. 'Wakey-wakey, mite!' There was scarcely space for the two of them, and he spoke with some excitement.

'How many hours slipped by you?' Bending an arm for me to read the face of a large wristwatch. 'How many?'

'Ten after twelve,' I read, once I had my head the right way round.

'So?'

The answer was plain to read in their eyes but my brain was still running too slow, slower than ever when my mouth opened wide of its own accord for a big ear-clicking yawn. Propped on one elbow to look more rise-and-shine, I gradually took in that Smoky was a tepid hot water bottle, that not just my head and throat ached but also my left knee, that Jesus was watching from the wall, and I was as naked as the day I was born. Yes, so how many hours had I slept in this big creaking mahogany bed with its fancy white embroidered counterpane half on the floor?

'We won Away Cup,' the younger one prompted. 'Remember?'

For the moment all I remembered was how he could arch the tail of an eyebrow. What had hit the floor was one of my hush puppies, the other being still balanced on the edge of the bed beside my pulsing knee. Seeing me eye both of them he collected them up and held them out for close inspection before stowing them beside a chair next to the bed. Odd, they looked almost as new as on the demob day I bought them. He liked my surprise.

'Remember now?'

Carefully stacked on the chair was all I possessed that wasn't still in a small empty room at the end of a winding corridor on the top floor of a lost hotel. Every item had come in for special treatment. My three-day-old shirt and vest and Y-fronts had been washed and ironed and neatly folded, my Army jumper looked as clean as it would ever get, even my weary jeans seemed to have recovered some of their blue. Atop the pile, perched on the packet of ten postcards of the Holy City, sat my woolly grey socks rolled in a ball. Someone had given as much thought to my turn-out as my own mother would have done. I'd have got wrong off her for blind boozing but she'd have done all the laundering just the same, though not half as quick. It hurt to swallow, which brought an awful memory.

The son seemed to read my thoughts. 'After,' he said, 'after the accident, and after the streets, you found too many stairs. Sit with me please, Tony. So we sit and speak, maybe one whole half-hour.'

'After?'

'Why aye man! After, after –' all five fingers of one hand dug inside his mouth to pull out a yard of imaginary tongue – 'after you spewk! Disgusting!' He looked delighted. 'Dad washed you good and proper. And at the end we put you to bed, with a nice hot water bottle. Remember now?'

Probably the burning need to urinate explained why nothing he said could jog my memory. The bed shook agonisingly as the two of them, mistaking why I looked away, made a dive for the pile of clothes. Son shoves a hand up one sleeve of the jumper and spreads his fingers to show the results of some very professional darning at the elbow, in near-matching khaki yarn and all. Dad holds my jeans up by their belt straps against his sturdy stomach for me to admire the knife-edge creases running down each leg. 'Prisoner of war,' he says in that distinct English, under the bushy brown moustache. 'POW Pasquino Pasquale reporting, Sir!' Clicking his heels and lifting his slightly bulging shining eyes to meet those of someone considerably taller. 'At your orders, Captain Bulkington!'

At this Antonio hoys the jumper in my lap and starts on a long story about how his father was taken prisoner after the tremendous siege of Tobruk, and after a very bad time in a camp in the desert but good treatment by a doctor in another camp way down in South Africa he finally finished up as batman, a very diverting word, in faraway India for an English officer named Bulkington, a good teacher of English and soon a very good friend, a friend for life unfortunately now dead, whereas in that first bleeding cold winter in London he, Antonio, before moving in with Suzanne always placed at least three hot water bottles in his bed, which by combination reminded him of something also very diverting about a man from Spain similarly named Antonio who shared the same gelid basement with the cook and two other workers from the Portofino and who so much hated getting up in the morning in that bestial British climate that once he convinced the landlady to serve his typical full English breakfast the night before … 'Okay?' he broke off, looking both worried and amused. 'Better when you get a good coffee in there, yes?' forefinger jabbing within inches of my ballooning bladder. 'Or tea? We have a nice big flowery teapot from England. Or coffee the good Italian way, with stacks of hot milk? The WC is …'

I was out of bed already, hopping bare-arsed on my best leg into my snow-white Y-fronts as I headed through the open door, the rest of my gear slung under my arm or round my neck. The bathroom was just across the corridor. Behind me, before I clashed the door, I heard good-natured laughter and the sound of shutters being banged open to let in fresh air. Barefoot on cold floor tiles, spouting like a burst hot-pipe, I stared in grateful wonder at the steaming remains of the past mysterious night of agony tumbling into pelted jostling harmless bubbles. When I lifted my head I imagine the look on my face was not so different to that of the survivor of a pit disaster who hasn't seen normal light and life for days.

The light was broad daylight, brightest in a slender gold sunbeam which sliced through one corner of a high-placed half-open window almost within reach of where I stood. The sky beyond the window was summer blue, and mirrored in the angled glass was part of the sun-warmed outside of the building, cracked orange plasterwork crossed by a brown downpipe. Normal life was this small white-tiled space smelling of soap and fresh paint, with bath and shower protected by a yellow plastic curtain part-reflected in a green-edged mirror screwed above a hand basin. Under the window, just a step away, was a solid wood box topped with pink foam rubber standing about eighteen inches high, the perfect height to give a normal-size person a leg up if ever he happened to fancy a closer look at how the day was doing. Fixed to the wall near my left elbow, at what would be a seated person's eye level, was a little joke tile with captions in Italian and a picture of what he would be sitting on.

Still tethered to the pan by running rope I edged gently round it towards the window. Now the open pane reflected a red ripple of tiles against the blue, and when I reached up and gave it a little push a line of nappies showed bouncing in the blue with brown arms going among them to add one more white flag to the row. Never noticed that before, that the sun can be shining through a pane of glass and it will still act like a mirror.

To my mind, at least in the next couple of minutes, no normal routine could beat sitting in the sun with my pants round my ankles and the extra diversion of trying to make sense of the four lines of writing on the tile. I didn't just read them with my eyes, I repeated them over and over until I felt I had the right rhythm, the true Italian rise and fall.

E' GRANDE IL PAPA
E' POTENTE IL RE
MA QUANDO QUI SI SIEDONO
SON TUTTI COME ME

Not easy to render half so tunefully in English, Italian being music to the ears no matter what its drift, all the same I felt I might have it in me to produce a passable equivalent. While working out my version I was put in mind of what a sergeant in the Education Corps, hence a fair linguist, had to say about beginner's difficulties when you first go over the water. We were chugging through flat beet fields in the middle of Holland and the packed troop train was stifling hot and me and Taffy were standing at an open window listening to this much-travelled sergeant-professor telling us how a modicum of patience is all it takes if you want to achieve the seemingly impossible, the rest of the battle being nothing worse than solid hard slog made more tolerable if eased along by an encouraging word or two from someone who has already been through all the hoops. His own words of encouragement included a consoling theory that there are three main phases all go through, dunces and geniuses alike. First comes the thrown-in-the-deep-end phase, when stunned by how simple everyone else seems to find the whole business you feel doomed to remain forever locked in stony silence, too overwhelmed by the weird situation and your own misgivings to imagine you'll ever express yourself, and yet if only you can summon the patience to sit it out you'll find there's no abiding cause for any such gloom and despondency, almost unawares you're slipping into the second phase, the accumulation phase, when even although the overriding sensation may still be that you're only more and more crammed full of outlandish sounds with no actual outcome in sight, all the while deep down inside you're amassing the vital basis for the great breakthrough into the third and final phase, when one fine day you simply seem to wake up and find all your exertions rewarded, with virtually no strain everything is flowing smoothly, there you are babbling away to your heart's content, Private Rowan, positively effusive. Well now, telescoping Sgt Wakelin's three phases into about the same number of minutes and a couple of inspired hunches, I eventually delivered myself of something which I felt ran fairly smoothly, and not even too short off the mark, as I now know.

GREAT IS THE HOLY FATHER
RIGHT POTENT IS HE
BUT MAMMA WHEN HE'S SITTING HERE
HIS TOOTING SOUNDS LIKE ME

Remember it has to rhyme, old Stick-in-the-Mud at St Wilfred's was wont to say, or bang goes all the music. Shakespeare could forget it, but none of you lot'll ever be Shakespeare. I cleaned up, hoisted my pants, and zipped my jeans humming 'Bless Them All,' the old buffer's favourite tune to hum beside the blackboard while fiddling with his switch and watching us lot write chopped-up sentences for him. When I pressed the plunger something looking like I'd chewed tobacco for a week took a couple of turns round the pan and swam off to find the shortest route to the Tiber.

And now let's have you, Rome!

Stepping up on to the pink-topped box I stuck my head out of the window, and with the cool sill-stone digging into my midriff found I was looking down from a good height into a big communal back yard criss-crossed with fresh washing at every level. The cobble setts far below were laid in curving patterns like in the lanes at home, and you could plainly make out their coggly shapes even under a long puddle covering one side of the yard. The washing lines were made of insulated wire all colours of the rainbow, a lot of them loaded with the Monday wash, our own household's too. A loop of apple-green wire ran from an aluminium pulley near my elbow to another cemented in the opposite wall beside another window, a reach of a good thirty or forty feet, and plum in the middle of our long line of laundry looking weirdly out of place dangled my khaki parka, like a headless parachutist come down among telegraph wires. A pair of scruffy pigeons clung to a balcony rail a floor below, pink worm-claws clenching and unclenching on the rusty rail as they sidled to and fro. From the constant narked downward twists of their necks I worked out that they'd been scared up to this height by a tiny tabby I could see trying to claw out something edible from a hole in a blue bin bag in one corner of the yard.

That was all the activity to be seen, but there was so much more to hear. The thick house walls were alive with a medley of voices coming and going behind the open windows and narrow iron balconies cluttered with plant pots and broomsticks and even the odd bird cage. Somewhere a doorbell buzzed, and not far off but out of sight a person or a canary set up a contented whistle, which caused me to realise I'd been about to do the same.

For quite a while I lingered there silently savouring the swarm of sounds and the warm smells of many dinners cooking, letting the good sun roast my hair. With one long heavy pang I thought of her at home in the heart of her family, then it quietly lifted along with the last of my headache, like a tight bandage being unwound. Smoky moped days and days for Scratcher, poor dead mutilated thing, but theirs was a simple and trusting friendship. The little tabby was patiently widening the hole in the bag, and meantime there was nothing those two huffy town doves could do but shuffle up and down their short length of rail between big white enamel basins strapped to each end, packed with greenery. Truth to tell, I was beginning to feel a bit like a peckish roof-roosting creature myself, in fact I was just as startled as the birds when a fresh white apple core having made the long trip unnoticed from a great height smacked the cobbles and spun to a halt under the puss's lifted tail.

Twisting my head to see where it came from I saw only a dazzle of sun. Then something moving in the sun, clearer when I shut one eye. It was a big wicker basket bobbing higher and higher above the roof line and underneath it showed the face of a woman with steady forehead and tightened mouth. Bit by bit she rose up full and straight against the glare as her feet reached the top of steps you could hear her climbing, clad in a dress as black as a nun's though shorter. The parapet at that point is no more than a foot high, but she strode fearlessly alongside it a good many paces before swinging down her basket and standing up tall again to stretch a damp double-sheet along a spare wash-line. The way she went about it looked so deft against that solid-seeming blue, she might have been sticking pegs in the sky preparatory to climbing up.

Not long before Claudia broke the easy routine of my post-Army life, some wet afternoon alone in the Essoldo in the company of Sophia Loren in a film called *Yesterday, Today and Tomorrow* was I think the first time I got the feeling that Rome might be a good place to live, and earn your keep as well, naturally, seeing you'd need something coming in to pay for a top-floor flat and ten square feet of flowery balcony on which to pass the time of day while in the sunny bed-sit at your back the bonniest lass in the district hums opera to herself while lovingly ironing your silk boxer shorts and blue Alfa Romeo T-shirts and boiling up the spaghetti and mince for dinner, leaving you to solve such knotty problems as why Roman cats seem to favour a windowsill in the shade over a warm tile in the sun, or why multi-coloured insulated wire is so popular for clothes line, and whether or not the lone bold widow on the rooftop knows that each time she bends down to haul up another bed-sheet from her collection the young Signor in the fifth-floor window across the way can see that in fine weather she likes to roll her black nylons below the soft white backs of her knees. Eventually a time will come, I mused, when you've lived so long around the same familiar yard that you'll need nobody to tell you what a person with a hidden reminiscent whistle is busy at, and it'll be no news that Roman pigeons can purr like cats, and you'll know at once the difference between the sound of a tight kitchen drawer being yanked open and a neighbour's little lass's quick squeak of laughter. And better than anything, it will require no feat of imagination to make perfect sense of every chance remark drifting on the air, so unlike that first Monday long ago when you had no Roman dinner times to compare things with and in the end you were so bemused that your head hatched a seemingly unconnected memory of sitting in the bottom of a row-boat in the company of a tin of red worms squeezed between a pair of wellies belonging to a big silent man fishing over the side, or long Sunday mornings in barracks when finally nobody shouts and the air is so still that lying in your pit at midday hugging your imaginary woman you can very clearly hear some poor bugger on fatigue filling a bucket from the red fire-point outside the guardroom a good two blocks away over the other side of the parade ground.

That doorbell was buzzing again, and I was starting to imagine a gassing inside when a low grunt drew my eyes to a small third-storey window much like the one I was hanging out of. Down there in the half-dark framed by the open window I spotted a solemn face staring upwards from under massive eyebrows. My first instinct was to duck out of sight, but sensing that his stern gaze had no interest in anything past the window frame I delayed the move long enough to realise he was keeping company with the Pope.

What a day! A blind man in a dungeon would have known it was special. I stepped down whistling 'Bless them All,' reminded by the fresh chemical odour of all that family washing that I could do with a good wash and brush-up myself.

The face in the mirror was a bit of a shock. A goggle-eyed intruder looking repelled by life and everything in it, starting with himself. You fly to answer the doorbell and instead of your friend someone you hoped never to see again is standing there after all these many years expecting to be let in. Cheeks as tender to the touch as nettles. Teeth the colour of morning urine, coated in something with the look and consistency of pease pudding. Stinking breath. Throat a sore red hole past a sick mauve tongue. Eyes bloodshot, the left more than the right, and creaking somewhere high up inside like a little hinge has snapped or requires grease, though a squint under both gory lids reveals no startling difference between the two. Snot-bunged nostrils sprouting hair like spiders nest in there ... Come off it now, aren't we laying it on a bit thick, after all I was only just into my twenties and close inspection was bound to bring some better features to light. To start with, I noted while rubbing the awesome stubble along my jaw line, a good many of the softening bristles had a bit of a reddish tinge to them, once or twice noticed that before, how they go foxy at the tips when allowed to grow. And though the whites of both eyes squirmed with tiny pink thread-worms each still floated a bonny bright iris of water-clear blue. Swimming-bath blue, in the immortal words of Debbie Piper, the first lass in the world to confess she had designs on Felix Rowan. At the choice memory I fell to wondering whether that touchy Claudia (shame she wasn't on hand to note I could think of her without a twinge or a thrill) might not possibly also be looking in the mirror this same identical moment, seeing it was one of her major pastimes. Aye, ogling all that dead skin and wondering what went so badly wrong, whether appearances didn't in fact count for a little more than was admitted at the time, and suddenly now so much wishing there was still some way of knowing whether something about the basic unalterable shape of the face had lost appeal (twisting it into untenable shapes to test the notion) or just some minor defect had caused offence but was never mentioned for fear of being hurt in return, curable without surgery, for instance a tiny fiery new pimple or the way the eyebrows almost mesh together – and then, and then so helplessly and hopelessly yearning to be given some acceptable explanation for how it can happen that a face which cannot change so very much in just a few months can lose all force of attraction for another face, its power to pull faces together, face over face, face eating face ... My nose was flat on the glass when I spat all over it, sorer in my throat than ever. I swore and swallowed and turned on the tap as full as it would go, informing her that after what she'd done she could put me right out of her head, what was once a face that I could never get enough of was just a blank.

All I could see through the spittle was the shiny shy face of young Debs who later married the surgeon who made a cock-up of Nana's hip but in second form wrote in her arithmetic book that the blue eyes of Felix Rowan gave her the exact same shivers she felt when she looked into the deep end of the Town Baths. Fear and attraction, Claudia. Of a sudden, and how vividly, I saw her surprising white tit the afternoon she locked us in their netty for a laugh, yes saw again the gingery soft hairs in her armpit and that extraordinary lump growing next to it, with a sort of ripening raspberry on the tip. Not yet turned fifteen, Claudia, and better packed than you'll ever be. Next I resorted to tormenting her with a good imitation of my first fan after the famed Mrs Perkins whispering in my ear, 'You're not seeing me other booster, Feelie, not unless you show what's hiding down there.' Now all this must have been getting truly unbearable for her, particularly now my face looked more like my own again, more than ever after I'd ducked it snorting under the gushing tap and pulled back out with that grand cold wet streaming from my water-darkened locks onto my flexing biceps and furry chest and my good strong back. That's our hero, lasses, the deep-end eyes all sparkly with water like a champion high diver climbing back out of the pool, and wouldn't yous all love to feel his foxy chin you know where, that burning fiery bush of a beard in the making, beard in beard, the very thing she wanted me to grow specially for her and now would never get to see, never ever again feel it scratchy how she used to love it, and fear it, prickly enough now to run another bare-bum *bambina* all the way up her wriggling spine from crack to nape and back again – rub 'em, red 'em, shriek 'em, hah!

Heeh! Towelling my fifteen-inch neck, fingertips massaging my cold-stunned scalp, I fell to crooning a kind of exultant ditty composed on the spot to the tune of 'Bless Them All' in honour of all the other birds in my life not omitting a few new ones from her very own city that she didn't yet suspect, in ninety-nine cases out of a hundred leaving me with far fonder memories than she ever bequeathed. A doe-eyed dish on a bus last night, flower, she'll never forget what it's like to be on the end of an eyeful from your bloody fine man of decision, and I winked in the glass in a way I knew she loathed. So what, it was my way, was it not, I was a free man again and could do as I pleased.

I waggled a corner of towel in a waterlogged ear hole and rubbed the hard edge of it across my teeth front and back to shift the worst of the pease pudding. Then, because that Roman tap water smelled so fresh and good but in my mouth tasted more like untreated sewage, I dared – shivering before the shock – dared to bite off a whole toffee-size chunk from the soft yellow cake of soap, old soldier's trick to sweeten the breath the morning after the night before. As I chewed it over, never wincing, careful not to swallow any of the spongy sulphurous foaming fudge, I kept on hammering away at her with more and more lurid revelations, in particular this pair of posh-spoken English floozies who took a big shine to us in a classy dive I happened to drop into after she pushed off, not quite the place you'd take a broken heart to, and guess what, them too educated slags were mother and daughter would you believe drooling all over us before ever I even made a pass, and if I didn't score the fault was hers, they were begging for it, all hers, both of them, not that anything like that would ever happen again now I'd flushed her right out of my system – aye, all hers for putting us down to make herself feel bigger, belittling us, insinuating and accusing, so that for instance last night when it was nearly in the bag and I was at my most expansive, yeah baby and right out of pocket too for their useless sakes which incidentally is a thing since it concerned the unmentionable she'd most likely have chosen not to heed being that tight with hers however hard up she knew I generally was and – well, I just went and contracted out ...

Soapy scum dribbling from my mouth tangled with the running water swirling at the bottom of the basin and then wound in a loop round the base of a big bubble which swelled and rocked transparent over the sucking black plughole, cold cruel as a crocodile eye, and on its shining dome I spotted my face upside-down, bug-eyed and menacing. Not even a photo for keepsake, *amore!* So saying I popped the bubble with a well-aimed squirt, and rinsed and spat and rinsed again until I had that city water tasting as fresh as spring water up among the moors at home.

Nobody's perfect, and that was probably your worse failing, Claudia, to forget it.

Still holding forth, and not too far off the top of my voice I daresay, I was by now wandering back in the direction of the open window, drawn to it by the sound of pigeons in a flap and an unaccountable screeching metallic shrill spiralling up from below, like a giant mosquito cruising round the yard. I had to step up onto the box again and lean right out to see the cause. A knife grinder was at work down there, sitting on a converted bicycle skimming sparks off a spinning stone. He had set up shop almost directly below, about a yard out from the wall, part-concealed by the balcony. His bike was jacked off the ground so the grindstone could turn freely as he pedalled, an upended Coke can dripping something dark onto the stone. A person with a push-chair stood nearby. All I could see of her was her black hair spread over the red jacket she wore, and her two hands gripping the bar of the push-chair. But I made a fair guess at her face when her baby girl looked up eager to share the thrill of shrieking sparking steel and the funny man pedalling nowhere.

Not a bad way to live, riding your old bike all over a famous city, turning into backyards to pedal your stone in the sun, pick up a few liras and new friends, pedal on ...

Someone was yelling my name, again and again, behind the bathroom door. Before I could call back that it wasn't locked the son had discovered as much for himself, bald patch and anxious face peering in.

No need to fret on my account, my friend. Stepping off the box I went to pick up my shirt from the watery floor, muttering by way of some kind of explanation, 'Knife grinder.'

'Knife!'

'A man sharpening knives down there. Years since I saw one in our parts, and possibly he was Italian too. *Italiano.*' And right on cue came the skirl of steel on stone. But he still looked a bit over-concerned on my account, I thought, even a bit accusing, so I was glad of one last quick moment all to myself tunnelling through my clean cotton shirt, a grey-blue bag smelling of soapsuds and bleach and the warm skin at her hairline. When I was through the neck he said:

'English is on today, Italian tomorrow. Remember?'

'*Grazia.*' This makes more sense than it sounds, for at the same moment he'd handed me a comb. 'The accent's my main problem. We had an Italian staying. She seemed to want to learn us bits then she didn't, and anyways –' clamping his steel comb between my knees and readying myself to pull my jumper over my head – 'all fell through.'

'Last night you remember it? Felix and Tony Baffone Bar Team. Spurs and Sunderland v the world. *Va bene Antonio.* Oh yes, mite, you repeat some good Italian for me. *Va bene, va benissimo, va benone! Evviva il Gran Baffone!* And remember? Please, please, Tony, let me walk with you. Why aye man, walk together, talk together. But English is on today, okay?'

'Walk?'

That moment changed my life for ever. I was in the throes of pulling on my new-patched jumper, straining to connect with anything he said I should remember, I could even see him through the stretched meshes out there in a khaki mist – when I was struck by a thought too good to be true.

'Or *work?*'

'Work.'

'No!' My mouth must have gaped as wide as the hole my head popped through. 'Never! That's just not possible!'

My dazed-ecstatic reaction had a strange effect. He turned his back on me and sort of cringed cold rigid. When I think about it now I'd say he resembled someone waking from a good dream to find himself bound hand and foot, and gagged too, neck veins near bursting in the effort to break free. Gag slips, thongs snap, out swings an arm, two, three ... Toscanini wasn't in it, Tony was a windmill of whirling limbs, and the *italiano* was going a mile a minute. And still he could not bring himself to look at me, eyes shooting every other which way as though some extra-dozy bluebottle had drifted in through the window and now scared frantic was skimming the floor and banging the ceiling and looping the loop to dodge the twists and turns of his furious verbals in hot pursuit. Not one word of it did I get, right up until he broke off abruptly and just stood gazing at the mirror in a lost sort of way as though his sudden fury had flown through the glass. Sighing, he scratched his bald spot, and at last recollected that today English was on.

'Wack – wick –wock! What you flippin' speak? Scotch? Never. Just not possible. Yesterday possible. Today no, today never ... '

In the tense air between us he looked to be dealing out cards only he could see, storming through the pack. 'Yesterday yes. Today no. Today never, never, never ...' Faster and faster, as though hunting for a lost trump, until finally he broke off and mimed a brief strangulation.

'Our offer is no good?'

'Best I …' My voice sounded very pinched.

'Best?'

'Better than I could ever dream, Signor.'

'Better, best …' I watched anxiously as he ran back over the exchange. Second time through he seemed to like it more.

'Last night we discussed it so much, so much!' He caught my timid grin, tried it on himself in the mirror and returned it in the shape of a full-dress smile.

I shook hands with him, shaking.

'I didn't know there was a vacancy.'

'Ha, you know nothing!' And he squeezed my arm where he'd thumped it the day before when we had tried to ring her. What a long way we'd come!

Passing the comb through my wet hair I wondered how it could be I had no recollection of their momentous offer. Entire chunks of the night seemed to have vanished like dreams.

'I'm hazy about things. You seem to have helped in so many ways, you and your father. He was good to me too? First I wake not knowing where I am, not even the country, next I've landed a job! And I thought I was hitching home. What happened?' I rubbed my thorny chin. 'What exactly happened last night?'

But Tony was in the window now, perched on the little pink box and leaning way out, temporarily reduced to smart brown brogues on tiptoe and dark serge trousers stretched from turn-ups to seat. I could hear him talking his language, debating the novelty with himself out there in the Roman sun, or maybe even passing on the good news to a neighbour.

'Espresso, Signorina?' I tried in the mirror, wiping it clean before sitting on the edge of the bath to pull on my socks and my smart hush puppies which I now saw had even acquired new laces.

'Won't I be needing some kind of uniform?' I asked when he turned from the window, arms full of sun-dried washing. I took the bundle from him. 'I've two good shirts back in the place I'm in. These old things, I only wore them to travel. Good white shirts from the time I worked in a London store. Also I did some bar-tendering in the Army, you might be pleased to hear.'

He stepped down, loaded from belt to chin, in no position to speak. Crossing to the door he eased it further open with the tip of a brogue and led the way out. We filed along the passage past the room I'd slept in (the big bed was made) and entered a kitchen filled with sunlight and silvery steam and smelling of something good that his father was stirring on the stove. I stepped through two bright sunbeams to dump my bundle on top of his, on a chair in a corner.

'Sit! Eat!' Tony slapped a sturdy table in the middle of the room. 'Felix is no English name?'

'It's more common on the Continent, possibly. Saw it all over shop fronts in Germany. But it's English all the same. Apparently my people were happy I was born, and it made me a pair with my sister they called Felicity.'

A white serviette was ceremoniously spread before me, and then arrived a large cup with a saucer placed lid-wise on top. Two white pills sat in the saucer.

'Coffee's all I need.'

Not that I fancied even that too much when under the

lifted lid I spied brownish wrinkled skin, bulging when I raised the cup, reminding me of something I didn't like to remember. But every mouthful went down to good effect, percolating slowly over the rawness in my throat, like tepid egg yoke.

The window was too steamed up to see through. So to fill the silence, and show some gratitude, here's me going between sips: 'Weather's cheered up, big change from yesterday. Sorry I gave trouble. More myself today I think. Or nothing your good coffee won't cure. Woke with a head first thing. Gone now. Though this knee comes and goes. Took a bit of a tumble, I remember. One of them little alleyways near your bar, not looking where I was going. Thanks for the laces.'

Tony, who had quietly drawn up a chair, was studying my lips very closely as I spoke. When I stopped, or rather petered out under all the attention, he said:

'Scotch?'

'Bit more south of the border. A little northern prison town. Not many know it, anywhere. The Roman Wall you'll have heard of though, and that's not so far. And Sunderland too, naturally, home of the great club. The Team of All the Talents.'

'I seen all the talents at White Hart Lane last year. Five-nil.'

'Okay, a game to forget. But a different story at Roker, right, and I saw every beautiful moment of that. We're a force again, we've all the quality to be back in the First Division. And that Brian Clough's a goal machine, good as any Italian.'

'Okay, okay. So only a little bit Scotch.'

'English, English. We've our own parlance, like everywhere. But it's basic English all the same. Though if to you I sound broad wait till you hear them through Newcastle. Or just my mother, for all she's done her best to improve, and learn me better too. Mine's a middle language, according to this Italian university person I knew. Partly, see, because with being a soldier I had to get on with folk from all parts. By which time I was already living down London, like I remember mentioning yesterday.'

'Yesterday you was from Scotland.'

'Just not quite that far up.'

'Why Scotland?'

'For some reason that episode escapes my memory. Could be some sort of misunderstanding. For instance if you heard me say my father originated in Scotland. Not that I remember him.'

'I understand.' A fingernail pinged the saucer. 'Medicine!'

'Listen, I'm fine now, champion. Alright, this knee aches a bit, like I said. Maybe both legs. But more down inside the shinbones like, down here in front. Pills are no use for that. I did a lot of miles yesterday.'

'Lot of bottle.'

'True.'

'And you did not fancy our coffee last night, eh?'

'Sorry. Sorry about that.'

'British people exaggerate to drink, man and woman. Why?'

'I was a bit under the weather like, also I'd had nothing to eat. And telephones only seem to be in bars. Then it was my luck to run into this twister who was already as tight as a scuttle. Though there was no reason to get that far out of my head. Sorry. And sorry about doing that on your floor. I was more dead than alive when I got back to your place. Felt a bit dizzy-like, I remember, and you thought coffee might do the trick then I think I blacked out. Did I bang my head? Sorry.' Like a nervous ravenous rat I'd clawed and chewed a hole right through a big bread roll I found at my elbow. Seeing it go, his dad set about supplying me with more to chew, using a saw-tooth clasp knife to carve thick slices from a massive round crusty loaf resembling an outsize stotty he propped against his chest, sawing at it end-on.

During and after my mangled confession Tony silently set slice on slice till he had fitted almost half the loaf together again in a neat mound beside my cup. Then he peeled and cut into a big knob end of salami, and his old man went to fetch a bottle of yellow wine from the fridge, a whole two-litre fiasco, though Tony signalled to him to put it straight back. But were those sandwiches good! Tough leathery layers of meat and grease and peppercorn between bread chopped so thick your mouth corners came close to splitting each time you went to get your teeth round them.

'This is something. Nothing at home compares. Hot sun on the fifth of November! And when I think what's to come, this brilliant job with you. My mother will be over the moon. Them holy cards are for her. Bread's different, good though. And the wine, just the smell, not to mention what we'd have to pay back home. Naturally I agree England's a grand country, in a whole lot of ways, only you don't know our little town where not much ever happens. No hurry to see it again, not now. And speaking of, Signor, speaking about this bar work you're so kind to offer, I'm thinking now it's almost like I was secretly trained up for it, right from early on. Saturdays and all the holidays I'd generally give her a hand, my mother, up at the prison officers' canteen. Yeah, let us loose on the tea urn when it was practically bigger than I was, though of course that's nothing next to that beautiful big coffee machine I will say I'm keen to learn. Providing that's all alright with you. Then again, as I say, while a soldier I spent some time behind bars. Sergeant's Mess first, then the Officers', so I know how you need to be on your toes. In fact I'll not be lying if I say that's the only job of work that gave any real satisfaction in all the nigh-on three years I was kept in, along with when I was a sort of army gardener. Party nights you'd draw upwards of four hundred pints apiece, all hand-pulled, which takes some care and consideration and a clear head for figures right up until the last penny's safe in the till. And they wouldn't stand for no drinking behind the bar. Which I fully approve, need I say.'

'Fifteen days behind bars.'

'Three weeks at the Sergeants', week and a half at the Officers', to be completely accurate.'

'And fifteen days behind bars.'

'When did I tell that story? I don't now recall my actual words but I'm certain I'll have said nobody ever mentioned you had to sign straight off for what you took out. Anyhow, I couldn't find the book, as I told him to his face when I was up on the charge.'

'To me you say: I nick their whiskey and in the nick I

go. This is part of my English lesson on the stairs. Then you say: Tony, I will be sincere.'

'Sincere?'

'Nicking is Army logic, you say. They nick my freedom, I nick their whiskey. Then you say a very nice thing to me. Tony, you give me back my freedom.'

'I said that?'

'The free life.'

'And this, all this was after -'

'After, after! First in the street you speak strange, all sleepy strange. On the stairs more straight a bit. Tony, your English is good, you say, amazing good. Not flippin' likely, mite, I say, Tony's English is like dog balls, all back to front! You laugh, I laugh. Spurs embraced Sunderland. Baffone United! *Viva Baffone!* Haway the lads, we're up for the Cup! We'll make it to Wembley this year!'

'Now that truly is amazing English. So it was like a bit my own idea, to help in the bar?'

'In bed, you know what you ask Dad? Haway man, who's the greatest?'

'The greatest? Normally I'd only accept one answer. Sunderland AFC.'

'No answer, mite. Eyes shut like this, quick, and away you slip.'

'And all this was after I –'

'Ha!' He pulled his father away from the stove, needing a full audience for this one, then acted out what all too clearly had been the big event of their day. Mere words could not do it justice, it had to be seen to be believed – a man transformed into a live volcano, a mouth-crater erupting in burst after burst of molten yuck as slowly he subsides in a quivering heap on the floor, bowking and gurgling a little while more before giving one last twitch and stiffening like a corpse right at my own feet.

'Grief,' I whispered, gazing down. 'What then?'

His eyes opened. 'Then no problem. Lemon with water and we march you home.' He let me give him a hand up from the floor, and then we watched him do a stiff-legged Frankenstein walk toward the laundry pile, observed also by a third pair of eyes, those of a pale-faced woman in a framed photo on the wall above a little glowing torch bulb.

'You make me look like a sleepwalker.'

'Sleep-walk, yes. Legs go automatic, and we accompany. But all the sleep-talk, mite! That blinkin' mouth never stop. And you are no help on the stairs, no bloomin' help at all. And before –' he sagged at the knees – 'before, out in the streets –' rummaging through the heap and then straightening jerkily and turning back to me with a white jacket hanging limply from one hand and the dozey-eyed look of Stan Laurel after he's caused mayhem once again – and I guess I might have found it comical if it hadn't been so serious. 'You remember now what is your sleep wish in the street?'

I stood up, shaking my head dumbly as he handed me the jacket, for still I could recall nothing, not a single thing, no matter how graphic he made it. 'Your wish is to nick a bicycle. See Rome by night, you say, navigate the Eternal City. But I am afraid, my friend, it is – it is a fixed-on-the-wall publicity bike! Cor blimey, mite, you say –' checking his dad's intent face for confirmation – 'Tony, me old cock, that there flippin' bike is fixed to the flippin' wall!' Every mysterious detail seemed to give him fresh delight, and his dad too, nodding at good memories and the merrily bubbling stew.

I pulled the jacket on. It didn't sit too well. The sleeves would do, just about, but fidgeting with the buttons I found space enough for a match-size football between my belt buckle and the middle button. While looking me over they spoke in their own language, then Tony returned to English.

'Last night Dad asked if you have no place here, no friend. There is a girlfriend?'

'She's no friend now.'

Funny, I didn't even feel especially bitter about it, the immediate reason being the sun shining bright red through one ear of the older man at the stove. His back was turned, but his clear voice came saying things I knew were intended for me, even before I realised he was reading from that paper he kept stored in the turn-up of his sleeve.

'Nothing of him,' he read. 'Bones in the water. Because I am bad.'

'What's he saying?'

'In the Colosseum lives my father. He is good, I am bad.'

'I said that?'

'Help me, Da, help me.'

'Sounds mad.'

'Father, father in the Colossal Sea. Help me. And weeping all the time.'

'Weeping?'

'Hands up!' Tony spoke surprisingly sharply.

'They were marching past the Colosseum,' I heard myself saying as he eased me out of the jacket and hitched it over the back of the chair, 'and he was long since at the bottom of the sea.'

'Sit down.'

But I didn't want to sit, not yet, not until I was sure there was nothing more to come from that paper, no more words in which his old man made me hear my own tears. The ear glowed red again.

'Help me, Da, hold me.' In my voice, but from so long ago.

'Why?'

Tony gripped my elbow so tight that at first I took the piercing pity of his gaze for anger

'Sit down!'

Now I did as I was told. Then he thrust his face close to mine. 'Your dad died when you was two. My mother died last year. And today one million Romans are without water, and at Prima Porta it come to here, the river to here!' The back of a hand banged his chin. 'Invading houses, Felix, invading mouths!'

From under a heap of onion skins and carrot scrapings on the other side of the table he tugged out a newspaper. ROMA leapt out in hand-high capitals above a picture of a bus bonnet-deep in water, with dark figures of people standing on the roof. Another picture showed what looked like a crushed three-wheeler straddled by an enormous truck. DILUVIO. He flipped to inside pages and more photographs. Bairns wrapped in blankets, perplexed eyes burned by the flash. Two firemen wading through water carrying an old woman balanced on a chair, her pale feet so bare.

'Read with me!'

When his finger traced the print even I seemed able to follow. 'City isolated. Lines to Rome intransitable. Water in houses, cows in trees. And the competent authorities –' his finger quit the print – 'what are they dreaming? I am very important person, vote for me, and tomorrow you shall have a beautiful barrier for all the water! Six years pass and no bloomin' barrier for the deluge that must come. And the cardinal with his big umbrello, what comfort is he? What this salame can make? Make potable water? Make dead persons live? Because what the poor people have and have all ways? Tell me!' His hand sawed at his throat. 'The aperture to the left, Felix, and the Tiber to here!'

'Look now! Look with me!' Again I seemed to understand the moment his finger stabbed the print. 'One man stop to help a man. Comes back. Finds no car, finds no baby. Read. Read his torment, please. Always we must call the thing by the name. Exists more your father or exists more this? My mother died last year. Excuse me!'

He almost ran from the room, leaving me staring at a cartoon of a shipwrecked sailor strumming a banjo in the shade of a single palm tree while three shark fins drew circles round his sanctuary of sand. My headache was back, I needed a shave, I could do with a bath. I had a hotel to find somewhere, a free bolthole for six more days. Maybe meantime I could pick up enough at the bar to take me out of that place of bad memories to somewhere which let the sun shine in. I don't believe I'd had such sober thoughts for days.

Tony was back, knotting the belt of a smart gaberdine, looking in much better spirits.

'I go to the bar now. Monday is cleaning day.'

'I'll come.'

'No. For you today is a holiday. We meet for supper tonight.'

'I see now what you were saying. Some never made it through the night.'

'Good.'

But I didn't want him to go without knowing what else was on my mind. 'I don't suppose there's any way I could stay, is there, stay here with you and your father? Just till I get settled. You could dock the rent from whatever I earn.'

'Stay. Talk to the guvnor. I come back.'

There was just one last thing to ask. 'Did we get to see the Colosseum last night? It sounds –'

'Tonight we see. I go.'

No sooner said than gone. After the outer door slammed shut I returned to the stranded sailor. A ukulele, could it be? So much had happened, so much to sort out, I almost forgot I was not alone. Only when I heard the stew bubble softer as he turned down the flame did I look up. He was watching me in a very close way. Comparing what he saw now with all he remembered from last night? Weeping, was I? I went back to the sailor and the sharks, while very clearly I heard his lips sucking the tips of that thick brown moustache. Then there came a rustle of paper. This time he held it under my nose, wanting me to read for myself. This is what I read:

My Dad is 22. I am 22. Marsdan Roc. It is k.o.

I looked at the broad thumb-end pressing the paper, the careful work of blue biro ink above. 'You wrote this for me?' Only when I spoke did I realise I was trembling. 'What's special about our ages?'

His thumb pressed harder, in the far corner. 'It is o.k.'

'It says k.o.'

Maybe I'd had some sort of revelation in the night, but unless he could help me recover that lost state of mind I'd never know what it was.

'I used to try to imagine his last thoughts,' I found myself saying. 'Is it true what they say, a drowning man's entire life passes before him?'

He released a warm chestful of vinegary breath, and I realised he had been holding it in so as not to miss a thing I said.

'I write for you. And because my English is bad.'

'It's not. But last night you didn't seem to know any English.'

'Last night, last night!'

'Your paper's right that he was twenty-two. But I'm still twenty-one. I'm sorry they didn't treat you right in that camp in Africa.'

'Hitler has a big family. In the camp was his little brother from England, we called him Adolfino. He burned in his tent in the desert long time ago. Come.'

He touched my arm. He had opened a door near the framed photo of the pale woman and was holding the big bottle of wine. 'Sometimes no water in Africa, only wine. And when there is nothing we must suck a stone. Come now.'

'That takes me back,' I said, stepping through after him and finding steep stairs to climb and not much light to see by. 'Someone I used to know said the same, best help for thirst in the desert is a stone. He got captured on patrol and he said when they all got shelled he ran off and the Germans purposely shot over his head. He had this bit of shrapnel in him, very small, like a blister.'

There are precisely sixteen steps. Near the top he turned round to face me and took the last few steps backwards, bending low in order to set his shoulder against an iron hatch in the ceiling, chin almost touching his knees. As he straightened bright daylight flooded in, so blinding that looking back I couldn't see the way we'd come. High above his head I remember a silver plane glittered in the even blue like a minnow in clear water.

Together we climbed out on to a wide flat roof inside a maze of washing strung everywhere, colourful cubicles and corridors in all directions. Swinging the fiasco, a squat figure looking as at home as a seasoned sailor on a tossing deck, he went ducking and zigzagging through the washing, and I followed. When we stood up all Rome was before us, tile and stone and brick on every hand, at intervals gathering into taller shapes I now know to call Santa Maria Maggiore, San Giovanni, San Clemente, la Macchina da Scrivere ... It felt like we two were standing on air, high as the far blue hills. If we could have gone back and begun again, flown into Rome on a day like this…

'And the sea?'

He didn't follow.

'The Mediterranean?'

A hand swatted the notion dead.

'You mean, we're not by the sea at all? Always I put the two together, Rome and the sea. Never pictured it otherwise.'

We had to shield our eyes against the sun. 'It was nineteen years ago yesterday,' I said. 'For him it was like an interlude in the war. A flying boat was to take him from Sicily to Africa and he was the only one they never found.'

I smelled wine, and finding the uncorked bottle under my nose, took it from him mechanically. 'Best not –' or some such thing was I muttering as he reached past my shoulder to pull aside the corner of a sheet. Like raising a curtain.

There it was, still there after almost two thousand years. No need for him to name it, the most famous building in all the world, how I imagined it and how I never could. Hard and round and empty, high as the highest roofs, a massive rusted bullet-riddled helmet of brick and marble left upside-down in the middle of the city. Robbie Rowan dreamed of seeing this, and all I could think was that it looked grand but not very beautiful.

I stole a long look at my companion, full of a whole mix of feelings. Curiosity, gratitude, embarrassment that he'd seen me cry in the night, certainty that this was the beginning of a long friendship. He seemed lost in thought, sucking on that shaggy upper lip, cheeks already sweating slightly under the power of the sun.

'One day,' he said speaking very clearly but I think more to himself, 'one day man must make a grand revolution against solitude.' Then he faced me.

'Now we can sit and talk.'

They keep a few deck chairs up there, stacked against the parapet. In a bucket flourishes an evergreen bush, I've never thought to ask what kind, also a big vine in a plastic barrel, its tendrils entwined in crossed bamboo canes nailed to the side of a wooden shack encasing the water tank. Pasquino Pasquale and I spent all afternoon on that roof in the heart of his city talking together for hours, like so many to come. He set his chair in the shade of the shack and the yellowing vine, I set mine in the sun. We hadn't been speaking very long before I had to strip off my Army jumper. Then, leaning back in my chair and looking straight up into the blue, I remember it felt like the earth had turned upside down and we two were floating in the sky above a calm sea that went on and on for ever.

SECOND HALF

1

All that stretch of the coast between the two rivers is like one long cliff, with every so often weird-shaped rocks sticking out of the sea. But Marsden is unique, because at Marsden stands this colossal sea-rock as tall as the land. To the very inch, it seems to me. Suppose here is land, cliff, right here where we're sitting, then that block there with the terrace where the kids are playing would be the Rock. That's how big, that's how close. In school they made us learn it didn't break from the land, all the territory between just got washed away in the long course of time. So now there it stands, separate, at the edge of the beach when the tide is out, half sunk in the sea when it's in. At first it looks a bit like a big stone head, with sea caves for eyes. But walk on, along the beach or up on the cliff, and you find it has a massive hole right through, making it more like a giant arch. My grandmother said in the olden days they told a tale that the Rock is all that's left of a bridge that reached right across the sea.

Scandinavia. Denmark. All way out there somewhere, by ship about twenty hours I've heard. And last time I was at Marsden was same as today, blue sky everywhere. But the sea was the surprise. One day this summer, way back in June, with that friend I mentioned when your son asked.

The no-friend, aye! No-friended by her own choice just yesterday afternoon, here in a room she rented for the two of us until such time as she regularised things with her family. Her own deliberate choice. And after months and months lodging in our house.

What can I say, Signor, it's the big unanswerable question! She decided to go off her head, that's all I know. Said she wanted another life. Best not go into it now, it would only spoil things. But put it this way, she changed identity. No exaggeration, I don't even see the same person when I think of Marsden.

We had fixed to meet outside this big library-place in Sunderland where she wanted to do some of her studying, and I was to come through on the one o'clock bus with stuff for a picnic. Which I did. She was waiting at the top of the steps with her bag of books, looking nice. So where do you want to take me? Marsden, I says, because Marsden's your sort of place, and we head out of town. Then at the top end of the bridge over the river near Roker Park, our team stadium where the atmosphere on a Saturday's unbeatable, this Electricity Board van pulls up. Must have been her presence, I hadn't yet even stuck out a hand. Anyhow, after a load of joking and singing along with his radio he sets us down in this lay-by at Marsden, and walking to the edge it was unbelievable. The power, the wildness. Same as now, not the breath of a breeze, yet monster waves were rolling in, bashing the Rock, pulverising the cliffs, each giving you the same feeling you get when a goal goes in. After a real big one everything would seem to go dead quiet, she said it's like all England's bracing for the next. Same as us two up on top there, holding our breath and each other and shouting as it came. Lick your lips, Feelie, you'll taste the salt!

That's what she said, her tongue all out. I had to kiss her.

Next she says she has to feel the actual spray on her face, and the daft thing starts down the steps, these wooden stairs going down the side of the cliff, right down, not noticing I felt a bit queer. And why I felt funny, it's what my mother tells about the time she saw my father there, long after he drowned. Stealing down the steps all soaking black, tight against the cliff, I was thinking this might almost be the day for something similar. Only there was nothing to see, water swallowed everything. No thanks.

Really and truly, no vino for me. Today I mean to keep a clear head. Get things back in perspective like. With your help.

When all that was, with Mam? Ten year back, eleven. So her memories will have been fresher, her memories of him. Stronger, fresher, you know what I mean. Despite other stuff on her mind. In particular a certain objectionable person I never liked but who was destined to dog our existence for years. That shrapnel man I mentioned. Like a little red blood blister it was, and only in the time we knew him it travelled from a bit above the ankle right to the top of his knee. He'd pull up his trouser leg, he liked to track its progress. I'm waiting for it to come out the tip of my cock, he'd say, and I hoped it would kill him.

Not that one, not that particular day. Supposed to be in school no doubt, or maybe I just refused to be her little chaperone. Because often I'd be dragged along on their little trips together, their outings, in the early days of it. Aye, more like eleven, because he was still driving the ancient AA van he got off his brother, an AA repairman who converted it himself. Oh he liked them initials! As for her, my mother, definitely she was working full-time in the canteen by then, the kitchen and canteen at the Prison Officers Club. Whereas 'Sir' never did a stroke after the war's end. Which didn't stop him calling her lad feckless.

Automobile Association. A national breakdown service, Signor. Which come to think is what she could have done with after Marsden, he being no use for that sort of thing. Or anything. Him I always see on top, parked up all neat and square to face the Rock inside that daft yellow van reeking of pipe smoke, the window wound just a half-inch down, chin squashed snug on his dicky bow, perusing the racing pages. What gives me the picture? She I always see underneath, down on the beach on her own, where on normal days normal waves just wash in harmless over the sand and pebbles. What happened next I somehow see in slow motion. Out of the water, she'll tell you, straight up out of the water rose the shape of a man. My man who now lives in the sea. That was her first thought, apparently.

A shock it most certainly was. Like the disciples seeing Jesus walk on the water, like in a mosaic I saw last night. And in fact it made her want to change her whole life, transform. First she ditches the Major, which was fine enough by me, and not long after she joins the Spiritualist Church over past the railway viaduct in our town. This P.O.'s wife told her they had a man there who could talk to the dead, talk like the dead. So enter Mr Telfer, the circle leader. They were all of them under his spell, George Telfer's whole bunch at his Sunday gatherings, and all dead envious of this new member who he certified had experienced a unique spirit manifestation. But you know how he hooked her good and proper, poor Mam?

I told you he did voices, the voices of the spirits of the departed all desperate to send down messages if they can only find the right living mouth to speak through. Well, I don't now know how long it was he kept her waiting and waiting but one day instead of transmitting her lost husband as she'd been all along expecting, hoping to hear how to lead her life, suddenly he's doing my dead sister's voice to perfection. Oh yes, back home in the middle of tea she's suddenly sobbing her heart out telling how at last we knew direct from her own little angel's lips that all earthly sufferings were but a distant memory, nothing could ever harm her anymore, unless it was a hurt to her darling mother. So now my sister Felicity was an angel in every way, for according to their set beliefs the moment a bairn dies it sprouts wings and flies up to the light realms.

Aye, poor Mam. Telfer had picked her very weakest spot, see. Nan always liked to say she was too literal-minded and too easily led, as is the case with all simple souls. She underestimated her intelligence a bit, actually quite a bit, but otherwise I went along with Nan, angels had scant appeal next to spacemen. But what happened to Mam at Marsden was another matter. It did things to my own brain too, Signor. In fact it got so I could stare at almost any patch of water and –

Short for Grannie. Nan or Nana. Winnie Rowan, my dad's mother, this extremely argumentative grandma of mine who sadly isn't with us anymore. The worst mistake she made in her life, she always said, was marrying the Quadruple B – that's all she ever called him – a big bigoted boozy bastard of a Scotchman, from a big bigoted boozy family. But that's what made her a freethinker, she said, and proud to proclaim it too, hands tucked in her armpits! And by a miracle it gave her a beautiful son, she always said, and exceedingly proud to proclaim that too. She passed away just this last January, leaving a big hole.

NON-nah. Same word, or just about. I say it for you and I see her trying it too, testing it like a new taste. She'd try anything once, Nan, it was a principle with her. Though if she didn't like it she'd sharp spit it out! Oh yes, my old *nonna*-nana always spoke her mind, no fear. Think for yourself, hinny, and say what you think. That was probably her favourite saying, we should have it on her gravestone. And seeing she was happy to have a go at anyone and anything, she thought nothing to telling my mother that unique spirit manifestation of hers was all in her own soft head – and proof of an almighty guilty conscience besides! Picture how that would set things off. Still, other times she might be prepared to back down a fraction, just a fraction, the great freethinker was prepared to concede the bit-late-in-the-day repentant widow really just might have seen something out there by Marsden Rock, not the beautiful nude male of her dreams, just something a wee bit out of the ordinary to bamboozle her silly mind. A seal surfacing, say, their heads can look so human. Or some trick of light with moving water. Wave spray spurting man-high a moment. Or a seabird, a whole flock of birds, the sun on all the white wings blinding her a second. Because Marsden's a paradise for birds, Signor. Hundreds and hundreds lodge in the cliff, crammed in nooks barely wider than an egg. And all up the whole face of the Rock, dotted around like big white flowers. While all along the flat top of it, sticking up stiff like its own black hair, stand literally row on row of cormorants. Cormorants or shags, never really known the difference.

Big snake-neck creatures, dark, no prettier than their names. Still, interesting. All stand facing the same way, like on parade. Rulers of the Rock. Some just look straight into the sun, their wings spread out like this, like black vultures. The other attraction is the pub in the cliff, the Grotto, where you get your beer in a cave.

No, it's a resolution! You saw what the drink can do. Not gabbling too fast, am I?

I know, I know, all spilling out as it comes. It's the relief of finding someone prepared to listen. Like a dam's burst. For months I've been living under the same roof as a person I care for, cared for, who in the end more and more only wanted to be in her own world. No admission. To the point I'm afraid of driving me crazy. Your paper proves that. What state was I in last night? My dead dad manifesting right here in the Colosseum, just like for Mam at Marsden. Yes, what kind of a state of mind was I in? And if I didn't bang my head, how is it I remember nothing? Not one word of what you wrote down.

No way am I wanting to make feeble excuses for last night, Signor! I know it's really the drink that hit my head. It's just I cannot get over the effect of your son there going all the time, 'remember, remember?' Like cases in football. At Roker I've seen it when two clashed heads, and another time our goalie collided with the post. He can even carry on a little while, even connect with the ball, next he's standing there like a redundant ref looking lost for even why he has his boots on. This friend of mine it happened to, my old pal Jackie one time we were all kicking a ball round as kids, he said it's not the pain, not that, it's gradually waking up to the fact you cannot explain a thing, not what you're doing or why you're doing it, nor where you are, almost who you are. People crowd round saying all sorts surely no one can forget, instead their every word only makes that weird gap grow and grow. You could have scored, it would be gone from your head for ever. Same with me right now, not one thing do I recall after trying to save myself with that coffee. And still, and still all these things the both of you tell, in some way I do feel they belong to me. So what I'm thinking might make my own sort of Rome manifestation easier to take would be if I was more like in some kind of dream state. He said I looked like a sleepwalker, your Tony, even acting it out. Is that your impression, does that match your memories of last night?

Wandering?

Wondering and wandering.

Like helping a sleepwalker home! I'll never forget that, never. And then you washed me, you put me to bed. Where would I be without you, Signor Pasquale? And before, before that, down there on the stairs talking me stupid head off, was it more like Tony says, straighter talk? Or more akin to sleep talk still, like the words on that paper?

Can't really say, you were running my bath! You know, hearing you tell me all these lost things feels as queer as being told my dreams. My own actual forgotten dreams. Every night we go wandering-wondering, but it's not something we can share. And that for me is the truly miraculous thing about last night, two unknown people finding time for a stranger in a condition like that. And you even took the trouble to write things down. Why?

Don't say that was the look on my face!

Truly like seeing a ghost. A ghost myself.

No, I do understand you, I do. You're saying it's like we have two sets of eyes, two separate sets. One for here, the world out here, and another for what's more or less for ever showing inside our heads. Then – is this right? – at times the separate so to speak wiring systems get crossed, can cross over, like you showed in front of your eyes weaving your fingers?

It's a help, yes. Shaping the words. Though to be honest I thought at first you were showing the path of my tears. So, yes, sometimes you can get something like – like a meshing, a meshing of both the sets, and at that point that person can see no difference between outside and in. The whole normal arrangement sort of gone all inside out.

No, they don't teach anything about the brain at school, though you'd think they'd all want to. But it's like you say, it's having one, being one, that's reason enough to speculate. And your double-vision effect happened for me last night. And Mam at Marsden. Maybe. Because as she speaks you see it all happening again at the back of her eyes. And no arguing. Who says I don't know the face and body of my man! So she'll go, if anyone dares pull a face. Then she'll likely tell how she had sightings before, ordinary sightings such as happen to anyone missing a person. He could sometimes go by on a bus for instance. But Marsden was his unique spirit manifestation. I suppose that's it, it all just comes down to terribly missing someone who cannot possibly be there.

Or fearing! Interesting point. Thinking of No Friend were you, when you said that?

Well yes, I do still have certain sorts of feelings. Almost like vertigo. Or no, like when a hidden fish pulls. But just one tug and that's it. Live contact for a moment, then the line goes slack and nothing's there. And now these tears. And now my dad. Mad. Yesterday was like one long nightmare, I felt so low I half-pondered doing myself in. Yes, how much of our own brains do we control? Even George Telfer, the great mouth for the departed, he's now well away with the show folk.

Certified insane, Signor. Victim of his own delusions, all them weird voices – and wouldn't Nana be pleased! She hated finding him nearly always round our house when she called, parked there on the settee downing cups and cups of Mam's best tea while maintaining he saw ectoplasms like fairies flitting in and out between her lovely lips as she breathed. Mam swallowing every word. Me too, at first, watching him count all so solemn and certain, one, two, three, each one of them clear to him as breath on a winter's day – or spuggies in and out a spout!

That's what Nana gave him to chew one memorable day, right in his face. A spuggy's a little bird. Made Mam hoot, I'm pleased to say, Lap Souchang all over the cream carpet! Which must mean her devotion to Telfer was on the wane, the major was likely banging at the door again. I told you I could never abide even the sight of that man, yet I'm bound to say he cured her of the spirits, if ever anything did. For Major Arthur Arthur nothing had a spirit. Day-dreaming of your friends the spooks again, he'd rib her if she happened to look a bit faraway, or just plain glum, all your men-friends the spooks! That's the type he was, happy to harp on anyone's sore points. He'd a funny high voice like you heard me do just then, tinny-like, specially when teasing, skitting her about all the money the what he called bitch-doctors make out of the gullible. And still she listened too much to the man. Must write that card. Mind, I'm not so sure she's seen the light even now. These days she's not too brilliant on her legs and still by preference she'll take the longer way home from the station rather than pass the meeting house where the old gang used to foregather on a Sunday, the odd weekday evening too if they had a speaker. Not the least bit scary to look at, nobbut a tin tabernacle with a stove-pipe sticking out the roof, yet she gives it such a wide berth she's likely petrified it's…

Eeh, sorry, rattling along far too fast, aren't I? Oh aye, holding forth like a flaming schoolteacher! Like I say, it's the excitement of having a person to share all these things with. Not just a person, someone who knows I may sound cracked yet I do mean to make sense. Whereas No-Friend claims I don't have the first notion what I'm about. And how did that feel? Like a great slap in the face. Still, I survived, you steered this daft sleepwalker home! And you knew, down there in your kitchen when you started reading them broken things, you knew somehow they must strike a chord.

2

The cards, the St Peter's postcards you will have found in my coat, I bought them off a man who seemed to want to make it his business to chase me all over this city. I was after something entirely different, only he didn't have what I wanted. Because can you imagine what would give my mother a shock at least as big as Marsden? Coming downstairs one morning and spotting a card of the Colosseum sat right smack on our doormat, just signed 'R'. Of course I would never dream of playing such a mean trick, but in a way we've waited nineteen years for it.

Once they were all out in Africa and the battlefront there came no more news, though Mam and Nan of course kept writing. Then after he was reported missing, months and months after, all of a sudden arrives a picture postcard titled 'Two Little Scamps.' It was one of a bunch she got for him before his unit left England, she remembers that very well, in fact she reckons there will have been others which never arrived. Two kittens sat close together on a cushion, the little scamps, so she thinks he had in mind my sister too. What travels it must have seen goodness only knows. It's dated the previous June and was addressed not to his wife and not to his daughter but to his baby son. And, Signor, I tell you if you could see it now you would see at once I truly was in his thoughts, because the letters are all big capitals, all nice and neat and square, like he imagined I was beginning to read or they'd be the very first thing I'd want to when I could. We have it still, so I can give you every word.

YOUR MAMMY WRITES YOUR QUITE BIG NOW MY DEAR BOY AND SPEAKING THAT MAKES ME PROUD WHOS THE MAN IN THE FAMILY TILL I COME HOME. BE A GOOD LAD AND LOOK AFTER THEM BOTH FOR US AND KEEP SMILING.
LOVE YOUR SOLDIER DAD.

But that isn't the end. More writing appears, normal writing, and much, much smaller, squeezed in like it came to him the minute before posting, alongside where he already had the address down. *Heres hoping next card big stadium where in olden days people fort lions.* Those are his last words, his very last, as the record stands. So naturally there's a family theory about them.

Not that the puzzle was hard to solve, remembering how history went and considering it reached England so very long after. He was still in North Africa, this they knew from the date stamp, after the last of the fighting but not yet over here in Italy. So they reasoned the extra message was his way of getting round the censor, hinting to home what was next in line for them all. Nana said it most probably meant the end of the war for him.

Where people fought lions, aye. Only in his hurry he wrote f-o-r-t. In other words the big day they'd have old Musso licked and all be marching past the Colosseum, a conquering hero every... Eeh, I mean no disrespect! It's just that it's so hard to get my head round, you two out there together under orders to kill each other. And when I think you must have already been in that bad camp...

Better than in his boots! Fair enough, fair enough. And of course you got home, eventually, thank goodness, or we'd not be sitting here. And the Colosseum never dropped through our letter box. His here's hoping.

You shake your head. But if it's because you're thinking how sad or something that would not be entirely right, not a fair reflection of the way things actually were. Not with me at least. I suppose I was too small to understand, consequently I think I probably never quite did. All right, sometimes I'd have a bit cry, because losing a father in a mystery accident at sea is an awful lot to live with. But it was a sort of adventure too, you see. For a kick-off, Nana made me promise that for her sake I'd one day make the long journey to see the big stadium which could not be named, where he said humans faced lions. But there's another thing, something even more important, something he wanted only his son ever to know. Our very own secret never to be divulged, not even to Nan.

Vivo means alive? So you guessed. Yes, Robbie Rowan never died. He went missing. Signor, how I latched on to that word! Colin, another lad in our street, one night his dad took his cap and coat saying he was popping out to the pub for his usual pint and ten Woodbines, and a year later he sent word he was living way down in Marseilles with a woman he had met there in the war. And cats go missing from time to time, do they not, but does it always have to mean they've been run over? They might just as well have found a better deal someplace else. Somehow or other it evolves. From I don't know when, up to say eleven or twelve, probably more, I built up quite a story, longer and longer and ever more involved, the key to it always being that for reasons known to himself he arranged to disappear off the face of the earth. And good reasons too, because somehow I knew they'd be plain obvious to all once he chose to reveal them.

Aye, quite a big notion for a little head. Going on telling yourself that for as long as grown-ups keep on believing one of the two people responsible for your existence is dead and gone then everything is running according to plan. When that notion first came, or when I realised it was how I'd been acting all along, I just do not know. All I remember is how special it was to be of an age to share such a colossal secret. No playmate of mine, not Colin, not Kelvin, not Jackie, not even Brian, could be trusted with a thing as momentous as that. And of course grown-ups cast doubt on just about anything you came up with, practically their every word was designed to bring you down from the clouds. Even Nana. All I knew was that the fate of the entire enterprise depended on me keeping my end of the bargain, all them silent promises to him never to breathe a word about it. Today, I'd go so far as to say I lived for him.

Now that's maybe putting it better. Two worlds. Your double vision theory again. Aye, simple as that. That way nothing could ever come between us, no one could interfere. Because losing a husband is not the same as missing a father. It was only right, Mam said, only right and fair to remember who's alive and try to make a go of things, hope for another good person to see us through. So for her, aside from Marsden and then the whole Spiritualist craze, he was just very sadly ever more dead and gone. And I didn't mind, not really, seeing I knew she wanted the best by me. Queer match. The more men she had the more I had my dad!

Queer but true. I know I tried to put a date on it just

now, but really I'd be hard put to say when it was I stopped having space in my head for thinking that way, stopped entirely. It had been around so long it survived in a different state. Not even a thinking state, if you see what I mean. In fact everything you and your son relay to me about last night seems to show that still lingering somewhere inside of me is the idea, not really hope, that the world hasn't heard the last of Robbie Rowan. How else to account for such antics?

Two separate worlds. It was a big help you putting it like that. Up until a certain age, at least in my experience, you can tell a lad a hundred times a special person died years ago, and he'll still have no trouble conceiving of a good swimmer floating on a bit of wreckage or some passing tree trunk until eventually he comes to land. Even now, even now I think some little part of me supposes he could still be drifting about the seven seas of the world, living off fresh fish and rainwater. I elaborated on that picture in endless ways, though always finishing with him coming home from his sea-wanderings. Just walking along the beach, say, or strolling up our street some otherwise ordinary evening. I could feel it so strong, right down to the stories he'd bring. Look at your own travels in the war, tales Tony likes to tell. And you saw India. Nan made me a present of his photo to hang on the wall, so I always knew what face to look for when he came searching for our door. And I knew who would have to be the recogniser, for of course I could see no connection between a baby and a boy. And now I'm almost sure you must have guessed what's coming next. But it too is true, like every word I'm trying my very best to tell.

Right from early on, very early, I suspect more or less as far back as I remember, the one unchanging thing I knew about what I'd do when I grew was roam the whole wide world until I found him. Kids get it settled in their minds, don't they, like it's all so simple. Hard not to admire. Even when things stopped being that simple, even then something or other could bring him back to life. Just about any new fact you get to learn about this existence of ours that makes it not so ordinary as it comes to seem, all these semi-miraculous things you get to hear sooner or later when you're growing. Round about when I first got suspended from school for bunking off a bit too often I heard how people can lose their memory after an accident, or some sudden shock, then another accident or another shock can bring it all back again. Even after years and years of forgetting, like I remember hearing of someone blind for ages getting all his sight back perfect after a chance knock on just the right spot on his head. So that was another new angle on existence, fresh information to solve the mystery. Why he went missing, why he never got in touch. The shock of nearly drowning did for his memory, and when he got to shore he just wandered off into the night and a new life. So the big hope had to be that wherever on this earth he chanced to be he'd walk slap-bang into a lamp-post or something. Or, like Nana said he often did as a lad, step in to halt a scrap, but take a surprise clip on the chin so the whole of his past would flood back in one big rush.

Oh lots more, lots! For instance, how many years was Robinson Crusoe stuck on his island, presumed drowned? Twenty-eight! I never forgot that. On the wall behind the teacher's head when he was reading that story hung this shiny oilskin chart, a big map of the world showing the Atlantic Ocean and the Pacific in all shades of blue, different shades for different depths, and arrows for trade winds, and dots big and small for islands and archipelagos and such, and as the words kept coming I could stare and stare at all them various colours and shapes until in my mind's eye we were floating together on one of the strong blue currents to some lone atoll that remote that only a ship blown way off course by a hurricane would ever pass close enough to sight any sign of human life. 'SOS' in smoke signals rising from his palm-leaf bonfire. A Desert Army shirt drying on a cactus on a hill. A long-legged man in wild goatskins waving and waving from in front of his cave, his home.

Company, yes. I'm pleased you say that. So nothing to be too mournful about. Company, a ready-made friend in the head, someone you can turn to. When Brian got called up for Korea and I think about only once got round to writing, Kelvin still idolised him. Always on about his big hero brother, fabricating this and that. Not too far different from myself, I realise now, acting like my missing dad and me had a hundred ways of tapping into each other's thoughts. So when I heard about telepathy it made perfect sense.

Telly-pah-TEE-yah.

I repeat it right? Man oh man, maybe there's some hope for us yet!

The telepathy was Telfer's doing. The day I'm remembering he was sat there again with his cup and saucer on his knee telling Mam and Nelly our neighbour how people can send mental messages to each other, if they're the right sort of people. Etherial telegraphs, he called them. Every brain has its particular own wave-length, he says, like different wireless stations, and all he found he had to do was close his eyes and open his mind and think about a certain person, think very hard, all the time repeating one short message over and over until in good time he'd get like a kind of suction between the ears, sometimes a hum, which signified he was being received, he'd got the frequency, and once connection was established it was amazing how easy you could sometimes get even whole brain conversations going. I happen to remember almost every word because of the very long silence that followed, it was that intense, the three of us sitting there mesmerised as Telfer sets down his cup and saucer and closes his eyes and joins them long fingertips in front of his nose like the vicar in church before now let us pray. Ever so softly Nelly finally asked who he was hoping to contact and he said that could not be revealed, utmost privacy was essential. Then after a very long wait he just opens his eyes and says I'm sorry there seems to be some interference, some jamming, and asks Mam for a fill-up. Well of course I couldn't wait to try Mr Telfer's trick, not thinking for a moment I was a long-time practitioner. I lay on my bed I remember and faced his picture and closed my eyes and joined all my fingers and almost straight off we had a brain conversation going about walking the Great Wall of China, me and my dad, then all the Andes of Peru I think it was. Just as for Telfer, it didn't always work, but often enough I was the right sort on the right wave-length.

Like praying to God, exactly. Only getting through, even getting replies. Like I say, kids have a place in their heads where they can rearrange it all. Even the hardest question, whether he was still in the land of the living or a skeleton at the bottom of the sea, generally the answer depended on nothing more than say whether I could race to the next telegraph pole faster than the double-decker charging up the street behind us. And who'd make a bet like that without any chance of winning? Which reminds me.

Bones in the water. Yes, like on your paper. So maybe I told it last night? When I seemed to see him under the sea. Practically the entire squad was there, only their eyes searched the top, since what went overboard would be expected to float. Whereas mine went down, like almost sucked down. No?

Funny, because I get a feeling like I've been over it before. Maybe with your Tony, in our big talk on the stairs. But I haven't even properly set the scene.

We were crossing by ship to Holland prior to three weeks of manoeuvres in Germany, and just basically all standing round on deck with nowt to do. Then. well you know how it goes, next thing a couple of the lads are improvising a bit of footie, kicking round this mate of mine too sick to care's cap for a lark. Deck football, old Taffy's cap being the ball. So of course before you know anything it's practically a full-scale game, everyone's joined in, consequently sooner or later it had to happen. Someone shoots wide and Taffy's rolled-up blue beret sails over the side. I was right by the rail, with playing wing, and close in by the ship was a whole patch of water quite different to the rest, like a floating sheet of glass, tipping with the sea...

Oh sorry, sorry, tongue running away with me again!

It's the relief of the words coming, even if any old how. The sea, Signor Pasquale, you know how when you're very far out it seems it has a roof, a thick dark roof, well at that moment it was like we chanced to be sailing over a window, a window smooth and clear as glass, like a big skylight, so that suddenly you could see deep down. Or such at least was my impression. Like fathoms and fathoms of water were no longer between my eyes and this thing down there they could see. And this thing that was so visible to me was inside the very same outfit I had on. BD, our battledress uniform, the standard English Army sandy yellow, you'll remember it only too well. The rest was white, greeny white, where the bones showed. And the head, the skull – and this is the worst thing of all about that sighting in the second world or whatever we want to call it – the jawbone was wagging, wagging up and down, and I could see the more you swallow the more you're swallowed.

Still not fully transmitting? It's not easy to believe, I know, and I admit there was more than just water in our water bottles, but I swear that was my impression. Even reduced to a skeleton he was needing air, still dreaming air, yet what he swallowed had long since swallowed him. That's the thought which has been lodged ever afterwards in my brain, a drowned man going on gulping all he can get of what's already gulped him. Generally in dreams it's someone I don't know, and still I wake in a panic like it's happening to me. And long after we docked at the Hook of Holland it kept returning, floating outside the train window so to speak, that underwater thing. And on the channel ferry only the day before yesterday, standing with that queer lass at the rail, sharp again came the memory of what I once seemed to see, a skeleton in a tattered BD wagging and wagging its jaw, then turning on its side and sinking away deeper, slow-spinning like a stiff dead fish as the waves flowed back over that window which for a moment was in the sea.

3

Fine. Honest, I'm happy in the sun. Let it sweat the muck out, soak up all the bad. But you're right, I'll boil alive if I don't get me jumper off. There. And who do I thank for mending the hole?

Batman had to learn to patch and darn! Seriously though, thanks very much, thanks so very much. Beautiful work, so intricate. You know, you've gone and rescued the very last souvenir of my soldiering days. The very last, because yesterday she took off with my kitbag. But what I might also do, seeing I can feel from time to time my head could do with a bit of protection, is shift my chair nearer your side. So. Now if I lean back I can sort of dip it in the shade, cool off …

Man alive, look up there! It – it's –

Yes, like drifting in endless blue! What is it about being up high? You think you'd feel heavier, instead you're so much lighter. Brilliant idea, coming up here to kind of very slowly get used to the new situation. Recuperate. Float above it all in your good company, at this for me most magical moment in time. With so much behind, and such a lot to come.

Aye, and so very much to celebrate!

No, save it for yourself. Truly, I'm not participating. Eh Nana, there's a thought – this is the day to take the pledge!

The pledge of the Order of the Sons of Temperance, Signor: 'Henceforth by divine assistance I pledge to abstain from all intoxicating beverages.' Dear old disgraceful *Nonna*-Nana, she loved to recite that before downing her first gin and pop. Her wee swally. Divine assistance! Picture how she could make that look, so tasty, so sinful. Tongue-end stealing out to lick her lips all round, eyes rolling to heaven ...

Some view!

No, I'm okay. No worries, truly. Just felt a sudden urge to – to exercise this bad knee. Stretch me legs a little bit.

A city the colour of peaches. The kids have gone in, the one shop looks shut. Your entire street's deserted, barring a window cleaner risking his neck. All so peaceful. Hard to believe it took such a battering, that yesterday was so bad for so many. Flooded houses, poisoned water, some even losing their ...

Them two there, didn't see them at first – who might they be?

Directly below us now. The two cock hats strolling side by side, one in the shade, one in the sun.

Waiters!

Ah right, that's police. Bumped into one in odd circumstances yesterday, but not kitted out like that. A pair of admirals in full regalia. But that's Rome. Even doorposts are marble, she claims, even kerbstones. Signor, it feels so sort of strange to be here with you looking over the side together like this, then thinking of me all alone trailing round these deep streets under that never-ending rain what amounts to just hours back. A dreich calamity of a day, Nan would say. Never have I felt so lost. I thought the entire city was my enemy. This priest took us for German.

Near which one? Because I see dozens. The silvery dome, or that curlicue tower?

Why, that's no more than three-four streets across the rooftops! You know, I wouldn't mind a walk over in a while, now that I've as they say unburdened myself. Aye, now we've had our big heart to heart. Get the feel of the neighbourhood, visit out place of work, see how Tony's doing. Maybe lend him a hand and all.

But it just doesn't seem right to start with a day off! I could polish round, shift crates, make myself useful for once. And who else should be giving that floor a good going-over? The very least I can do, after walking in and behaving like that. And you keep it so sparkling. I'd go on my own, only I'm not too sure I could find it unaided, even with a good picture of where it is from here, even though I was twice there yesterday. The fact is I don't quite trust any of my memories of yesterday. All I know is I described a big circle. And more by luck than judgment.

Oh aye, the luck was finding the two of you! You didn't want to speak, I remember. I'm not surprised, must have looked a sight, certainly felt so. But we shook hands, I remember that, remember it vividly, I could hardly stand. And when I think what went on next to happen I've just got to wonder how you can put up with my company now. A disgrace. I should have seen it coming. Far too much booze, no food, and an endless train journey where I hardly slept. And I'm not sure my stomach quite got over the Channel. Even back in England, just the thought of Rome was producing butterflies. Out of fettle for weeks. Not myself. And then, pathetic, she shoves off and I have to overdo it in that predictable fashion, sample a fair selection of all our national beverages. Whiskey in desperation first, grappas galore off your son, and beers before that, and I don't know how much gin and wine in a sort of submerged nightclub full of oddities all after us for one thing or another. By which time I was that pie-eyed and washed-up I let myself be parted from all of my savings. But it was parting from the lass, that's what did it, not handling that situation too well.

You mean you heard it all last night?

Not all. Well thank goodness for that, because the less said the better. Still, over the worst now, more or less. Water under the bridge and all that. Just one of them things. Aye, on the mend now, surrounded by so much –

Not me! Never! I just don't believe it!

No, I get the picture thank you, the full awful picture. You made me look about age ten. So not content with bawling my heart out for my dead dad I went blubbering through all the streets of Rome for – for – for that… Emotionally immature, she claims. Mind, she herself wasn't above shedding a few crocodiles when –

Some windows have eyes!

She's watching, she's watching us all the time! That's what it felt like, that's why I had to sit. The queerest feeling, still tingling all round the back of me neck here. In waves, in waves it comes, and always her last blank look…

Forget it, Feelie! Let her do what she likes. Forget her, man. You're free as the wind now, aren't you? Forget her. Aye, that waste of breath can do what she likes. And who, and who! Somewhere out there lives a namby-pamby pianist I know would do anything to have her back. And in some penthouse lives a conniving old fortune-teller who has her dangling like a puppet on a -

Sorry, I wasn't completely listening, I didn't quite...

Why, you've deliberately turned the subject! And it just so happens to be another fairly painful one. Not worth spilling an ocean of tears over, all the same ... God Signor, the faces we make when we cry! So hopeless, so helpless. But so what if I did revert to age ten? There was a kind of purity then, wanting nowt to do with females, wanting only my dead dad. And just to prove my extreme immaturity I'm going to share a funny little picture that just popped into my head. Yes, you know what I'm savouring right this moment now? I'm savouring the thought she could walk back into my life by accident, this new life with you that's coming, one fine day step into the old Baffone and find the three of us working side by side all parlaying away in Italian! And oh yes I'm savouring it, assuming it's like pubs in England and we're not obliged to -

Sorry, Signor, sorry! Over-reacting again, I apologise. Enough of her, I fully agree. I'll not mention her ever again. Not ever.

Back to that! But I did say it happens ... Still, true enough, you've about summed up my general attitude, my previous attitude. I don't know what else I divulged last night on that particular sore topic, but the plain and honest truth is I've had no form of regular employment since I managed to discharge myself from the Forces, which will be fourteen months this next week coming. Or more truthfully, no employment, full stop. Happy just drifting along. Which isn't good, I know, not so very promising-sounding to a prospective employer, if that's why you bring it up. But that was England, see, this is Italy. And I mean to pull my weight, I genuinely do.

But that's hardly the point now! Still, you have to make it, you're the guvnor. And you know what I say in reply? What with all the time they made us waste in the Army, and as you rightly say a bit too much dilly-dally after, I'm one hundred per cent certain I've stored up a lot of energy in that direction. Two hundred!

The employment direction, Signor, what else! God's honest truth, I swear you've nothing to fear where any kind of job of work for you is concerned. I mean, would I ever even have contemplated such a big upheaval if I didn't intend to reform? Word of honour, I feel it in my bones just sitting here. Wasn't I only a moment ago wanting to get cracking this very minute? That hasn't changed. You say the word and I'll be on my feet. I really do mean to be totally open with you.

Now how can you say a thing like that, you don't even yet properly know that side of me! Today's a new day in a new country and I intend to make a new start, simple as that. Fair enough, I've got nowhere yet with my life, I concede that, concede it fully. And I'll be even more open with you. After quitting the Army I got into a bit of a rut, a rut so deep I doubt I'd have thanked anyone for pulling us out of it, in fact I'd go so far as to say I'd probably not have accepted even your kind offer while still in that frame, not this incredible chance or any other. So now that's right out in the open. But as I say, as I keep on saying, that was me at that time and this is me at this time. Today I woke up a changed man. Yes sir! For one thing even as I speak I can tell my head is working better, so naturally will my hands, as I know from good experience of myself. For another, if I may be allowed to say it, everyone deserves the benefit of the doubt when starting afresh. Just ask your son there if my reaction to the wondrous news doesn't prove how much I truly do appreciate the chance to be earning my living again. Yes, I left a lot behind with the white cliffs of Dover. Whereas the Army, the Army gave me one desire only.

Freedom, Signor Pasquale. Freedom, freedom, freedom – this great unending craving for freedom!

No, it's a fair question, perfectly fair. Freedom not to be ordered about, for one. Will you ever learn to use your head, soldier? That was a favourite with them to say, to shriek, while only recollecting you had a head was tantamount to mutiny. Because your common soldier's head is presumed empty, right? At the command change magazines, change magazines! On observing a fire shout, Fire! Fire! Maybe it would have been different if we'd seen some action. Oh I don't mean like you, and not like him. Not for a minute am I saying we want more wars, or I don't, it was just another way of saying that of all the torments they can devise the worst is the boredom, the excruciating boredom. Use your head, use your initiative, use your imagination! So they go, while keeping you nonentities. Traumatic. On fire piquet did we even once get a fire to fight? All I seem to have done while serving my time is fall in and fall out on the same parade-ground each and every morning, and lay me down on the same pit in the same billet every blessed night. Barring the one short break in Germany.

I'd not been long in, maybe a week, when it began to dawn I might have signed away five years of my life to no purpose. That's nigh-on a third of my entire existence up to then. All right, I'd more or less reached a dead end by the time I took the step, the fatal step, and I've not done very much to boast about since, but to my mind after a long ordeal like that a man has a right to revel a little while in his newfound freedom. If only to guard against making some similar mistake on impulse. Because that's how I went and enlisted, Signor, on impulse. Never mind the circumstances now, suffice it to say one freezing February morning I was screamed awake in a big barracks way down in Kent. Which is about as far as the crow flies from my point of origin. Dover being just forty mile down the road, to give the idea.

Volunteered, oh aye I volunteered! I know, I know, the dafty's head needs examining, as my mother would say. Even more when you consider she had the foresight to bring me into the world in time to escape national service. That's the call-up. Every poor bugger over eighteen had to do it until the government agreed it was pointless. With having the bomb, A and H and all the rest, they decided to drop it.

Oh you heard me right. And never a truer word. Though just as a point of accuracy it wasn't myself who coined it in that connection. No, *traumatico* was first applied to my Army career by a certain person who worked in the one place you'd least expect. A fairly unusual character at the

Dole office, one of all the officials paid to hear how hard you're hunting for a job when they already know three in ten are out of work. The Dole Office being where you have to go to queue for your National Assistance, or Benefit as they prefer to call it now. She says you have and you don't have anything like it over here, though likely she was only looking for one more way to put us off. I tried to get her to explain what arrangements you have for the out-of-work and what you need to do to qualify, but she's clueless in these sorts of vital practical … Hah, this should tickle you! Guess what line I finally took with the Dole people.

Declared I was contemplating emigrating, quitting the bloody country like I quit the bloody Army! Looks prophetic now, though it was pure fiction at the time, just one more survival ploy. Because you have to learn to stretch the truth a good bit to earn the pittance the unemployed are owed, and that can be well-nigh a full day's work itself, waiting your turn and telling your tales and filling in their forms, in other words perfecting the art of grovelling for what is rightly yours by the law of the land. Same land, mind, I was prepared to sacrifice my life to defend. While Signorina Brentani with the well-off family behind her, cause of them wasted tears, she'd tell you I have no business complaining when half the world is starving. Which I don't deny, mind, naturally I don't. No, all I'm saying is our country likes to call itself advanced and according to me the system's nothing near perfect yet. Not for the man on the wrong end of the begging bowl, that is. Doesn't take him long to work out how finely his benefit's calculated to be the bare minimum, so long as he doesn't have to pay for the roof he sleeps under and doesn't have too big a drink problem.

And another thing I know, and most definitely does she, it's nowhere near what a person young and straining at the leash in directions other than pure survival requires, if ever he's to begin to think what they call positive. So tell me, where's the benefit now? Mind, I'm not denying it gives a better feeling for a day, any coat sits comfier for a couple of quid inside your ...

Eeh sorry, I really am so very sorry, I don't know what I was dreaming! Away off on one of my favourite rants, like she's sitting right here too. Why can I never leave her out of it? No wonder you preferred your own thoughts. And now I'm afraid I've gone and got…

Traumatico! Grazia, grazia. Seems I have a knack of telling everything back-end on. Also, I don't know why I had to get a bit hot under the collar with you like that a little while ago, I'm ashamed of myself, I truly am. You've given me a life-line, you've every right to press. Put it down to the sudden revelations about all the weeping and wailing. Unbelievable me going to such extremes, and after the tongue lashing I had to take from her yesterday. Well, I'm fighting back, which I think is what you want. And it's helping, it's helping. That's what a good sound-off can do, in the company of someone you know you can open your heart to. And old Lacey, for all he did do us a good turn or two, was not quite that someone.

4

That oddball at the Dole Office I mentioned. With him you had to watch yourself a bit too much, and watch him. Besides, he's a Newcastle supporter, so we differed on a few other essentials. All the same, I did for a time feel he genuinely was taking a bit of a fatherly interest.

Known some other cases, says he at our very first encounter, I've known other cases where the Army has put paid to a well-adjusted youngster's natural-born will to apply himself. Happen not only the bright ones get the sensation they're going nowhere fast, even for a relatively simple young lad like yourself it can be tolerably traumatic, if they just cannot learn to adapt. Traumatic, and in the end soul-destroying, as with any occupation where they won't leave you alone to work for yourself. I could hardly believe my ears. And when you think where we happened to be. Traumatic! Soul-destroying! You're telling me, Mr Lacey, I says.

Oh yes, quite a study. Bit moody-like at times, a bit unpredictable beneath the bluff exterior, but in no way run-of-the-mill. Never once did he give out the drill about the bad old days when he was young and only too glad of any bit of work to come his way. In them days, all the other old fellows are that keen to tell you, they didn't treat you soft like nowadays, oh no, lose a finger in a roller and you reported back the same afternoon with it sewn back on, and there were no government hand-outs to keep idlers snug in bed, not then my fine young man, if it snowed overnight you made sure to be down there first thing outside the Labour Exchange to collect a shovel and clear the Council Chamber steps. All because he was fed up with his own, if you ask me.

His own job of work. The reason he could see the other man's point of view, identify with the traumatised, spot the soul-destroyed, look not unkindly on the skivers. One time I took the liberty of saying that going by the types of job on offer for my sort I might as well have never left the Army, did they honestly suppose my horizons were no broader than that. I mean, we saw Germany, I said to him, also bits of Holland, and only just two months after achieving my release our entire mob went and got shipped out to Hong Kong. Hong Kong, send me there and I'd never come back! I endorse those sentiments, laddy, murmurs Lacey, I too dream of them whorehouses.

Aye, some remark! Like we said, the man's a study, quite a turn, and cut from the same cloth as Nan, one of them rare souls who don't really seem to mind what they say. As you might imagine, if ever I spotted old Lacey up front I'd be certain to stand in his line, and sure as sure almost every time, like he had no recollection of ever having mentioned the matter, he'd start in all over again expatiating on the subject of willing young infantrymen deadened by senseless discipline, on one occasion even going so far as to divulge that the same thing afflicted – right at this moment I don't recall the name – anyhow his brother-in-law's son by a previous marriage who likewise signed the yellow-brown warrant for his own apprehension, if you take my meaning, though in his case he was that simple he went and set his name to a nine-year stint and of course after serving the full whack still comes out the private he went in, same as yours truly, though in my case that's because I opted to take on the entire Army. Anyways, forgetting that bit of a long mouthful, for fully twelve month after demob this same lad, goes on Lacey dropping his voice so I got the impression the lady official next-door wasn't intended to hear, this same near relative of his displayed no interest in any job of work or anything much else in life apart from his step-daughter – Lacey's, the new wife's grown lass – and then all at once after this kind of long gap-year doing sweet Fanny Adams what does he go and do but surprise one and all by quietly fitting himself up with a plumb job lifting upwards of thirty quid a week as an all-night croupier in a Newcastle casino! And who can ever guess whence came the tip-off for that nice number, eh?

No, no, every word I'm saying is still on the all-important topic we had words about a while back, I swear! Maybe it sounds like I'm only going round in circles, maybe it seems I deserve a whistle for time-wasting, but not for a moment have I lost sight of my own problem. My problem that was, that is. Not for one single moment, Signor. Because the very next time I'm up before Lacey and well-launched into the usual rigmarole about how hard I'm looking for anything to suit my hidden talents, all the blind alleys I'm exploring and that, he cuts us off in mid-flight and once again embarks on this let's face it pretty revealing private family story regarding this other bolshie ex-squaddie who chose to make the most of the freedoms of Civvy Street before all in his own good time toeing the line in that miraculous fashion and – and this is what it's all been building up to, see – I could hardly help but draw the conclusion, could I, that in a not even so very roundabout way I was being advised to indulge in a similar prolonged period of adjustment, and more or less with official backing and all. Which goes to show, in the most unlikely places you can sometimes find the most understanding people.

Oh he's a one-man entertainment, old Lacey, well worth listening to, so long as he hasn't had too many and you've learned to take his banter, and I only wish I could reproduce his talk for you. A sort of born pontificator, very educated-sounding, though for all the colourfulness he can come across as a mite patronising, even indifferent beneath it all, that's another thing I'd need to capture for you. Bit on a par with this mouthy fake Irishman, come to think, who chose to go off with all my savings last night, someone who likes a good audience. Lacey's slower-spoken, mind, otherwise likewise a bit over-fond of oiling his wig, another full-time boozer as you see at once from his jammy eyes, and it's a fair guess it's the side-effects of that which did for him as far as progress up the ladder goes. I mean, even I could have told him he'd do better to be more tight-lipped in that line of business, a bit less liberal with the bonhomie. Same story in the Army, isn't it? Because didn't you also find that of all the many types of people who exist to make others fall in line, time and again it's the quieter ones you need to be more wary of, they're the ones who get the promotion, the softer-voiced types who sew along the inside of their creases, not the blood-and-thunder lot forever barking they'll have your guts for garters?

Right enough, you always know where you are with them. Though on second thoughts I think maybe I'd put

Lacey somewhere between the two. A little bit of both. Also he had a very interesting secret, as I discovered.

Never trust a dog that doesn't bark? I'm sure, pretty sure, we've some similar saying in English. Personally I don't trust any dog. But can I mention what it was, Lacey's secret? It transpired I wasn't the only misfit to be taken under his wing, oh by no manner of means! In fact I found he has a whole band of drop-outs gathered round him, in the inner circle upwards of a dozen professional dolemen who all look on him as their lord and protector in exchange for standing him the occasional pint if ever they happen to run into him, which is easily arranged once he lets on he's partial to a liquid lunch in the back room of the General Gordon, any weekday. Oh yeah, quite a devoted little following has Mr Gerald Lacey, almost any day you'll find at least four or five of our town's happy losers keeping him company over a jar round the coal fire that's always blazing away in there. A nice quiet out-of-the-way place, the Gordon, yet only just over the river from the Dole Office and a bit up the hill. And I don't mind admitting I've whiled away a canny few hours in the snug there myself, what with the good football crack, and old Lacey musing on all our foibles.

According to one recent situation report, his sit-reps as he likes to call them, I'm what amounts to a not unusual variation on the common case of ditherer between croupier and life-boatman. Seen a good few in my time, says he extending loving lips to sip the froth off the fresh pint of his beloved Brown I've just bought him, seen 'em come and seen 'em go, day-dreamers like your own good self, Shorty, forever dithering between love-thy-neighbour and the tantalising gleam of far-off mountains of brass!

Oh aye, well-oiled already as you can hear, for it was hard to see how any of it related. Take your time and let them have their full say, I always think, all authority-types, never hurry them along, keep on nodding while thinking hard to yourself through all the preamble so you're better prepared when finally they get round to whatever it's all working up to. Because anyone could tell it was working up to something. And right enough, just as I'm thinking I'll maybe have to be getting in another, suddenly he's dropping a heavy hint in my ear about what he terms a recent grape-vine SOS for a half-dozen bright young lads willing and able to do ten-hour shifts six nights a week as croupiers in a little place a certain close acquaintance of his would soon be opening somewhere down Sunderland docks. Now as he himself well knew having long since planted the idea, that was the one job of work I might have been prepared to take a look at, what with having so dutifully modelled myself on what's-his-name's chequered career. Mind you, I had other reasons for contemplating almost any job right then, though that's a different matter. They weren't after French, he also let fall, not even Maths, just quick hands and quick minds. Half-pay training was to begin any day, he says behind his big hand, even conceding name and address. But guess what.

The fly owd bugger was only taking us for a ride! Of course I know it's neither here nor there now, not now I'm signed up with the Baffone, Signor, but to be honest even as he whispered in my ear, 'Hedley, Jubilee House, Whitburn' I had my doubts, and in fact in the same breath that I broke the news at home I took the precaution of saying sending off an application was likely only a waste of the stamp. And was I ever right! Up until the day we left, that's first post Friday, this close acquaintance of his who he, Lacey, knowing full well the effect it would have did not fail also to confide happens to be on the management board of Sunderland AFC, still hadn't got round to so much as acknowledging my letter of application, the best thought-out and longest piece of writing I ever wrote. And believe me, Signor Pasquale, believe me I truly did desperately want that job, and every penny with it. Yet I don't suppose his close acquaintance had the patience to read one single line I wrote once he'd checked the name at the bottom of page three rang no bells, for you can be certain Gerald Michael Lacey MA never put in a word on my behalf, for all his hints that I should have long worked off the trauma effects by then. Ours not to reason why was all I could winkle out of him, if ever I happened to let fall I was still awaiting his Mr Hedley's summons.

Absolutely not. No tragedy now, absolutely definitely not! In fact I don't know why I go on about it so. Maybe only because it shows I was doing the right thing after all, secretly plotting my escape to Italy, clearing out to where no-one has any ready-made notions on my account. That's why I never got on so well at new schools, always arriving with a bundle of complaints from the one before.

But man, oh man, what a daft dunce I felt waiting and waiting for my great casino offer after giving up two promising days by the rising river to put together this great long screed close-packed with just about everything anyone could ever wish to know on my account, even without an interview! A history of my various doings from the day head teachers lost the right to make us attend school, and close on one entire whole page proving my undying support for Sunderland, plus some passing thoughts on the merits and morals of gambling, and as good a justification as I ever yet concocted for why I broke my contract with the Army. Not a particularly eventful life, I give you that, but worth getting down all the same, and in certain respects I have to say I enjoyed it. Not the writing, never that. The mulling over and the taking stock, that side of the process. And I truly still do believe it was well-pondered, and pondered from the heart. Yet you know what was her opinion when I gave it her to read? She said she's never known such a talent for making a mountain out of a molehill, and will I ever learn where to put a full stop.

Aye, let her write it for us, if she's so know-all. Equally, mind, sometimes I wonder whether it didn't show a gratuitous need to put me down for encroaching the tiniest bit on her scene. Yet what's she ever had to fear? I told you, the whole act puts us off. Seldom do I fail for words until I have to set pen to paper, when invariably by line two I've lost the thread whereby the whole tangle seems to somehow mostly manage to more or less hang together without too many worries when you're speaking. For me, having to get it down spoils all the enjoyment, breaks the natural flow, like at times even speaking came to be when forced to wonder how that woman I seem incapable of stopping myself bringing up might chance to be secretly thinking of whatever I was endeavouring to put across at the time. But we'll never get into her head. All I know is writing means the world to her, in fact I'd even go so far as to say it's her one true love, her dad possibly aside, though seeing the agony it caused her what good she supposes she gets out of it is way beyond my wit and comprehension. The more I knew her the more I got to hate it. Time after time it came between us, and frankly in the end I just had to learn to stand aside and watch it get on top of her, again and again. How can a thing that does that to a person be more important than living? But then, I ask, would she ever want to handle that beautiful big espresso machine in front of all the bottles in your bar? Wouldn't see the challenge even. Ta.

Just a taste.

Oof, not bad at all! And now straight back to you, that's all I'm touching. Oh no, keep it by your chair, if you don't mind. Breaking my resolution doesn't alter my determination. If I go mixing alcohol with all this sun and novelty I'll sharp be losing the plot again. Mouth just felt a little bit dry for some reason, and you could see I had to sample it. Which is one more thing she'll never understand. About the strongest drink I ever saw pass her lips was a lime and lemonade.

Eeh, will I never stop going on about her! What's the good of this useless hankering?

5

Window-cleaner's progressed a floor higher, I see. Brings along a whole other set of memories watching him there, things that seemed to have a habit of coming almost automatic if ever I started fantasising about the perfect job.

Down by the river wending through our town stands this big old warehouse, derelict for years, and one time me and my schoolmate Kelvin forged sick notes for ourselves again, in the spring, we happened to be wandering along the path on the other bank sharing this packet of crisps and kicking an old can around, and looking across we saw someone had decided to brighten it up. It was the music that drew us, the song that goes, 'How would you like to be …' He was perched in a top-floor window, sat right out on the sill in his painter's white duds, just like him over there now, legs inside the room, all his top half in the sun. So we stopped to watch. If that's a painter's life, says Kelvin, and I tell you he took the words from my mouth, I wouldn't mind giving it a go. Smoothly, patiently, expertly, we watched him spread this fresh wet green all up and down the old window frame, a bright duckweed green, his radio playing for him from somewhere inside the room, and under him a drop of at least forty feet to one of the fishiest parts of our river, this deep slow bend before it widens right out to flow over the weir. On that side, in front of the old brick parapet by the warehouse where it's sort of sluggish-running but still clear enough so long as there's been no heavy rain for a while and no breeze is frisking about, it's easy to spot them in the spaces between the waving waterweeds, practically every fish there is. Sharp as sticks they stand out against the sandy bottom, if the sun decides to shine. First find his shadow, a darker streak on the bottom ripple, then lift your eyes a fraction and you'll spot him there, the lighter form of the actual fish floating right above his shadow. Dainty little dace for the most part, or maybe a roach round as a stone, but I've also sighted massive salmon lurking in there at certain times. The right times like, round the back end of summer.

Were that me, I says to Kelvin, were it me paid to paint up all of them windows I'd be tempted to run a secret line out, you know set me up a good long ledger reaching right down into the deepest part of the flow, then just see what happens. You're not supposed to go after anything fifty yards either side of the weir, see, consequently some fish in there grow that tame that honestly, Signor, I remember once this lady leaning over the parapet to flick ash off her cigarette and a good-size trout, one of the biggest I ever saw, tailed almost half across the river lazy as may be in the slow water for a good long close-up of what was drifting by. Such sights make you ponder maybe having a little go at night, and I must admit I've considered it, for I reckon you could pull them out with near enough anything on the end, I mean I've seen them nose an empty crisp packet, not to speak of how they all gobble the bread for the ducks. Once upon a time in the big pool below the weir lived this massive goldfish, some kind heart must have originally let it loose after a win at the shows, and I swear even at a hundred yards you could already see him glowing like a copper kettle rolling round the bottom. Every year he grew twice his size, finally I'd say as big as a good two-three pound carp. Gone now. Goodness only knows what happened to him, how he met his…

Signor Pasquale!

Well no, actually I was under the impression you might have dropped off.

Wandering a bit, yeah. Wondering and wandering! On account I suppose of this good gentle siesta-ly feeling percolating now, less cars about and all so relatively quiet. This drowsy sun. Still, true, I did have a question in mind, though nothing specially important. I was just wondering whether you ever happen to see people out fishing along the Tiber and catching anything. And for the matter of that, where exactly is this famous River Tiber everyone talks about? A bit of a mixed-up English lass I bumped into last night spoke of trees and islands and bridges and that, which makes it sound quite a big affair. Big enough to do a lot of damage, from what Tony said. All them sad pictures.

Grand lad, aye. I'm looking forward to when I know him a lot better. Passionate. Takes things to heart, doesn't he? All yesterday he was the one and only person who seemed to want to help, barring possibly that same lass with a terrible mother. And now I know where he gets it from! And seeing he was off to the bar, I should have remembered to ask if by any chance he still has -

Big? But not *grandissimo.* So a middling-size river.

And filthy! I can well imagine, with a city this size. Not that it could ever be muckier than the last fifteen mile of the River Tyne, fish stand a better chance on land. Though, mind, you should have seen the disgrace out own little river was this summer.

Angler?

Not a fisherman. Is there some other word perhaps?

Now that's good, that's unbelievable! You have your arm going exactly like an eel. So what was that word?

Slippy, yes. And greedy, greedy as hell, consequently almost each and every time it's his fate to hook himself right at the back of the gizzard, if not way down the stomach.

And no, no one likes killing eels. So am I right in thinking you would be a bit of a fisherman yourself?

Aye, curls all about the line and pulls and pulls. Hoping to break it, no doubt. We could go sometime.

You and me, after the eels. Some other day-off like. Or some night after we close. Did you see the elvers ever, the eel babies, wriggling upstream? Nothing daunts them, full spate or trickle. To me it's one of the wonders of nature, water creatures even prepared to cross land to get to where they need to be. Now who'd have thought, the common eel in the mighty Tiber! Makes it practically big brother to our little river. Yes, I wouldn't mind a bit of fishing, in the territory of the Romans. Assuming it's okay we share tackle till I've earned sufficient to accumulate my own. Because I'm afraid at present I haven't two liras left to rub together, all thanks to that double-crossing Paddy painter. Plus my own idiocy.

That so? With the sun this strong it's no good in my experience either, they lose their appetite, though I wasn't sure if your fish would be quite so averse to the heat. That was the trouble this summer, the long heat wave, or the excuse the Water Board gave out when just about everything in the river got the plague. I don't suppose it made news over here, but in the north of England we'd not a drop of rain for weeks and weeks. We'd a job persuading our live-in Roman that seventy or whatever days of non-stop sunshine is not the rule but the exception. Still, to be fair, she said she too just longed and longed for rain.

Mind, she needed her eyes opening to a few other facts of life where we come from. Her dad's a teacher of English in some big school here, and apparently he drummed into her since she was so high that nowhere on earth compares with ye olde England, though insofar as I understand things he only ever set foot in the place but once in his whole life, and that was his honeymoon with his wife just a year or two before the war. She's half English in fact, the wife, by all accounts the result of an encounter on the wrong side of the blanket between some high-born English officer and a local lass high up in the mountains somewhere near Venice during the war before last. Bit of a funny result too, because from all I hear you'd reckon the mam and the dad switched origins. He's totally Italian but adores our language and dotes on the place, whereas the mam says she feels one hundred per cent Italian and doesn't see why she should have to know English. Character-wise, though, it's more as you'd expect. She's more withdrawn, he's the expansive one.

Shame we'll never meet. Because the truth is I speculated quite a bit about how we'd all rub along. Going by his picture, the great *professore*'s no more than a wisp of a creature with a big round nose and sunglasses in an Oxford duffle standing next to a marble carving you have in a museum here, one of them old carvings my uncle Harry who was a bit of a wag would call a perfectly armless Lady Godiva. Yet just by the tilt of his chin you can see he reckons he's the bee's knees and loves to be professor-thissed and professor-thatted, while all along he's nobbut a ruddy schoolteacher! Still, I shouldn't mock. Out here I'd be more lost than ever were it not for a book he put together to give not very advanced beginners like me some guidance with the lingo. The wife by the bye, her mother, she was in the same line of business too, a schoolmistress herself, in fact that's how the pair of them met I'm reliably informed, until at some point she retired on the edge of a nervous breakdown. Still is, if I've pieced things together correctly.

On the edge like. And a bit retired into herself now and all, by the sound. Even more than a bit, seeing I gather she's known not to utter a word for days. The daughter's taken a leaf from her there, mind. And she takes after her in other ways too, far as I can tell from things she says. For instance this kind of waxy yellow her skin can go on her off-days. Also a hair colour you cannot really describe when it's natural, which it almost never is, though it went nicely down her back when she first arrived in my life. Never asked whence she gets the eyes. The mythical grandad, who knows. Big, greenish, beautiful. They change according to the light, or just the way the mood happens to take her, anywhere between browny green and greeny blue. I chalked up a big point with her when I compared them to all the colours of our river when it's fining down. But you know what I reckon, you know what I've decided?

Reading between the lines of what's the name of it, the book he wrote, all the fancy shops and sights his Mr and Mrs Smythe-Jones make for on their big trip to Italy, and all their small talk, the only sort of Englishman he'd consider halfway good enough for his daughter would likely earn her a po-face picture in one of them glossy magazines you only ever see in dentist's waiting rooms. Lady So-and-So pictured on the occasion of her recent engagement to little Lord Fauntleroy type of thing. Or in her case more like some randy rich businessman three times her age to keep her permanently in books and cigarettes and hair-dye fees. Because she has a thing about decision makers, see, the type of man you can tell at a glance knows all he's about and where he's going. So she'll inform you only moments before walking out on you, the green orbs finally gone no colour at all. Aye, out the door and into the arms of a dotty old astrologer, or a cardinal's nephew, or I don't know some toothless midget millionaire nightclub owner with breath as terrible as a dog's fart and hands he ... *Vacanza in Italia!*

How can such a simple thing slip the memory? I seem to have almost perfect recall until it comes to a language which isn't mine. On my tongue-end all this time and it just wouldn't come. It's her dad's effort. 'Vacancy in Italy' I called it for a tease. I had a good look at it on the train, in part because she intended it to be another of her little schemes for humouring Papa. It's only just come out in England, see, and she thought we could use it to make a great big fuss of him, swearing it would make him ever so pleased if I asked him to autograph it, having by coincidence just spotted it brand new while we were queuing at the station. Victoria Station, just this Saturday morning gone, the queue for the boat-train happening to wind right past this massive bookstall they have there, and I only wish you'd seen her face the moment she spotted her dad in print at last in his promised land, why it lit up proud as punch, rosy as the covers of the book! I'll be sure to let you see it when I fetch my things over from the hotel, if ever I find it. I happen to know it took him years and years.

Actually, I'd be interested to hear what you make of this book once you've had time to get to know it. What I reckon must be just about unbeatable is the lengths it goes to give all the words for you exactly how they're meant to sound, which is the most important thing I reckon if ever you hope to get through to people in another language and expect them to stick with it right to the end. *Vah-CANT-see-yah een ee-TAH-lee-ah* type of thing.

Acceptable? Bit odd-seeming at times, but according to me it works, and it's even quite good fun. Otherwise the whole strategy is pretty obvious. He puts the English on one side and the Italian on the other in a whole variety of fairly normal situations. Trouble is, I also happen to know it's not all his own work, in fact I have it on good authority he could never have finished it but for a lot of help, most of all from the immediate family. Apparently he quite often gets himself in a muddle or just downright discouraged, and even though our language may be his pet obsession I hear his command isn't all it could be. For instance she let slip he quite often turned to her for advice and was very grateful for it. Hers, her command, I have to say is brilliant, though maybe just a little bit stilted seeing so much of it comes out of books.

And you know something else? I personally can vouch his leaves something to be desired. Yesterday afternoon, the first time I landed in your place, your Tony got through for me on the phone and this man on the other end I'm now almost sure must have been her dad only managed about five real words of English. The gist being I was on no account to show my face. No come round, mister, understand, no come round again. I tried to be extra-polite, I truly did, thinking how he was likely feeling, and in point of fact he did sound peeved, not to say pretty aggrieved, which in spite of everything is still I think a bit much considering all we did for her in England. Like I say, he's the only mortal person I believe she really cares about, never in all these months did I hear a word against the man, from Papa after all flows love and money. Yet the more she told the more he sounded like another character ripe for study. I mean, his sort are dying out fast, even in our own land. His shirts he gets tailor-made some place like Windsor, and every other year or something a new suit turns up from Savile Row no less. All performed by post, goodness only knows at what expense. So now you see why we two weren't exactly made for each other, yours truly and the precious only daughter. Not very well suited! Hah! Nice.

No capito? She and me, we no suit. Bad fit, Signor. Never mind, just another of my terrible jokes. Even so, maybe it's a sign I really am on the mend, not to fret about cracking a shocker like that, see it coming a mile off and still not be scared to use it. Why aye man, as your Tony says, seems the old boldness might be creeping back. And not just thanks to your blanco.

Well, they do say the hair of the –

Dooh! Lovely.

And while on suits, right now I don't have anything resembling one but in the hotel I'm meant to be in is my bag and in that bag is some more presentable gear I could wear for work. To go with that top of yours, unless you can find one of Tony's, wouldn't want to let the side down. And tomorrow, I'm also thinking, the great tomorrow when I'm thrown in the deep end, if ever I seem to you to be wrestling with what exactly people want from me I'm hoping you two will cover for us. I mean, when the *italiano* really starts flying around. I've picked up bits and bobs from that book, from her too, but I'm just a dead loss when it comes to stringing them all together. But bit by bit, I suppose, day by day. Yes, how long I wonder might it take a potential avid learner to get to be almost a native speaker? Because that's what I mean to be some day, with your kind assistance. You have the right approach, you and Tony you encourage people who aren't good. Whereas that green-eyed carrot-haired woman of Rome, if ever I endeavoured to get my mouth round it she'd accuse us of massacring the world's prettiest tongue!

Man, your wine's having an effect. Better lay off, stronger than I thought. As you say, suck a pebble.

Which, funny, reminds me of the best story I could ever find to tell about my father. Unless it came up last night? The desert dentist story?

Well just stop me if you find it did.

Okay then. First, by way of introduction like, I need to say that when the Army found he already knew all there is to know about electrics and radios they decided to train him as a signals man, a wireless and telegraph operator, posting him off to a camp near York to learn every kind of code. So once out in Africa he gets attached to the CO in that capacity. The Commanding Officer, a lieutenant-colonel no less, who years later relayed the whole story in a famous letter which came as a total revelation. Anyhow, so there he is, Signaller Robbie Rowan, the top man's driver-cum-wireless operator, running him round the front in a jeep and keeping everyone in touch over the air ...

Eeh, what a case – I'm forgetting again! But Signor Pasquale, this isn't about who won or who lost, it's about survival, pure survival, and could be about anyone in similar circumstances. You see the colonel contracted a terrible toothache, abscesses presumably. And the point is it happened when they were stuck somewhere way out in the desert, the wrong side of the Gazala line as the famous letter put it. You know it, you nod. So now imagine the situation, their jeep jammed axel-deep in sand in No Man's Land, the all-important wireless similarly out of action, and the gaffer near out of his head with unbearable pain. So what does my dad his driver do to save the situation, very possibly his life? Goes ahead and pulls them out! The offending teeth, out by the roots, ripped from their gums. Just like that. These two uppers we have next to each other up front in the top row here, after splitting the remains of a bottle of whisky. And if all I'm telling sounds resourceful, wait for what comes – and remember it's all of it true, every word is written-down fact. Not wanting to leave the man with a dirty great gap at the front of his mouth, and stuck there for who knows how long twiddling their thumbs waiting to be rescued or slaughtered as fate would decree, and the colonel also added maybe a bit to make up for the fact the wireless had even Signaller Rowan foxed, my dad Robbie goes and makes him a present of a set of new ones!

God's honest truth, I've seen them with my own two eyes, these thin sharp ones we have here, like rabbits, fashioned out of whatever happened to be to hand. Some metal you can maybe melt down and work before it hardens, anyhow manipulate one way or another, cut and shape and polish. Not lead. Tin? Aluminium? I just don't know about these things. Why do I think resin, not rubber, is something else he used? For a bed to help them sit softer.

Is that a fact? So the war made the desert a good

scrapyard. I bet it did. Major Arthur, that more or less geriatric boyfriend of my mother's with the bit of shrapnel, he had a very similar trophy to the one you describe. A clever little brass lighter he claimed an Italian POW made special for him out of a spent cartridge case and some vital part of an airplane engine. It's the artistic genius in them, he'd say almost every time he flicked it open, though they're all too damn individualistic to make worthwhile soldiers. Shit, me foot's landed right in it again! But you know me, you know me well enough by now, Signor, I take both comments as a compliment. And coming from that man.

I know, unbelievable, absolutely unbelievable. I mean, you can just about conceive of drawing your CO's teeth in the absence of a dentist if he truly is in mortal agony, but who else on his own initiative would set to work and in such circumstances to figure out how to fashion artificial new ones that craftily slot into the plate the man already wore in his mouth? All that, and never having studied a word of dentistry! Even, who knows, my dad was that handy he could perform the entire job with nothing more than an intricate combination of plier work and hammering, prior to bedding them in that reddy-pink resin or whatever. Because we're talking about a real inventor here, remember. And he part-trained as a coach-builder before the war, which may have been further inspiration.

Oh, if you'd seen the work that went into them! Resourceful isn't in it, to me it's nothing short of a miracle. And all confirmed in the famous letter.

Never will I forget the day. Coming in from school or wherever I see Mam standing sort of rigid in the middle of our back-kitchen with this look on her face, this very strange look, staring with her eyes wide open and the tears building in the corners, weird, so I just stopped where I was in the doorway and stared right back. And then, ever so slow, from out of cotton wool in this little battered old Player's tobacco tin open on the table next to that letter on sky-blue paper she picks out the colonel's bone crunchers like this, like a jewel, holding the mystery right up high to the light for me to see. Made by your father. That's all she said. Made by your father. Of course I hadn't a clue what I was looking at, but I knew it was momentous. Because it proved our secret was true, I'd been right all along, he would get in touch when the moment came. In her fingers, in the sun, it glittered like a little present of silver from Alaska.

Bone crunchers, you heard the words right. It's the jokey name the two of them must have concocted for the new teeth, what the colonel also liked to call his desert gnashers. It was written right there on the tin, inked on a strip of sticking plaster stuck on the lid. First the colonel's name and rank, then underneath: 'GNASHERS', in bigger letters, 'GNASHERS, upper, artificial, bones for the crunching of, TWO.' Like tiny twin chisel tips welded together, I was thinking as I fingered them, heart pounding. You're alive, Dad, you're alive, you're coming home, you're coming home!

Then she said to me to sit down. And she read out the letter, the long letter on sky-blue paper, line by line, page on page, signed at the end yours very truly Lieutenant-Colonel Ronald Sandyman. And it gave an awful lot to think about. Too much, very likely. Because it didn't tell just the wondrous story of the teeth, it also told what led to my dad losing his life. He'd been thinking of putting his war memories together, the colonel, and in the course of various enquiries it had chanced to reach his ears what fate had befallen his desert dentist, as seemingly he liked to call him, never at the actual time having received word about the accident. And it just so happens he should have been one of the very first to be informed. And for why? It's all there in the letter, which unfortunately we don't have any longer now, how he had sent over to Italy for his one-time signaller-driver, the maker of his desert gnashers, the famous bone crunchers. They'd earned him more renown than anything he ever did to beat Rommel, he joked, but also they were giving him a little bit of bother, so when he came out of hospital after being patched up following what he called a rather disagreeable encounter with a Jerry landmine he decided to take himself off to a top French dentist, in Bizerta I remember it was, to get that gap filled with something which might also be a better camouflage. His exact words, more or less, and all there in black and white for years inside the cigar-box in the glass cupboard where Mam kept it stored along with the other mementos, the original terrible telegram, and Flight-Lieutenant Leonards's note, and my picture postcard, and of course the teeth in their tin, before she posted it and them off to the War Museum, though that's a whole other chapter.

Yes, we finally had our answer. What on earth a solitary infantryman was doing on a seaplane. The colonel had decided he wanted him over in Africa for the celebrations, his new teeth celebration party. The top chap in Coastal Command here in Italy owed him a favour, he wrote, likewise he had had little trouble prevailing upon his successor, the DLI's new CO, to authorise Signaller Robert Rowan to be flown out from Sicily during what was to be logged as temporary leave due to a bout of battle fatigue. So then of course when his special guest didn't show up for the party he just assumed his various ploys hadn't worked. After all there was a war on. Still, going on all he wrote he sounded genuinely pretty put out, that due to his whim his desert dentist met his end in the Mediterranean Sea. A good soldier, he wrote, and above all a good man. Yes, you could tell he felt a good bit knocked up about it. And then not only going to all the trouble of writing, even parcelling up his sacred bone crunchers, and so long after the event.

No, I don't condemn him. Don't even blame him, not anymore. Now I just put it all down to chance. Besides, later we heard the old boy himself had passed away, and a pretty decent fair-minded bloke by the sound of him. Appreciative. Even a bit of a friend to my dad. Similar perhaps to your Captain Bulkington, not the least stuck up like the generality. In any case, why condemn anyone? Once we start down that road we'd wind up with the day he was born.

6

You're very patient. I wouldn't normally ever monopolise the conversation like this, gabbing away like there's no tomorrow, leaving almost no space for you to get a word in. But already last night you saw how much I needed to unburden myself, so please just read it as a sign I've suffered in silence for far too long. All these past weeks my mind hasn't seemed to move at all, today it's racing, and somehow I just cannot stop my tongue going with it. Something very similar happened once before, in fact didn't end too happily, and if it's all the same to you I'd quite like to tell about it, now we've got the ball rolling. But just remember, if ever you start to feel enough is enough you're free to shut us up, any time you like.

It was the very end of my second week in the Army, the Sunday night coming up for midnight, and the lot of us were fair dropping with sleep and yet there we were, each by his bed or in it, all still bulling our boots by candlelight. The big inspection was in the morning, see, and I don't know how often we'd been told the true measure of our progress as soldiers would be the state of our boots. The British Army in its wisdom, as I'm sure you know, chooses to commission footwear with a million pimples in the leather then decrees all must go, so with any luck after slaving over toecaps and heelcaps fourteen nights in a row you should be just about ready to show your platoon sergeant the proverbial shine that's good enough to shave his face in, squeezing and squashing and smoothing out every single one of them bleeding pimples with a metal spoon handle applied red-hot from a candle flame, like a miniature flat iron. And anyhow, that night for some reason I just got to gobbing on. On and on and on, like some all-night news service, bloody Book at Bedtime!

Goodness only knows what got me started or kept me going, the weird silence after the barracks wireless went off, the general need for background noise, and of course an awful lot was bottled up inside all of us, for not once had we been let out of that gate since we first reported, each with his little suitcase. It was just suddenly so very quiet, see, everyone having lapsed into silence long since, each man absorbed in his bootwork, same as myself. Aye, in many ways I was equally oblivious, even after it started, lulled by the sound of my own voice, tuned to the running radio that was me, entertaining and entertained, as though in the middle of all our separate private mullings a knob in just one head had turned to think-aloud, and otherwise I was as much in the dark as the next man as to what was coming. How long I'd been at it I couldn't say, long enough, because at a certain point this normally timid lad from Swansea, Taffy Hughes, the one whose beret we were playing passy with on the boat that time and who to tell the truth I'd barely noticed up to then, from right down near the far end of that great long hut they stuck us in, dead quiet and I imagine taking careful aim over a good six or seven beds while the rest of them must have been watching and waiting mesmerised, all the way through the air he hoys his own git great black shining ammunition boot.

To knock off the human radio, aye! And of course with me head who knows where and the candle flame right in me eyes I never saw it coming. The heel end caught us right on the hip here, here where the bone's just under the skin, for days and days it was tender. You've a big ladle, Geordie, he goes, the biggest we ever heard – and that's for your sodding big Geordie ladle! And with one accord the whole hut splits its sides. Nothing ever gave him greater satisfaction, so he said later, for in the course of time we became good mates, me and Taffy Hughes. In fact once or twice he even got us to partner his sweetheart's best friend, to get her out from under their feet a while. After dark in the park on one or two occasions, forgot all about it till now.

Agony, agony! And of course I couldn't let on how much it hurt, could I, not with the entire hut creasing itself. Next morning on the great parade it was all I could do to set one pimple-free boot before the other, and I don't suppose I opened my stupid mouth for a week, save to admit food and drink.

So yes, things can all get a bit traumatic, can't they, not least in those first weeks when you don't yet possess a single what you might call friend and there's no one from your own particular part of the country to let off steam with. Because like I said, the outfit I landed in was in the deep south, way down in the bottom right-hand corner of England where they don't talk faintly the same, as some got a kick out of reminding us. Or I got the kick. Not a few were all too happy to act like they were under orders to bully what they miscalled the Geordie out of us, not that I was the only foreigner they reserved their special treatment for, not one bit. In fact it's how I acquired a few pals along the way, Taffy for one. Still, you can see why that was not perhaps the best moment for it to happen to me to start to wonder whether I really knew anything at all about Signaller R. Rowan, maybe no one told the whole truth, all they ever gave out was the censored version, as tends to be the case when people are no longer around.

In your experience, in your own army, when they were bawling you out for this or that, say not lifting your knees to the height of your belt when marking time, what sort of thing used to run through your head? Personally I couldn't help wondering whether it was any better in his day, whether their whole discipline quirk hadn't once or twice made him too feel like jacking it in. After all, it was in good part on his account I volunteered in the first place, consequently I was bound to ponder what passed through his mind in the identical position. And one thing I didn't like about these difficult head debates was that certain days all I could get out of him was the standard patter about square-bashing being the time-proven way of toughening the moral fibre of the great British fighting-man, and how all stood rigid to attention on deck as the old Birkenhead went down. Which might be heroism, just possibly imagination, but hardly initiative. Right up until he vanished from the record book who was to say he didn't revel in every blessed moment he wore khaki? He only got top reports, I'd dismally recall, even at moments pondering whether my unknown father might have been one more Adolfino like the rest of them. Did I mention he was up for sergeant before he went missing?

Then consider my own brilliant career. Wike up, soldier, you're why-sting our time, this particularly nasty East-Ender would scream an inch off your nose whilst you hadn't to bat an eyelid though he was sprinkling your face with spit. He'd shriek so high his voice sailed clean off the register, like struggling to play the bugle. You 'orrible idle individual, you bleedin' little clown Brown, whatever yer effin' nime is, don't you know you're why-y-sting our time? Theirs! And what were they making me do with mine? Like I said, it was fall in and fall out on the same parade-ground almost every day until they saw fit to grant my rights of discharge.

The shame, the great shame is I was so slow to twig I had any rights at all, and most important the right to get out of it. Thereafter, that is about once a month until the day I walked out of that gate a free man, I was paraded in front of the CO or his stand-in to be served the same fare every time. Terms for other ranks desirous of purchasing release presently under review blah-de-blah – spouting the same old passage once the adjutant's finger found it for him, the same old passage from the same old battered blue WO manual open on his desk with all the hundreds of amendments pasted in – so frankly my good man, in view of the circumstances I suggest you make the best of a bad job and condescend to get that finger out and knuckle down to it like all the other chaps. A lot of them I find don't seem able to see you very clearly with their eyes, like only having to look in your direction makes them weary. They leave the job of looking at you to the other-rankers, any non-commissioned hopper-headed little Hitler only too pleased to yap at your heels all day. I mean to say, how could anyone expect the likes of a man like that to listen to a reasoned account of all the hard labour I was already doing? All the exercise his kind get is twiddling a swagger stick or lifting a phone, and their right forearms every night, as I had good occasion to observe during my spell as assistant barman, before the whole lot ganged up to frame us.

I know, yes I know I sound resentful, but that's because I joined up in a different frame of mind, with different expectations. Maybe I did rush into it, but only because I was that keen to give it a go. I wanted to do what I thought he'd expect of his son, show I was as good as him. Often

I used to think along that old groove, maybe you'll say I took overlong to grow up. But I see from your eyes you're remembering something too.

Did he just?

Bastard. His little bit of fun, eh? Still, he got his desserts. And how long did he keep you doubling up against the wall under the African sun before you dropped one by one?

Man, how is it they can want to get their pleasure that way! You wonder what warped them at the outset.

All prisoners of war! All! Brilliant, must remember that. So can I take it that when I decided to buy myself out you'd have been in sympathy with the general object? It was my big dream, see, the only way I could think to keep sane. And I had time enough to live it, the dream, having heard eighteen months was the earliest you can start the process, though later of course they made out it was twenty-four. And being the way I am, I didn't only have to bring Mam and Nan round to my point of view, persuade them both to contribute a few shekels to the fund, there was a lot of inner negotiating with my dad. He had to be swung round too, the phantom corporal in the Colosseum.

In the perimeter fence at the back of the cookhouse was a good-size hole, handy for any on the fiddle to sneak stuff out, and I'd duck straight through and into the trees. Then walk. Three-four miles at a go, six, not caring where I was heading the first one or two, too busy straightening it all out in my head, then theirs, trying to get all concerned to feel what a better character I already was for being at least temporarily freed, so they'd appreciate the hundred ways I'd make good once I truly broke loose.

You asked about freedom, remember. Well, a taste of freedom was my attachment to the brigadier's garden. That was the best break I got, Germany aside, and before life as barman went sour. The brigadier's outdoor batman had got himself knifed in the groin by this Cypriot lad from Gravesend, and the brig plumped for Pte Rowan to replace him. Oh yes I too know what it's like to be Batman, despite the criminal record! Because, yeah well, I have to say your Tony got it right, fourteen days I did in the guardroom jail. But on the flimsiest of evidence, I swear. One solitary bottle was all they found in my possession, untouched at that, when it was my luck lockers got spot-checked the same weekend fifteen cases of Scotch mysteriously went missing. The old man, you see, was one of the few who never, no matter what they were into themselves, acted like I was a danger to others' property. He knew anything belonging to him was safe with me.

Quite impressive to look at, big and dignified, if a bit on the mournful side. I used to think of him as a cross between a heavier-built Anthony Eden and a taller version of a reasonable teacher who took us for football at the last school I had to attend. The sort you can imagine sending you into battle feeling almost good about it, with the shits in you like before a big match, but still all keyed up and ready to go. Jack Hawkins, John Mills, that type. Also I think he may have kind of merged in my imagination with Colonel Sandyman, the one whose wireless he worked and teeth he pulled. A top-ranker yet someone you can actually talk with, to a point. I mean, once he as good as admitted there was more than a grain of truth in what I unfailingly claimed, some likely lad had to be found to take the rap when they could pin nothing on the quartermaster's little syndicate.

First thing after morning parade I'd be off to the brig's, out that barracks gate and down the long road and round the corner, only then slowing down to savour the full relief of it, maybe popping into the newsagent's for a bit of chocolate and a packet of tabs, for by then I'd resorted to smoking again, so keen was the boredom. You had to be in his garden by o-nine-hundred sharp, but you were not to report at the house itself before ten, and on the dot I'd be pressing the bell and like as not he'd have us inside for one of his milky coffees and maybe perhaps a ginger biscuit, admittedly at the price of a little pep-talk certain days, but the kind you can sit through. And it wasn't even as though there was much to occupy a gardener in his garden. Cinder a path, weed a patch, chop kindling, rake a leaf, deadhead a rose. And I had some smashing bonfires. But best of all was this nice little greenhouse I had all to meself, tucked out of sight round a curve in the wall, good shelter from the wet and well-warmed with a paraffin stove you had to keep going for his late tomatoes.

Sundays were special. Oh yes, at times seven days out of seven I was putting in of my own free will, so fond was I growing of my place of work. He always popped the backdoor key under the same wobbly stone, so on a Sunday morning with some excuse such as a can to fill I'd softly let myself in. Doesn't sound much now, reminiscing about it with all of Rome spread before our eyes, but all considered it wasn't a bad a way to pass the time, entire hours off the Army. Certain Sundays I could stretch a morning to the best part of a day, all being well. Brew a surreptitious pot of tea, even fix me a slice of bread and marge, put his battery radio on low then sit me down beside the radiator to read the soccer reports and sex cases in his News of the World and all the rest of the sport in this small-print big paper he got similarly delivered of a Sunday. I had a couple of rules though. Never a tab, no ciggies indoors, and I never touched the toaster, and if I felt like a coffee, because whatever the impression I may have given last night I do very much like a cup, it was always my policy to use the fake stuff since as I hardly need to tell you the genuine article will leave a whiff behind as tell-tale as tabs. Oh, and once or twice I have to say I even indulged in a dirty phone call with Taffy's lass's friend back in Swansea, who was getting to be a lot more passionate on the phone than out on the grass. Ann or something.

Scusi, scusi, I should have explained! Sunday being the Lord's day, see, and the brig a bugger for church parades, though the actual reason for that I never discovered, for not once in all our time together did he bring up God or Jesus in our little pow-wows. And the best about it, Signor, the best about it for me of course, was he was capable of spinning out almost an entire Sunday clear of the house, first marching off to church at the head of his God-botherers and reading them all a lesson, then knocking back gin-and-tonics at the mess and likely stopping for his dinner there, or even better moving on to some place he favoured in town. Some Sundays if I was in luck I'd not be slipping out the back at the sound of his key in the latch till gone three, half-four one time I happened to nod off. Well, all that of course got us to thinking it might not even be a bad idea if she could afford it to have that game Welsh lass back down to Kent some weekend, only by the time I got round to endeavouring to propose something of the sort Taffy had dumped his side of the bargain and she likewise wanted no more to do with a soldier. Liz.

I wonder now whether he'd have greatly minded his outdoor batman entertaining himself on his territory, for I think he was as near pals with me as anyone else he knew. Not a natural talker, no great fund of stories despite all his experience, in fact a born old solitary, really. The wife off somewhere warmer with someone younger, and of the three kids two were grown and gone and the last was miles away at one of them schools where they pay to have them taken off their hands and educated up into officer material. If you want my opinion he was more pleased than not to be shot of the lot, the wife and all three lads. Not that we ever went very deeply into that sort of thing, not like you and me. That said, there did in time develop what you might call a reasonable type of understanding between us, and once I learned to swing it right he seemed happy enough to stretch a point and write a weekly chitty to the effect that I had much too heavy a workload with him to have to do parades and suchlike inessential duties, though after the first frost and then the snow even he could see there was less and less in his garden for my spade.

Still, by then I was well installed in his greenhouse, my home from home. I had this broken armchair he very kindly produced one day, so I'd sit me down and maybe toast meself a bit of bread over the heater while eyeing the rain or sleet and thinking my funny thoughts, then maybe do a spot of reading, for by the end I'd practically a library of his books stored round the place, good war books, good murder books, good sex books, and his tomatoes were coming on beautiful. Mind, don't get me wrong, even a temporarily improved situation like that was no reason for altering my opinion that the best years of my life were going to waste on the Army.

No, no, go right ahead! My fault for keeping you up late. Mine, my yawns, generally got classed as sure proof of idleness, hers as overwork. Even hunger, which is a bit of a laugh considering who had the appetite.

Signor, I just have to say it to you again, it's such a big relief you don't mind that my sole ambition as a soldier was to be idle and 'orrible. Like you say of yourself, I wasn't made for their way of life, the one you put in a nutshell a moment ago: What else are all soldiers in any army of the world but prisoners of war! Brilliant. Nan always said a good idea's no use unless you can find the right words for it, so it stays in the head.

Under duress, mind, and only under duress, I'd have to confess certain bits weren't too bad. The in-between bits such as just now I was trying to convey, and such for instance as the great day me and Taffy and two other pals imported an entire cask of ale to the greenhouse to celebrate our first eighteen months in. That was the Sunday before the big Monday when I thought I was at last free to announce I intended to buy myself out, funds permitting. Though of course I might have known, you don't just purchase a ticket to freedom at the guardhouse or something, it transpires that aside from the usual reams of forms they like to choose to leave you to kick your heels a good while just to see if you won't want to change your mind, in other words until such time as a special panel of officers sees fit to make the necessary arrangements to agree to sit round a table and begin to start to look at your case, then similarly your appeal. I mean, just about any bleeding outfit in the world would fall over backwards to accept the resignation of a reluctant worker who patently has no flair for the job and doesn't attempt to hide the fact, even to the extent of stating in writing he's willing to pay through the nose for the sack. But that's it, we're not dealing with any other outfit, we're dealing with Her Majesty's Forces, where the first thing you learn is they do it by the book. And a mighty queer old book it is, Queen's Regulations, the first doubtless going back to Boadicea: hold on hard to whomsoever ye hath inveigled in! The moment I broached the subject of my premature release someone must have ruled that helping the old man dig his Morris Minor out of the snow was too soft a dodge for a deserter, for the very next morning as I was making my customary toast and dripping and musing about how many pints might still be left in that good cask a little deputation in the shape of this exceptionally foul-mouthed Paddy sergeant I already knew far too well and a jumped-up arse-lick lance-jack I also never liked marched us out of my little home-from-home and down the drive so fast I never got the chance to even salute the old boy farewell. Later on though, I did happen to hear he put in a good word for us when my appeal came up for consideration. Off his own bat and all, and taking the very same line I did, testifying to the effect that the Army would be no worse without us.

In wartime if you commit a misdemeanour there's the front line waiting for you, don't we know, up to your eyeballs in mud or sand. In peacetime it's the cookhouse, up to your elbows in swipes and grease, and long before the day dawns that it's revealed you're permitted as many fried eggs as you please you've gone off the slimy things for life. Which I should say just about covers the next stage of my heroic career. And leaving out a whole lot more which would truly send you off to sleep, when one particular day I would not do what I saw no reason to do, in other words when the cookhouse sergeant and myself didn't see eye to eye over his interpretation of a certain minor regulation, he personally prevailed upon the RSM to devise a special roster for Pte Rowan. Frog-face bastard!

Eeh, sorry about that, I didn't mean to give you a jump! But with your permission is it okay if I just skip back a second? Because I cannot resist very quickly telling about Christmas dinner under his auspices – Frogface that is, the cookhouse sergeant – just for the nutshell picture it gives of what I had to contend with for months and months. And it's not a bad story at that.

I don't know if it's the same in your Army, but with us Christmas dinner is when the tables are turned so to say, when the men get served by the nobs. Except that since they don't do the preparation or the cooking and virtually the entire camp's on leave it's a total farce from the outset. So well, after the CO kicks things off to wild applause bearing in a couple of plates of soup on a tray, and a bunch of subalterns trundle in the rest, the Brown Windsor and in due course the turkey and sprouts and all the other stuff we all did, finally, eventually, comes the big moment for the pud, and naturally Frogface reserves that honour for himself, doesn't he – you know, setting the brandy alight and parading the big fellow in, all aflame. Now I should have mentioned before that by previous arrangement the privilege of the lowest of the low was to knock out the lights, prior to his grand entry like, and anyhow as I'm stealing back to my seat in the dark I cannot imagine how it can have happened but the clumsy clot manages to tangle with my extended left foot and the entire flaming pudding goes flying, landing plumb bang in the middle of that great long table, like an incendiary bomb, see! So well anyhow, when all's over bar the nuts and tangies Frogface gets to his feet and inserts in his overlong arse-lick of a speech a pathetic joke to the effect that he's well content in his job but he'd be even contenter if he could be spared having to put up with a certain dozy Geordie comedian every day until next Christmas coming. Which was unfair to say the least, seeing that even on a supposedly free-for-all occasion like that unless you count for something in the hierarchy you have no more licence than any other day to get to your feet and finally set the record straight. And truthfully, Signor, I could have entertained them all to a ripe old tale or two, such as there being more spit than sago in the quartermaster's pudding plate every Thursday dinnertime ever since he declined to let Frogface have his way over a little consignment of prime beef in fair exchange for a load of field tents that Frogface maintained he could find a good home for. See the type of thing I'm talking about, Signor?

Signor!

No, almost done, I promise. But I mean, what is there to shout about? Can none abide an honest man? Coalhouse, cookhouse, shithouse, that's how it went, this new special roster of mine, week in and week about, five days out of seven, when after the Xmas pud sabotage and then Frogface maintaining I'd gone AWOL one afternoon that I went walking in the woods instead of peeling more spuds they saw fit to have my weekend pass removed. Absent Without Leave, in normal language. No use ever trying to explain some folk have an urge to see something other than bricks and concrete from time to time. Because once they get a taste for being on your tail they never get off it, do they? Some days I felt like I was the only man working at anything like full stretch in the entire British Army, the rest being paid to watch. So that's why when the opportunity finally came I didn't at all object to the live-soldiering, stalking over peat bogs on Luneberg Heath with a clip of dummies up the spout and more packing our pouches, or a twenty-mile route march through one entire wet night, and finding out the hard way how to pitch a tent in a hurricane. Just like old times, even better, times we had when we were kids, when in the streets and fields and woods at home we went on fighting the last war long after the actual armies had packed up and gone home.

Well, I'm pleased to hear it, I must say. And seeing it met with your appreciation might I just keep you a little bit longer from your siesta with one very last very short anecdote which similarly might give you cause to chuckle? Sitting right here beside you is a veteran of World War Three! Nuclear war, aye, like they had us all lined up for just a week back. It was the last day of manoeuvres and literally only moments after being congratulated for wiping the floor with the opposition suddenly out of a motorbike sidecar hops a captain in a blue armband shrilling the Reds have gone and pressed the button and we and all life roundabouts including the German village over the hill have just been flattened Hiroshima-style. So after he scoots off and we're digging out our spam sandwiches they gave us every day, presuming we're out of play for the foreseeable future, along comes another official surprise in the shape of another puce-faced blue armband jumping wild saying only the dead can eat and seeing our mob's all live casualties we've to lie down right where we are on the wet ground and groan and moan and start imagining what it's like to have our clothing and skin and hair and that all roasted off, and our eyeballs frying like butterpats in their sockets I remember he also said, and then right on cue up runs a bunch of stretcher bearers to give us each a pretend jab and parcel us up from head to foot so that when they're finally finished the lot of us look like a load of stand-ins for *The Return of the Mummy*. Each finger had to be wrapped separate, my personal medic said, to hold all the veins on, and when he had ears and nose and chin similarly under wraps he very kindly goes and feeds us bread and spam in bits like a baby through the slit. But then next day it was back to Blighty and my old duties all over again.

And returning to barracks one last moment if I may, and remembering a soldier's best friend is his rifle as they'd have you believe, then I was issued with some mighty queer friends on that special roster of mine. Listen. Mondays my best friend was a coal shovel, Tuesdays a spud peeler, Wednesdays a toilet brush and squeegee, Thursdays back to the shovel, and Fridays sinksful of greasy pots again. Coal dust in your hair and up your nostrils and fingernails the first day, thick grease the second, and I'll leave you to guess what the third. Spread that over my final months and you see what I loved about the Army. Listen.

Me mam!

7

Gone.

No, it begins again! What's she on about? Honest, she sounds just like my own *mamma* bawling us in when I was a bairn.

It's that double vision thing all over again, I hear your neighbour and I see my mam. Still do. One floor below us and just over the churchyard wall! First her head was shoved out the back-bedroom window where later we put the bathroom in, then this last time she was in the yard letting fly after clashing the poker on the down-stack by the kitchen drain. Often she'd do that, take the poker, though her voice alone was capable of scaring the crows out of the trees for miles around. Haway on home Feelie, yer mam wants yer! We were building the tree house, me and Colin and Kelvin and a few bigger lads like Brian. Brian was generally an ally because his brother Kelvin at times took his tea at Nan's, their own being one of her cronies, their own nan, and so long as Brian was anywhere round they all had to let us play in the old yew tree. Brian, I told you he got sent out to Korea.

Again! She'll bust a blood vessel. I swear to you she's the perfect Roman version of my old lady.

It's that crack at the end, hers split in the identical same fashion when it could escalate no more. Fee-LEEE-EEE! Same as when she was belting out the hymns along with Mrs P at St Wilfred's on a Sunday, jumping for the high bits no one else could reach. The Ada Rowan and Agnes Pattinson duo, heads up, mouths wide, marching as to war, with the CROSS OF JEE-EE-sus going on before!

Mrs P until her sight got bad kept the corner-shop at our road end along with her husband George who never ever uttered a squeak except to ask her the day's prices, yet for all her inventive arithmetic she was generally well-liked since she'd do anyone a good turn and she loved relaying the gossip. Mrs P in fact it was who coaxed Mam back to church after the Spiritualist craze, in part no doubt because she missed their old sing-alongs, though a few on a Sunday would still look askance, wondering what gave a woman like that the right to share the same house of worship. So blessings on Mrs P, I say. Nicest daylight robber in history, Nan called her, saying the only true religion for Mrs P was pledged on a Monday and redeemed on a Friday.

Again!

Signor, how it used to make me sore anyone could publicly bray for their kid like that and expect them to do their bidding. But it was strong as pike tackle – aye and with a sharp treble on the end and all! – and no matter how big I acted in front of the others its barbs went deep, very deep, way down deep in the gut like in the case of them poor eels we were speaking of. From the very first screech I was on and how easy then she could reel us in, slow but sure. There she goes again, Shorty, hollering like a old witch. Bugger her, she is a witch, and what's she after anyroad, sodding done the pots already. To skelp you for swearing, and who said you could climb our tree? Brian, and I'm not coming down for no one. Haway home, it's babby's titty time and he messed his pants and we don't want your stink round our house no more. Before you did. Gan away home, kiddar, says Brian extra-gentle, else she'll murder you. Bugger it, bugger her, and crap bugger shit all o' yous ... Thick ivy went all up the graveyard wall and to shin over you needed first to climb on a high stone slab, the lid of a tomb, a big boxlike affair with a two-hand sword cut deep in the lid, a favourite cat lick and bird bath with queues of twitchy-bells and tiny black slugs stuck all along inside the old carved lettering. It wanted elbows as well as hands, knees as well as toes, and that day levelling with the top my eyes come up just in time to see her shaking out a yellow duster in the yard and turning to go back in. She didn't need to wait, see, she knew I was well-hooked. What a carry-on for nowt, I'm no doubt thinking as I slide over, too fat to fetch the coal in or a forky-tail's wiggling in the sink and she's too scared to squash it, even wash it down. Oh aye if I know me I dragged my feet every inch of the way to our back door. And then I hear her voice from inside the house, all soft and different. Come away in, pet, your granda's gone.

All that stored in the memory, waiting to come back to life right here! Something sets it off, then the chance to talk about it brings the whole lot back. That's the day your neighbour lady has got us reliving, and who knows when I last gave it a thought, the afternoon she bawled us in from Tarzan and broke the news my granddad up in Glasgow had died of an overdose. Not, mind, that I had the foggiest what that meant, most likely thought it was one over the eight, and inside I daresay I'm going something like: So what, who cares, screaming us away in because her old dad-in-law kicked the bucket who never remembers me birthday. That was a favourite refrain with her, see, any time there was a bit of a bill to pay she'd bring up old Tighty-Fist-Scotty up there in Paisley made of money who never spared his only son's widow a thought, not even the bairn's birthday, never once in all these long years. Nelly from next door was in there with her, a naturally kind person, sat close by Mam on the settee and patting her hand with the yellow telegram in it. So that's all you shouted us in for, I can hear meself thinking, for a witness to see how cut up you're not. And Nelly keeps on, there now Ada he'll have had his reasons, and if it says he was dead before the ambulance come likely he never felt a thing. A tragedy needs time to sink in, you pop round and tell Winnie and I'll see to the bairn's tea, I've a nice tatie pot just sitting waiting to go in the oven. Would you fancy that, Feelie my darling? peering over her big specs as though she's very, very sorry for us, like I'm suddenly seriously ill. Well now, finally it's beginning to dawn I've got news that's sensational enough to gain instant re-admittance to the tree house. Me granda Quadruple went and killed hisself! And out I scoot shouting, I'll have that tatie pot, Auntie Nelly, when it's tea time!

Well, I'm not sure I'm the very best person to answer that, I wasn't in the cookhouse to cook. On the other hand I've watched them in the making, seen it done. Nelly's a champion cook, so was Nan, and Mam's not bad. What you do I think is you take a fair-size oven dish and fill all the bottom with mince or chopped steak, or you can just open a tin of bully beef if you like, and then in go all your vegetables, your diced vegetables, carrots, onions, leeks, anything in that line you've got, parsnips if you're partial to the things, oh and a good quantity of brown gravy, and after that sliver by sliver careful as you can you build it a solid roof with as many sliced taties as it takes. Potatoes. Then you cook it.

No, not specially. I still feel all that good bread and salami inside. And that pot on the stove can look after itself, can it?

That good-smelling stew simmering away in the kitchen, it won't spoil?

Just thought I'd remind you. Because, see, personally I wouldn't mind carrying on just as we are. So as not to break the spell, I mean. Stay on up here a little while more and see where things take us, like you intimated at the start. For today's just got to be one of the most amazing days of my life, like my whole brain's set on dictating its memoirs, like the old colonel, the way one thing touches off another, and all these strong memory pictures that come. I mean, that episode is at least fifteen year away and a thousand mile ago! And even this minute now I notice my head's again in two places at once. This time it's the way them little white clouds are building up, banked over the mountain there. Because for all I'm set on making a new life here I can still tell there's bound to come times when sunny blue skies will make me miss home a bit. This last summer was near continental, true, but home when I think of it is the opposite. Home to me is big grey clouds skidding over row on row of little brick houses. And Mam of course, now Nana's gone.

Oh you'd get along famous, I know you would. Men do. More women now too. Maybe I make her sound hard as nails but I tell you deep down she's soft, practically soft as a baby. Aye, she'll be seeing off a few hankies herself and all, I guarantee, once she gets wind of yesterday's farce. Our great bust-up. Mind, next breath she'll claim she had a premonition. Right from the start she was dead against my coming out here, even speculated that once the lass was among her own kind she'd likely want us off her back. Well, I think we know the answer to that one.

When I told her I had a mind to be off to Italy too, that I'd even secretly procured passport and ticket, just by the set of her mouth you could tell how much she hated the idea. And sure enough next day at tea she's playing up like we two had not just the English Channel but the entire Atlantic to cross in an open boat. I'd been out all night it just so happens, and temporarily leaving the lass in the middle of a crowd split like opposing armies screaming Bomb Cuba or Stop Nuclear War I nipped home to catch the football results like Mam always knows I try to do of a Saturday if I'm not at the match, though truthfully this time it was just as much to patch things up, Claudia having reported she was in a right state. And for a fact the tension at home was near as bad as on the streets, for I found her hovering in the kitchen like a two-legged stool with my ham sandwich already set on a plate by the radio, just waiting to start straight in on the current state of ferryboats.

Right. Too dead right. And thank goodness both sides came to their senses in time. In point of fact the day in question was the twenty-seventh, two Saturdays gone, just a matter of hours remember before Mr K backed down and the world breathed a sigh of relief. All on tenterhooks, weren't we? Mam being no exception, though she kept it strictly personal.

Ancient out-of-date tubs, she goes, after demanding why I didn't even know the time of sailing. I told her she hadn't the faintest notion how things are nowadays, if I remembered rightly the last time she took a ferryboat was over to Arran with my dad the same week they got married, to see his island relatives. And so what, she snaps, it was blowing up a gale and still they took us across. Good on them, I go, what people won't do for money, turning up the radio a little more. That's what I'm saying, scatterbrains, she bounces back, don't you tell me they have any qualms about putting people's lives at risk if the company stands to be out of pocket. Shut it, Mother, I says, but nicely, or I'll miss the scores, anyhow when the weather was on I don't remember him going on about no gales at sea or nothing, at most a touch of fog. Daft ha'porth, she goes, did you never hear of ships going down after colliding in fog? I held my tongue, having just heard we'd gone down ourselves, 4-2 to Norwich City. Give over, man, I says, and says no more. I mean, that was two priceless promotion points down the hatch and right up to then we'd been unbeaten in twelve consecutive games and I just couldn't see how to explain it, we're far and away the better side and yet it seems we just weren't there, missing simple tap-ins and defence all over the place. It was a weird day, admittedly, all the same I was tempted to blame everything not just on the general atmosphere but my very own self, on account of how I spent the night before. On top of which, I also happened to have made a secret agreement with myself, call it a kind of cautious wager, that with being an away fixture even if all we could do was hold them to a draw it would still mean a future for us in Italy.

Mothers all alike? Maybe so, though I think mine's still a case apart. Persistence is her middle name, as her old Arthur liked to say, and for once how right he was. I mean, would you believe it, the poor old thing was still harping on about the hazards of modern-day travel a whole week later when we were finally stood there on the southbound platform with the luggage all round us and the 11.05 chugging up the line. Hardly seems real now, No-Friend squeezing my hand, and squeezing back the tears too I could easily see, and Muggins the eternal dreamer imagining what a miraculous time was about to start. While Mam, bless her, I just hate to think what she was going through.

Wouldn't let up for a moment, poor soul, even with the brake squeals in our ears, even while giving us a hand up with the lass's big bookcase, she's still telling her Shields ferry story for I should think the tenth time we must have heard it over all that last week. How with one thing and another, her man away in the war and Nan down London, she decides there's nothing for it but to go and look up her flighty old dad and his new woman in the hope of a little bit of a Christmas handout, and – Claudia flower, listen – our Felicity was not yet four but already so high and still showing no sign of what was to come, and this little one a terror for crawling off soon as your back was turned, consequently it was as much as a woman on her own could do to keep tabs on the pair of them and – looking up so sort of terribly sad at the two of us in the open window – Claudia pet, all of a sudden I see this one like a skinny bit worm squirming breakneck on his front across the deck like he's set on slipping through the railings, and the other's toddled off to stick her head into Lord only knows what moving machinery and – goodbye, goodbye, look after the lad for us – imagine, imagine, it was that bad I stood rooted to the spot on the slippery deck of that rolling raft affair in the middle of the big river and just screamed me silly head off, and I tell you still in nightmares I see him about to plop over the side. Lost one, she's just about crying now as she waddles after the moving train, and it would kill us to lose another. Kill us. Write, both of you, write, write, write, and flower you promise to take good care of him out there in your country. I promise, comes the reply. I promise, Mrs Rowan, waving her arm out the window. I promise. Pat as that. And I'm considering sending it off to the News of the World to win a quid for the saying of the week.

Oh she's a canny old soul when all's said and done, Signor, a very nice person. And as I say I bet you two would get on famous, supposing you could ever meet. At the PO's club all the talk is she's in line for the top job now the big chief's due to retire, and if that's the way it goes you can be sure she'll be far and away the most popular manageress they ever had. They like someone they can talk to and joke on with. Mind, she's worked for it, she's grafted, and considering she's not now as young as she was it's surprising what a lot of go there is in her still.

Not big, no, she's my mamma after all. On the small side, if anything. Very small actually. But nice and compact-like, if you know what I mean, round and warm and neat and very proud of her bust, though she does now fret the peroxide's thinned her hair. Maybe with one of them sort of fairly lived-in kinds of faces you see a lot of round our way, but a smile to make up for it, good and warm again, the kind where you see straight off a person's heart is right where it should be. Healthwise though I will admit she's going down the bank a bit, not weathering so well as some. Bones wearing out too fast, the specialist says. And it's beginning to show, some days for instance she's not too clever on the stairs. And getting ever so very slightly bow-shouldered too, I've noticed, here, this one side only so far. Though just try telling her to wear the corset they gave her for Christmas! Thankfully Nelly promises she'll be straight off in touch if, well you know, if…

Tony mentioned that. Terrible. So it's her in the kitchen?

Terrible, terrible. The same thing that killed my grandmother, so I know how she must have suffered. And you. And Tony too, you can tell how much he misses her. So when you spoke of solitude was that the reason?

It must be, it truly must, and remembering the two of you worked side by side all them many years. That's how she manages too, the way my mother deals with being on her own now, the loneliness and that. Lives for her work. More than ever is she wedded to it now her funny Arthur's gone. And just as well, I suppose, seeing I'm not any longer going to be around to keep her company, come evening.

Oh you're right, you're so right, she's the one you should be employing, not this daft ha'porth! And listen, Signor, for all the worries about her state of health I want you to know she still has plenty going for her. Plenty. Not for one moment do I doubt she'll get her promotion. Nowadays she's accepted in all circles, just about. Half the town turned out for the big do she put on in Arthur's memory at the PO's club where the president of the Rugby Club's address made her sound like the official widow. Mind you, the man has his beady eye on her, word is, and barely widowed himself. But not to worry, she says we don't have to fret about that.

Aye, go ahead and sign her up for the old Baffone, be nice to have her with us too! I'd love it, she'd love it, and I'm almost sure you'd love it.

Now where do you get that from? Next you'll be saying

I think it's a shame Tony doesn't have an irresistible sister!

Never, never, never! Of course not, of course I don't. It was only a flash, believe me, a totally unrealistic flash – one happy family in the Bar Baffone. But in the workplace, Signor, not in the home. Only for her love of work did I cite her, purely that. I mean to say, how could you dream I'd ever suggest anyone could replace your wonderful Angela?

Pulling my leg!

Man, you caught me out there, I genuinely did think you were mortally offended. Still, you're right, she's not bespoke. So in theory, yes, in theory she could be the next Signora Pasquale. Only the pity is I see no way we could ever tempt her out here, a bag of nerves just at the thought of travel, as you've already heard. Besides, she'd tell you straight how much she values her independence now. Freedom at last, she says, and memories galore to live on! Dream on, Mr President!

Aye, and dream on Mr Pasquale!

Why of course, feel free to ask. I'm just so glad you like the sound of her. And after all that.

Ah. Well that was just her idle Arthur's pet name for her. Partly for her whole attitude to work, definitely that was all part of it. But he had a more special reason too. And thereby hangs a tale, as we say. It takes us right back to the colonel's teeth in fact, the other half of the story.

Remember, the last we saw of the famous bone crunchers was the day she posted them off to the museum, the Imperial War Museum down London? Still in their tin of course, tucked up in the old cotton wool, and along with that good letter, plus a covering note from her about how they and her inventor-husband earned a special mention in Lt-Col Sandyman's memoirs of the Eighth Army? What I think happened is one day her Arthur said he'd heard the museum was advertising for trophies of the Desert War, unless it was that he just couldn't live with them any longer on the second-to-top shelf in the glass cabinet behind his chair, I told you how he hated anything to do with her past. Anyhow, as you would expect, every once in a while she'd wonder aloud why the museum people never sent so much as even a note of thanks. Even so, it must have been at least a good two-three years later, not so long in fact before I took off for London myself, that remembering Arthur would be passing through on his annual visit to his sister in Bexhill she prevailed on him to look in on the museum and check out the display. Well he goes through every room, does the major, every single room he said, and no bone crunchers did he see. So then the game was on.

First she gets on to them via the phone at the end of our street to hear all their reasons for why they weren't on show and why nobody even ever had the civility to acknowledge her parcel, and when they said they prefer people to write in if they have a complaint she fires off a furious missive, a mini-masterpiece in my estimate, and the major's too of course seeing he had a big hand in its composition, to the effect that that precious testimony to human ingenuity under extreme stress and the historic document accompanying it were at once to be put on show by express order of none other than the interested party himself, which I'm afraid was not quite true, who wrote entire gripping pages about his famous bone crunchers and their famous inventor in his famous book, which later we ascertained was equally untrue. Anyhow, whatever, by the end, when all she could get out of the museum was that she should have checked with them a lot nearer the time and in any case had no business sending a package like that unregistered, and their replies got shorter and shorter and fewer and fewer and of course eventually stopped altogether, Old Persistence was accusing them of all sorts, such as not even knowing their own job and in their incompetence mislaying a treasured family relic among the junk from all the other wars cluttering their cellars – which by the bye is how Mam taught herself to type, sort of, bashing out all them wild epistles with one finger on a machine she found at a jumble sale at the Institute after the major finally convinced her no one these days has the patience to read anything handwritten – and no doubt that's what I should have done with that letter to Mr Hedley, come to think, if the old machine hadn't fallen to bits long ago. Anyhow.

Anyhow, in the end, picking up on something I think Nana must have said, Old Persistence what does she do? Demands her precious property's instant return to its rightful owner, or full compensation. And when of course they still didn't want to know she at last decides the time has come to enlist the real live Colonel Sandyman. Twice at least she wrote to his address, probably more, the address on his original letter, and then only a long while after even she had stopped dreaming of ever getting a reply suddenly comes word from a solicitor in Torquay or Torbay, I forget which, saying the late Lt-Col Roland Sandyman MC burned all his papers before dying somewhere out in India, which was apparently the country of his birth, and another of the many faraway places you've seen.

So never were there any gripping memoirs, or all went up in smoke, which I suppose comes down to the same thing now. A bit of a shame really, for we'd all of us over time developed a great belief in the colonel. And now of course my mother never stops blaming herself for not getting in touch with him at the very outset, right at the time of the original letter and parcel, because then at the very least she could have told him that going on the way he wrote to her he should never have dropped the idea, it would have made a champion read. And personally I wouldn't mind still having that letter. Because just as you were saying about your Angela, nothing is entirely over and done so long as you have strong memories to keep you going. Failing that, if it's all written down so you can go back to it any time and live it all over again.

Could I trouble you for the fiasco?

8

So many of these things we've been saying seem to concern people who should not be dead. Long ago, you know what I used to think? That we only die when we want, and if we want. A time comes when we'll settle for it, like my grandad up in Scotland. Do me in today, Death, type of thing, better six feet under than live on in the clag like this. Or the opposite, but similar: Thanks for everything I could want from life, there's nothing more I could wish for, any time from now you can peg us out. Comical, what kids make of it all. One day I put myself in the way of a train, or that was the intention.

So many of these long-gone things I worked out for myself after I went for a soldier, when I had maybe too much time to mull over what led me to volunteer for the life he knew. And most of all when under lock and key fourteen everlasting days and nights stretched out on my iron pit between the piss bucket and the weeny window near dead from boredom, when suspended so to say in a state of non-existence between old memories and the far-off day of my release bits and pieces from the past kept floating up and in the end I could not help start trying to see if somehow they fitted together to explain how I got to be where I was, and how I came to get this mixed-up head I seem to have.

Choosing to die, that's how it looked in the case of my uncle Dick. He lodged with us a while and I have to say I liked him well enough, actually a lot, in fact my first two-wheeler I got off Uncle Dick, and he learned us to ride it too, and just as good or maybe even better we went together on this special bus to see my first Sunderland match, and it was Len Shackleton and Dickie Davis running rings round Sheffield Wednesday. Davis was a Sunderland great, he was the orchestrator, but Shack was our hero, Shack was genius. Breath-taking. There's nothing Pele has all the world marvelling at now that Shack wasn't already doing with a ball way back then. Flick it, chip it, curl it, lob it, head past and nip round and collect, even sit on it! Shack was different to all the rest, he didn't just take every sort of chance, he had his own way of doing things, and above all he was entertaining. The Clown Prince of Soccer, they all liked to call him. Uncle Dick got his signed picture and put it on the wall right next to the one of me dad. But his going and dying in hospital after an accident that killed my cat changed all that.

No one said Dick was hurt so bad that he needed hospital, so of his own will he had himself admitted, seemingly without a thought for anyone else. That's how it looked to Mam too I think, like it amounted to desertion, though she never forgave herself after. You see, the doctor on the scene had said there was no real damage, nothing broken, at most a touch of shell shock, so sent him home. So then Uncle Dick he raised hell, howling like a shut-in dog all night long in his room right under mine, and in the early morning I ran down and finally she went out and fetched a different doctor to do his bidding. He'd had an awful shock, me too, but acting like that was so out of character. He was a quiet man, see, exceptionally quiet, Mam said ditched by his wife for that very reason. Of course now I know the accident set something off in him and he was just cracking up. Still, it was such a massive change and happened so quick you can see how to a child's mind it might look like adults simply arrange to go.

And my dad, did he similarly choose to suddenly give up living? Maybe that's another reason I came to resent Uncle Dick, why I switched to hating him so. Because as we were saying there seems to be no place in a young head for the fact a good person can stop existing, entirely stop. Or it takes years and years to sink in. Too good for this world, you'd hear them say of some person who died before their time, and definitely Mam believed that about my sister.

Yet not once did I hear anyone say anything of the sort regarding him. Okay, Nan thought he was good, probably totally good, but not so good that he was not meant for this life. The opposite. Me, all I knew was he was far too good to die, and it was my business to make sure he never did.

I'll have been no more than about seven when I went off with Nan and Mam and Nelly and Hakes on a special coach trip to see his name in brass among hundreds of others, maybe thousands. I thought the brass was gold and we were looking up at the names of all the people let into heaven, though still that didn't seem to alter my opinion that somewhere was some kind of island he swam to. A man, I don't now know who but definitely not Hakes, this big man lifted me high up with him onto an extremely creaky platform at one end of that massive building, then higher still, so we could look down together at this great big open book made of the whitest paper I'm sure I've ever seen, simply colossal, with all the page-edges trimmed in gold and name after name written in ye olde black pen writing, thick-and-thin, and buried in the middle of one long column we found his name, the only name I could safely read. Most were killed in action, he said, but some were unaccounted for. And after his name half the same as mine was written with a different nib, smaller and freshest blue: '*Missing, Mediterranean, Nov 4, 1943*.'

I know that's exactly how it was written because Nana copied it onto the back of his photo straight after we got back home, his Army portrait I had to promise her to keep unfailingly, where he's sitting looking a bit uncomfortable I generally think in his DLI cap and uniform, and you can just make out the two crossed signals flags on his sleeve.

Yes, definitely I was already seven, for our Felicity must have just passed away, seeing Hakes told us all to kneel down and pray for her soul as well.

Missing. That mysterious word. Then the very difficult one for where it happened, the longest word I thought could ever be. At times I had to be careful not to say it, even think it. And for why? Some type of magic, I believe. For fear of saying it wrong and losing it, making it nowhere. Other times I could say it and think it almost too well. And hear it, Signor, filling up my ears, great rumbling Mediterranean, more black than blue. Oh and here there's like a kind of link with you!

The man who made the Mediterranean fresh blue again, blue and calm and safe for swimmers, was the first Italian I ever knew. Pete we call him. Pete promised there were no sharks in the sea anywhere round his country, not man-eaters at least. He had postcards of the sunny blue Med stuck up all over inside his van along with the Madonnas, same as now, and he promised where it's really bad for sharks is the Red Sea, and I don't need to tell you how that made me imagine it got its name. Pietro Dimambro, brought over to England with his entire family when he was six, from somewhere near Napoli. Then when the war with you came along they interned him with his sick old dad and his younger brother Danny, and poor old Pete he went on to lose a son fighting for the same country that put him behind barbed wire. Danny runs the family café now, a bit like yourself, but old Pete's indestructible, way past seventy and still doing his rounds, still serving up his ice cream cornets through the hatch of the same old van labelled Supremo Ices that's haunted our back streets practically since time began, the only novelty being that now he's got a contrivance on the roof that tinkles out 'Greensleeves', a song we learned to murder in every school I ever went to.

So, well, being brought up by his two biggest admirers you can see how I came to acquire a headful of my dad's great doings, all his famous deeds along the way, from the time he crawled into the coal scuttle to the night he stepped out of a sinking seaplane in Augusta Bay. Nan always liked to tell what a help and blessing he was when she took him back down to England after the Quadruple B beat her face in for speaking to his best friend out of turn, and how hard that lanky lad of hers worked to earn little bits extra for the two of them. He was barely thirteen, yet from almost day one he was never out of work. Boyhood stuff at first, paper rounds, tatie picking, snagging the beet, then helping out in a bike repair shop until he could get set on at the pop factory, bottle washing and sorting first, then loading. That's where he taught himself more about the ins and outs of engines, for in return for keeping the waggons clean they let him drive round and round the yard and help them with repairs. And soon as there's no more to pick up there he's off again to a laundry firm and cleaners doing deliveries all over town and up and down the colliery managers' houses, going from strength to strength in almost no time, from delivery lad in the back to man in front at the wheel. And by the end he's doing night school too and passing exams, having decided to go for mechanical maintenance, and then one day a coach-building set-up of his own maybe.

So that was this brilliant father of mine until the war came along. By which time he was a married man of eighteen with a baby girl on the way, and soon enough a boy, driving for Woolworths now and doubling as store detective at seventy-five shillings a week, and all the while filling up Nan's backyard with every machine and implement he could raid for parts to build his coming inventions. See, the feeling for machines was in his make-up right from the start. Even before they quit Glasgow he could take a radio all to bits, Nan said, then put it together again good as when it left the shop. And his first motorbike he built entirely from scrap, a three-gear affair, she remembered, just one cylinder and a side valve, yet that powerful it could sail up near enough anything in top gear. Oh he knew he was made for something special, my dad. At the pop factory, the day he left, Nan always said he showed them he could lift four crates at a time, standing there in front of them all in the loading yard. Two crates per hand, each packed tight with pint bottles, so what weight are we talking about, for goodness sakes?

Oh. Thanks. Helps things along I do admit, oils the wheels. Still, I leave it in your safe keeping. Now none of these snippets I'm telling may seem so very much in themselves, but it's what they all amount to, it's how he was always held up to me. Plus the plain fact of his not being there. Nan used to say at least we have to be thankful we have written proof he got out of that flying boat affair, at least we don't have to think of him trapped inside an old machine rusting at the bottom of the sea, at least we can think of the lad as somehow free. All the same, two films gave me hard thoughts when I was small. The first was *Captains Courageous,* for the way Spencer Tracy has to lose his life. The other they also showed at the Institute. I forget the title, but it's about one of our submarines sinking loads of enemy shipping until it too gets crippled, knocked out by depth charges. You see it very slowly come to rest far down. Tanks punctured, generator gone, something of the sort. Anyhow, immobilised. Then you watch their faces as it dawns they're down there for eternity. One makes a joke and all laugh, then no one can think of another.

Of course. It affected her, of course it did, Signor, in different ways. I've already said how she – oh I see, you want a potted history of her as well!

On the contrary, happy to oblige. Remember the living, that was her attitude too. I was too small to build up very much in the way of memories of my own, all the same I do know that the early years after he was reported lost at sea were none too easy for her. We carried on living at Nan's, but that of course was never going to work, and in fact after a final showdown she says she hoyed little me and a few belongings into the pram and grabbed our Felicity and stormed over to our Great-Auntie Teresa's, her dad's unmarried sister who she says turned out to be even more of a pain than Nan, and a professional invalid to boot, and that arrangement ended when Mam declared she had no wish to live the rest of her days as chief cook and bottle-washer for a fat healthy creature installed all day long on a couch in the parlour like a sentry watching over her comings and goings. The mouth on her, she always says, the mouth on that terrible woman it was forever pulled down at the corners with disapproval, like permanently clenched on a yawn. All the same, but for the terrible Teresa things would have had to wait a long while longer before taking a turn for the better. And here's I think how the story goes.

Following Great-Auntie Teresa's, and a long lapse of

time wandering from one cheap-rent place to the next, we were apparently right at the top of the waiting list for a council house when this other great-auntie I also don't recollect at all, known as Maggie Sixpence on account of the knick-knacks shop she had where nothing cost over sixpence, one day suddenly decides to drop dead in the shop with a clot on the brain and the funny part about it is the other sister, the terrible Teresa, had gone and died only just the week before or something, having moved in with her once she did in fact become a full-time invalid, that's over the shop itself, half-paralysed after a stroke and with no powers of speech at all, see, and Mam, who had been in the habit of fettling for the pair of them two or three times a week seeing it was a lot for her on her own, Maggie, what with the shop to run as well her sister, always says that nothing she ever tried could help her make her peace with the terrible Teresa. Even in that deaf-and-dumb condition the woman wouldn't let her near, if she went to feed her she'd lie rigid as a statue with eyes averted and that mouth clamped as tight as ever. And yet you know, Signor, my mother herself would be the first to tell you the terrible Teresa saved our lives. Because right after the double funeral imagine everyone's surprise when this one-legged Irishman who used to help out a bit in the shop discovers in some drawer upstairs Maggie's latest will and testament stating among other things that a certain house in Lowery's Lane which unbeknownst to all had come to her along with her sister was to be split between the two nieces upon her own demise. The next-of-kin, in other words.

That's to say, if you followed all of that, our actual present house, the very last at the very end of this long terrace right on the edge of town. The shop and the flat above it went to that Irishman while the terrible Teresa's two-up and two-down which as I say up to that moment no one even knew was in the family went to the brother Eddie's two daughters, Ada and Amanda. That's to say Mam and the long-lost sister she never had a good word for.

Now Amanda, if she's still on this planet, is older than Mam by ten years or more, and just about all I otherwise know about her is that some time before the war she sailed away to Canada with a Canadian and stopped writing even before granddad Eddie and Nana Edith died, who were by then anyhow separated. So Mam, having no specially good memories of her sister reasoned that, one, it was not Amanda who'd cleaned for months and months for Maggie Sixpence and put up with the terrible Teresa, and, two, like everyone else she could have no inkling of the existence of number 53 Lowery's Lane.

So there we moved and there we've lived ever since, in the last house at the back of St Wilfred's churchyard, sandwiched between the prison wall and the graves. The Lane started out life as pitmen's cottages but now all that's left of them old times is the round shape of the pit heap past the prison all overgrown with gorse and grass where we all used to play. When we first arrived most houses in the Lane were taken up with prison warders' families, but there's been changes in recent years, in fact we've heard even our place may be worth a bit now there's development all round and the jail's finally been condemned. Gone long ago is the big field across the Lane that sloped up to the farm. From top to bottom's all houses now.

I think your latest yawns could be telling me I cannot go on much longer putting off the difficult part. She had to live, Signor, a husbandless mother of two has to get by somehow, doesn't she? She was friendly with all sorts before, so I've heard, but none on such a very regular basis, if you see what I'm saying. Till number 53. Then, well then all of a sudden she found herself with a room to spare and a chance to earn an extra bob or two. Which is how it started. The first to move in, the first of a long line of lodgers, was a car salesman everyone knew as Jackie Mack on account he never went out without the same old brown mac, though more than that or him I remember the cat he also brought with him, this beautiful big ginger tom he said lost the best part of his tail in a fight with a fox cub. I cannot be sure now how long he lasted, Jackie Mack. Not so very, I think, because I know that once he got himself married he wasn't seen nearly so much round the house. But his cat Scratcher stayed right up until the day he died.

More or less round the same time as Jackie, Cousin Harvey enters the picture, some sort of second cousin or something to Mam. I have a clearer recollection of Cousin Harvey Quinn who already in them days had longish silver hair and beer burps loud as barks. Lying in my attic bed at night I could hear him weaving his way home by all the back lanes, practically the entire journey from the Market Tavern to our end-row house, shattering the silence every minute like a perishing dog. According to her, for all it seems to me he was around the place a longish while, Cousin Harvey was of no importance and brought only problems from the start, the biggest being how to get him to go. Still, going on how I remember things, Cousin

Harvey knew how to make her laugh, laugh till she cried. Because same as Nan in her time Mam finds it almost too easy to laugh if anyone has a way with a joke. Me too, I suppose. Maybe I'm forgetting bits, maybe I'm muddling with somebody else, but I honestly do not recall anyone objecting to Cousin Harvey, barks and all. Not Mam, not Jackie. Then again, I don't expect I even really saw much of any of them, for when not forced to attend this school or that I was roaming the streets and fields and woods with a gang of lads my own age and more. The Merry Men gang. Well of course the whole Lane knew the truth or guessed it.

But, listen Signor, you have to know it wasn't so much her worries about what the Lane might privately be saying, more a terror of getting into trouble with the National Assistance people if ever they should get wind of the fact she was taking in lodgers. And still no one ever shopped her, and that must say something for the depth of feeling in our neighbourhood. You know the excuse she gave out for the fact Cousin Harvey happened to be tucked up on our settee reeking of ale one morning the means test man called unannounced, and for all Jackie had moved in with his new lady a quantity of his things still happened to be living in the big wardrobe upstairs? She said the things upstairs all belonged to her deceased husband and she just couldn't bring herself to throw them out, and the gentleman unwakeable in the living room happened to be a close relative who just occasionally dropped by when he'd consumed too many to wend his way right across town to his non-existent residence way over by the station, and who was she to say no to a member of the family drying out on her settee!

There's someone else I believe must have lodged with us a fair while round about that same time, because recently she said he was more regular than some with the rent. A very shy man by the name of Wilf Robson, though just about the only thing I remember about him now is he played the tin whistle, same as my dad. Apparently I was forever on at Uncle Wilf to give us a tune, yet all that comes to mind now is one time after dark I was making my way in by the back from over the graveyard wall, and it was such a surprise I had to stop and listen. The lilt and quickness of it I'll never forget, though I think just as much the reason I remember it so vividly is that I only had to take one more step toward the light in the kitchen window and his music stopped clean dead. I was just a nipper, yet so fearful was Uncle Wilf that I could switch him off, like a bird. However.

However long it was Uncle Wilf or Jackie Mack or Cousin Harvey stayed I cannot be sure. A year, just months, weeks, time is not the same as time when you go back that far. In fact I've noticed I can never remember being at home and being at school on one and the same day, the two run on different tracks, eternally apart. Myself, I think I even missed their company a little bit, leastways in the light of what was to come. As for her side of it, whatever she says I'm still of the opinion they all did her good. Made her feel wanted, to put it simply. Proof being that when all went their separate ways I'm afraid she had one of her what she now calls wild times, which not beating about the bush means they came and went so fast she's likely forgotten the names, no doubt even the faces. She doesn't care to dwell on that period in her life, not surprisingly, and fortunately I cannot tell you much about it either, for I was kept well away, most nights stopping over at Nan's, or my friend Kelvin's.

Nan, you see, by then she had come back up from London where she'd been hoping to marry her insurance man and was set on trying again to make a go of things in the hairdresser's trade, though in the end they said she was too set in her ways and had no idea how to speak to customers. Nan had a quite awful tongue, true, and wasn't too clever at keeping it in check. Mind, her own version was that that young cow of a boss just couldn't take the fact she knew how to stick up for herself and anyone else being sat on. That can be a devastating combination, a quick brain and a sharp tongue.

Anyhow, as I expect you can imagine, Nan naturally wasn't above hinting over my head when members of her gang dropped by just what she reckoned to the way her poor dead son's widow was carrying on, particularly now she had a nice house to flaunt. Not that that type of talk had the big effect on me you might suppose, I'm pleased to remember. In fact when I look back I have to say I quite like myself then, for I never took sides, or so it seems to me. It was good to hear from Nan about the doings of my fabulous dad, in fact I could listen to those stories for ever and a day, and she had a great gift for telling them, all the same I believe I never was in any real danger of being won over to her opinion of my mother, her estimation of ways she chose to live. For never forget this, Mam in her own way cared for me just as much and even more after my sister was taken away and eventually died, which was such a great sadness to her and possibly as good an explanation as we'll ever find for why from time to time she let herself go. Both loved me, that was all I needed to know, and though neither very often had a penny to spare both spoiled me rotten. I don't mean toys, I mean listening and asking questions, and filling you up with food. And so long as I had two homes to lay my head where I knew I was wanted, why should I trouble? Maybe I had two mothers really. And playmates aplenty, leastways at that particular time.

One thing though. Looking back on it now it seems to me Mam didn't have quite the same energy then, not always the same vitality which as I was saying I think you'd find she has in abundance today. Not so surprising, I daresay, when you think what she had to endure, the general battering from life. Even so, I cannot honestly remember a time when she didn't count for something in the Lane, whatever some chose to say behind her back. Their problem not mine was her refrain, certain people should consider themselves lucky others give them something to prattle about. Live and let live was the general philosophy round our place. Up until she got religion, that is. Hakes and religion.

She had to pay for it, though. I know one morning the police brought her home in a pitiful state, because I overheard Nan reporting it. Blood and things. After that a few would turn their backs but most still spoke civilly, and not only ones near enough in the same boat. And Nelly of course never failed her. For all the Lane's now changed almost out of recognition and it's no longer even on the extreme edge of town, by and large it's still the case that if someone's poorly or in trouble differences get forgotten and folk rally round. Always someone on hand to cook and console, and that she says was good to know in the bad old days, no matter what their private thoughts. Know what I mean, Signor? There but for the grace was the general attitude, and nobody was left long to mope or starve. Particularly if they had bairns, right?

I see you nod.

La donna è mobile. Isn't that how the big opera song goes? Well I suppose it was the case with my mam too, if *mobile* means mobile. Or no, on second thoughts it wasn't as simple as that. She wasn't the one to set the pace, she didn't flit from one to the other as the fancy took her. They did the flitting. So, no, I'd not describe her as so easy-come-easy-go as I maybe made her sound. Definitely no Madame Butterfly! Never was it a case of the more the merrier, not unless you're going to count the rare short couple of times she took what might be called a holiday from everything. To my way of thinking for what it's worth her only real sin was a very common one, always hoping for something better to come along. And what's so shocking about that?

And please always remember everyone says there's nothing she wouldn't do for our sakes, both before and after Lowery's Lane. Cleaning anywhere they'd let her bring two bairns along, the Three Hearts of Gold on a morning, then Maggie's, and a big old house down by the river with a trio of unmarried sisters and these giant spiders under all the heavy furniture, and how she loathes spiders! Then too, please also take note when you come round, Nana wasn't without a few faults herself, glaring ones, and even although just about anything Mam said or did would set her off she was far too fond of us bairns ever to say a thing like that in front of anyone. I mean like, well, like she was a pro. There, I've said it. Not that she was, I've long since convinced myself of that, no matter some tales that follow her around. Even in her wildest times she was really only playing about, I'm absolutely sure, just too unhappy to care. I'm only asking you to see it from her point of view, that's all, though I do wonder whether I'd have gone into it this deep if you hadn't happened to be suddenly so dead to the world.

Please understand. She had to live, she couldn't survive on memories, she had to try other things once he was presumed drowned and the government cut her allowance from thirty-eight shillings to only twelve-and-six a week. I do know after the difficult time with Great-Auntie Teresa we shifted about a lot from address to address, trailed everywhere by his black tin trunk, as she'd not fail to tell you. It was part-packed with his civvy clothes, the rest being all half-finished gadgets of his devising. The clothes got sold off once she finally accepted he'd never be back, and sadly eventually the trunk itself and every invention inside it went for scrap. Which always seems to me a terrible shame, not to have it here now to open up and explore. The one and only creation of his still in our possession is this little sailing boat he made for my sister's bathtime, and you can still just make out the name he painted on the stern. *Coral Maid.* Apparently he liked to say if ever he got the money together he'd build it for real and we'd all sail the world.

What a difference to what she had to endure after he went missing! I'm told most landladies wouldn't ever allow her in their own bits of the house, only condescending to speak the day the rent was due, and it was on the nail or out. In one place the cooker was on the landing and the only water off a tap in the toilet. Another I sort of half-remember I'm almost certain had a good crab apple tree in front, and other tall bushes, and now it seems to me I was scared of getting lost between all that shrubbery and the crazy paving winding right round to our door at the back. Behind was similarly wild, all dandelion and docken, and in my memory the tortoise she told I got off a man-friend of hers left a tunnel right through it from end to end. It's still in existence, the house not the tortoise, though now the windows are all put out and the roof's just beams and tatters, like a bust umbrella. Poshest address we ever had, she says! That whole street's been due to come down for years, but you can still see how it was once the big house at the top of the row. To hear her, the old chap who let us have a bit of the basement meant no harm, he just had the same attitude to his lodgers as he had to his bits of garden front and back, leave things to fend for themselves.

Whenever she gets on to them times, which she doesn't too readily, always into my mind's eye comes a very tall building with an unforgettable smell where it seems to me we're installed in one bare room at the top of flight on flight of echoing stairs and the entire place is empty apart from us. She says we never lived anywhere that quite fits that description but I'm likely remembering a dump near Sunniside. I'm a bit doubtful about that, because it doesn't seem to me I'd retain even the faintest memory of an attic where apparently we didn't last a week and I was not yet four. But I smell it still, that ghost of a smell you find in old biscuit tins after the biscuits have fled. She says at least I'll not be wrong about that, every room we rented had that same identical smell, gas and mouldy wallpaper, and likely it's what did for our Felicity.

So there you are, my friend. And what odds does it make now anyhow if she tried her best, or had the most ridiculous high hopes of almost anyone she had dealings with? And if before you drifted off maybe it sounded to you like I might be a little bit blind to some things, that's only because I was what I can only describe as very special to her when I was small. Oh yes, wee Felix was the big power round the place! You see, losing Robbie and then knowing so long before the event what fate awaited our Felicity gave her these almost boundless anxieties for her remaining bairn, and the upshot is it gave us more or less a free hand to be the little terror. Aye, think of the fun I spoiled! All I knew was I had some sort of power, consequently I never needed to stop to wonder what it was. Most things you don't ask yourself at the time, just take for granted until things go wrong.

Of course I don't yet know what your verdict would be, but never once, and do please bear this in mind as well, never ever once before packing me off across to Nan's on a night time did she not whisper deep and tickly in my ear that I was the only man she loved in all the whole wide world, me and my darling dad in heaven. And Sunday mornings, Saturdays too later in life if I was due to give her a hand at the canteen, and all the school holidays, I'd hammer and hammer on our door till down she'd skip in her rosy night things to open up and get a second breakfast frying for us, chips and all!

9

It was no more than a year or two after we moved into number 53 that she started her long connection with the prison. If you'd not chosen to be napping I'd have made sure to tell you how bit by bit she tried to settle for a quieter life, still taking in lodgers but all above-board now and strictly one at a time, since there was really only the one room to spare. In a word, she wanted no more than one man muddling her life. Also at long last she had the makings of a proper job, and one she meant to keep. Better prospects all round.

Hakes being one, worst luck. I'll get him out the way as quick as I can, because up until the Major's arrival he's the only one of all our lodgers I cannot find even one good word for. A God-fearing widowed warder, or in my opinion a devious heartless bastard, one of Adolfino's understudies. Goodbye to power. He'd a way of setting her against us, much like her Arthur later. Nothing you ever did could please the sour sod, only for a kid to exist was a crime, he'd clip your lug for nothing, or just nip it. Only for the exercise, like he was a frigging schoolmaster in a previous existence. And mind, that hand of his, with long years as a pitman before he was a warder, it was iron hard. Hard as the back of a cricket bat, and he preferred to use the back. And I know Mam felt the hard of it too, more than once. Still, one good thing we can say for Hakes is he didn't last as long as he might have, not much more than one cold winter of beatings and bible readings, because like every man she ever cared for barring Uncle Dick, maybe even Arthur too, he walked out on her one fine day. On his job too and all. Things were getting a bit hot for him in there, they say. In any case one day he just embarks for Australia without a word, where now he's doing champion by his account. Aye, even seems the man's holy conscience came to prick him later, for you should see the quality cards she gets off him come Christmas, and what fond messages he pens, to the extent you'd almost agree with her that somewhere under the big chip on the shoulder simmered the glimmerings of a human heart. Almost.

Never for a moment did he let us forget Newcastle beat Arsenal for the Cup that season, while we got knocked out in the third round. And he forced us into the Church Lads, you know. Oh of course I know if she heard me going on all resentful like this she'd sharp be onto you about how at least we have to be grateful to Bill Hakes for getting our family back onto the road to respectability! He it was, see, who got her into the vicar's good books after our Felicity finally died, then off the National Assistance by fiddling her a bit of cleaning at the Institute, then kitchen duties at the prison officers club and canteen. So now, after about ten more years hard skivvying and a part-time catering course at the Tech she's graduated from Church Institute char to assistant manageress at the P.O.'s club. Not bad going, eh?

Nearly all our lodgers, following in Hakes's shoes, and after Uncle Dick, were prison staff, single men or married on temporary secondment, and naturally as time went by she might start getting on reasonably friendly terms with one or the other, because I don't mean to hide the fact she didn't care to sleep alone. I suppose after her very short time with Robbie her reaction was that something in life was missing without a man, then rightly or wrongly she started to get this reputation, though mostly only stemming from the relatively long-ago times when some of the worst used to seek her out. But we've been over all that, and by these other years I'm talking about now she'd set herself to live it down. Which granted isn't easy. Being her, the best way she could think to do it was to hook herself someone respectable and show the whole town she could keep him. Even Hakes I suppose, then Uncle Dick, men older than her by maybe twenty years, and neither much to look at. Who knows, maybe she thought that too would put an end to comments. Some hope.

Now it just so happens that from round about then I seem to have a more regular run of memories, I mean from when she settled for this new regime, even maybe a bit too steady and churchy from my perspective. Being set on showing she could run a good house and bring up a bairn as well or better than the next woman she made a regular hostage of her lad, and I had to stop with her practically without a break, and that naturally rekindled full scale war between her and Nan, though already the free-thinker and the vicar's prize exhibit were hardly speaking. So then do you know what she went and did? Turned our old accommodation arrangements upside down! Yes, once Hakes's reign was over, and Uncle Dick's, lodgers got my attic room and I had the run of the entire front bedroom. And honestly I didn't know what to do with all that space, once I'd put up two nails for my fishing rod and another to hang my bag. And his Army photo of course, and the wondrous Cup Final drawing.

Uncle Dick. Now he was something else, and not just

because just about anyone would have been an improvement on Hakes. Take football, never were two more chalk and cheese. Hakes, I told you how he was devious, well he actually switched allegiance from Barnsley to Newcastle after the Robledo brothers got their transfer, the first and last time I ever heard of such a thing, whereas Uncle Dick though long settled in Hartlepool was by family tradition Sunderland through and through. And I'm happy to say such great loyalty was well repaid that year, for we were in the title race all season and put more in the back of the net than any other First Division club. Eighty-three goals, and like I say I'm pleased for the poor bugger, that being his last ever season. His one failing according to Mam was he could talk politics non-stop, for all he was normally so very quiet. I'd understand if he was a politician, she'd say.

When we were talking before, before you fell asleep, I'm not sure I made it quite clear enough how fond I was of my uncle Dick. More or less right from the start things were on a fairly good footing between us, and I don't doubt they'd have gone on better and better had I not let myself get blinded by the notion he made Scratcher die in place of him and just didn't care. That's the cat that installed himself along with Jackie Mack, remember, and fought the fox cub to the death. And that bike by the bye, my first ever, I didn't even mention he saved it from the Hartlepool emporium he tried to set up with a pal of his after losing his job at the docks for sticking his neck out too far, before coming to our town with high hopes of starting afresh, though he never did. Anyhow, I was wanting to say Uncle Dick he went all the way back to Hartlepool for it, and being of course too big to ride the thing he walks it the entire way home, would you believe, which is miles and miles, and then somehow he goes and keeps it hidden until the morning of my ninth birthday, after secretly painting it up in our team colours. I opened my eyes and it was under the window, a three-speed Raleigh gleaming red and white, just beautiful, with a big note saying it was a present for making him such a careful copy of the 1937 Cup Winners for his own birthday. But all that stopped when the truck failed to see Uncle Dick at the crossing and our Scratcher died.

That big warm smelly beautiful-natured stub-tail creature, you know, he was in many ways my best and definitely oldest friend. We were taking him up to the vet's, me and Uncle Dick, Scratcher being bad with ear mites again, and then this had to happen. Uncle Dick only had a little smudge on one side of his face and just looked a bit dazed, though really it was an invisible injury, internal. He sat there on the grass staring into space not even looking at my cat that he was carrying in the special box he made which I thought he had used like a cushion to save himself. Yet Scratcher's jaw was torn clean off and his red blood was splashed all over the road and the side mirror where the lorry must have caught him. People wanted Uncle Dick to leave go of what was left of Scratcher and get to his feet and speak to them, and instead he just sort of grinned, and I turned against him from that moment on. Now when I think of my grown-up friend Dick crouched there with that daft brave smile on his face in invisible pain and little me shouting every bad word I knew because he went and killed my cat, it all seems a terrible shame. And I knew some choice words courtesy of Hakes. But that's the thing, isn't it, you get used to an animal. At home I still look up when I hear the kitchen sneck rattle in a draught. Mam too. Smoky doesn't do that, see, just sits and waits, but Scratcher he'd bump and scratch at the door when he wanted in. Hence the name.

Uncle Dick killed Scratcher and nothing could change my mind about that. Mam couldn't even drag us to the hospital when he was a whole two month lying dying. That's when she started caring for him, really caring. And for years to come, times even now when she's low, you'll hear her say she'd not have minded a man like quiet Richard round the house for the rest of her days. Funny old game. Mind, sometimes I'm more cynical and I think to myself it's because he never got a chance to move on like the rest of them, that's why she got to talking about him more and more, until he risked being almost in the same class as my dad. I mean, right after the funeral what do I see but Uncle Dick's photo go up over the fire, straight off the coffin to face their wedding one. And later, when say for example some new man was in the process of being settled in or just making enquiries, she could spend the best part of a morning telling about her wonderful inventor husband that died and this lovely gentleman called Richard who was a famous union man and sadly also passed away, and me forced to sit there like a stuffed parrot expected to back her up in every lull in her natter, the new bloke's eyes shifting from her to me and back to the two dead men on the mantelshelf, the tall gangly one next to little Mam all in white and almost unrecognisable to me since she looked no older than some lasses at school, and the dumpy one with his hair all stuck up in the wind, squinting into the sun outside his sea-front junkshop that went bust. Aye, some old game it certainly is!

Oh I knew all about it when Mam had a new lodger. Basically it meant she had a lot less time for her own flesh and blood, while she fussed and fussed to make the stranger feel at home. Not that I'd lack for anything, only I'd know it wasn't totally for my sake I had to make sure and be in for every meal, and better meals too, and although she still made out she liked hearing about my stuff I didn't really any longer have the same free run of her time. I don't know how well you'd say I'm putting all this if you could hear it in your sleep, and in any case it's quite hard to think right through in one go, but I really do not mean to convey she was fatally attracted to one and all. Even so, if memory serves, after Hakes's vanishing trick and Uncle Dick and all the tears, there came another quite queer period for her and I preferred to move back to Nan's.

Nan by then had given up her council flat after she became quite friendly with a fairly unusual man who let her move into one half of his bungalow, down round the back of the Bramley's massive back garden. Not much more than a wooden shack in actual fact, but very neat and cosy and covered in red ivy from top to toe, from old white-haired Mrs Bramley's back lawn to right round the chimney stack, the very same place Nana said when I was small I thought was a house built all of leaves. Lovely to stay or visit, and almost always smelling of Nan's good plate pies and date slices. As well of course as leathers old and new, the leaf-house's owner being by profession a boot repairer.

In fact with all this warm sun toasting us now I don't even need to close my eyes like you to see the green and crimson leaves thick-growing round the porch and the big pink and blue hydrangeas like Nana's best hats, and their two white pints waiting on the doorstep if I arrived early enough in the morning. And the cat sat on the mat of course, old J.W.'s immaculate black and white she-cat known as Matt the Mat. Never ever have you seen anyone care for a cat like that. Towards the end he was even pre-chewing her little bits of meat and fish seeing she had almost no teeth, and finally all she'd take was maybe a lick of beaten egg off the tip of his thumb or similarly a spot of warmed milk. Matt loved that. But having seen other cats go Dummy knew the moment. It was horrible to see, she was breathing very bad, gasping for air but still trying her best to get up, so then Nan wrapped her in a nice warm towel off the radiator and Dummy carried her into the yard and held her feet apart over the flower bed and for the last time Matt did her business. She'll be there still, tucked under the wall where Dummy dug her in. But in her best years what Matt was really mad about was pilchards, often I'd arrive with a tin, incidentally also one of our Smoky's favourites along of course with sardines, in oil not tomato, though another all-time favourite Mam lately found is chopped ox liver, but mixed in with breadcrumbs to stop her getting the runs. It's all gone now I'm afraid. So's Nan. So's J.W.

Even before, the bungalow must have been a bit on the small side for him alone, yet he was happy enough to arrange it in two halves, one more or less entirely for Nan, while on the other side of the partition he lived and worked, her peaceful companion, the deaf-and-dumb boot repairer John Wesley, though we all called him Dummy until I knew better. A gentleman, she used to say to people if they looked at her in that way, and a gentle man. Her own Uncle Dick you could say, though I'm assuming she was too old for that. Or maybe not, I don't know, Nan used to say she loved the Kirk Douglas dimple in his chin. She kept an easy chair for him right in front of the telly when he got her one, and of course she could have it as loud as she liked, herself being a touch hard of hearing by then. Also she loved doing him a good Sunday dinner with all the trimmings and trappings, and I of course was careful not to miss too many of them, for no one I ever knew could do a Sunday roast like my nan.

Come to think, there were some other routines they shared, for instance she liked him to okay her turn-out when she was all dressed up for the bingo, with her best coat and white gloves and flowery hat. His side was the shop where he worked and slept, and all hours you'd see folk trailing up and down the pebbly path round the edge of that big lawn with their shoes to be cobbled or fetched. All their needs had to go down on a pad which everyone knew lived on this shelf in the porch. Well now, seeing most folk had been dropping by for years as often as not they liked to enter into a bit of an exchange with old J.W. if he was in, and as like as not he was, and naturally in due course some quite long dialogues might ensue on that pad seeing Dummy couldn't get out a sound anyone save Nan perhaps could comprehend, and so you see bit by bit and week by week that pad would slowly be filling up with half the tattle of the town, because although he may have been deaf as a post just as much as anyone else Dummy liked to know what was going on. Ah but then, and this I'm sure would make you laugh, once the pad was filled up real fat the next caller might look for it and not find it on its shelf, because of course my gossipy old grannie had fetched it away to read for herself, all that mix of scribblings. And the best pads she used to kid on to Dummy and me she was storing up, claiming we had the makings of a regular Domesday Book on our town! Happy days.

My bed was a little pull-out she kept under her own bed. And early on a morning what did I like best? To crawl inside the warm tent of her bed and make her start all over again every single story she told the night before.

Yes, it was a nice life. Yet I have to admit in some respects Nana was not the best companion for me, right at that particular point in time. Not that there wasn't as much love for me as ever, there was, and fierce too, and of course I had no bother returning it. But the thing about it is I was growing, though still not much in height, whereas she was getting more and more housebound and set in her ways, and as time went on it came to be like my dad her son only died something like the week before last. Result, he became more of a legend than ever, and consequently for all Mam was long back on the straight and narrow it was now as though she had even less of a right to make a go of things in ways she chose. As for my own side of it, with growing came changes and with the changes came trouble, and so more and more I found he was just so very hard to equal. As ever, I aspired to her idea of what he'd expect, but for the first time in my life I could feel a sort of gap between us, and that gap it was widening all the time.

But keep Nan off Mam and not too much on my dad and she was still the best company. There was this marvellous memory she had right up until the last, and which she absolutely had to share, more than ever since it was mostly lost on old J.W. And I mean she'd been around a good bit, Nan, and done some thinking as a result, first the long years up in Scotland, then her years down London after and during part of the war, all them long days and nights of the Blitz when they practically lived in the Tube, which was where she met her insurance man she always hoped to wed, and then finally back up to our area again. And she it was by the bye who fixed for Hakes to take us up to Glasgow on the train that time our Felicity was due to be brought home to die and be buried. Couldn't face her old man again, see. Nan never forgot or forgave.

Fierce does describe her, both the worst and the best of her. Last year, when she was in the wheelchair and only a week or so before she got finally hospitalised, I took her down to Leeds to see this old girl from munitions days she used to visit regular once a year, and what for me was so like her was how she refused, just absolutely refused, to be separated from her wheels, consequently the railway people had no option but to dump her in the guard's van, both coming and going. And that was all a bit painful, to be honest, seeing Nan in that big push-chair affair hadn't affected us too much up to then, but something felt so wrong about the bare steel cage they stuck us in, and the rails beneath making too much of a clatter to hear ourselves speak. Consequently she spent a lot of time just gazing at her grandson. Which was difficult. Of course later I found she already knew she was due for the second operation, in fact that's why she had to fit in Leeds ahead of schedule, for one last good old reminisce with her pal Nora from their golden days making bombs together. And she was right to have a premonition, because when the time came they took just one quick peek inside and sewed her up again and parked her in the ward for hopeless cases. Aye, like we were saying, I had two mothers really. And would you know what she once came out with on that score? Said I could learn all about people from the two of them, but only one could learn us how to think. Fierce!

Oh she could go off like the bombs she made. One time I'll never forget. All I was doing was leaning up against a telegraph pole waiting for her to come out of the post office where she was in collecting her widow's mite as she called her bit pension, and honestly, coming out the door and down them few steps and seeing us propping up that old log did she let fly! Come away off that, goose, don't you know it's full of electricity! No use telling her if that happened to be true I'd already have been dead of shock.

Another thing I must tell you when you come round again is her famous wise words the morning of my first day at real school. We were nearing the fatal gateway, and what does she say when she makes us let go her big warm hand? Listen here young man, she says, listen to your busybody old grannie now. If they ever dare to pick on you, if a bigger lad goes after you for no cause, remember you haven't to run and you haven't to cry. Keep the tears behind your eyes and look him straight in the face, but watch his hands too. If he really is a lot bigger and he's already thumped you once I suppose you can even turn the other cheek, like your soft-head mother and her silly friend the vicar say, because I won't deny it might be a smart thing to do. But listen to me now, hinny, if he's mean enough to smite that cheek there's but one thing for it, and you can tell them both from your bad old Nana Winnie that Jesus forgot to say it – plump the clever-Dickie hard as you bloody can! And go for him here, just above the buckle of his belt. Never below, mind, that's not right.

Jesus forgot!

Signor, one day we found a puddle reflecting the bright sky, any round puddle in our path, can look like a hole right through the world. So me and Nan we'd stand there and act out like we were looking all the way down to the sky above Australia. Then of course I had to show her I dared jump over Australia. Or was that only her canny ruse to keep me boots dry? The year of that game was the winter it later froze so hard you could walk across the river, and day after day over the farmer's field facing our house the snow kept on falling and falling until by the end there was nothing more to see but very slight bumps where his Brussels were. In my memory all I did that winter is watch snow through windows. I was in a window when it stopped, the kitchen window. One minute all was the same yellow-grey, next minute out pops the sun to make the bricks in Nelly's wall glow bright pink under a great big pillow of silvery snow. Until then even the cats preferred to stop indoors, Scratcher and Smoky hated to tread in cold snow, and we'd sit in the window together watching the swirling flakes and the famished robins hunting for scraps by the ash tip, little round living lumps of clinker hopping about leaving prints behind like the arrows on convict suits in my comics. Some mornings it'd be hard even to get the doors open, front and back regularly iced up overnight, and this one particular time I must have been sent to fetch in the milk just moments after the dairyman's float had been and gone, for when at last I got it open there was a long deep orange trough of horse piss steaming in the snow like only a second before someone had emptied out an entire urnful of tea.

So really then it was mostly Nana who kept him alive for me, after the Spiritualist craze died down and virtually all the years of the Major. She'd sit with me by the fire after tea at Dummy's, hands in her lap so like yourself now, going over all the endless stories with that special faraway look, the blue eyes glowing almost red from the coals, and not always above shedding a tear or two. Imagine the effect that had, with me growing older by the day and dreaming away alongside her of all the ways I was going to make good, and please her and please him, surprise everyone, to the extent that once I even went up and asked my old enemy the farmer if he didn't happen to need a hand howking his taties on account she was so fond of reminiscing how as a lad my age he'd picked the fields for a shilling a day and as many spuds as he could carry, staggering up to their door every night with a sackful, and ten pence in every shilling went straight to her half-sister Hilda who I remember was good enough to give them a roof when they first came back down to our town after the big love affair with Scotland turned sour.

Funny how it seems a pattern now. Nan with Grandad Quadruple, then her insurance man. Mam almost every time. Now me. Were we born unlucky from that point of view? Or simply bad at choosing? Or too good not to let ourselves be used? Aye, dig deep enough and there's a daft soft side to all of us. Specially Mam, hope springs eternal and the rest of it, never so bad it cannot be worse.

Maybe we're all much of a muchness there, only a woman has a harder time through it. I mean, why else does she harp on about Uncle Dick right to this day, near as much as her blessed Arthur? In certain moods she'll even claim she showed him the door, Major Arthur, though that's putting a bit of a fine point on it, since to everyone else it looks like he took himself off to Bexhill as usual, then for his own reasons stayed put there right up until he pegged out. There's a picture of him on the bedside table and snaps in the trophy cabinet, but I think, Signor, I think if when you wake you were to ask the likeliest reason why her Robbie and then Richard are the only two to earn a niche above the hearth, I'd say the answer has to be that the sea took the one and the other died in her arms.

10

So there's me growing apace among people no doubt with problems enough, while meantime I'm gathering plenty of my own. Not that I really went looking for mischief, most of it was only sky-larking, if you want to ask me. Alright, some are more easily drawn into it and the smarter ones capitalise on the fact, but I'd still contend I was no greater a sinner than the general run I consorted with. It's once you have a given reputation, deserved or undeserved as the case may be, that's when the unfairness starts in, suddenly there's no dearth of folk who reckon they don't have far to look to finger the culprit behind almost any misdemeanour. Take the example of a window breaking. They have this picture in their heads which sends them after you almost automatic, so dead keen to match you with the picture, and under such attention no matter what the truth any normal bairn is going to act shifty. Shifty or defiant, which to their eyes mean the same thing. Older people slip easily into that habit, I found, eyeing you in that presuming way, like for some any stray cat is just asking to be stoned, watching for any excuse to wipe that shifty-defiant look off your face just to prove themselves right again. Hakes being the supreme case in point.

Mind you, I'm not trying to claim I was some kind of angel in shorts, I bust my quota of windows. And okay maybe I was a bit of a handful at times, I accept that, same as just about anyone else at that particular stage in their lives, but all the same from my own personal standpoint what I had to put up with in exchange was extreme, justice was no different from the olden days when they made you stick your hand in the fire and you had to show it would not burn before anyone would dream of entertaining the notion you might be innocent until proved guilty. And another thing I'm tempted to say, if this little tirade is getting us anywhere, in the Army it reverted to something very similar, and just when I thought I'd outgrown attracting that kind of morbid attention. It's a fact, Signor, while what you call a prisoner of war I likewise never consciously went looking for trouble no matter what anyone else might have you believe, not even in the matter of that one solitary bottle of Johnny Walker which for the life of me I cannot imagine why last night I should want to go and make such a big confession about. I took the whole case, Signor, as a perfect illustration of the general point I'm endeavouring to put across, that had it been anyone else they'd have assuredly let the matter slide. But by then, see, the trend was set, I'd collected whole queues of stone-throwers who one way or another combined to make sure I was never going to get a fair hearing. Most weeks I was more on than off jankers, I tell you.

Jankers. I wonder if that was the word they used when you had to suffer under the same regime, along with the added excuse you were enemy? As you rightly said, with any institution nothing ever really changes, save maybe the words. Fatigue, defaulters, detention, jankers. That's it, aye, jankers is no different to treatment meted out to dunces in school, keeping you back after hours to write lines, making you parade in full kit for the entertainment of some vindictive twit who seeing everyone else is happily off in town putting the memory of the Army temporarily behind them takes his resentment out on you by making you double round the parade ground or stand to attention under the pissing rain, or as you yourself confessed leaves you marking time for hours up against the shithouse wall, we're brothers in misery there, while meantime he nips off to keep a weather eye on you through the guardroom window warming his backside over the four-bar heater. I've never really properly understood how it is, why with some people these things just seem to happen to happen. Which I don't mean as an excuse, of course not, just a statement of fact. Many's the time I've asked myself if I was so often in trouble because I'm a bit of a dreamer, or a bit dreamy because I was so often in trouble. The chicken and the egg.

Certain people attract trouble and I'm one, I'm one. Can we leave it at that?

I wonder if ever in certain circumstances you longed to be invisible, such as we sometimes achieve in dreams? You know the kind, they don't see you and they're coming after you with knives. I still get versions of that old one from time to time, only now as a rule it transpires I'm bollock naked and everyone's only pretending not to notice. A story we once had read to us at one of my schools told all about this lad with bottle-end eye-glasses called Peter, I still remember the name, who by some lucky accident invented invisible paint in a chemistry lesson and then proceeded to use it to get back at everyone who had ever messed with him. Did you never have that wish? Did you never dream that dream?

One day it was sheeting down and I was running from the farmer on his tractor. I don't now recall exactly what I'd done, probably nothing worse than trespassing, though I may also have hollered something that didn't delight the shite. Normally he'd not have stood a chance, but that day his field was like an ocean of mud and my boots were soon clagged this thick with the horrible stuff, heavy as fetters and twice normal size. I did all I could to keep on legging it along the tops of the rows, terrified of slithering and sinking down deep in the sloppy quag waiting there like wet cement in the long furrows stretching uphill right to the sky, and all the while I could hear his big tractor gaining fast and sure. I'd staked all on his mean streak, you see, hoping he'd elect to keep steering straight so as not to squash too many of his precious turnips, but when I was near the top and I swerved for the stile he swung over too and aimed the dirty great thing straight at us. So then I had to turn and double back the other way, racing like a frantic rabbit close along the fence where the grassy edge was harder but the barbed wire was like out to catch us too, and then, well then suddenly I knew I was well and truly done for, because looking back over my shoulder I saw the tractor standing all alone with its seat mysteriously empty and of course next moment out round its big back wheels he comes shooting at the speed of a greyhound. I don't know whether I yet know you well enough to be sure you'd approve of what I did next, when there was no more strength in my legs and no more breath left in all of me chest and nothing short of a miracle could save us. I tried to perform the bloody miracle! You know, put their great mind-over-matter theories to the test, see if a combination of praying hard as you can and believing it utterly sincerely will cause a git big fire-breathing turnip farmer to drop dead of a stroke, at least snap an ankle, even just fall flat on his face. Jesus could do it, and Mr Wouldhave who took the Church Lads made amazing claims for ordinary mortals, and every school I ever attended was rampant with how the spirit can beat the flesh and faith move mountains and all the rest, and kindly also don't forget I happened to be guilty of nothing unforgivable, or not in this instance. So I quit running and stood stock-still right where I was with my feet together under all that rain still coming down like stair rods and my eyes tight shut and praying so hard to my dad and Jesus and my sister, and let him just come on. And on he came. I could hear him running and I could hear his tractor running, so then I had to go for the impossible, silently scream in the dark to all of them to make us invisible. And it happened too, or so I thought for a minute, because I could hear him panting very hard very close by and his boots not squelching anymore. Well of course he was just standing there gloating over his victim, silently savouring his power, and when I opened my eyes he grabbed me ear and near twisted it off.

So there's another thing that takes us straight back to my father. He was never too far off when things weren't working out. If trouble followed us all the way home, if Mam was vexed over something I most probably didn't even recall until I spotted her standing on the doorstep tapping her foot and puffing on a tab with her arms folded over her famous bosom, it was as good as sending us off to talk it all over together in my brain. I already told you, remember, for a long time my chief concern in life was to remind him he had a son worth coming home for. And the surest test of that was whether it was war or peace between me and me mam.

I wonder if I can explain how it went. At the start he'd be no better than other grown-ups, not really even listening to what you had to say for yourself and always siding with his own kind, so then I'd need to remember to take it a lot more slow, make him see for instance that although from the outside it might look like quite a bad thing I'd committed it was not without good intentions, seen from the inside. And knowing all sides, the good and the not so good, hence ultimately prepared to listen, it was normally only a matter of time before I'd talked him round. Or no, wait, there was more to it, it was more complicated than that. He could see ahead, yes, my dad could see far ahead. He knew, same as myself but so much better, that lots of things I did or said were almost bound to be taken in the wrong spirit at the time, for the plain and simple reason that nobody could possibly yet know what would only become crystal clear in the far distant future, when all the world would see how the bairn they took so much for granted connected with the unusual person none but the two of us knew I was due to become. So that was another advantage of having him for company, as you so rightly called it, this shared prior knowledge that somehow I'd make good in the end. And now my thoughts are more in their stride I think I should be able to illustrate better how I remember it used to go in my head.

Things might start, generally did start, with him being one hundred per cent in her favour, content to echo her every Hakes-inspired word and consequently make his long-lost bairn feel twice as small, what her Hakes would have called a right little godless maggot. But in the long process of walking it off I'd find ways to get him in a more reasonable frame, bit by bit make him prepared to attend more closely to my less simple version of events. I remember inside my imagination it would be like I'd sort of choose to hang back to let him almost unawares catch up, get him as it were to fall in step with my own approach, that at least one member of his forgotten family might be worthy enough and loyal enough to maybe consider thinking about once in a while, maybe in exchange for swallowing yet more excuses for why he was currently a little bit too over-involved to contemplate the long trip home. Finally, naturally, I'd have him listening fully to all my problems and promises and we'd part good pals again, not least because, as he never needed too much reminding, the two of us had one long-standing complaint in common. His long-lost wife, my mam.

No, still I make it sound too easy. The fact is that sometimes these sorts of very long head debates could run for days, plugging in and plugging out so to speak, carefully working over every word I felt he'd most likely want to say and what he'd want his son to say and what I'd actually want to say and then all the places we could go from there, until all in good time I'd have it talked right through pat to all parties' satisfaction. Even, oh yes, even to the point of no longer needing to fret over-much about whether or not he even anymore existed. If he did, leave him to his own devices, so long as he never forgot the prime reason for wanting to make his fortune was to accumulate enough for a one-way ticket home from wherever on this almighty planet he was at present, panning for gold in Australia, hunting the Abominable Snowman, fighting in the Foreign Legion, building the world's fastest motorbike, tracking down Hitler who we two knew for certain never died in the bunker, whatever was the current attraction.

Generally our long walks would take us in a big circle, beginning past the prison wall and extending right round town by all the back ways. Other times, since the more drastic the case the wider the sweep, I'd slam furious out the front door and over the Lane and up the cut between the fence and the field and into the woods and on, on, on. All weathers, the worser the better, exulting in my pictures of her all alone in the kitchen still mouthing off to herself though secretly more and more worried sick for my safety and finally able to stand it no more and racing out to the box at the end of the Lane to dial 999 in a panic sobbing that her only surviving child could this very moment be expiring stabbed through the heart in a pool of his own red blood deep in the scary forest, or just perishing of neglect on a cold hillside after snapping an ankle down a rabbit hole, till in the end without necessarily even planning it I'd find I was steering a roundabout course for home. Then, arriving back, no matter whether from just round the churchyard wall or right from over the top of Windy Bank, seeing the familiar long row of houses next to the bright grid squares of the prison windows and the friendly glow behind all the curtains and every chimney pot smoking away against the black nothing of the graveyard, why then suddenly after all the solitary miles of crutty paths and giant trees I knew for certain how sorely I'd be missed once I was old enough to run away for good and ever.

11

Now all this must be taking us well up and into the years of the Major. He's dead now, the useless sod, so I ought to watch my words. But when did he, so why should I? If I have to think of him I think of a little yappy terrier, a short-legged wiry grey creature whiffing of sweet shaving cream and the stink of a dead pipe. He's what put us off smoking for life, or most of it, serious inhaling. Having his foul ash up me nostrils all them years. He had no connection with the prison though it was at the P.O.'s club she first got to know him, where he was a bit of a well-known character, having the proper sort of posh voice for calling the numbers at the Wednesday and Friday night bingo. And he was quite a leading light at the Rugby Club too and all, another place where the beer is cheap.

When she took up with him he had the run of his brother's retired AA van, as I remember recalling way back, and for as long as they were as you might say still in the courting stage she often made him take us along. Seaham, Roker, Whitley Bay, you name it, and once or twice maybe even as far as Redcar, any place where the two of them could hold hands under the table in a pub after posting little nuisance off with a few coppers to get lost on the slot machines. Marsden too, because until her big shock that was another favourite spot for them to park up and dig out the thermos and look at the sea. Man, the times I've sat in the back of that daft vehicle munching a cold bacon sandwich and passing the old cracked yellow mug to and fro, the three of us without speaking, just gawping through the windscreen at the grey drizzle and the old Rock head remote under its bird hair! In the back was only ever the spare tyre to sit on, or his lumpy tool bag, and he of course must have felt he had a miniature policeman breathing down their necks. Hope so. Choice memories. Chomp of jaws, patter of rain, and no one with a word to say.

Mam of all people, tongue-tied! A serious sign, take it from me. As for us two, little Major Arthur and wee Feelie Rowan, from day one there was an unspoken agreement that neither could abide the other, always awkward in each other's company, a state of affairs that only grew worse as time went on. I wouldn't call it jealousy, not really, after all I was well used to sharing her. More a fatal combination.

No back-answering your mother, boy, not as long as I live under this roof!

With that prick in residence I couldn't wait to be out the house on a morning. Oh I'd be first through the schoolyard gate for once, would you know, if I didn't just bunk off for the day, a situation that more or less lasted right up to and including when I got my first brain-wash job packing boxes and watching machines at the new plastics factory up the Sunderland Road, before I finally chucked that in and went down London for a total change of air. The owd sod cast a shadow over everything, took the place over, not to speak of our actual lives. I tell you it was like a throw-back to Hakes's reign, from the day Major Arthur Arthur darkened our doorstep he acted like he was cock of the roost. Once, and once only, though right before her eyes I'm sorry to say, oh yes with my own mother standing there transfixed in the doorway with her finger hooked through the handles of three teacups, he whips off his leather slipper and gives us a terrible thrashing, me, a little lad hardly half his size. And all in aid of what? Apparently I'd stepped out of line by not giving him his regular good-morning-sir. And he enjoyed it too and all, you should have heard his grunts. While she, she said nothing.

Scared to lose him. I'll say this though, he never tried it again, so I still like to think she had a word with him in private. At any rate, after that little episode my thirteenth birthday was a total farce, and next day of my own free choice I moved in more or less permanent with Dummy and Nan. And when after various reconciliations finally nothing she tried could lure us back, you know what she did, what my own mother went and did? Turned my big bedroom into his study! Leastways that was their grand name for it, and a misnomer if ever there was, because I can tell you all the owd sod ever studied in there was the racing form and his secret store of dirty books. God only knows what else he found to mull over in his little mind up there in that room which was mine, apart from his smut and cross-doubles and all his supposed glory days in the war. Never got close enough to discover, thank goodness. All I know is that if ever I happened to drop round there was always an invisible notice on my own door saying don't disturb. Hours on end, whole days, he'd spend shut up inside there, and my own mother like a tame poodle dead on the hour trotting upstairs and down with pot after pot of tea and plate-loads of buttered toast spread with his favourite Gentleman's Relish. Her ministrations, he called them. Fussy about things like that, which had the effect of her fussing over him. Man alive, you could have set your watch by the two of them!

Just tap on my door, boy, what else am I here for but to listen.

Only once now do I recall taking up his tray, that time she said she was so loaded with cold she was petrified of passing it on, though they of course slept in the same bed. Well I duly tap, and when I get no answer I stick my head round the door and there the owd bugger is, snoring away with his mouth open and his stockinged feet on the fender and the paper practically in the fire. Did he honestly suppose I'd take my complaints to him? As much good as sounding off about the quality of barracks food when the duty officer comes round the tables asking if there are any grumbles. From the word go, or as soon as I divined the lie of the land which was anyhow soon enough, I kept well clear. As suited the both of them, don't doubt. I'd only have to hear his cough at the front door or the putter of his stupid motor and I'd be out the back and over the wall to Kelvin's or Jackie's, or grab my clobber and push straight off to Nan's.

Are you daft, boy?

Daft was my name. The sod knew every warder, same as Mam, and before he gave up on his notion of my education he almost convinced her it wouldn't be a bad line for her son, the prison service, if ever I grew. You didn't need anything very much in the way of written qualifications, he told her, only a certain height and a certain attitude, the same no doubt he dreamed of thrashing into me. Which is no doubt the main reason I didn't, why I just could not seem to grow, the hidden reason I delayed my one and only growth spurt until I was ready to strike out on my own and his days as a force in the land were fading fast. Easy for him to sit in judgment up there and dictate my future, he who had a good war by his reckoning and could afford never to do a stroke thereafter, his old man having left them property all over town. What has a boy to learn from a man like that, I ask, who never understood for a moment what I was about? Didn't even follow my reasoning when I declared that was no way to live, stopping others making a run for freedom while you yourself are locked in. At which he just resorted to growling about it not being long odds I'd end up in there anyroad, only in another capacity. Or worse.

I wonder if you'd appreciate his full meaning. We're not as civilised as you, we still like to do people to death, and at that time they topped them a bit more often than now. You'd see a huddle of warders whispering together in the Lane, next morning they'd run up the black flag and a notice would appear on the big jail door. And they didn't die quiet, not always. One of my nightmares is waking again like early one morning long ago when I heard a terrible sound the other side of the wall, a sound to make your blood freeze. And do you know what to me that voice seemed to be saying, or sobbing? SAFC, SAFC! On and on and on, I swear that's what I made of his garbled gargle. I was no more than eight but I know I did not dream it. I had the bedclothes pulled tight over my head and I could still see what they were doing. I managed to more or less bury the memory, then it came back in Germany when a cockerel scared us all awake in a barn.

I'm warning you, boy, I have eyes in the back of my head.

Even at the time of his first occupation of number 53 he must have been nearer sixty than fifty, so what joy she got out of it I find hard to imagine. Neither can I see what possible need there was to move himself into our little place, what with him having a massive house out by the river road sitting in its own big garden and just his younger brother there once in a while, practically a mansion, one of the likely-looking places where in the old days we used to make a point of calling for a penny-for-the-guy. Their old man was still alive then and he kept this huffy butler for jobs like that.

He was her dream of respectability, or I reckon that's a big part of the story. Respectability, stability. Otherwise not in all these long years has she been able to say what it was about her Arthur, though I suppose knowing my views doesn't make her want to go particularly deep into the matter. She'll say things like, fair enough he was an eccentric old codger, maybe even a bit of a tyrant, but by no means the worst of the bunch, conveniently forgetting there were no other contenders by that stage. Least not that I know of. The truth is she thought it grand to be seen around town with a nob, when he let her be seen. Even I suspect never so very far from the back of her mind was the hope he might as they say make an honest woman of her, for let's face it another marriage might have changed everything for Mam. Then also, to be totally fair for a moment, maybe I could have done with a heavier hand as I got older, in fact who knows whether from that point of view it might not have worked out okay between me and almost anyone else she wanted. And I will say this too, still putting myself in her shoes for the while, it's not hard to see that my attitude didn't make things any easier for her. All I can otherwise think to add in mitigation, thinking back on it all from this safe distance, is that my never-ending resentment was possibly a touch unfair, the constant level of it. But then again, who could ever rival my own real dad, for ever an adventurer of twenty-two?

Nana in this whole question for once wasn't much of an ally. She tended to say a no-nonsense type like that was what Mam had always needed. And fair enough, I have to admit he must have cared for her in his way, I concede there must have been some feeling there, or why else would she have let him get away with murder? As I said, he took the place over, infected it like he infected her, everyone had to do the old dog's bidding, and the atmosphere could be terrible. If he didn't get his way by snapping he got it by brooding, and either way set nerves on edge. Not cheery at the best of times, unless after a drink, finally he'd get himself into such slumps of gloom he'd stop talking even to her, and at long last he'd take himself and his big old suitcase back off home. Even then, though she was all over the house with bucket and mop muttering good riddance, anyone could see the way she pined, worse than a cat that's lost its kittens. It was just another routine with them. So even with him off the premises a little while life wasn't worth much around home in a deadly atmosphere like that. Consequently I took more and more to wandering off.

What else can I think to say? The one and only time I felt just a little bit sorry for him was years after, the time I managed to get home on embarkation leave before the war game in Germany, and even though I found him once more well installed on my territory, watching him there at the table and afterwards by the fire skulking behind the paper, just by studying his hands you could tell how he'd aged beyond belief in only the ten or so months since we'd last clapped eyes on each other. He looked old and he acted old, wheezing on the stairs, repeating himself more than ever.

Yet he scared us silly in that dream. Man, what our brains choose to lay on for us at night, even horror films! Every inch of him was right, the springy hair, the silvery dandruff on his collar edge, even the mix of pipe stench and shaving soap. Left to itself your head can come up with all that, seemingly without trying. Aye, forcing it gets you nowhere, Claudia. Remember what I told you Uncle Harry used to say? If we could only take a camera into our heads we'd all win an Oscar!

Lot of truth in that, eh? Liked to hear us going over old times, didn't you? Me and Mam having another set-to on my pet hate, you with your Mona Lisa smile and your head to one side, storing up every word. We could write a book.

Phooh!

Phah! Good stuff this, slips down so damn easy. Just a bit past the halfway mark now, I see. Best lay off, leave the man his due.

Why did you change so, lass?

What got into you?

12

'Mad Karoo' he'd hum to himself while staring out the kitchen window at Nelly's wall, just so I'd know he couldn't wait for me to be off to school. That was another catch with the owd sod, he was an early riser no matter how much he'd put away the night before. An awful lot of time, as I recall, was spent musing through that back-kitchen window of ours, sucking on his windy pipe stem in that foul old felt dressing-gown, I suppose because in the early years he didn't care to be seen at the front. Sunday mornings was the worst, that's when he took it on himself to get their special matey breakfast in bed, another ritual with the pair of them. I'd be up extra early, if I only could. Up and out.

My own company was best, and school or no school I'd

take myself off to the river, that being what I liked more than anything at the time. Aye, fishing even outclassed football. People like you imagine angling's dull and boring, for all I've often enough told you how for me it can be electrifying, and not only after dark when any stretch of water looks as deep as the world and stocked with monsters. Daytime too, as you remember from our walks, just a mouse moving or maybe a frog can give you a little jump, can't it, a quick one, almost as much as a good fish showing. So imagine what it's like to be all alone far away in your own thoughts and a lanky-legged moorhen plops in off the bank when you're not expecting, or a pair of wild ducks scoots splashing and skidding neck-first in a panic out from where they've been quietly feeding hidden among the reeds, if you suddenly move to reel in. And I always enjoy watching the water rats paddling about their mysterious business, just eyes and noses showing.

Look at him. Blissful. He could be having a fishing dream himself. Of course you say you cannot bear the thought of harming any living creature, barring one I presume, so you wouldn't even know the pleasure. Next time he stirs I might ask whether it's the same sort of simple delight with him, or if he'd be more like my uncle Harry despite the one arm, someone with more of a match-fishing mentality, where it's all about breaking records. For me, as I know you've tired of hearing, time by the river helps get things sort of a lot more in proportion in my head, at the very least in a state of suspension. Just hunting out some secluded piece of riverbank and setting up me bit of gear with the feel of a whole entire day ahead, that's all it takes to free my mind. I know I often used to say I wished you'd consider coming, thinking of us together in the long grass of course, but once by the water I honestly don't think I've ever minded being on my own, never missed anyone, I think because of this all-absorbing sensation of a sort of slowed-down long adventure ahead, dreaming of what might be, not knowing what I'll find. In the river, in me head, as it comes, while quietly settling down to study the patch of water I've animated with a couple of handfuls of tempting ground bait, craftily plotting out my day.

This last difficult period too, with all them things to say we didn't say, some I probably even didn't like to think, tortuous things, I found myself resorting to the same ploy as long ago when Mam first got her Arthuritis. Similarly certain mornings it was best to be up early and well clear of the house, particularly after you said you didn't want us in your bed ever again, two pairs of socks inside me wellies, this same jumper under that same coat you affected to hate which is presumably still drying on the line, a bit of bread and cheese in my old fishing bag and maybe an apple or two, making my way to the river. Opening the door extra-careful not to make a sound, stepping outside, that was always the hardest moment, thinking of you too deep asleep to recall I even existed. Most mornings these last weeks have been on the chilly side, generally with a bit of mist about, thick in the dips, thinner on the higher fields. Cows cough on account of it, in the wet grass chomping away alongside the crows and gulls, the white gulls never moving but the black crows waddling about all over the place like they all have ruptures, after the worms. And that too can give a special shock, I find, a big crow or jackdaw or something perched unseen on a fence pole alongside you suddenly going 'croak' in all the stillness. The morning I'm thinking of the mist was coming off the river like smoke and that sudden creaky croak was like someone cranking one of them old-fashioned brass fishing reels only a few feet away, hidden in the mist. You need to watch out not to tread on the slugs in the wet grass, shiny black as liquorice, fat as a thumb. Remember me telling you and Mam I saw three hares out there, no fox this time, well a few years back unbelievably a stag waded the river right before my eyes, not the least bothered by a human. Times to yourself anything can happen.

And similarly them long-ago Sunday mornings when not you but the owd sod dictated the mood in the house I'd be on me way to the water well before even he could get himself downstairs, and doubtless none too pleased to find the special streaky he'd set by for their breakfast departed inside my sandwiches. I've more than once taken you the route that gets you fastest to the river, I've shown you the nettly cinder track round past the back of the big house him and his brother used to have, remember, with the big long windows right up against the fence. Same as now the curtains would always be drawn, but in the big garden at the back I tell you there were whole beds of strawberries and raspberries and currants and gooseberries going for the asking in their seasons, and apples and pears galore, all good eaters. Long before the top of the path I'll be walking faster, for I'll be thinking of them already biting and be scared of arriving too late, after they've come off the feed, though thankfully it's not that far to the white house where remember I told you Colin's nana used to live, and rounding Windy Bank all sprinkled with sheep it's only a matter of minutes to the river. But not until your boots are ringing on the iron bridge itself do you get your first full view of it, the old river at last, all them millions and millions of gallons of water slipping down to the sea making only a quiet trickling sound.

Come winter, and not only Sundays but Saturday mornings as well if I wasn't playing football with the lads, for still I had daft hopes of making a career by it, I'd be out of the house long before it was even properly light. At that time nothing could equal me with me, us with us an entire day, never mind the cold, never mind the rain. Rain brings the worms up. Aye, pet, even hunting worms I hate to remind you I do enjoy, pulling them up between the back yard cobbles by torchlight, two at a time if they're stretched out together making love with their free ends stuck fast down neighbouring holes. You have to step light, you have to be quick. Worms are nervous lovers too, see.

A bit of an unusual thing comes to mind and I'm not sure I'd even mention it if you really were listening, and not still stuck here in my head out of long habit, for sometimes these sorts of things intrigued you, sometimes not. There are these trees, wild cherry trees, maybe half a dozen, younger then, their straight trunks dark silver red and smooth, growing in a clump near the old iron bridge I was saying you have to cross to get to the other bank where access to the river itself is easier. And the thing is just about any one of them trees could give you a feeling, when you went to touch it. Rough-smooth cherry tree bark, I used to do that. What I invented for myself is I'd take my hand and lay it softly on my chosen tree, tenderly round the trunk, keeping my eyes closed so as better to feel the feel, and directly into my mind would come very strong sensations to do with Nelly's four girls, the middle two in particular. You know how I've been friends with Doreen and the others for almost as long as I remember, well from when I was around I suppose eleven or twelve I began to think of them in a different way, and different sisters different times, and of course as time went on and it got to the point where I was dreaming of birds nearly all my waking hours, my dreams of the sisters mixed with them magical trees.

Claudia, oh Claudia, I don't have to tell you I could drive myself mad all night thinking of the four of them two to a bed right next door, and in the early morning I'd creep up and secretly touch their smoothnesses, the silky trees by the river near where I'd jump off the side of the bridge with my bag and rod at the ready, to drop down to the river bank proper. They were all of them a tease, and all at various times said they knew us far too well, and I suppose that's what led to my taking my sort of solitary revenge. One night it might be Maureen I could not get out of my head, or Charlaine in that short white frock, and next morning to touch my tree, stroke it along its so to speak body slow but sure right up to where the first branches part could bring her alive together with me in all her naked glory, glad of my hands gliding over her smoothness up to the crotch where the bark slightly splits, bumpy rough. You liked that too, admit. Another time it might be Doreen, the younger of the middle two, particularly after I heard Jackie say Brian said she already knew what was what, and all I'd have to do is maybe trace a finger up along the curving bark and slightly move it round to know what it would be like to go further than any of them would ever let us, past the tantalising point where my sleep encounters broke off every time, all my let-down wet dreams. Weird what you do or imagine doing without thinking how it might seem to anyone beyond yourself, never feeling funny about it until you have to tell it. And yet it is so easy surely to understand it was only my need for the actual living form and feel of them, no more to be tormented by my yearnings for the unexplored territory, what we all called the penalty area, everything hiding in the forbidden private gap between the start of their tits and the tops of their knees.

Nelly it's said never wanted even one of them, her four daughters by three separate fathers, each so different but each as bonny as the next. Remember Mam telling how other women used to say it wasn't right that Nelly tried everything to get rid of her bairns before they were born, while others desperate for a baby would have something or other go wrong? You looked at the floor, remember, and I knew what you were thinking. Well Mam could also have told you how Hakes used to maintain that one night peeking through his bedroom curtains he spied Nelly sitting in that same old rocking chair in her kitchen and whenever the bairn started kicking inside her she thumped it with a rolling pin, right on her bulging stomach. Mind, I'm not too sure I believe that story now, I've told you the sort he was. Still, as you undoubtedly also remember, Mam says it's true she did try practically everything to lose the fourth, little Lorraine, swallowing concoctions, jumping off chairs, even the coalhouse roof though it caved in under her. And no matter what she did or didn't they all come out perfect, every one. Perfectly perfect. And I grew up next door. And that sodding Arthur would not even let them in the house. Not even Nelly, Mam's oldest friend, just so he could show who's boss.

By, the tension on a morning before school! Get cracking, he'd go, meaning eat that boiled egg. He'd a whole store of suchlike conversation stoppers. Manners maketh man. Greed not need. A place for everything and everything in its place. And his special one for evenings, hen in the pen, hub in the pub. If those are pearls of wisdom I'm as much of a professor as your dad. The only time of the day he'd loosen up just a little bit was at the prospect of a drink down the Rugby Club, or the Prison Officers', then on his return if I hadn't managed to get away to my room or off to Nan's he'd not be above trotting out what he thought highly comical versions of 'Ding Dong Bell' and 'Mary Had a Little Lamb', chanting away like a tiny mad tipsy vicar chortling at his own infantile wit. Mary had a little lamb, the midwife had a fit, that was the level of it. And a great one for doggerel was Major Arthur Arthur, he knew every verse of 'The Face on the Bar-room Floor' and half Rudyard Kipling backwards. Boots, boots, boots, marching up and down again! Boots, boots, boots! So he'd go, stamping out the rhythm on the floorboards, marching about in time, wanting little me to parade all round after him, littler even than him. It was I suppose all part of his strategy to win her over, beguile the nipper, while still under the impression one didn't come without the other, that it was the whole package or nothing.

And let's not forget his Standing Orders now. Wholescale mock parades, a foretaste of the Army, so nobody can say I wasn't warned. When addressing an officer, boy, stand to attention like this, legs braced, arms forced behind the back by the shortest route, thumbs along the crease. Those eyes are roving, woman! Because he'd want her playing along too, up on his feet himself of course, at times on a chair for extra height, three parts cut conducting the entire regimental band then breaking off to harangue Mam and me and the cats about his wonderful war, how he put one over this side or that, whole glory episodes he'd enact right through to final victory, his sharp voice yapping away at all the other voices he'd set in motion against his own. Too small to stop a bullet, the bugger, too light to sink. By his account an entire Abyssinian tribe surrendered just to him, laid down five thousand spears in a great pile before his nibs the mad major, and one shot from his pistol over a stretch of empty-seeming desert would have scores of your lot popping up out of their slit trenches waving white hankies like the last train for life was leaving. All so pleased with his little self, so eager to be seen in charge, and how the eyes did shine. Eyes of a terrier, a rat terrier, or a rat itself, and his chin was twitchy and his laugh a squeak. Clever at card tricks, mind. But not the faintest interest in a kid. Small, very small, hardly bigger than Mam, and finally not even as big as myself when I finished growing. Yet surprisingly strong, as I found to my cost that time he bent me over the settee.

Listen to him now, chuckling in his sleep. That's something I only learned with your help, that sleepers can show they're amused by what their dreaming. Thirty-two months in barracks never taught us that. Nowt but snores and shouts and farts.

Heeh! Signor, I tell it wrong if I give the impression my mother took everything lying down, I wouldn't want to perpetuate only that idea. Admittedly not often did she give him the end of her tongue but you should have heard it when she did! The case I have in mind is the time she found his store of dirty books, all the nudie mags squeezed in behind the old mirror in my room. Out go the lot along with him. I was over among the graves playing tiggie-on-high with all the others, and when we heard the screams the lot of us ran to shin up the ivy on the wall, because I wasn't the only one scared she was being murdered. Shriller and shriller rose the screams, then the back door flies open and out scampers the owd sod himself, out the hole and up our entry dragging that stupid bulging suitcase after him over the concrete, and next thing Mam comes storming out on his heels to hoy the whole collection at his bent back, at his fat arse. And even that wasn't enough, not for her. Long after he's no more she's still chasing round the yard wherever they dropped and ripping out the pages and shrilling up the empty entry: Get back to the toilet where you belong! All them shameless tarts offering their bums for a wipe! And that's how I like to remember her, the day the major got his marching orders and Mam was boss.

He was back soon enough of course, and it was all lovey-dovey again, likely even worse than before. No wonder it got so we couldn't be in the same room together, let alone the same house. And I could barely even speak to her. She wouldn't even hear of asking him a penny of rent, you know, and the man only owned half the town. And eight whole years he haunted our place, Signor, with longer or shorter absences, and no one on this earth could make my mind turn quicker to my dad. Home or school the atmosphere was no different, hemmed in by authority types. More and more I took to wandering off.

Likely my schools weren't that bad as schools go, and no doubt I was the real problem, but there's times it seems to me all we learned was how to sit up straight with our hands on the desk and look a grown-up in the face without taking in one word he said. How else could I think the equator is a menagerie lion what runs right round the earth? It's right there in my geography exercise book with a picture to prove it. It turned up in a box of things poor old Dummy brought round after Nana died. Three months later he too let go.

Now that's what I call a real couple, a genuine marriage of minds, like you say it was with you and your Angela. Two people as different as can be, but good with each other and good to be with. Not Ada Rowan and Arthur Arthur.

That last Christmas was unbearable. Yet it was not until the last Thursday before Easter that I walked out of my mindless job at the factory and took off south to see the world, me and good old Jackie. Daft as a brush was my old pal Jackie, ever good for a laugh, the only reason I stuck plastic cups as long as I did. When he showed up at the roundabout anyone could see Jackie Hazelgreaves meant to take London by storm. He had on the whole Teddy Boy outfit, pea-green jacket to the knees of his drainpipes, bootlace tie, and the only pair of blue suede shoes in town. We got in at dawn, riding high in the cab of this big articulated which took us right the way from Scotch Corner to the exact centre of Vauxhall Bridge. And what a memory that is, opening our eyes as the driver pulls over and says, this do yous two? Then grabbing our bag and jumping down for our first sight of London Town, half-six on an April morning with the famous shapes all bluey gold in the smoky mist, Big Ben and all the rest, and the tide racing out beneath as me and Jackie empty our bladders one hundred feet through the parapet.

Normally you only ever think of who puts up a city, but at times like that you catch yourself wondering who dreamed it up, old Christopher Wren and them, Michaelangelo and crowd, all the different shapes they choose to give it in people's eyes. Maybe for that to happen you have to be at a bit of a distance, up high like us today, or Jackie and myself that morning. Marra, everyone dreams a city, says Jackie, smoothing his velvet lapels and combing up his quiff like all London is his mirror. And now we see where we fit in, Feelie, come on. A relative of his when last heard of was supposedly doing okay in his own spare parts business up the Lillie Road and Jackie reckoned he might have room for one more, even two, at least be in a position to put us on to the next-best thing. Well, we enquired and we enquired and no one thereabouts had the foggiest notion what might have become of this Smart chappie, such being his name. But that's London, isn't it?

I wonder now whether your Tony formed the same impression. In the end I decided it's not that they mean to be all that unfriendly, or not half as much as some make out, it's just that interest in other people cannot stretch so very far, the place being much too massive for the time and continuity that requires. Look at rush hour. The bigger the crush the more they pretend not to know each other. When the Tube comes to a mysterious standstill in the middle of a black tunnel no one breathes a word, it's a major crime if eyes meet, yet they're all crushed up against each other like in a frozen orgy. On the other hand a bus can be the opposite, momentarily very warm and friendly, times it was standing room only you could hardly keep up with the repartee. And naturally I used to wonder why that was, and the difference between above and below ground is all I could come up with. But there again, out in the open can be as bad as down the Tube. Walking back to our B & B she threw up all over the pavement and no one stopped.

Still, maybe the best example of what London does to people is Jackie and me. I see no other particular reason why we're no more in touch, whereas in a little town such as where we started out that's about all there ever is to do. And are Romans no different to Londoners, *amore*? Didn't take you long to lose us yesterday, did it? Then look at this kind gentleman here, think what he and his son have done. Without asking. Then take a good long look at yourself, perhaps.

Signor, I tell you it was like a little rehearsal for yesterday's full explosion, pushing us away and flopping against the wall with her hands on her stomach waiting for the rest of her Greek supper to appear. White as a sheet, hating eyes. Don't touch, don't touch me! And there was her own pink sick all over my sleeve. Right up to then she seemed to me to be definitely in love again, we'd kissed a bit, we were holding hands, and I was wandering along sort of all happy and oblivious thinking about what we'd soon get up to back in the hotel, by coincidence reminiscing about old Jackie and myself finally in the city of our dreams and how gleefully we escaped northerners polluted Old Father Thames. And then this sudden change, all resentful again, as though somehow I could be guilty of making her ill. I'd a mind to ask whether she didn't object to the sight of me only because it made her have to face the fact that if there was any change it was all inside herself. Anyhow.

Anyhow, anyhow, and fucking anyhows!

Swinging our one bag between us we walked all the way up the Vauxhall Bridge Road and over to Victoria Street, to book into this big Sally Army place which that friendly ex-marine Durham truckie had told us about, each being assigned a cubicle with a bed, and a bible and a good breakfast too. And next day but one, following our exploration of the joys of Soho and when similarly nothing came of the Lillie Road, one of them very helpful bible people took us both round to the nearest Labour Exchange only to find that most jobs for our age bracket and qualifications were for watching machines or packing boxes again, or for night watchmen or night cleaners, or if you happened to have any exams for watching night cleaners clean and night watchmen watch. Jackie had Biology I believe it was, anyhow claiming about six more passes and upping his age a good bit away he goes to have it off every night, if you believe him, with heaps of sex-starved cleaning lasses in office blocks all over the city. Jackie Hazelgraves, now he was one of life's real chancers!

And God I miss the lad! He'll be a millionaire by now or a con with a record as long as my arm. For how many weeks did we share that cellar with a single mattress in Camden Town? The mattress was for Jackie to sleep it off in the day, consequently I had to be up and out at the crack of dawn when the streets are still all empty and weird, and with the excuse of job hunting I'd wander miles and miles, wherever the fancy took us. You know, I shouldn't be surprised if I've travelled the equivalent of something like half round the world, jumping buses and following the canals between one tunnel and the next, or dawdling through the parks for a sight of the office girls sunning themselves and whatever animals are visible in London Zoo from the wrong side of the railings. Once I rambled along the river right the way from Charing Cross to the Tower, then all over Dockland as well, because I was contemplating setting sail on one of them big ships you could hear booming so yearningly in the dead of night even from below street level in Camden Town. It was the travel bug I suppose, all London wasn't enough, likely Rome was pulling even then. Of course when I made enquiries they said you needed seaman's papers before you could hope for an interview.

Well, my friend, naturally eventually reserves ran out, and when even Jackie refused us the loan of another dollar there was nothing for it but to don my smart-boy-wanted kit every day for real, this blue serge suit which came my way via Uncle Harry who's earned several mentions but I don't think I ever got round to saying quite enough about. Lost an arm down the pit, did Harry Crosthwaite, the left, or three-quarters thereof, which may be why he always dressed in immaculate suits and shirts and had Mam forever washing and ironing. Otherwise if I think of Uncle Harry I think of how he liked her to set a basin of hot salted water in front of the fire to steep his feet in before tucking them into his fender-warmed slippers after coming in at night, huge fleecy things, Harry maintaining it was mortal agony being on his pins all day, though all the labour anyone ever heard Harry did was hover by the fruit machine calculating the right moment to pounce for the jackpot while earning himself the occasional free pint by collecting up the empties and all bids for the twice-nightly sweepstake on behalf of Mr Webster and his two sisters in the Hotel Victoria saloon bar and lounge where he was by way of a permanent fixture, so much so that behind his back everyone called him the One-Arm Bandit. Being curious by nature I was dying for a view of that stump which lived out of sight in an otherwise empty sleeve with the white cuff of it always pinned neat to his shirt front. It could flap the sleeve, the stump, but never did I get to see the actual thing itself, though Mam once said it bore some resemblance to a well-risen individual Yorkshire pudding, which is apt enough when you think, or a raw white sausage end she said another time, I doubt not unlike that salami your Tony sliced to go with all that good bread of yours, and who knows with a similar skin knot in the end and all.

Harry doesn't know the meaning of hurry, she'd skit Harry, and Harry'd just laugh. You know what Harry is, he'd say, Harry's a certified armchair philosopher, so why should Harry chase time, even a duff clock's right twice in 't day. Unfailingly calling himself Harry. Each morning somehow there was a fresh flower in his buttonhole as though he was just off to a wedding or every day was a holiday. And he was another who had a good war, joking he'd never have been wounded if he hadn't volunteered to go back down 't pit soon as peace was declared. He wasn't Army, Uncle Harry was Navy and very, very proud of it, serving on convoy duties that took them right up to the Arctic Circle and beyond, and that of course supplied him with no end of tales, such as what monster salmon Harry and his good friend Eskimo Nell pulled out of the big hole they cut in the ice outside her igloo, using hooks made from polar bear claws and seal gut for line. Harry took his

Nell on all his adventures, cunningly smuggling her aboard inside his kit bag, and on a top-secret sledge expedition to track down a Nazi doodlebug base near the North Pole what great cook-ups had Harry and Nell, roasting sizzling joints of arctic wolf over a campfire they had to feed with chunks of whale blubber due to the dearth of trees. In short, Uncle Harry could spin a golden yarn, and of course I hung on his every word. But time to get back to my own adventures.

So there's me in Uncle Harry's navy best with my hair flattened down knocking on staff office door after staff office door in every department store to be found in the neighbourhood of Oxford Circus. For some reason I was partial to that area, mostly only I expect because there's always plenty going on, though maybe there's a connection with my dad here too, because I'm almost sure before you dozed off I happened to mention somewhere that they employed him as a store detective in our town, being that tall he could see over all the partitions in Woolworths. Naturally I wasn't expecting anything of that sort, just sales assistant or something, though finally all I could persuade one of them places as big as palaces to pay us a pittance for was to go round picking up the days' droppings, or in their words maintain all floors and lifts and stairways litter-free, and as a special reward for good behaviour first thing on a morning help polish up the brass and glass bits and bobs in the knobs and knockers department, for nine hours a day at ninety-two shilling a week.

So when not a sort of roving fag-end collector that was my territory, knobs and knockers, first basement, one stop down the elevator. Ah but then after about ten weeks did

I not rise to be one of a little team of expert hooverers of thick pile carpet, of which they had acres and acres. Neat little machines they had, very nifty, sort of mini-versions of them mechanised mowers you see groundsmen riding round on at football grounds. Plug in, start up, steer about, nae bother once you get the hang. Trouble is, for a bit of a lark me and this even dafter cockney lad Joe Lamb from second basement jump on our two machines on Christmas Eve and act out like they was dodgems. Heeh!

Joe got the sack.

I got second basement.

Ciao.

13

It's the other side of your chair.

Just something I was remembering. Didn't know I was laughing out loud. Mind, you seemed to be having quite good dreams yourself.

True. More relaxed now, a lot more. In fact on top of the world.

Oh that helped too, I daresay! Had a bit, I'm afraid, after you started napping. More than a bit if I'm quite honest, though there's still plenty more to go I hope you're pleased to see. And I'm just so glad you managed to get in your siesta. Watching you snoozing, sipping the old vino with your city that is my future right in front of my eyes, filling in the time as best I could, it's been a good combination. Just what the doctor ordered in fact.

Nothing much really. The whole afternoon's just floated by. Sun moved round, clouds retreated, city slowly woke up again. While me, I've been as I say happy enough drinking it all in while pondering this and that, all the funny things that happen to happen, waiting for you to come back to the world. Oh and once a little bird popped by, no doubt hoping for some crumbs. Hopped all round our two chairs like we were long acquainted.

Yeah, be nice if he showed up soon, to make the team complete. Actually I happened to be thinking of him only a moment back, in connection with quite an amusing little London story I reckoned he might enjoy. Concerning another total foreigner in the city, before reality set in. Very amusing in fact.

Sure?

Absolutely sure? Then first I need to ask if you'd be familiar with what I'd have in mind if I speak of a sandwich man.

Now that renders the picture even better! *Uomo sandwich. Uomo*'s the filling, boards the bread slices, as I know from actual real experience, believe it or not. One board hangs down your front like this, right from your chin to below your knees, while joined to it by two leather thongs is another for your back, only also with a upper part reaching high up in the air, this-a-ways, so people can read both sides of you without your face getting in the way.

That's it, a walking advert, a man disappeared inside a load of words, and with scant leg room and all so your top speed's a shuffle. Some do it off their own bat to advertise the fact the end of the world is nigh, and they will have been out in force until a week ago. But this assortment of old gadgies I'm remembering just have to parade their boards for shoppers to read where to shop, or where to find the Railway Lost Property Office if wanting a brolly or a briefcase or what have you.

Me and Jackie, this bosom pal of mine from home, we'd been drinking all morning in this pub, possibly over-drinking, so when they call time off we toddle in the general direction of a bite to eat, in the course of things happening on a back lane behind Regent's Street where it's a bit of a mini-red light area, and this hidden-away caff we find turns out to be the very one all these old tramps like to hole up in between sandwich rounds, if you take my meaning. Well now, over our pie and beans Jackie being Jackie soon gets talking to the only one who seems in any way prepared to engage in conversation and of course eventually for a laugh goes and asks if we can try a couple of Lost Property boards for size, of which a stack is standing by the toilet door. See the situation, Signor? Being the sort who'll try anything, and because plainly not one of all them glum gadgies looked faintly bothered what happened, Jackie gets mugs of tea all round and they seem content enough to let two loons do a circuit for them. Jackie's that friend who got the knock on the head I told you about, remember, the delayed concussion, this time we were kicking a ball about when we were all lads together in the Lane.

The official beat, that old fellow explained, was Regent Street – Oxford Circus – Piccadilly and back, to and fro, to and fro, the only rule being the police prefer you to keep close to the kerb, if not the gutter proper. That's where we belong, he says, shuffling along between the traffic and the humans. Which we then proceed to do, shuffling off toward Piccadilly feeling about as conspicuous as two giraffes, for that of course is the very heart of London and you've never seen such crowds. So anyhow all goes according to plan until Eros heaves in sight, at which point Jackie, typical, says why not do the grand tour while we're at it, Trafalgar Square and that, and right down Whitehall and maybe finish up outside Number Ten or somewhere equally ridiculous. Which we agree, Jackie betting he'll be first and soon looking to break the world record for man-sandwiches. Only, halfway down Haymarket what happens?

Jackie, having drawn a good way ahead and at a lick that doubtless could not fail to attract an expert eye, gets hailed by a big ugly gent in a bowler hat, very red-faced braying at him from right across the street, who unfortunately turns out to be the gaffer. Lord Sandwich, as Jackie joked after. And now you'll probably be wondering about me. Well me, spotting the two of them just up front there having a good go at each other, verbally only as yet, I slow right down and shuffle by in the wake of a bus, hoping he's not yet cottoned on to the news there's more than one daft northerner larking off with his lost property. Success! Maybe my boards belonged to a different outfit or possibly I didn't cross his immediate line of vision, with Jackie able to talk the hind leg off a donkey, or just possibly he couldn't even tell I wasn't the owd gadgie he thought I was. From behind, in that get-up, nobody can tell you even possess a head, I was just a shuffling shaft of words, and the backs of me shoes would have earned us the job without inspecting the rest.

Honest to God, Signor, I just ploughed on! The weather was nothing like we've had the benefit of today yet I was well and truly sweating, and not just from the weight of the blooming boards. Still, I did the entire circuit, the whole blinking grand tour we set ourselves and more, every paving stone and zebra, always praying Jackie was about to show up to witness my triumph before I got nabbed by each and every copper I shuffled past, though equally I was more and more convinced that must be what was delaying him. Still, luckily most of the bobbies in that part of London are only looking to show you across the road, or get their picture taken.

Hand on heart, every word you hear me tell is guaranteed fact. All the way down to the river I went, right down to Parliament, by which time I was that full of it I'd have crossed Westminster Bridge too and all had the wind been a bit less strong. It took a little while to get the hang, at the start I could all too easily imagine the edge of a board getting clipped by a passing double-decker or something, they all run that close to the kerb, even a madman shoving us in front of one, though still more was the terror of just keeling over like a sailboat because of that tricky wind, or only the sheer bloody weight of the things. So in the end, what do you expect, I broke the one rule and quit the kerb, by degrees took more and more to the pavement proper. And this is the queer thing about it, the queerest thing, no one even seemed to notice, like I was just a shuffling pillar box or something, and as time went on I stopped sweating and started to enjoy it. Enjoy it a lot. Nobody seemed to realise there was a living person inside the writing, even when they could be bothered to read.

Brilliant outfit for a spy, says I to myself. The invisible man, like I used to dream. And there was life visible all around, life abounding. Birdlife, to quote Jackie. Some lasses in that part of London are so magical it's heart-stopping, and they come in all shapes and sizes and colours. Aye, bit of a shame it wasn't the start of something, that would have made an even better tale to tell. Sandwich Man Fell For Me Confesses Chelsea Bun! Good old Jackie, that was one of his prize witticisms, picturing it headlined in the Standard. Jackie paid every pint that night, conceding I won the bet, and all evening the two of us just couldn't help going off into fresh fits at the memory of every wondrous moment, embroidering it all. Much like us up here today, except that was lousy London ale and this is Roman blanco! Didn't pop anything extra in it, did you?

Some sort of magic potion, I mean. Because it sure feels like it.

Laughing gas! Now that's a good one.

Jackie? She asked the very same question when similarly I got on to reminiscing about old times, when we two were in London just this Friday gone, where we had to overnight before catching the boat train. And all I could find to say was the last I heard the lad was taking the money in a bowling alley having dropped his married lady typist in favour of a figure skater all of fifteen. London's bursting with crumpet, Jackie loved to quip, here there's more birds hungering for it than there's peckers to feed round Nelson's column! While me, I'd been getting a lot more of that at home, quite honestly.

Which takes us back to knobs and knockers. Or rather carpets, two flights down. Because, see, I'd finally managed to find myself a job in this big Oxford Street store, though then at Christmas I went and blotted my copybook. They docked my wages for half the breakages, which near broke me too, and confined me to what they called the bowels of the building, second basement, floor coverings and kitchen ware this time, pots and pans in the one half, rugs and lino in the other. Being mid-winter by then, I never saw the natural light of day save if once in a while I surfaced in the dinner break, the staff canteen being similarly underground. Dark when you clocked in, dark when you clocked out, good as down the pit. And don't ask how they made it pay, Signor, in the bowels, where it was more a show than a sale.

Take carpets. The costliest we hung on the walls, with little tags for hundreds of pounds stitched to their undersides. Once in a blue moon someone might happen by and visit one and maybe stroke it, but if they seemed in danger of falling in love you only had to reveal the under-tag to shatter any illusions and they'd wander off muttering about going away to think about it. Still, it was a sight quieter than first basement where I started out, and had it not been for Blinkin' Sod I might have stuck it long enough to see what £199.19s. 11d. looks like going in the till.

Blenkinsop, Signor, the floor manager. Almost nothing needed doing down there, only instead of taking it as given he took it as a challenge, priding himself on never failing to come up with something to keep idle hands out of mischief, as he was a bit too over-fond of saying, such as for instance wiping over the stairs each and every time he floated up or down them in his creepy rubber shoes. You might think that kind of regime would have been a stark warning to me, for isn't it the very thing you're up against in the Army, only that there you have to contend with not one Blinkin' Sod but scores? I doubt he had even three year on us, if that, and in time I might have cut him down to size. Instead, before the month of February was out that life and that prat drove me to commit what still ranks as the biggest mistake I made in my entire life.

That's right, Signor, that's right, this daft ha'porth upped and joined Her Majesty's Forces! And now let me tell you how it happened.

In the dinner hour, or forty-five minutes as it only really was, forsaking the canteen in order to avoid certain faces I was already seeing too much of, I took more and more to patronising a nice little pub just a short way up and off the Edgware Road where they always had these excellent grilled sausages, fat and crisp and peppery, perfect with a pint, sliced in half and wedged inside a soft bun spread with ketchup and mustard, practically good as a full meal, and cheap. The trouble is, trouble was, the road to it chanced to take you past this Army recruitment office, and one fine day around I suppose about one-thirty as I'm wending my reluctant way back to Blinkin' Sod, in other words having stretched forty-five minutes to around seventy-five, I just seemed to come to a stop on the pavement dead opposite the fateful place, transfixed. It was like I'd never even seen it before. And it was like he'd appeared from nowhere too, the man sat behind the desk in there, and putting on my best limp I crossed the street and walked straight in.

No, I tell it wrong! The truth is I hovered a longish while outside, just across the road like, keeping him in view in the mirror in this barber shop window and debating it all out between us, between me and my soldier dad, in that identical way I always used to do as a kid, figuring out what he'd have done in my shoes. And I hardly need tell you it was like he was urging us on, like he was all excited too, and no matter what objections I could muster when the moment came it was like Corporal Rowan himself marched us over the street and through the door and up to that desk where all this time it was like he had sat waiting for us, balancing an India rubber on the end of a ruler. I looked him straight in the eye and declared I was considering the pros and cons of carrying on the family tradition, beat heel permitting, and before I'm even halfway done he's up and out of his chair and rounding that desk to wring my hand like he's wanted to make my acquaintance all his life. As you know, all I ever dreamed as far as my long-term prospects were concerned was what I reckoned he'd want by me, only right up until that moment in time nothing very precise had suggested itself, or nothing on which we could agree. Now all at once I felt I had his full backing, I was born to pursue the brilliant career his regrettable accident cut short.

So that's how this turnip who says there's no such thing as fate delivered himself into the hands of destiny! Mind, there's evidence I wasn't all daft, the preservation instinct wasn't totally dead. That limp, you see, it was in the nature of a wise precaution. And I can do a pretty convincing limp too, for when I was fifteen I got such a hack in football it did for my heel ligament, and I've not played a full game since.

Well anyhow, just my luck, that man so warmly pumping my hand was about the most decent-seeming NCO I was ever to meet, and not ten minutes later I'm strutting out of his place with a big fat envelope of particulars under my arm and my mind already made up, poor daft goose, dazzled by the revelation that a routine medical and a simple intelligence test was all that stood between Felix Rowan and the gates to free world travel. So before going back to collect my coat and give Blinkin' Sod two fingers I go round to the Lion for another pint and another sausage butty, and carrying them over to an empty table I fills in that harmless-looking khaki form right there and then, cheerfully sentencing meself to five years in, selected out of the full option of five, nine, twelve, and God forgive them twenty-one. Oh aye, even at that high point a degree of caution did prevail, there were limits to even my gullibility, specially when you consider he'd said the longer the stint the better the pay. Still, it all shows how father-struck I still could be. In crisis times I'm afraid it tended to be stronger than ever, the bruised bairn's dream of one day coming home having made himself into everyone's acceptable version of a man. But who doesn't dream?

My mother reckons there's a fifty-fifty chance he'd have opted to stay on after the war, remembering the big impression he made on the colonel. Personally I prefer to think he couldn't wait to get back to his pre-war plans, the coach-building scheme and the pigeons, and his boat, and all the half-finished things waiting in the black tin trunk. Yet even Nana used to say her Robbie never looked back once he joined the Army. She said the depot near York where he learned to send and receive in all manner of codes soon got to be like a home from home to him, though that was maybe just to get at Mam.

During basic training, out on the parade-ground with everyone screaming again, I used to reason with myself that being extra-tall he must have stuck out like a sore thumb, so either he had to put up with more than the usual brunt of attention or he was a more adaptable sort than I am. Because as I don't need to tell you, neither the lofties nor the short-arsed can quite manage a natural Army step, being just a mite too tight for the one and too long a stretch for the other. Added to which, right from the word go, with everyone dressing off tallest-on-the-right shortest-on-the-left, and assuming there were no rival six-foot-fourers, the entire rabble must have had to fall in on my dad. Now, from my own experience of square-bashing and from studying the examples all around, I reached the conclusion that there are basically only two ways of reacting to such over-exposure. Either you slope along more or less as you always have, or you lift your head up high and step out smartly to become a leader of men. Okay, and so which was Robbie Rowan? Did I know a thing about my soldier dad when all's said and done? He'd have towered over the likes of you and me, so maybe the whole world looked different from his height. Or maybe we have to consider the possibility that everyone when they speak about my father lies.

So why go on inventing, you'll be thinking, why go on wanting things to be different to how they almost always are? I felt the call of duty too, let's not forget. Also I freely admit I was hoping to make up for ways I'd hurt her too over the years, my long-suffering mam, who when it comes down to it helped put these powerful things in my head. Whatever, something queer came over us as I stood there across the street from him.

He had a poster in his window, a big colour poster of a bunch of tanned squaddies in shirtsleeve order in an open jeep driving past the feathery shapes of coconut palms and a long column of camels strung out against a white beach and the bluest sea. 'Oh, the sunshine and the palm trees and them tinkly temple bells!' to quote ruddy Kipling, so maybe even old Major Arthur was joining the chorus in my ear. Queer indeed, it was strong as anything I've ever known, my knees were knocking together, I had to speak to him.

Well, I might have guessed. Because doesn't the same poem later go, 'There ain't no buses running from the Bank to Mandalay'? Aye, seems some have to learn the hard way never to listen to *la forza del* bloody *destino* and never trust such sorts of dangerous feelings, remembering they're almost certainly a sure sign your brain's stopped functioning, just as I found to my cost you're not much use to a woman when you get similarly over-emotional. And besides, who knows what might not have gone on to happen if I'd just stayed put in London and never heeded the bugle call of destiny? Big cities have endless possibilities, and I was only at the very beginning. I was pretty sure a lass in Lingerie was making eyes. Everything's possible until the final whistle goes, that's my philosophy, right up until nothing more can change the score line.

And that's what I tried to argue with her, with No Friend, countless times. I mean, who can ever be certain, completely certain, what will happen in even say these next few minutes? Until last week nobody knew whether the whole human race was coming or going. And maybe that too is why I blubbered like you said, like a lost bairn in the night. Not just for her, not just for him. 'Father, father in the Colossal Sea!' Today, in the daylight here, that sounds like a desperate attempt to make him stronger than ever he can actually be, the start of some sort of hopeless prayer. Wanting him as strong as, well I don't know, God or something. But Nan always said there's nothing in the whole wide universe as large as life. And don't thank God, she'd say, thank goodness. Well, well, no matter, not even his ghost was a help, eh Signor? I don't suppose even all the dead bones in the stadium where people fought lions could ever spell out what we're to make of it all.

Not hard to think of it filling up with bad memories, is it, now the shadows are getting longer. Gladiators and Christians, emperors and slaves. And I say pity the poor animals too. In his photo he looks a bit awkward I always think, a big man but no danger to lions, not kitted out to kill. Whereas a uniform makes some feel a lot bigger, doesn't it, as though they've just acquired another set of muscles, an extra suit of bulging muscles. Ah well, we were never all meant to be the same, as Nan would say again, and thank goodness for that! I think she's getting to be as big a miss as him.

She said two inventions in particular obsessed her Robbie. A wireless telephone, but nothing as clumsy as a walkie-talkie, something that would almost fit in your pocket. I could get nowhere with that, knowing nothing about the secrets of radios. The other was the total opposite in scale, some notion he had for extracting electricity from traffic. That's all she could say about it, yet I still found it could exercise my mind a bit. In a city like London, a city like Rome, full to overflowing with traffic such as we hear this moment now, isn't it all an awful lot of energy going to waste? So the question he must have asked himself was how to tap it, how to save something of all this never-ceasing motion.

Think of a road anywhere, any very busy stretch that you know round here, isn't it all so much vital power going to nothing? What I saw, what I saw one night in Camden Town as precise as in a dream, was the flat surface of a road with all over it spread these like little pedals poking up, and all somehow so craftily anchored and sprung that they could be pushed down by the wheels and then pop straight back up again, the full weight of the wheels, and of course each one wired up to some colossal generator that can turn that continual to-and-froing into good electricity. On the dynamo principle, Signor.

No?

Look, I don't necessarily think they would all just snarl up the traffic like you say, at the most slow it down, but only fractionally. Because each pedal, see, each one according to me would only need to project maximum an inch above the road, even a half-inch, just enough to find the traffic but not break the flow. Like cats' eyes, no higher.

Still no? Man, you're worse than the brigadier! When I tried it on him he said my problem was I took no account of the law of diminishing returns. That was the first time I heard the expression and I tried to grasp it with his help, so as to find new ways round. But no matter what I came up with, just like you he said we could extract some energy from the traffic, yes, but in the process the traffic would lose a lot more. But is that always true, and does it even matter? I agreed my notion was still a bit crude, only the beginnings of an idea. So by degrees we set about refining it together, two heads always being better than one, and in the end if I remember we had our pedal plates reduced to very low little ridges right across the road, all rubber-padded so the turning tyres noticed nothing, or almost nothing, similarly the passengers, and our springs were so fine-balanced it only wanted the slightest pressure to set all our wires humming …

No, but listen now, listen to all this din, then imagine it could be what lights up your whole city tonight! Every street, every shop, every office, every factory, every home, every bar, the picture houses, the stadiums … I'd be useless on the engineering side, that would want someone such as given a chance he'd have become, yet never will I give up believing something useful could be made of this endless racket.

Think about it, anyhow.

Bit chilly, aye. Time for the old jumper again. Seems more special somehow, now you've put your own touch to it.

Agreed. Supper can wait till Tony comes. I'm for staying up here to witness my first sunset over Rome. Also, we've not done full justice to the bottle. Aye, not quite got to the bottom of it yet!

14

There's a man in this city. A wise astrologer, or so she maintains, not seeing any contradiction in terms. Her own sort of father confessor, I suppose. I'm told he entertains the select few in a form of top-floor studio in some very old part of town. Something like, who knows, one of them long attic windows where you remember I thought I saw her face, above that second line of roofs there, where the slanting gold sun is burning in them now.

She had to know that he'd always be on the end of the line for her, latterly more and more. Even late as just this Friday morning I caught her at it again, hardly an hour before the train. I'd been given to understand she needed to take a last book back to the library, instead I find her in the box at the end of the Lane locked in talk with her astrological bugger, and with only about forty-eight hours or whatever before she could see him in the flesh, her horny old sage with the white goatee. It escapes me now what is his particular zodiac, but you can bet he didn't have to consult no star books to find the two of them were made for each other. Aye, saw it all in his crystal ball, I bet. Gemini has monster row with Capricorn, then in scene two she's all happy back in Rome sat on his knee sampling his box of Black Magic. The Ram, was it?

Don't go in for this star stuff carry-on, do you? Signs, houses, conjunctions and the rest? Well, thank goodness for that. Turns people into zombies, I said when I saw what her calls to Rome were doing to her. And how star-gazing can sit so easy alongside religion don't ask me, ask Gemini two-minds!

Same here, Signor, same here – as if life isn't already complicated enough! The nearest speck of a star's something like a hundred thousand million billion miles away, tell her, so why not start with what's the score in the real world, beginning with what's right in front of your nose? Nana would have sharp sorted her, same as she handed it out to the Jehovah's Witnesses when they started coming round the doors. Whereas Old Persistence who's supposed to have stopped believing in anything that isn't visible and verifiable, she'd say I should attend to what more better educated people choose to think, they can find proof for all manner of things ignoramuses like to laugh at.

Yet you know what's no laughing gas? I've as good as convinced myself old Hocus Pocus here advised her to dump her English appendage. And told her so again in that final morning call. Only she couldn't find the heart to break it then, not after sighting that same nuisance of an appendage through the glass, signalling like a mad thing that it was time to call the taxi for the train. Coming out of the box she looked I don't really know what to say, radiant, like a great cloud had lifted. A woman besotted, anyone could see, and of course I was daft enough to think the object was me, more than ever after we squeezed back into the box together. Yet the bare fact of the matter is it was always Italy or England, him or me. Why else spend pounds phoning him every week at the same queer hour, five minutes to ten on a Thursday night?

Studying her, Signor Pasquale, was like studying him. For instance listen to this. Before leaving England she suddenly wanted a fresh forecast, and he of course obliged, telling her she'd come home with something not so big but very precious she didn't take with her. How facile, I said, that could be just about anything that would fit in a suitcase. Only you see being who she is it got to be an obsession, the key to it all, just the way he hoped it would.

Not big but precious. She of course wanted it to be her baby, her precious thesis, this convoluted great tome she'll likely never finish, not for even a moment thinking it could equally apply to me. As to my shame I hinted eventually, only to be informed she'd changed her mind, now she knew precisely what it signified, and very precious it truly was. Still keeping their little secret to themselves, naturally, and looking a bit smug and even a bit mad I thought when she said it. But that's the way you go about it, see, you plant the seed then just leave your victim to develop it.

Recipe For Disaster is what I called it, this sort of remote control technique of his, and the day I found the name I also told her if I was as twisted I could make a good living by it too and all. Because do we really honestly have to believe it when she says a man who cares that much for her would take nothing off her?

Take nothing off! I mean, pennies aren't the only form of payment, are they? Pennies! Just listen to me now, the bare thought of her lecherous goat causes havoc in my brain, every time! Why could she never see he's an insult to her level of intelligence? I told her I might not have read the books but it's plain enough to me how the recipe does its dirty work.

Rule one, never give too cheery a forecast. In all her time in England I happen to know he never once supplied her with even a middling good one. And for why, for what plain obvious reason? To turn her off the place. Off Mr Appendage, that is.

Well why not, why not, seeing I'm now almost certain he persuaded her to run back home? Yet, you know, when we two first met she was fair bursting with England, and specially our bit where family legend says the mystery granddad had a castle, though that was more likely only a tale to get granny into bed. Aye, plain daft about the north she was, even our coaly little town. The first morning she steps out of our front door she looks up at the sky and announces to all the world she'll never forget the mingled smell of soot and rain. Sniffed it in too, deep, before coming under my umbrella. Old Pocus knows her through and through, see, it's the gloomier sides of things she goes for, leastways it's one big part of her make-up, all of our normal wind and wet and murk. I mean, right in the very middle of the heat wave, back in July, what does she go and do but produce a longish thing about the Lane, a poem all by her where our brick and slate terrace in the drizzle turns into a line of brown saucepans all steaming under their silver lids or something. She loves our language, see, even our down-to-earth version. Three she knows, three separate tongues she speaks which aren't her own. And it's easy to see she has a good ear, actually see it. The way she listens with her head to one side, like this, how a bird listens, and with that little hidden smile, so you almost see the words coming alive in her ear. Entire long evenings she used to love to spend in our back kitchen following the crack, writing down all sorts from Mam and Nelly's natter. Mine too. Listening and asking, asking and listening, one time saying it was like we'd all sung for her all evening.

That poem by the bye, it was a tiny bit inspired by thick old me. Not any special feeling like, just the fact that apparently some particularly windy day I happened to say the washing flapping on Nelly's line sounded like horses cantering by. Oh yes indeed, a poet and didn't know it! Mind, she'd likely even hear poetry in Nelly having one of her good shouts at Lorraine. Seriously though, the night she produced that thing and wanted one of us to read it for her we thought it amazing, well-nigh incredible when you consider it's neither her land nor language. Who knows, maybe it runs in the blood, the long-lost granda was really a Geordie bard! All written by her, all thought by her, yet she wanted yours truly to speak it right the way through, saying her own voice would spoil the effect she wanted. Cantering. Funny word when you think about it. And it just came out like that, and she remembered it. Never forgets a thing. Unless she wants, mind. Anyhow. Where the hell were we?

Yeah, the recipe. So that's the first rule, see, the first trick to it, never give too cheery a forecast, play down the bright side, feed all their little worries, otherwise they might just dicky off and act like humans have a will of their own. Which takes us straight to rule number two. Undermine their confidence. These poetic souls are fair game for the notion they're accident-prone, always in the distance an ambulance siren. But never predict the worst of course, nothing fatal. A patch of depression, but only on a level calculated to drive other folk to suicide. A bit of a fright, but no actual unwanted surprises. Till maybe next time.

And so to the last rule, vital number three. Never forget to stick a cherry on top, a nice juicy red cherry, the faintest chance of a happy ending sometime in the far future. And there you have it. And once you have it go catch your fish, any sucker in deep water waiting for something better to come along, and there's no end of them. Bait up, cast out, any famished creature on the bottom will fall for it, hook, line and sinker. And once on it's easy enough to play them along, from bitter experience I know the moment they've swallowed the recipe they'll never again dare make a move on their own, not without full consultation, even on something as simple as does he like me for myself or only for what he cannot get. Otherwise all they'll ever want to hear is when will the run of bad luck we've lined up for them begin to start to relent a bit. And that we just cannot put a date to, can we, or we'd sharp be out of business. So keep it vague, keep it mysterious, mumble wise words about brushing of teeth, the whole point of the exercise being to keep scaring them off life, convince them they're not free agents but walking problems.

Eeh, never have I put it better! And why could I not come up with that when it was wanted? Every blessed day I struggled to think up something new to bring her to her senses, prise her from his grip. Oh aye, too late now, the old spider's got her. And just possibly we're looking at his hole this very moment. And just more than possibly No Friend is regaling him with her skewed version of recent history. And how I'm coming across I dread to think.

Whenever she'd been on to him you could always tell, every time. More absent-seeming, eyes like missing Rome. Fantastic company one day, hardly there the next. And still I could never seem to make her see what Pocus was doing to her. To both of us. Aye, some weird notion of intellect she had, living all week for her Thursday long-distances, and every Sunday morning off to St Cuthbert's to worship Father Brendan again! For all her book-learning I was sometimes tempted to wonder whether she had any more sense than Mam when she got Spiritualism, a pushover for any Mr Telfer. For her, which means him of course, all that happens must be mapped out ahead, like an architect and a house, she'll try to persuade you, or a composer and an orchestra, whereas in my case when I know my head is right, times like today, each and every moment seems primed to go off in almost any direction. Life makes itself up as it goes along, that's more or less my whole philosophy, and that's what I enjoy about it. A game of football, not a concert. And whatever happened to the great element of luck, you try and ask her. The ball flies by and the nearest player jumps on it, or doesn't, and the best your holy coach can do is shout his blooming head off from the side line. But oh no, Feelie, there must be more to it than that, she says, there surely must be a lot more behind this whole muddle than appears, otherwise it would have no point. She'd like to give the impression we're all of us unbeknownst singing along to *La forza del destino*, her favourite opera, something or someone is surely masterminding it somewhere, like old Pocus here pulling all her strings. Myself, I prefer to be kept guessing right to the end, while she wants everything decided beforehand and all act accordingly. And how can anyone live like that, hope like that, if what seems new is really a foregone conclusion? Nobody would have a life of their own. Not her, not me. Not Felix Rowan, famed free thinker temporarily nuts on a nutter who has to consult the oracle just to hear it's okay to ease springs! That's the crazy world I've had to contend with these past months and months. Recipe For Disaster for what's in store, Father Brendan for how to mend it after. And purely as a matter of interest, what business is it of theirs how we choose to live?

Sometimes, after confessing all our sins to that soft-eyed padre of hers she wouldn't let me within a mile, even turned the key on us one memorable night, all shy and virginal and twenty-four. That was not even that very long ago, the first days of the new regime in fact, when she proclaimed it's a nobler thing to abstain, if that's what she was endeavouring to say in her funny way. But after setting up such an infinite craving what else could she expect from her man? As likely to succeed with me as her own efforts to quit smoking. Yes, what the hell else could she possibly expect, eh? And that was fucking then so what about fucking now, after all that's happened? Aye, bugger-all use anyone ever trying to tell me she can seriously still be expecting -

Eeh sorry, excuse the outburst, excuse the language! Must cool down and think before I speak. Still, at the very least it shows the pressure I've been under. So why can I not just thank my lucky stars I'm shot of her and leave it at that? Mam could see things were not quite right with her, more than once she said how worried she was about a person already so far from home spending such long times on her own, shut in with the same old excuse about needing to think, needing to read, needing to write. What book is that good? That night she turned the key I must have spent no exaggeration two hours parleying with her through the door, and she wouldn't open up even to run to the toilet, not with old *amore* between her and the stairs. And still I'm almost sure it was not just resentment at me, it was at herself as much, her ten rising twenty a day, fresh spots on her bum, or her hair again, no wonder she resorted to saying she felt sick nearly every morning. Recently she's looked that washed out and pimply you'd think she would have lost all attraction, instead I'm afraid I was even more crazy after her. Crazy to prove I still am her cure, as she used to like to claim. Three shades of hair she's had just this past month. Off-yellow, yellow, and barely a week back this almost unbelievable reddy-yellow. Like the sun in them windows again. Who was she hoping to be?

Every time, surfacing from one of her self-sessions as she calls them, long hours dwelling don't you doubt on the sorts of gloomy stuff normal people wouldn't want to think about even for a minute, she'd be so very careful to say it wasn't just me she needed to get away from, it was everything. But surely no matter how engrossing whatever happens to be occupying her at the time something has to be done about it, in the end a person has to be reminded others exist and not just their own soulful eyes in the mirror. What have you gone and done to her now, Mam asked out of the blue, as though I could possibly be to blame. The next time she asked whether the lass might not be in some sort of trouble I had to get her at least to try to begin to understand that giving the impression you're not particularly well or happy can be of some concern to other people, particularly if you happen to be sharing the same house, not living on separate planets. Even that had to be spelled out on paper and shoved under her door.

I'm thinking, Signor, I'm just thinking now I really ought to mention that the first lock-out was actually way back in June, the twenty-first of June to be precise, the longest day of the year in more senses than one. Hours and hours she stayed barricaded up there in her attic room claiming a midway date in the calendar is a good time to be alone with oneself and reflect on things. And it was such a fabulous night when it came, right up to eleven she could have read her book by the light of the sky had she so desired. And next day no change.

So what would any man resort to, when day followed day of this sort of nun's existence in the attic? No, I didn't seek consolation elsewhere, not then, I told you she was my fixation. What I did, what I did during one of her longest disappearances in the toilet, I crept up the stairs and into her room and just waited for her there behind the door. Almost an hour I waited. And back in eventually she comes, even apparently quite glad to see us after the initial shock. And I truly have to say the end result seemed to be that we were back on a more even keel, at least that was my impression. I say end result, because she said owing to the nature of things, the mysterious calendar she keeps, she wouldn't be available for a few more days. And when was the last time she'd let us get a leg over? Three days at least. Four? Man, I was desperate, I can tell you. Yet you know what she said, after? She was touched by my sincerity, she said, and my very own natural truthful voice again, though to me now that sounds a mite condescending. Anyhow, did the same tactic work next time it reached stalemate? I'll be blowed.

The sincerity points by the bye were earned for saying my desperation over being banned admission did not alter the fact I was genuinely worried about what such a regime of solitary confinement might be reducing her to, health-wise and what have you. No actual love is the ruination of a healthy relationship, all the sex manual maniacs agree. And luckily so did she, that famous night when it finally came. In fact she conceded there might be a flaw in the entire starry system, even. Aye, stupefied that Capricorn could even begin to want to fancy Twins when Crab's in Venus. Something along those lines. Ah well, nice to know that at least once in your life you got one over a billion stars!

15

Twins makes me feel I could probably be a bit more honest with you about the reason for her midsummer retreat from the world. She was worried she might have got herself pregnant. She only brought it up a long time after, and I was careful to say I was sorry if she'd had a scare and that, very, but is it enough to claim a woman always knows, what actual facts made her imagine she really was, and anyway how could she be so sure I was responsible, wasn't there this college lad she was seeing long before she even knew I existed? She laughed a bit of a queer laugh, said I was the first, in England anyhow. Ah so then naturally I asked whether it didn't go back a lot further. There was a baby, she said, and it was yours. What baby, I said, be reasonable.

Well, at that point I'm afraid I had to listen to a terrible story. It was the most horrible thing she'd ever known, those two days alone in her room, she said, first terrified by what she managed to convince herself was happening inside her, then all of a sudden bleeding and bleeding so much she was certain she was losing not just blood but the beginnings of a baby, one clot she passed was massive. I'm sorry to mention these details. Of course I didn't like to say that sounds a bit big for barely a month old, for I was just so thankful that having had to hear such a story she'd kept it all to herself at the time. Also I thought it's good she's got it off her chest, now she can start to forget it. But no such luck.

Because I'm sorry to have to say that was not the only time I had to wonder what I'd do if I was actually going to be a father. And this time it was very definitely a real alarm, a genuine worry for both of us. Her periods aren't as regular as the moon, don't always arrive to order, in fact as far as I can see are sometimes happy not to happen at all, sort of skip a month, which is one more reason you never know where you are with her. Of course I left her to count the days and that, obviously, but I must say I did secretly suspect something this time, the fact her monthly never quite seemed to come. In fact the night she broke the news she said it was such a huge relief to share it. Instead I am afraid I panicked. We'd made love, quite good love I thought, and so I dropped off like a log like you do, and then for some reason I woke and I was certain she was crying. A sort of mewing. I didn't stir, thinking how much she'd hate to be caught like that, because whatever else you can say about her the lass has a lot of pride. Also, as I say, I'd already guessed what might be the reason. All the same when faced with something as shattering as that I think it's maybe fairly normal not to want to know, keep hoping for as long as you can that you could be wrong. But then she spoke, said she knew I was awake, and out it all came, the reason for the tears and how she'd fought to spare us any anxiety as long as she could, remembering how I was the first time. The pillow was wet through.

I don't think I'm getting this across too well. It was actually a terrible talk, there in the dark, and suddenly not daring to touch her, anywhere. She said she couldn't stand the unfairness, she wanted rid of it. Destroy unfairness with unfairness, she said, that's the rule in this dirty life, she said, how could we ever let this happen to us twice? Hey Feelie, what do you say? Because up to then I hadn't said anything.

Of course I'd been thinking quite a bit, glad of the dark, thinking what they'd probably have to do to her. It's hard to know what you expect us to say, I said eventually, suddenly springing it like this. You never want to face anything, she says, but now you have to decide. Last time it was nothing, I tried to soothe her, touching her hair a moment seeing her head was still turned away, wait a little bit more and you'll see. Hoping, admittedly, some similar mechanism would cause her to go through that messy business again. It was not nothing, she says, I aborted. You mean, I finally managed to get out, you actually helped it happen? She made a horrible sound, so loud I was scared Mam might hear, saying she wouldn't know what a woman on her own should do, take a scalding bath, jump off the roof like Nelly, stab it with a knitting needle, she'd likely kill herself as well. Decide, decide! Look, I says, I know exactly how you feel, naturally I do, but you're not giving us a fair chance, sounds like you've made your mind up already, anyhow it shouldn't even really have to be my decision, ultimately. In that case we don't want it, she says, we didn't give it a thought and that's how we'll treat it, and for that matter who'd want to bring one more helpless bairn into this hideous world. She definitely said bairn. Or do you want it, Felix? Tell me, do you want it? So I said I'd help get the money.

I was hoping to spare you all this, I knew it would spoil the atmosphere, likely ruin the entire day. And spare myself too, because it's no fun talking about these things. In fact now I don't know why I even started, I really don't, except that with you I don't seem able to hold anything back for very long. In fact to tell the truth it's why I wrote to Mr Hedley, the real reason for writing that careful job application I told you about before your long sleep, and for meanwhile also starting to hoard my benefit, seeing Brian said they can ask anything up to fifty, even seventy quid to do it. I suppose none of it seemed particularly relevant at the time, and I have to say I feel no better for telling it now. Besides, the fact of the matter is I really never even needed to embark on it, because I'm pleased to report everything panned out painlessly in the end, and in point of fact those sad savings were destined to become my Italy ticket.

No pain, yes. Leastways no permanent damage. The bad stuff had a happy ending, so to speak. Because after days and days of meaningful looks but no more direct talk about it as such, and at least three more furtive calls to Pocus, when I happened to mention I'd put by nearly seven quid and still had eleven in the Post Office from all that Nana left us, she suddenly said forget it Felix, what you feared isn't going to happen, so don't you worry your head about it no more, all the same I don't want you in my bed ever again. The first part was cause for relief, naturally, while the other I hoped was just another of her temporary whims, as though two aren't always involved. After all, wasn't whatever happened inside her this time a lot better than what we finally agreed that awful night, and in any case hadn't I just proved I truly was prepared to help, if the worst came to the worst? But unfortunately she did mean it, the second part. At the time the only way I could seem to explain it was that she wanted her man to suffer as much as she considered she had. Also I thought between them they maybe even quite enjoyed playing cat and mouse with my feelings, her and that conniving old bastard in Rome, despite knowing how my nerves were already in shreds. And now of course it has me wondering if they didn't actually just dream the whole thing up between them. Because that wasn't all. There was an even bigger announcement to come. That same night in fact, in the course of reinforcing the ban, she announced she didn't need to do any more writing in England, she was rounding off all her researches as quick as she could and was leaving for Rome.

No, no – I told her I respected her decision, it's a free world after all. What else could I say without cracking up, or strangling her?

Something of the sort, Signor Pasquale, something of that sort. Yeah, just one of them things I suppose. Whatever, from then on I found more and more I was living with a different person, her whole behaviour grew more and more of a mystery to me. She couldn't wait to go, that much was plain enough, hardly putting in an appearance at home except to catch up on a bit of sleep. So one morning I did what I realised I never did before. I told her I loved her, loved her to distraction. Which I still maintain was true enough, leastways at the time. The morning was dark as if the sun had never risen, out in the yard it was pouring. I'd heard Mam leave, call ta-ra to Claudia and the front door clash, so I stole out of bed and crept down just in my knickers and saw she'd had her breakfast coffee, and her smoke, and her bag was sitting on the table beside her stuffed with papers, and her cape, and she was in the process of pulling her boots on, the long zip-up Calamity Jane boots she got with the money her mam sent special for her birthday. And me, well I stood right there in front of her like at school and blurted my piece. She tipped her head, that way like a bird. Her attentive angle, remember, so I knew she wouldn't yet say a thing, not until some more came from me. I waited, thinking hard. I know I'll love you for ever and ever, I said, but I know you don't love me. I actually said it. It's not love I need now, she said, it's support. She straightened her neck, pulled on that big rain cape thing, picked up her bag and went for the bus.

Even long before the ban I think I was making more of love than is probably healthy. With me, previously, it never used to be much of a problem. My head kept more or less out of it so to speak, barring the planning stages naturally, content to let the body have its own way and say. Knowing her has changed all that. It's drawn us deep into these what I can only call mental contortions, the commonest being a creepy sort of feeling I'm watching the entire proceedings over my very own shoulder so to speak, wondering what I'm up to if you see what I mean, my own bodily actions, so that in the end more and more I find I can seize up, on account of my body like I say catching my head wondering what's going on. I even told her about it once, in different words. She said that's very mature, *amore*, but I just find it ruinous. Don't fret, don't fret so much, she'd almost always remember to say after that, if ever she detected my interest was waning, most probably it's my fault, not yours. But that, seeing I was head-over-heels and out to prove it, always seemed so self-defeating and I just longed to tell her it's not the interest, it's once you start to make me feel almost apologetic about what it's fairly obvious we're made to just get straight on with, both of us, it's when you give out this feeling I cannot put a foot right in your eyes, so more and more quickly it gets to this stage where as I say my brain starts interfering and these two what I would call normally friendly halves of myself are pulling apart, so that from the point of view of my thinking half, the action seen at a distance, or maybe perhaps too close to, it begins to feel as though I'm only going through the motions, and pretty senseless monotonous motions at that if you stop to consider, so in a word it's not possible any longer for the other fifty per cent of the equation, the vital other half, to enjoy it simply for what it is, for all the normal good feelings and that, and relax ...

Man, where in hell did all that come from!

16

I don't know if these things I'm endeavouring to think right through almost as fast as they come into my mouth would manage to make even half as much sense to her as I hope they do to you. Because it's hard to formulate what you think and never say. Right now for instance a simple thing running through my head I wouldn't have minded sharing with her is the notion that all we needed was more time. More time to ourselves I mean, quieter times secure. Instead so often there was Mam to think about, nearly always about the premises when the lass too was home. She doesn't go out that much, not anymore, Mam of an evening, with this general concern for her bones. So we had to have a regular routine whereby one or the other would carry on at tea like it was a case of having to be out for part or all of the evening, to get her supposing only one was stopping in. Which is all well and good, but then how can your hearts be fully in it later, when half your attention is taken up with not making a racket? I don't know whether I have a sick mind or what, possibly I do, maybe it's that mental contortionism, but for me love gets to be not nearly as good if you cannot allow yourselves a bit of noise. Mind, I used to like a dangerous game, the need for stealth could be a good turn-on too, but I find it gets to be a lot less so if it's almost always the case. Maybe all would have been different if we'd had a car.

More than once she said she used to like my company above all as what she called a born entertainer, when I still seemed to be able to find a hundred ways to amuse her. Her clown prince. Then somehow as things went on and things got worse I think both of us grew a bit too serious and wary about what we once enjoyed, to the point that at times out of desperation I found myself dreaming up what you might call guest appearances, inventing so to speak new acts and parts for myself, all to get her a bit more involved again. Only I find the trouble with that sort of make-believe is that in the end you're not even really too sure who you've talked yourself into becoming, if even it's you she's letting have his will of her at long last, not the fantastic stranger you're impersonating, one of the five hundred she'd prefer. And just to give you an idea of the company she keeps, she said one morning after a big party somewhere in this city she woke up in this massive carved four-poster with crowds of saints and angels on the ceiling looking down at her lying starkers beside an unknown creature with a big black beard and a dirty great *cazzo* out to here. His uncle was a cardinal, he said, and they'd screwed all night in his bedchamber. Forgetting the language, is that even strictly allowed?

Well anyway, it could not be more different to how we two met. Me and *la donna di Roma* met on the Sunderland Road bus, it was as romantic as that. I hadn't even noticed anyone was standing there until the driver brakes a bit sudden as he's pulling into her stop and she lands plum in my lap, and it just grew from there. She laughed oh and I jumped off in pursuit only to find someone was waiting for her, this college lad I half knew from football days, but who when I mentioned I was contemplating a drink in the Kicking Cuddy she gave out a distinct feeling she wouldn't object to being rescued from. She was looking for a room to rent, he said once we were all inside, probably remembering Mam used to be in that line of business too, this bed-and-breakfast she was in being over-dear. So that's about all there was to it, just about. Plus the fact we couldn't seem to take our eyes off each other.

Of course now I see why he might have felt quite easy about being relieved of her. She's different, agreed, but still a handful by anyone's standards, as all this time I've been endeavouring to get across. And frankly she's not even so very typical Italian either, all warm and shapely and outgoing as we imagine all your women to be, like old Danny's three black-haired lasses we all tried to get off with at their dad's espresso bar. No Lollobrigida, put it that way, possibly due to her part-English origins. Not, mind, that she doesn't make an impact when you see her. No one particular detail, except the eyes, and maybe the very thick dark eyebrows, it's more the way she carries herself, straight and proud, leastways it always seemed to me something that set her apart. Whatever, she was a mighty rare captive to bring home to Lowery's Lane.

Mam had her suspicions from the start. Oh you should have seen the here-what's-this look on her face the afternoon I walked Claudia over the doorstep! Equally, you could see she was a little bit thrown by this unknown foreign woman who goes straight up to her and kisses her on both cheeks, smack, like an old friend. I'm afraid it's worse than Paddy's Alley, dear, says Mam looking sort of wildly round our kitchen which is never anything but spic and span, he didn't say to expect a visitor and today the place is all out of shape like this old out-of-shape body of mine. The lad's father, my deceased husband, was out there in the war. After which of course there was no stopping her, she was well away. The lass likewise.

The fact is Mam took to Claudia like a house on fire, right from day one she thought the world of her. Otherwise do you think she'd ever have let her move in like that, right the next morning, and the very first female we'd ever had to lodge? And foreign to boot! Tantamount to a major revolution, I'm telling you. As for myself, you know how it is, I may have been dead broke and jobless but it gave us a bit of standing with the lads, having a real Roman at home, though of course I had to kid on we were having *mucho amore* long before she let anything like that happen. Later, I must say, she guessed I was telling stories, the very sort in fact which were going the rounds. Which was extra encouragement, she said, to stop them coming true. Mind, I don't begrudge her that, not now, because the fact is I never felt too pleased with myself when I had to face her after a long session down the pub.

She seemed to have a knack of knowing things where I'm concerned. Though maybe that's all to the good, maybe it means I'm a lot less mixed up than she is. More than once she claimed she could read us like a book.

Now having Claudia on the premises had its difficulties as well as compensations. Mam in the main. My mother has certain pretensions to live up to, so you can guess how she was for ever getting after us. The very first morning, just as soon as I'm back from showing the lass where the bus stop is at the end of our street, she sits us down on the settee and won't let us up again until I've sworn never to take advantage of an unattached young foreign lady living in a room ten short steps above my own. Only imagine if Nana in her free-thinkers' heaven happened to be tuned in to one of them solemn sermons on how much store they set by their virginity! I can just hear her crow: Maidenhead, as though you ever knew where that was, Ada Rowan! Even so, that's how it went, right from the very start Mam formed a high opinion of her, and she never wavered, never, no matter what. In part I suppose it was the long line of books she stood up in the window and along the skirting board in that room at the top that used to be mine, and our combined efforts to explain why there's nothing like a real bookcase in all our house. In part too it was the old Catholic bit. Made us think as well, mind, when she wanted a nail knocked in right above the bed to hold this fair-sized silver crucifix. The creature with the beard purloined it from his uncle's collection, I heard later.

Looking back, it's funny she never turned it to the wall. Sometimes in our terror we thought Mam must think the old house was rocking with an earthquake, and yet right up until the day we left we weren't one hundred per cent certain she knew the inevitable had transpired. Us two going the whole way I mean, Signor, and what ways! We'd turn the radio up high, then next day I'd maybe mention the lass happened to be learning us the twist.

Before, in the awkward days when we were still getting the measure of each other, I never knew a thing like that could go so slow, or not since school crushes. Almost storybook stuff. Little walks together with the excuse of having to look for Smoky, hands touching as though by accident, me even prepared to listen to the crackpot philosophies of her old star-gazer or the ravings of this keen pianist over here who made her swear to come back to him undefiled. I wasn't even always too sure just how seriously she was nibbling at the worm, except there was that way of tipping her head and fastening her great green eyes on you, a way which said to me it's not just her tales of being enthralled by the quaint local voice that makes her let us prattle on. Still, that's more or less the way we went about it, all very patient and respectful, after she beat off the first direct assault. And when you think we two were living in the same house, I mean I could hear the bed creak every time she turned over!

It was when she started missing out on libraries, sitting awful quiet up in her room, that I started to be near certain we were having the same thoughts and that maybe she really was growing mad-keen. She's deep, see, she prefers to keep her feelings to herself, or they don't always show in ways you would expect, but I did seem to detect signs that she was more soft on us than she let on. Meantime I had other distractions, one or two old faithfuls who didn't play so hard to get. The novelty of having one upstairs was the challenge. She aroused my curiosity, I couldn't not have another go.

Finally came the Easter Monday holiday when Mam was away on a mystery tour with the Institute. We two were at each other's throats at the start of that whole long first free day in the house together, and passionate lovers by early afternoon. She'd been going on and on about when would I stop living off my hard-working mother and find some sort of job of work, so naturally in the end I couldn't help saying who exactly did she think she was to be talking like that, what money was she making, and after a bit of a scrap things of course got on to her father the great professor, how she loved him to bits for believing in her work which really was work, and so at some point for some unknown reason I said whether or not he was long dead I still kind of loved mine to bits too. I got a kiss for that, our first, a good long real warm kiss, even a little tear too, so then of course I thought to tell her the whole story. And that's more or less how it went. But here I have to report a thing that may surprise you. I wasn't the one who took the leap, she was the one to jump into bed! And despite everything that has happened since I still class that as probably the best moment of my life. Nice if we knew we could say the same thing for her, even now. Still, from then on it did I'd maintain go from strength to strength, weeks and weeks of unbelievable secret loving. Because, see, that's how she always wanted things. Mam was never to know, like her own dad and mamma back here.

Oh she was well and truly smitten, she told me so that

Easter Monday, and other times too when we could still laugh and joke about anything. Mam soon noticed the house was full of her singing, and now I'm managing to speak of her in this fond way I never thought I could again, it does seem to me I'm almost speaking of another person. There was this fresh expectant look lighting up that bonny face of hers every morning like the sun, as though I was all those green eyes ever wanted to see since she first opened them on this world. You see, it was so free and easy then, during love and even as much in the afterglow, which I know now is the real test, lying quiet together in her bed in the deep dark of the night, skins stuck fast with what she called our love glue, listening to her funny heart and my funny stomach, and of course whispering all sorts of rubbish. And sharing a bath when Mam was out. And comparing toes, comparing moles wherever they happened to be, comparing everything. One early morning she stole down to my room with nothing on but my famous Sunderland scarf round her middle, and thank goodness I could hear Mam suddenly snoring. Because, see, she liked to sleep in something of mine if she couldn't have me. This ancient shirt you so kindly washed is another relic of all them magic days. Even in the heat wave she wore it to bed, unless I pulled her out of it, to the extent you'd think that yesterday she might have claimed it as her own.

All these things that suddenly come to mind and tear us apart! Just think, at times she could even come over all jealous, like if we happened to be out together, even just down the pub, say the Two Hearts with my old friend Charlotte behind the bar. Seething jealous, in that particular case. Charlie would only have to pass by collecting up the empties or something and you could feel the lass tense up, like our normally gentle Smoky if another cat shows in the yard, when her eyes suddenly catch fire and she hisses like a cobra. What else can I say, it seems we've got to the point where we have to face the facts and ask what happened, what went so badly wrong, possibly even before that messy midsummer business.

Certainly not something I could plot out for you all neat and clear, working steadily through it step by step and day by day, but here's one way I try to explain it to myself. She may have cooled down just a very little as she got a bit more used to the situation, and if all I did was stay the same temperature I always was the result had to be that as she came down from say boiling to warm at some point in the process I'd have overtaken, without even noticing at first, either of us. Early on, during one of our famous walks, she said that one thing she specially appreciated was the way I put no more than a certain degree of effort into being in a woman's company, no more and no less, while the trouble with that lovesick pianist of hers back here in Rome was that he could not seem to take her even a little bit for granted. Set out too hard to please, in other words. So isn't it starting to sound like I should have taken more note of a thing like that nearer the time, meaning she never wanted our show to get as dead serious as it did? But back then how was I to know she'd get under my skin, until it was like a sort of disease?

Not only her books had claims on her, as she upheld, in the end I had to accept she just didn't want us in her hair all the time. Not that she was getting much down on paper, to compensate. The day after she moved into our place she showed me and Mam how much she'd done, in this thick blue exercise book, and it was precisely seventeen pages of that round writing of hers, I remember it well. Then the day before we left, just this last Thursday sitting round the table after the farewell spaghetti tea she made for the three of us, and the special pretty song she sang, she thanked Mam for everything and said she was pleased to announce she'd covered forty-one more sides under our roof, which unless I'm mistaken makes a grand total of fifty-eight, forgetting all the crossings-out. Oh aye, that's what she had to show for months and months of labouring to keep old *amore* at arms' length, all she could excavate from her mountains of notes! What's it add up to per hour, shifts she was working? Ten words? Five? She might not have looked quite so chuffed if I'd asked her to do that sum.

She calls it work, this writing of hers. I concede it may feel like hard labour to her but I still wouldn't call it work, not unless we're going to say the same about a dog and a bone. To start with, I'd point out, it's how you choose to spend your time, you even claim to love it. Work's the opposite, only people get paid for it. I mean, I could go right ahead and set myself up too, sit right down here now and start scribbling away, but who would ever dream of funding a fit-for-work person just for saying he'd be happier doing that type of thing? No more than if I said I wanted to spend all my waking hours fishing, I says to her, my own personal hobby I truly love and you refuse to understand. Some people get paid to fish, she says. That's another kind, I says, and there's no art to it. So there you go, she says, one person's hobby is another's job. Okay, says I, possibly falling into a bit of a trap, maybe I wouldn't resent it so much if it actually was your job. Then call it a vocation, she says splitting hairs again, and sticking her nose right back in her writing. In the end, undoubtedly to get us off her back, she teamed up with Mam to drive us out of the house almost every day to see whether there was nothing in the way of work in town, which of course was as good as sending us straight out to the Gordon. Her own, I discovered, her own apology for work entails no more than digging out bits and pieces from a hundred books and shoving them all into a new one of your own. Why not just reprint one of the best of the old ones? Besides, whoever's going to want to read her effort at the end of the day? The kinds of books she gets out of libraries, I happened to notice, seldom have anyone else's date stamp in them.

Not born to it, even I can see that. She'll chew the same sentence over and over, same as a fingernail or her pencil-end. Often watched her do that, turning the same string of words inside-out and roundabout behind the big frown on her forehead, the black eyebrows sort of knitted together tight like this. One night I thought to call it her game of cat's cradle. She liked that, funny, though it's apt enough when you see a page after she declares it done. One colossal god-almighty tangle only she can possibly unravel, and even then not always. At that time, see, she was still wanting to let us in on her English writing, supposing I had some sort of natural born advantage. She'd read out maybe an entire page of writing when finally finished, even just a couple of sentences, in her excitement needing an appreciative audience like no doubt we all do with something we feel we've achieved, but then like as not the moment she was done she'd want to try it a different way. And of course I'd appreciate, never letting on that no matter what she did with it I still saw the same old piece of string.

I can see me now, stretched out on that bed that for all my early years was mine, maybe with the radio on extremely low so as not to vex her overmuch, and our Smoky finally settled down purring behind the door since I'm afraid cats don't agree with her and as a consequence Smoky always wanted to sit in her lap or plonk on her papers, watching her there chain-smoking away at the little table in the window and tugging at the front of her hair, oblivious to everything, even to that, the so-serious eyes flicking to and fro, to and fro, me finally drifting off on my own thoughts as well until maybe she'd suddenly look up and ask about a word. Our little attic hideaway would be reeking like a coke works by the end of them long study evenings, but what did I care, it's when I had her to myself. Otherwise, she was so often out of the house and away.

Listen to me, man, just listen to me, I told her once, you know what I'd do if I was you, I'd get me of one of them what-are-they-called thingumajigs you see murderers spouting their last confessions into in the films, and talk and talk my way through my whole thesis more or less any old how until I could not find so much as even just one more word left to say. Then play it all back, copying out and tidying as I go, and lo and behold in possibly not much more time than it takes you to do a perfect page I'd have my entire book finished. Because certain days, Signor, not just a rare think-aloud one like this, all manner of things can somehow start moving in my brain with no control like dreams and just the thought of having to slow down and write them all out would stop the momentum, I'd never get to find what new things might be coming and –

Fair comment, fair comment! She's a pen-pusher, I'm a babbler. The one's for reading and writing, the other's all for up and doing, and no use ever hoping to combine forces. When it comes to writing I don't have her mental discipline, she's right about that at least, not to mention the mental wherewithal she has in abundance. With me, it's the old fear of making mistakes, straightway I'm back in school. Sit me down in front of a piece of paper and put a pencil in my hand, and my mind which can be teeming up to then it just goes blank. Even when I might seem happy just sitting by the river watching my line I still like to do little trips up and down the bank from time to time, see what's round the bend.

We're total opposites too in that I happen to have a need for other people's company once in a while, whereas I think more congenial to her is her own sort of busy form of solitariness, if I can put it so, long spells where she seems content to lose herself in her own head. I mean, she could be right here with us now, we could be talking away like this together and even looking straight at her and still wonder where she is. And at this point I think I should reveal what is her greatest aim in life.

Nothing!

Experiencing nothing, for goodness' sakes, and not the least ashamed to proclaim it. She possesses entire whole books about nothing, the all-time favourite being a special present from her star-man, about as thick as this and still all dog-eared, page on cross-eyed page black with teeny print about how to make a mental journey to nothing and nowhere. I told her personally I can wait till I'm dead, he wants you in that zombified state just so you're easy meat for his jiggery-pokery. Man, the stuff she's consulted on all the ways and means to empty that brilliant brain of hers so as to reach this witless state called enlightenment! I could just about understand the need to stop my brain performing, I said to her, if like millions and millions of your beloved Orientals I didn't know where the next meal was coming from. With starvation staring me in the face even I can see the wisdom in training myself to contemplate my navel.

One time so earnestly she said to me she'd finally reached the desired object by gazing into her own eyes in the mirror for hours on end. She looked very queer when she told it, having been to nowhere and back. Green orbs gone almost black. I thought about it a long while, all afternoon in fact down by the river talking to my float, then when that night I tiptoed as usual stone naked upstairs to her to win her over again, I sat on the edge of the bed and gave her everything I'd accumulated in my head, everything to put him firmly back in his place in Rome. I told her I saw no mileage in it, right here is where I want to be, and anyhow what made it such a great achievement in itself, was she not making a sort of big virtue of a deficiency? Meaning, she's enough absent-minded already. It was a bit of a risk, but she took it graciously by the end. It made her sit right up, see, sometimes she likes a genuine challenge. We two don't need no mumbo-jumbo technique for forgetting, I says repeating my lines but scenting victory now, the present moment is all that counts for the living. Flower, I whispered slipping between the warm covers, life's too short to long to rise above it, this whole night for ourselves won't ever return. All my powers of persuasion must have had some effect, because three times she wanted to make love before morning.

But is that a way to have to carry on night after night, when they start taking even longer to settle than a cat on a cushion? I'll wave a banner for women, always, whatever they choose to think, but I don't believe ever again it can be for only one. That way it degenerates into analysis I find, and from there into suspicions and accusations. Unless that's what they all prefer to love? And I mean, is it never a case of the pot calling the kettle, save that being built different they hide it easier? Because, Signor, I do find it *un poco* unfair, women having all the advantage in that compartment, how in their case it's not fully exposed to the naked eye and doesn't normally reveal what they're feeling until practically the last moment. I've even sometimes thought that if I'd happened to have a hand in the matter I'd have kitted out man and woman each with what the other has, both the gap and the attachment, then we'd straight off know everything about what our opposite feels, thus sparing all the current fuss and bother. Mind, other times I'm not so certain about that notion. Maybe it's still only skirting the issue, it might turn out we'd not need each other for nothing.

And now I see that what all this is coming round to making me admit is that one way or another she got me so wound up that eventually it reached a stage where I had love constantly on the brain. Not a relaxation, more a perversion. So then the big question has to be why did I put myself through all that agony when I could see love was less and less a priority for her, and when anyhow originally she was meant to be no more than a stop-gap in the awful vacuum after Nana passed? The good times, the good unthinking times, went by so fast, so fast. Even when we managed to recover our balance after that bad midsummer episode, too many mornings would see me back in my own bed fretting away in an empty house, part trying to banish the memory of the night before, part planning next night's salvage operation, how I'd be the world's greatest lover next time round, forever dreaming up new angles to take her by surprise, casting about in the more colourful corners of my imagination and the tired literature under my mattress and behind the mirror for some novelty to put the sparkle back in her eyes, those big green eyes that seemed to be more and more only drawn to what's on paper.

17

Don't get me wrong, I've nothing against books if they happen to be the only distraction. I devoured tons in the Army, some this big, and nearly all of them good reads guaranteed to pull you in and carry you along. But never her sort, schools being designed to put folk like me off them for life. Open a study-book and all I can see is ink on paper, whereas in my kind of book almost from the word go you've slipped between the lines, you're right inside, part of everything that seems to be going on. I've sometimes wondered how they do it, but hard as I look I cannot see where the trick lies, how they manage to get it so transparent. Of course it's a gift, you have it or you don't, and it gets my full respect. We have it when we dream, all of us, and that's why I know that one day someone will have to build my dream-machine.

A machine for recording dreams, Signor. Sit down, switch on, and up comes last night's entire entertainment, all the weird and wonderful things your brain lays on when it's free to amuse itself. It never ceases to amaze me how it can just go projecting picture after picture after picture, and new people in new situations or old ones in new situations, and all their different voices, and always a special atmosphere, and still keep on springing more and more surprises. Is it because with being trained always to look and notice things it cannot switch off so very long, if we don't give it something to chew it has to invent its own scenes to get to work on? Shut your eyes, young 'un, and just see what comes, world's best picture house and seats are free! So my uncle Harry used to say when packing us off to bed. I've even fantasised, I suppose a sort of dream inside a dream, that my dad if he hadn't died so soon might have been the kind to build it, or start to, because no doubt it would want more heads than one to get the entire way there. He studied codes, he studied signals, and he loved inventing, and this surely is the century for it. One night in that lone prison cell I woke up staring full at the shining moon and that same moment it struck me the place to start would be to combine a television and a lie detector. Who knows, maybe I've produced an idea there for someone brighter than I'll ever be.

I happened to mention the notion when Pocus told her to start keeping a dream diary, apart from her ordinary one, only she didn't seem even remotely interested in what

I was talking about. My timing was wrong, I suppose, by then she wanted no intrusions. Same story with my I still do believe reasonable suggestion about getting a dictating machine, there's the word now, keeping it for instance close by her pillow at night, which she agrees is when the best ideas come. Might take a while to get used to, nobody likes the sound of their own voice at first, but I'm certain it would get easier and easier as you trot along. Look at us here, if we'd had one of them machines with us today who knows what we could have made of it sometime in the future, listening back. But I might as well have saved my breath. Books are made from books, that's her position.

God, Signor, without her never would I have known there's that many libraries in our region! If she heard of another she'd think nothing of travelling fifty mile and more, bus or train. We live a bit on the fringe of things, for her purposes too, so no matter what she had to get herself all over the place, near and far. Newcastle of course, Sunderland too as you may remember, plus any number of smaller places all with their own libraries and such, even right up into Northumberland which she soon found has more old houses and castles than I ever thought, and where it seemed the old professor thought she might turn up some long-lost clue about her mam's mystery dad. So now maybe you can see why I came to loathe what books can do to her. In the end all she seemed to care about was spending longer and longer in one blooming library or record office after another, once even practically a fortnight devoted to visiting a private library hours away where she said just for her sake the man kept it open late. True, I did wonder about him, though all she said was he had his own very difficult book to finish. What a game, eh?

I spied on her once. All these past weeks she's almost always been getting an early train through to Newcastle where there's this ancient library they call the Literal and Philosophical, quite a mouthful, and seeing the trips getting that regular I'm afraid I fell to wondering whether she was really even going there. To that building, for that purpose like. So after bailing out of bed one morning and stealing upstairs to lie in her empty one, which I'm afraid was getting to be a bit of a bad habit, I could stand it no more and ran out of the house probably not an hour after her, caught the next-but-one train in fact, and found the place and walked straight in. It's not far from the station, very old-fashioned looking, imposing, with Roman-style heads all over the entry-way and that. I told the man I was interested in consulting the section on mansions and manor houses, and he asked straight out if I was a member. I must have looked sick at the question, at any rate he suddenly relented and said I was welcome to have a little browse round upstairs if it would help make up my mind about taking out membership at twenty guineas a year. So up the big wide staircase under these mammoth oil portraits I creep with my heart thumping and thumping, and at the top I position myself just behind the big open door. And of course there she is, and of course doing just what she said. The one soul in the place, sitting at a long table tugging away at her yellow hair strand by strand in the middle of a great heap of books, and it was plain her mind wasn't on anything outside the usual worries, all the pages where she thinks the answers are. Queer lass, she did try hard. But at the time I have to say I wished she was tying knots in her hair over some of the things I was thinking as I watched her. Hidden in the doorway, with only that little gap between us, I could measure precisely how far from her thoughts I was. All the way from there to here.

Naturally I did hope she sometimes asked herself how it might feel to be the likes of me, having nothing to occupy myself with but thoughts of her, but if ever I hinted at something of the sort she'd brush it aside, even claim she envied my free existence, never considering how that might be an argument for maybe taking a day off once in a while. To tell the truth I gave up explaining how I filled my time. Waiting for her would have been the only honest answer. Yet she said to keep her I had to let her go.

And didn't I? Lately on an evening she's not been getting back from the city before eight or nine, half-nine even. Dog-tired too when finally home, eyes keeking out from behind red lids like they don't any longer know where sleep is. She even started misremembering what time she promised to be back, and we had frictions enough already without extra provocation like that. Even Sundays, the one and only day of the week without libraries, I hardly even saw her, the best part of the morning spent on bended knee in church, the rest up in her room again, treating her lonely lover like a trespasser in his own house. Always another book to read, always another page to write. And more and more she took to falling back on the old excuse that her heart's not quite right, though I happen to know she told Mam the doctor said it was nothing the new pills couldn't fix. It saddens me. How about my own heart, I ask, what she was tearing in two?

Did you I wonder never go through such a disaster of a love-clash, in your younger days like, before being so happy with your wife? You know, where the both of you seem to have lost the feel for all the ways there are to get through to each other, yet always with such great hopes of a sea change, and always back to square one, and always still kidding yourself you'll somehow still contrive the earth-shattering explosion that will put everything back together again? When in fact there's nowt more to be done. Humpty Dumpty had a great fall and that's the end of it. And when you're that far gone, that obsessed, isn't it the very reason you've lost your grip? That, and the perpetual fear that in her face you can read you're relegated.

Because when she was finally home what did I get? *Caro,* just give me a little more time to myself. After eight or nine or ten hours book-worming already, and still claiming she hasn't yet quite done all she set herself to achieve, her target for the day ever on the increase. And as I've said to you already, never a thought for how you yourself might feel at the end of yet another day on your tod filled only with dreams of having her back. Every night out of terror of losing her for good and ever I had to learn to hold my tongue and let her make her usual black coffee in this miniscule metal pot she brought from home, then wander upstairs with it and maybe a sliver of toast, and shut herself in. Later on she'd run a deep bath and likely fall asleep in it. People have drowned themselves that way.

Lately her timing has been so erratic that Mam despite her own private worries about her even gave up leaving her supper on the warm. While me, I had more than worries, I was fast going to pieces, to the extent that sooner or later I was bound to make a fool of myself by asking if she wasn't seeing someone. You know, if she'd found another attachment. Such a Charlie you feel, the moment you've uttered the fatal words you know nothing can ever be the same, you've as good as admitted you deserve what you're bound to get. Time you noticed I'm in no state for that, she muttered, which if it means what I think it means was grossly unfair considering all my obvious concerns on her account, another put-down, anyhow very off-hand and no real answer. Later to myself I said don't fret, don't fret, that's her way, she's the kind who'd tell you straight out if she really was playing away. Trouble is, I already knew that fine well and was dreading the day. And anyhow, wasn't it just possibly about time she noticed the state I was in? Not once had we made love since that terrible night I tried to describe, when I woke and found her crying. And love I'm afraid is the only test I could imagine for showing she had any feelings at all outside books.

Which gives me a sudden memory-picture of a bit of a wild night after a big Sunderland win. Saturday nights were my only drinking sessions all week, ever since for her sake like I told you I started saving bits from my dole money. And I stuck to that even after the baby scare was thankfully all a thing of the past, just to show her I knew the meaning of discipline, though privately of course it was to keep back scraps from what the government owed us for my secret Italy adventure.

Now that particular night, which incredible to relate was no more than just three Saturdays back, do you know what she came out with, you know what she actually says on seeing us walk in when I doubt it was even a minute after nine o'clock? Look at him, misses us so much he gets rolling drunk down the pub and claims he was sitting all day by the river! Claims? Every word was true. And rolling? I never walked so straight, I says, pointing out that was the first and only time I'd set foot in the pub since the week before when we held the Magpies to a draw at St James's Park, and what did she think of the wondrous fact that today we had made history again, thrashed Walsall at Roker and the goals just would not stop coming? Five! Miraculous. Even Mam was glued to the radio, I informed her, and we danced all round the kitchen when it was over. Five-fucking-nil, man! But what's the good? She'll never ever understand what it means to be a true supporter, the loyalty, the passion, the undying devotion. And listen here, I says when we were safely shut in her room at last, is a man not allowed one little drink to celebrate easily our best win this season? Cloughie got two, first a header and then a real cracker from thirty yards out, they chaired him off the field, and our other top scorer Charlie Hurley wasn't even playing, for the past two games on the casualty list, but you wait for Norwich City next week when he's back rocketing them in! She claimed my pacing up and down was interfering with her concentration, so I said okay lend us ten bob and I'll leave you in peace for the whole of the rest of the night, I promise. And after a bit of dither she did. Here, she hisses, and don't ever ask again. Which is another unfortunate side to her make-up, never likes parting with the professor's money without a little bit of a show, as though when your best friend happens to be doing nothing for a living he's still somehow expected to provide for his occasional few luxuries himself. And if you find your way back, she says, spare us having to see how straight you can walk.

You'll see, I says, you just watch this, I'm walking straight out of the almighty presence and back down there where it's warm and welcoming to get really rolling! Because she was way off-side, to use the terminology, for since when had she herself been seen at home any earlier than round about the same hour? Also, she knew fine well if I took myself off to the river it was because I couldn't any longer bear existence in that empty house, the two of them out at work the entire day and every room lifeless. I didn't go for the fish, that's easily proved, for there nearly are none. Back in the heat wave, all them I don't know how many days the rain never came, our poor river sank so low it started to stink like a sewer and just about anything still left in was floating wrong way up.

But she couldn't leave it at that, oh no, always has to have the last word, see, because down at the Hearts still ringing in my ears was what no doubt she thought was a very smart parting shot, to the effect that although I might like to say my head is full to bursting with goodness only knows what bright notions that still didn't alter her opinion, and my own mother's too she said, that I never want to learn to use it, my burst-full head, since I'm incapable of ever delving deep. Ever was rich. And even if I dispute the fact, and most definitely I do, tell me who does it not apply to almost all of their born days? So okay, maybe I didn't acquit myself too well right then, but after another two or four at the Pot – not the Hearts, sorry, because Charlie said she wouldn't be on that night – I come storming back up those ten sacred stairs shouting

I want one deep-delved thought out of you right this minute, egghead! Maybe it sounds to you like I really was rolling by then, but I wasn't really, no, in fact I'd sat down very carefully with myself and used the time to plan out the whole coming contest, and hopefully conquest. Right now, egghead, right this minute!

She was sitting cross-legged on the bed just the way I'd left her, oriental-sage-like, pretending to be deep in her reading, and when she didn't look up I knocked the flaming tome right across the room. Come on you, I says, and remember my personal definition of a deep-delved thought is one nobody can ever have had before, because I mean if she's only struck on dead writers and random patterns in the stars and thinking herself to Nowhereland how can she ever dig up anything new like I swear I do from time to time, even if I cannot give you an example just this instant? And look at me when I'm talking, you'll not find it there! She was picking up the book. It's in no book, mate, which by definition has been in minimum one head before. Or to be truthful, no fucking useless book, which possibly deteriorated from the intended effect. Following which this is about the gist of what I said, with all due allowance for the heat of the moment. A live thinker, my own humble notion of a truly great philosopher, would never sit hunched over other people's words all day and night, it's his own particular unique set of brains he endeavours to rack until they come up with some fresh angle on existence. Because you have to exist it, existence, how else would anyone ever find even one good reason for it? Aye, ask me the one and only sensible purpose for your unreadable reading and I'll tell you it's to check any new-seeming idea isn't as old as the hills. She couldn't find an answer to that, nibbling a nail and turning pages faster than a genius can read.

I'll have to try and hurry this along, because something tells me I'm beginning to weary you a bit. It's, well, it's just that you never can tell how things will turn out at the time, so almost any little thing acquires importance, looking back. Or are you going to say that even after having that frigging door slammed in my face it still looks like I don't ever want to free myself, she's destined to grow into a fixation almost the same as my dad? But to answer that you'd maybe need to say whether all them useless tears I spilled in the night were by way of a pledge or a purge.

Cautious remark. All up to me, in other words. Time and me. Well, never again's my attitude, as you know. Got to be. I even agree with her, agree totally now, by nature I'm not equipped to understand a woman. Specially that one. All the heart-searching, where's it get you at the end of the day? Where'd it get her? Where me? It comes to be like you're watching yourself too much, as I've said about ten times before. So I'm going right back to my old position before this one pathetic attempt at love, the same attitude as Jackie. How did that joker-lad put it now? Who cares what goes on inside a woman, it's what she's inside of! Perfect recipe for no tears, right? Come to think, Jackie also used to say the thing he found hardest to abide in women is the way they can drop into what with a man would at most be a passing mood and just decide to stop there, like they never intend to come out. And how right can you ever be! No doubt it's for the effect it's meant to have, leastways that's a big part of it at the start, but in the end it gets to look like even more of a punishment to themselves than their man. As in fact she herself more or less conceded, finally.

Anyhow, forgetting all that for now and considering everything else I've been trying my level best to explain, would you say I've managed to home in on what was the basic trouble between us? Our incompatibility, as a quite experienced lady I met last night happened to call it when she finally let us talk a moment?

Here, that's hardly fair! Naturally I don't put it all down to books and writing, that's only the most blatant example. Like equally she'd say of me, football bloody football, fishing bloody fishing. But still, you're right in a way. I know full well all comes down to the plain fact we were born different and in different corners of the earth, and consequently we feel different, we think different, we speak different, we act different. And the daft thing is to neither of us would any one of those differences have mattered a toss had we never got together and stirred them all up. *La forza del destino* all over again. Though let me say this too: look at a peg and a hole, or a palm and a fist, some opposites are made for each other.

That wild night by the bye, I think all I was probably attempting to get across is that she doesn't all the time have to think of a thought as sort of lying there along the path waiting to be picked up and stored like a used thing the last person dropped after having no more call for it. But she'd have none of that, need I say. Ideas come from ideas, books come from books, she must have repeated it I don't know how many times, then and earlier when I was still angling for my bit beer money, and honest it was as though she'd read even that somewhere.

Okay, okay, I told her when I was finally back from the Pot and well forearmed, that would be all fine and good so long as every idea going had happened by nineteen-hundred, but this is progress, pet, this is the twentieth century and we're way past the halfway mark and I for one believe that since the Russians and now John Glenn can sit up there in capsules coolly circling the earth we'll all soon see a man in the moon. I told her for a fact that somewhere or other I read there are more ideas hatching now per year than ever before in the history of humanity. And what's so wrong with hoping to be a little part of that? According to me it's modern life by definition, new gadgets are being dreamed up all the time, and by and large it's for the better if ever you think how people used to live and a sight too many still do, and anyhow that's how it is and that's how it's going to be, so long as no one sees fit to blow us all to kingdom come.

Yeah I know, I know, getting carried away again even now. But that was the same week, see, the Cuba thing started rumbling. The Pot was full of it that night, everyone talking at once about World War Three after the telly came on before the match with the news they now had photographic proof old Castro truly did want to go nuclear like everyone else, and Kennedy telling Khrushchev to forget it, and Khrushchev saying bugger you. Also, and I'm sorry that I forgot to pop this in where it belonged, you'll never guess what she said when I came back the first time and told her the place was buzzing with talk of the four-minute warning, not even looking up from her reading. Let this shitty world destroy itself, she said, it might solve a lot of things, she said, good news for the universe, she said, ever since man first heard thunder he's wanted to make a bigger bang. Her carefully considered comment, incredible to report. Not the least moved or bothered at the thought of goodbye to a billion or whatever years of evolution. I meant to mention it earlier, but lost my place when I got side-tracked by the feeling you wanted things speeded up.

Mind, the universal scare did work on her by degrees. By the end of that queer week she'd actually come right round to my way of thinking, that with the world on the brink of extinction maybe our own crisis looked a bit daft. Not only that, she even decided she wanted to do something about it. Yes, she suddenly said she wanted love again. And you could tell she meant it, she looked like nothing must prevent it, not even if this was to be our last night on earth. Specially if. So I did what I'd been dreaming for weeks. We didn't steal up to her room, no, the moon was full and I took her down to the river to this lone boathouse which on my solitary wanderings I'd found a way into, and we climbed in by the broken window at the back and piled up all the punt cushions. Nothing was between us that night, we were mad lovers again, better than ever. She opened up at last, said she was sorry, said she knew now what was wrong with her, she'd gone through a very long depression, and when you're depressed the worst about it is you feel superior to other people because they don't seem aware they all have to die, you have this horrible secret knowledge about life that everything is diseased. Unforgivably superior, she said. When steps on the towpath woke me next morning her arms were still tight round my bum. I didn't move, timing my breathing with hers so as not to wake her, breathing the smell of her hair, thinking let him walk in and find us like this, so what. The steps stopped, but then went on again, and through her bright new hair I watched the sun rise. The colours in her hair, Signor, they were all the colours of the sky.

Still, destiny again, just as this sun here must go down as we watch it now, I have to report that was the last night we spent together, in our total way. Because in the B&B full of mirrors near Kings Cross she claimed she felt too sick and I had to promise to keep to my side of the bed. Come morning she acted like she still felt funny, anyhow we had to grab breakfast and practically run for the train.

Too late now to dream of getting back at her by revealing she wasn't the only woman I had that momentous week the end of the world was nigh.

18

Doreen Finnigan. The lass in question. Number three of our neighbour Nelly's four. I never cheated on Claudia before, not once we were going steady, and never at any other time through all the long lock-outs, since it was only with her that I had to prove myself. But what did it was this.

Two days before, the Thursday Khrushchev terrified everyone by talk of a thermonuclear war from the very first hour, when I finally got myself up I found a note saying she'd gone through to Newcastle again and might be very late home since Father Brendan was holding a meeting at

St Cuthbert's to support the Pope's appeal for dialogue. So I stuck to my plan, my original secret plan, and went over to the station and bought my ticket to Italy, paid for as you know through much stealthy skimping and saving, plus I admit a little bit extra from Mam's special purse lent without asking – but don't worry about that now, I made a full confession before we left – and for a sort of surprise I put it with my passport to sit there innocently in the middle of her pillow for whenever she finally got in from church. All hidden there inside this big envelope saying Please Open Me. Well, so up she goes with her coffee as usual, and not a minute later she comes running back down looking very surprised, genuinely, almost crying, saying she never imagined I had it in me. Fingering my brand-new passport too like she could hardly believe her eyes, claiming in the photograph I looked like my old self again, happier than for ages. I said yes, pet, yes, because out there everything's going to be different, it's going to be just like it was all over again, wait and see. By then it was way after ten, so I knew she must have phoned Pocus before coming in, the usual Thursday night briefing, yet still I raised no objection when she said she fancied a little walk on her own to think things over, get more used to the idea. Of course I knew she was going straight down to the box to ring Rome again, but equally I knew how much I needed that meddler on my side now. In fact she was back in record time, wished Mam and yours truly *buona notte* very nicely, and before heading upstairs whispered I'd given her some very interesting things to sleep on. Very interesting. I decided that sounded promising.

Well, next morning when for a change I was first

downstairs it was only too plain she'd hardened up again, for no reason to do with myself as such, or not that I can see. I blame him. Definitely nothing untoward was said by me, in fact seeing that sour-puss face again I was as usual careful not to open my mouth, leave the eyes to do the speaking. As for her, about all she said, and it was more to Mam, was it had been a packed prayer meeting at St Cuthbert's, very inspiring, and she'd worn herself out listening to the radio half the night because she feared her friend in Rome was right, the Americans were about to invade Cuba any moment. Then after telling me twice she didn't want a second coffee she went for the bus. So that's more or less how it came about. After what I thought was a good reception the night I broke the news, when I found her all solemn-sides and sick-pale again on the morning, I said to myself to hell with it, if she won't accept even this as proof of my full support I'm getting the bus myself and I'm looking up my old friend Mrs Doreen Heron where she now lives out in the collieries, hoping to catch her in.

I hadn't seen Doreen since the night of my big twenty-first birthday knees-up in the Hearts, but I had reason to think she might be available again, having heard down the pub that she was now semi-split from her pitman husband who's been half off his head ever since he got a big fright at work when the cage went out of control. She was kind enough to let us have what I came for, for old time's sake, though I could tell she had him on the brain, and naturally I did Claudia. Still, we got a good bit closer as the day wore on, and in fact now I look back on my pointless trials during all that longer-than-Indian abstention I could kick myself for not seeking out such an understanding friend and ally sooner. So well, what else do you expect, I ended up staying the entire night, and that was a first too, when things got later and later, way past the last bus, in their great big bed upstairs, with the curtains tight drawn but the window wide open in case her Harry suddenly showed.

This isn't the first time I have a feeling you know what I'm going to say, as though by now you too can claim to read my mind. Yes, we did have a good long talk together, me and Doreen, a right old heart-to-heart, and a lot more constructive than anything we experienced on the same settee, quite honestly, for I badly needed to unburden myself, and similarly I realised after a bit did she. Nothing seems to change the way it is between you and me, I said, we're still like brother and sister, but in this Italian woman's case something has affected my mind, infected it, and I've never felt so ridiculous. Earlier, when I'd say to her like you decide, country houses or Felix, we'd generally make up after a bit of pull and push on both sides, even if next morning she was off again, same bus or train as usual. But now thinking of the way it's gone on from there I actually pity myself, Doreen, I have to, recalling my long morning lie-ins, maybe waking a moment to hear the front door go and not always sure even whether it's the lass or Mam, then dozing off again with only dreams for company, my private cinema we used to talk about, remember, though now generally only programming stuff I can never seem to make end happily, and those terrible drowning dreams have begun again. It's come to be a pattern, this living in separate worlds, and worse now with Cuba on top of everything. I think I'm even in danger of losing interest in fishing, not to speak of football, now it seems mostly only hunger can get us up to face the day, and only the requirement to sign on ever seems to get us out of the house much before noon. We've not done it for weeks, Doreen, weeks and weeks, she doesn't want us ever again in her bed, and although it's torture it's also I do concede a kind of relief. You know how I am in that department, normally no worries, but instead love with her was getting to be almost crippling, each and every time I was starting to feel almost like I was on trial for my life, as well as perhaps being a bit of a pest. We hardly even talk now, yet still I know we both have the same trapped feeling, that far I can see. And it's not as though she doesn't need anyone, it's obvious she herself is in a mess. Mam says the lass's heart has started racing again, and she used to put my hand on it here like this to feel the funny beat, saying only I knew how to cure it. I think she's most probably decided she wants to be ill, actually decided, though not enough to prevent her going out. But even more it's her general attitude, and I don't mean just to myself, to everyone. Mam, and you know how she is, even Mam doesn't seem to like to say anything. I look across the table if for once she's actually there and I can see there's something ever more sort of inward about her, like she's nursing some special secret, something unreachable, something no one can fathom, maybe herself least of all. And it's all having an effect I don't fully understand, a truly big effect, in fact if you were still next door I think you'd struggle to recognise your old mate now. I mean to say, certain times I've caught myself almost revelling in my lot, not just my unfair banishment, even my normal woes with the dole people, like I just invite trouble and sort of almost like it now. For instance, when finally up and fed I don't generally mind doing the last night's dishes if neither of the women has got round to them, I even seem to get some sort of masochistic pleasure out of tidying up after the two of them, even just putting out the rubbish and suchlike, and I've been known to run the hoover about the place, and this week I started putting paint on the stairwell for Mam to finally pay her back for keeping us all this time and well fed, and just a few days back after coming across a remnant of canary yellow in the shed out of the goodness of my heart I dabbed it all round the lass's window frame, my little tribute to her new yellow hair colour which I wrongly read as a sign things were maybe finally due for an upturn. And now it's got to the point where I've started on the whole kitchen as well, like remember you and me and Maureen did for your mam that first time she was in hospital long ago, and I mean to make a proper job of it too, woodwork and all, primer and two coats. Mam can see the transformation alright, even commented I seem a reformed character. But that Italian could not, will not, and the truly pathetic thing about it is I don't even like I say completely mind, all the time having the consolation of my own little secret up my sleeve, see. Oh aye, all this while I've been quietly storing up my benefit hand-out to add to the last of Nan's post office savings she left us, bit by bit accumulating the necessary for a new start to life in her country. But God I'm so blind, Doreen, how could I not see she was hoping to make a desperate bid for freedom, and now she's terrified I'm coming after her?

I don't know how much help all this was to Doreen, having to listen to my long tale of woe even after we retired to their bed proper. She has one or two problems of her own, see, what with being in the family way as I next discovered, and her Harry gone AWOL since she claims a man's first instinct on hearing a baby is on the way is not to want to know. I suppose it was her being in that condition, probably that's what made her ask if perhaps I couldn't have got Claudia in the same way too, thinking it might explain a lot of things. I said forget it, I told you it's by invitation only, and I've been granted no more than a peck on the cheek for practically as long as I remember. Still it was I must say quite perceptive of her all the same, so I went and told her about what I finally got around to admitting to you, about the two false alarms, explaining how it could lie behind why she took to communing with herself so long in her room, when not just keeping clear of the house. I don't know any of the details of what she went through this last time, I told Doreen, and quite honestly I don't even want to know and anyhow it would be unfair to ask, but I do know the first occasion was quite bad, quite lonely and upsetting, pretty painful and bloody in fact, so I reason she's suffered enough without being made to divulge these very personal things all over again. All I know is it was a near thing, very, and beyond that I'm just not going to presume on her privacy. The poor lass, it's terrible, sounds like she might never be able to have a bairn, says Doreen, which I must say did give us pause. It's a delicate subject, obviously, I said, you can tell that by how she stares at the wall, but since I'm desperate not to lose her I've settled for thinking it's best to wait and let her get over it in her own good time, like the first occasion, and so bit by bit win back her trust, no matter how long it takes. That's been the hidden logic behind all my strategy, my game plan so to speak, although I must say it doesn't stop us feeling worse than useless, and though she may not think it the very best idea just at present at least I know I'm doing something constructive, if I go with her to Italy. Besides, remember I told you how I always promised Nan that one day –

Sorry?

Oh. Well on that particular topic Doreen took what in effect was Mam's angle too, best policy was to let the lass go free if it's what she seemed to want, then maybe see whether she tried to keep in touch, even think of coming back some day, use that as a test. That's when I suddenly twigged she was pregnant all along, Doreen, seeing she hadn't produced a French letter like on my birthday night when she proclaimed she never lets a man near her without being so equipped, for all I tried to tell her it's a comical thing I feel detaches us. So anyhow, when I could feel she too felt like maybe making a better go of it a second time I thought I'd best bring the whole subject up, and after a great big laugh she told us she was nearly three months gone and anyway what did I do about my Italian bird and protection, considering we all know the Pope hates seeing his people wearing anything. That's the religion for me, Doreen, I says, they put out a calendar of safe days so your woman can make all the necessary calculations, and the rest of the time you're expected to look for other ways and means and as a result we've tried just about every combination in the book, tongue-and-groove, lollypops, even backroom boy. That made her laugh a good bit I will say, I hope you're not offended like. Still, as I said, it was quite perceptive of her, and a big relief too to get all these things off of my chest at long last, talking as man to woman, and one with whom I go back so far. And of course such talk can only lead to more of the same, right? Aye, daft not to have looked her up a whole while sooner. Because that wouldn't have a made a blind difference to my ultimate fate, would it?

Instead almost every day I'd sooner or later down my brush and fetch my rod off the hook and go out along the river, miles along sometimes, to walk off my frustration and keep away from the temptation of the pub. Because, yes, as you know only too well I have this regrettable tendency to drown my sorrows, and for that matter celebrate anything worth celebrating, like a Sunderland win. Aye, Signor Pasquale, it's just possibly a little bit ironic that today's wee swally with you could be seen to celebrate the miraculous fact I'm finally free of her and still in one piece, whereas that particular night it was the triumph of achieving my ticket to Roma Stazione Termini and my sudden rediscovery of my old pal Doreen. In fact I was still pretty bleary-eyed when she threw us out at half-ten next morning saying some nosy neighbour was due to call by to take her round the shops to look at baby clothes. Standing at the bus stop I suddenly felt back in the real world, and in no hurry to face Claudia with my tail between me legs.

Now that of course was the Saturday morning, the day the two Ks looked more than ever set to collide and take us all with them four minutes later, true to their war of words. So you could say there was a kind of double emergency in the air, our future and the ultimate fate of all mankind, each hanging in the balance. And well, *amigo mio*, what happened next, we couldn't have written it.

As I'm hopping off the bus by the Market Tavern who should I sight but my old pal Kelvin kitted in khaki disappearing inside. So then of course in I nip after him for the hair of the dog and to hear what he makes of a soldier's life in the age of atomic war, and when finally we emerge after suitably celebrating our reunion and our joint departure, he to Cyprus, myself to Italy, there before our eyes packing the entire Market Place from end to end is a near riot of local warmongers and college student do-gooders split in enemy halves shouting fit to roast each other, bad as Sunderland v Newcastle. And who to my amazement do I spot standing together right there in the middle of the fray, and hand in hand at that, the two of them shrilling We Shall Overcome as passionate as a pair of opera singers?

Claudia and Charlotte, my anti-nuclear soul-mate and my stubborn lover now sporting unbelievable red hair, when up to then my one impression was neither could abide the other. Their side was chanting Stop Nuclear War, U.S. Missiles Out Of Turkey! while the other was going Missiles Out Of Cuba, Don't Trust The Reds! some running right up to scream it in our faces. Ours, yes, because when I see Kelvin dive in to get the nearest lot going Traitors, Pacifist Traitors! suddenly I'm between the two lasses and Father Brendan, Claudia looking I can only say over the moon to see us and squeezing my hand, good mates again, and myself soon going full throat too, electrified, all of us pouring our hearts out with that big number Down By The Riverside fit to burst, like it might really be true that when people get together like that they actually do have the power to save this world from its own madness. Make Love Not War, I'm thinking to myself, we're united again, it's Felix and Claudia for ever and ever, Peace Co-existence Talks, and we're obliterating Norwich City this very moment, so I thought, and the old boathouse was swimming before my eyes, then Rome, because hopes combined as strong as that can surely keep any finger off the button.

19

After that, all that, our last week was actually a bit of a non-week. The world as you know woke up next morning to find it could breathe again. The two Ks had made a kind of peace, and so had we. Things felt better after the boathouse that night, a lot better, though she still wanted us to sleep apart, for Mam's sake she said, and because after all that had happened so quickly we needed time to adjust. For we read she. But fair enough, I wasn't going to risk another confrontation with just days to go. The calls to Rome continued, in fact multiplied, and for all I felt we were close again I still couldn't help agonising about what the two of them might be cooking up between them. So, basically, after the excitement of the Saturday night, the winning her back, I more or less resumed my patient line, calculating that any new developments could wait till Rome. Bit of a miscalculation, given the outcome.

I'd explained my general plan for the two of us after the first magical release of love in the boathouse. Seeing she said she thought all of a sudden adding a boyfriend to the equation would get at best a mixed reception at home, I said why not use the remnants of my savings and anything extra from her usual sources to set up a temporary base over here somewhere cheap as possible, apart or preferably together since that would sooner force her people to face up to the reality of my existence, then hope her famous leverage with the professor plus his soft spot for anything English would by degrees resign them to the new addition to the family, so to say. After a bit of debate she agreed with my every word, make no mistake, the skin of my neck was between her teeth as she said it, right here where my finger is. In fact it took a whole week, until Kings Cross in the morning, for every trace of that love bite to go. So was it not forgivable to greet it every new day in the mirror as her signature to a contract, our great Rome contract, her signature in blood? And if privately she thought otherwise, why couldn't she say so before it was too late? In all else she would stick to her guns, to the point of dogmatic.

So there's not really even so very much to tell about our final days. Hardly saw her, to be honest, forever out trawling libraries. We had a bit of a disaster on the Wednesday I'm sorry to report, third round of the League Cup, and I thought what a performance for my last match on my own soil. Went fishing twice and caught precisely nowt, wrote a jokey card to Kelvin to sort that out, resisted the pub, resisted Doreen, wondered what to take and settled for one bag only so as not to scare Mam overmuch, and finally finished doing up the kitchen for her, in fact kept her company a good bit, Mam, seeing as you know she just hated the thought of us leaving. Smoky likewise, because cats can sense things too. Pulled up a welter of weeds while saying a sad farewell to Nana's grave on the Thursday afternoon, and old J.W.'s right next to it, and our Felicity's just round the corner now so overgrown it's almost disappeared. And that in fact was the same evening she at last made a long call home in the course of which I gather she let slip that the landlady's son was considering coming to Italy too, might even be on the same train. Oh, and bumped into good old Pete Di Mambro who stood us a double cream cornet for old time's sake, and wished us *buona fortuna* ...

Ref peeking at his watch, I see. I know, light fading, game flagging, time for the final whistle and all that. You must be thinking how much more can he go on using us as a kind of punch bag in her absence, will he never stop, but I promise I'm only asking for your patience a very short while longer. Because somehow or other I've got to finish the job, having run this far with the ball. Aye, now I'm this deep into the opponent's area!

Our final clash was about nothing. That's still my position, whatever she might want to say had she not chosen to absent herself from proceedings. Which, like it or not, leaves her permanent failure doing lone battle with the truth. That middle-aged English lady I mentioned speaking with last night imparted something to me about the truth, something very clever, but for the life of me right this minute I cannot recollect what it was. In which case we'll just have to make do with one of the One-Arm Bandit's wisdoms. Never forget, young 'un, there's always three sides to 't story – yours, mine, and the truth!

Always on the boil. That's as good a place to start as any. I know it's what she said because I couldn't very well not hear, not in that confined space. Mumbling, but it's what she said. On the boil. Always! Yet if I remember correctly I'd only just extra-gently inquired what was troubling her, if again she was feeling funny. All this is yesterday of course, Signor, yesterday somewhere hereabouts in a weird hotel in a weirder room, somewhere between three and four in the afternoon.

Okay, I says to her, okay so tell us what you said if you didn't say that. On the ball, I said on the ball. Claudia speaking. So what, I says to her, so what blind difference does that make, it sounds all the same the way you say it, anyhow I heard the first time. For some reason it got to me I'm afraid, maybe because she wasn't looking my way right at that moment. And where can such things lead to but a scrap? Boil or ball, a scrap's what she wanted, and of course I fell into the trap.

I was unsure about that room myself, I admit it now, though equally I'm not the sort to fret over-much about such things. In any case why should she? We'd agreed anywhere dirt cheap would do for us while she went to work on her dad, it was all part of the contract, also I know for a fact the deskman told her it was the best bargain in that whole ramshackle place all corridors and stairs and doors so quiet you just know there's people behind them. And you could see why he wasn't asking much for it. Barely space for the bed and the basin and a plastic bidet, and the only window was for examining the lift shaft. All the same, and still speaking solely for myself, it was somewhere we could call our own at long last whatever it was like, and anyhow her room in our house, mine before hers, was no bigger and I don't know how often said she loved it. Also, as

I sat there on the bed watching her change into something else right before my eyes, I just somehow couldn't help recalling one unforgettable summer's morning when our usual five o'clock alarm went off under the pillow following the most unbelievable love night, shrilling it was time to creep back down to my own bed before Mam should wake, and happy-naked as we were she hugged us extra hard and said she was going straight back to sleep to dream of a warm dark den, dark so we'd never need to know there was a world waiting, warm so we'd never have to wear a stitch again. Not, I suppose, that it would have greatly improved things had I been minded to look round our new den right at that particular point in time and recite those famous lines of hers, because when just for a joke I said since she'd checked the sheets were okay how about testing the mattress, she switched to her other tone of voice and went off to find a bathroom with a fed-up face. Her high and mighty tone, I mean.

When she got back you could see she still had her judge's wig on. You could see it best when she was painting her eyes in the little square hand mirror she keeps in her purse and had stood on the basin, the hotel having forgotten to supply anything to see ourselves in. Unless, and it only occurs to me this minute, unless maybe she was intent on camouflaging the fact she'd had a little cry to herself, something I can only suspect now I know everything that was set to happen. I was still on the bed, in actual fact stretched right flat out by now, shoes off, hands behind me head, watching those great eyes in the mirror and wondering what to say, and to be honest feeling a tiny bit foolish. Anyhow.

Anyhow, to cut a very long story short, rightly or wrongly that's the moment I chose to pop my shoes back on and traipse back down all five flights to fetch up the last of her luggage, her almighty bookcase, which as a point in my favour I'd earlier said I'd be happy to manage on my own, on account of her heart, her supposedly weak heart, this well-nigh trunk-size case jam-packed with all of her books and papers, calculating also she could possibly do with time to cool down on her own and recognise there was nothing the least disrespectful intended in anything I may have said, the very opposite, being I should think a fairly understandable reaction if you're in love and no love for a full week by then and nigh-on two days stuck on a train cooped up with strangers, and in truth I did indeed end up giving her easily time enough to think it over seeing the idiot on the desk minding the bookcase's English was as good as non-existent and still no way was he going to let *el signor* get a hand on it until I'd used up every scrap of any language I know including sign luggage, language, to make him finally begin to accept I don't happen to possess a single acquaintance in all of England who might be able to fit him up with a job in London, or Southampton he for some reason also insisted, all the time promising him at least five times that if anything occurred to me I'd notify him pronto, and so armed at last with that ton-weight of print and scribble all the way up them hundred or whatever stairs I sweat and struggle and all along the winding corridor to our little hole-in-the-wall I come– only to get what sort of welcome home?

She jumped down my throat, she bit my head right off! And you know what was almost my first thought? That in the course of just them ten or fifteen minutes some Roman acquaintance of hers had slipped into the room and put her up to it. Aye, had there only been a phone you'd have sworn she'd been on to old Pocus to complain about the vibes. Because the things she said, the things she said! Always making selfish claims on her yet never one real thought for herself, her self, her own actual thinking and feeling self, that was somewhere in the first long mouthful, whilst I'm standing there flabbergasted having only just salvaged her bleeding bookcase for her. Selfish, superficial, insensitive, immature, some men should be kept away from women all their lives, she says, or shouts, or locked up, locked up forever on their own in a horrible cold cell like this. Though that bit may have been later. Anyhow, just pulling any old thing out of the air to suit her argument, and with not the slightest provocation on my part, I swear. Insensitive, immature, unperceptive, never will he change, and no understanding of her own deepest feelings, no interest in them, no notion what she's about or for that matter what he's about, most probably even who he is, and no sense of direction, oh not that again, and it's in one ear and out the other, and never will he change, never, never, never ever, and all the same too big for his boots and with sights never set higher than the physical, and no tenderness, no damned fucking tenderness to be completely honest, and so thick-skinned and thick he cannot see the plain truth even when it's staring him in the face, and so blind, so blanketty-blank blind, never will he ...

Signor, if I could remember even just the half of it we'd be here the rest of the night. While me, I was only about six words into what I'd been endeavouring to explain, the reason for the very short delay which I already took the trouble to explain to you, and out it all comes in one long pitiless harangue. And that I think was the most frightening thing about it, that she never once stumbled though she was screaming. So was it all off the top of her head, or all cooked up lie by lie while we were stuck together on that never-ending train? I cannot decide, still cannot, though a tirade like that must take some preparing. In any case, can anyone in all honesty say it was even remotely justified, to that extent, after everything I've gone over with you all this time? To that extent?

You can hear I'm wavering. Even now something in me refuses to accept she can have planned it all out to end the way it did. Not like that, surely not like that. Call it love, she said, I call it loathe, loathe, loathe! The way she snarled, it made every hair on the back of my neck rise, right up. Yap-yap! You used to understand, you used to help, you used to care. Yap-yap-yap! Apparently now I never help, never understand, never care, never think. She means care for her, think only of her. Good grief, as though I've done anything else all these past long wasted months! I couldn't believe my ears, truthfully I could not. Never mind ears, I couldn't believe my eyes. Trembling all over she was, first white as a sheet, then more and more sort of almost black, a dog would have been lathering. And myself, alright I was trembling too, not an inch of me wasn't shaking before the end of it. And no wonder. Three times at least she must have shrieked she'd given up waiting for some change. And what could I begin to say to that when week after week, month after month, I'd waited for some faint sign of a change in her?

Unless you're now wanting to tell me it was some kind of last-minute warning, a sort of desperate ultimatum? If so, it was all a bit one-sided, was it not? With all that shite flying, all them sudden hysterical accusations, how could she ever suppose that was an acceptable way to go about laying down terms and conditions, shrieking the long odds on whether there was any future for us in Rome? I mean, if that was really the case she should have minded more how she put it, if ever she expected a man to be able to engage in civil argument, let alone think straight. Venomous, vicious, vitriolic, and well larded with four-letter words once she was really going her ends. I'd only survived on sufferance, that was the general message. And I could hardly be expected not to do nothing, could I? Surely she understands that, surely she sees that now she's had time enough to reflect.

Yes, as I hear myself saying these things, all the untenable things I'm saying she said, I still cannot keep from wondering what she would make of them now. Would she not want to alter even one word of what I put in her mouth? Hearing herself speak through me now, but this time knowing the outcome, would she not want to revise at least some bits of all you hear me say? If she's anything like I am she'll have been over and over it almost every single minute since, so let's just hope that now like myself she's capable of seeing it all a little bit clearer than she could at the time. Even, who knows, our separate versions practically converge. But that I'm afraid would make it one long tragic farce from start to finish. Because I mean, if she's now finally coming round to endeavouring to understand things a little bit more from my point of view, that by and large she has just as much herself to blame for anything I may have done, the pity of it is there's no way we're ever going to know. At the very least I wouldn't mind hearing her concede I did do everything to keep control of myself as long as I could.

Which wasn't easy, I tell you, once I knew her mind was as set as her face. Though that's also when I knew more than ever I had to keep a hold on myself, so as to get all that rush of revelations better sorted in my head, prior to carefully demolishing her point by point. Which now brings us to what is I think the most devastating thing about this whole unequal contest. When at last I had a chance to speak I just somehow didn't seem able to come up with even one of all the many things I've found to say to you today in my defence, yet yesterday was the time they were really needed. I told you she's clever, very, and I do admit I was a bit knocked flat by a lot of the things she said, though I think even more it was the full force of them all coming together at once that was the real shock, such a tremendous shock to me, as I think you can detect even now. But worse than that, worse even than that, I suddenly realised my only hope of survival was not really a matter of anything I could ever find to say, only the way I said it.

I did try, naturally I did, but it came out so weird-seeming. It was like I couldn't get enough air in my mouth, or enough wet, and so my voice went way off-key, like breaking again. Yes, at the crucial moment my entire speaking apparatus let me down. I'm not normally stuck for words, but I do know now what they mean by tongue-tied. And when you have to contend with an encumbrance like that, what could actually be a knot in your tongue, and at the same time you're struggling to do all you can to try and keep your head above water enough to attend to how you're coming across to someone waiting so intently on what you're next going to say that suddenly you feel you're being expected to justify nothing less than your entire existence, it's not exactly a simple proposition. And I couldn't stand there and do nothing and just watch her pack and go. Could I?

She waited, I'm not sure how long she waited, long enough, holding her peace at last so as to let me have my final say, eyeing us in that old way with her head to one side. And when in all this time nothing in my own defence came to me right there and then that I could manage to put properly into words she slowly turned her back and started gathering up her last things, her cigarettes, the little mirror from the basin, all very, very slow, because even then I think she knew how hard I was still searching in my mind for the truest and best thing to say about how I felt, and felt about her. And now I also think it was more than anything the sadness of it all that hindered me, the terrible sadness of knowing everything was coming to an end, no matter what we did or said, either of us. I feel it again now, I live it as we speak, and on top of the memory of my abysmal failure at the time comes this extra almost unending sadness that says to me that once I'm through going over this most problematic patch of my life with you it will truly all be over and done for ever. For ever. And somehow I just don't even yet feel quite prepared for that. All the same, the plain truth, the plain and painful truth is there's so very, very little left to tell. Only I wonder if I can, I just wonder if I can. It's so difficult to do without her.

I think it was only the need for some sort of light relief, possibly also a desperate device for delaying the inevitable, I cannot really say now, but I do know I thought one way forward might be to try not to appear to take everything so seriously, even make an elaborate joke of the whole affair. For what can you do, in a tight spot like that a man cannot be thinking of all the possible consequences of every move he makes, not while at the same time anywhere inside his head he's grabbing for every last reserve he has. I do have a sense of humour, you know that, I'm partial to a joke, in fact it's something I know she used to love, but still I have to say that one totally sunk us. Way long before I finished I knew for certain it was the beginning of the end. Yet I did mean well, I believe, all in all I did try to weave into it a hint she might be feeling a bit fragile after the very long journey to here, not to mention her worries about the family, plus no doubt the state of her heart ...

No, I'm afraid I cannot bring myself to tell that joke. I can see that anyone might consider it one too many, and it doesn't seem even remotely funny now, and in any case it was so mistimed. Suffice to say I thought I was about to score the equaliser, instead it was an own goal. And so. And so now without even wanting it I've come to the part that's hardest of all to tell, even to you. Yet I've got to have a shot.

Remember how I said that before that sad attempt to be a clown, and partly during it too I must confess, when at last I did have some space to put in a word for myself like you've kindly given me all this long time, no matter how I strained and strained I could not seem to generate a proper voice, could not so to speak connect my mouth to my feelings, remember, and all because so acutely aware that time was fast running out and that anything I said at that late stage was going to sound not good enough, or plain wrong? Well, while more and more at a loss for words, even just one right word, my eyes all the time were following her as she packed, her every act and action, patiently and quietly removing every last trace of herself from my life, and with me still there, and when that awful miss-hit seemed to confirm her worst imaginings and I could stand myself no more, I'm afraid I pulled her bookcase off the end of the bed and tipped the contents all over the floor. It was I suppose to show all the many things that had split us apart, though probably most of all it was just to stop her doing that anymore, her deliberate torturing of me. And when I saw even this produced no change in her silent rejection I did the same with my kitbag she suddenly decided to appropriate on our very last day at home together, my old Army kitbag with my own number on it, and after emptying that out too I tied a knot in the cord so tight I thought never would she be able to undo it. But in the end, when at last she had remedied even that with no help from me and I saw her standing up in front of us there looking all smart and nice for her family, and her famous Calamity Jane boots for the weather, and I didn't myself have much actual real packing of my own to do to stop following her if I so chose, though I'm sorry to say already by then in a state of complete undress, unluckily, and seeing her rain cape still hanging on the hook but knowing it would be the last thing to go preparatory to her leaving …

I sound muddled, so damned desperately muddled. But that's because now I'm at the point where I cannot stop and equally I don't know how I can go on.

Why did I do it? The memory of her assault, partly. The volume of it, the level of her language, the wild exaggeration. For in a black mood like that you've got the stubborn energy to flatten anyone whatever they might care to want to say for themselves, whoever you really know them to be. In other words, a fright like that puts you too much on the defensive. And all things considered maybe I'm better in attack.

But why, you're sure to be wondering, why do that, why take his clothes off? Why strip? Wouldn't it ruin every last chance he had? I think it's only because I thought there was no other way to keep her. Maybe not even that. Maybe the simple fact is I thought there just had to be something else I could do, anything, after I found I could not speak up for myself. And it didn't start, I swear it didn't start until I could see no other hope. Also some things she said, I thought they showed she herself wished things could have worked out different. Besides, there were tears in her eyes. I should have said that long before, though of course it's only one more thing that told how her mind was set.

But more than that, Signor Pasquale, much more than all that was this dreadful sad feeling that took hold of me. This last-moments feeling, this feeling of living again what almost everyone on earth lived through so recently, and could so easily have become reality. And if it nearly happened once who's to say it will not happen again? We two, we could be sitting here together like this with our thoughts absorbed in these very private things and all of a sudden we could be shaken by a solemn public announcement that the end of the world is due in precisely four minutes' time. Repeated and repeated until we know there's no escape. What would be left to do when clearly there's no way out, if it's closing in fast on every side, like a dream I had on the train, when any way we choose to run can only be toward the catastrophe? Even then, even then don't you think we'd still hope there's something left that we might share, if only the catastrophe itself, and possibly in such extremity our bodies are what might best speak for us, against all the pain I don't believe we ever really want? Why else would she be crying?

I wasn't going to do that, not then, I couldn't bawl, I knew it would not solve a thing. So what else was there to turn to, what else, when by then the tears were running like open wounds and still her hands were filling bags, like two things she had to obey? That end-of-everything feeling welled up once more so strong from so deep inside, so strong I don't suppose I was even really thinking from that moment on. Now I wonder I didn't go stark raving mad.

I remember the words, or some of them. But it's no particular thing I said, it's what I was driven to. Hold me. I know that was in my head, I remember it clearly. And it's not so untrue it seems to me even now, for where else does all start and all end? Hold me, hold me! And when still she would pay no heed, no heed to me stone-naked and ridiculous and still so desperately wanting her to reconsider her final judgment, rethink all her supposings, what did I have as a last resort other than my own body I live in, which she once liked, I think possibly loved, short of a weapon to pick up?

I am. This also I remember saying. Hold me, I am. That's all that I suppose I wanted her to accept, since it seemed to me she once cared to know. I am. Plus I think I thought she might like to say she felt the same.

Well I could not have done worse. The way she acted you'd have thought it was tantamount to rape. A man, an unknown man, a naked hairy ape loose in the same room! And I thought what does she have to be scared of now, hasn't she had us a hundred times before? Not that I wanted that, not then, not at first. Like I said, it was that end-of-everything despair driving through me, which I realise now is also a kind of strange desire. She's the cause, I thought, she unleashed it, so I don't see why it should frighten her any more than myself. There, I've said it now, I was frightened too. Scared of myself, scared of me, about what a person can do to another person. Yet in the end I think all I wanted was only another look in her eyes, one that still took us in, right in. And when it didn't happen, when it couldn't, I tried to pull the clothes off her as well, just so there need be no difference between us, to make us two the same at last. And it must be then, and for that reason only, that I caught her by the hair, that crazy beautiful new red hair I thought she went out and got herself to celebrate the fact I had my Italy ticket ...

How she contrived to hit her head I do not know. It was the doorpost, I tell you, only the doorpost. All right, yes, my hand was raised, but not against her, not really, only to make her turn her face. But she hit it hard. I heard how hard, I felt the impact in myself.

That's when I finally let her go, let go of the bright hair still tight in my other hand, when I could tell how badly she'd hurt herself. No blood, but a lot of pain. After that of course there was nothing I could do. For one, gone was every trace of a tear, and prior to that I told you they were streaming. For another, the hurt was in myself as well, an agony that never left hold of us all of yesterday, at times today. This moment now. Inside here, here where she tore herself out of us, leaving a gaping gap she used to fill. And there was the other hurt too, the fact I could see she actually thought I could do that, really thump her, to the extent that now it is immaterial whether or not I did. And still she was standing so close, this close, but I knew I could not touch her ever again. Nor could I have said then and certainly not now what she was thinking. Her eyes in her skull were gone too far away. All I can say is what their emptiness made me feel, and of course it's something I'd been dreading for a very long time. For her I'd disappeared. I never was.

EXTRA TIME

Lovely, aye. *Bellissimo,* this last light. I was watching too, very glad of it while speaking. The way it makes all the architecture stand out now, along with the glow from the street lamps below. And look up there. Still blue as midday aloft. But deeper, cleaner somehow, and all the stars are coming. Ink-blue, she'd call it. And traffic's wilder, ever more hoots and toots. Sort of makes you want to go down and live the night, join in. Not like yesterday, stuck with people deep in their own world before ever I could begin to get mine sorted.

Fine weather again tomorrow? Well I must say that's good to know. Because what's to come is all that counts for me now. This always was my imaginary city. Strange to be in it, living it now, what you only ever imagine. Knowing this is the place.

And this the people, oh aye! All your doing, Signor. How can I thank you ever?

You showed the sea of roofs in front of us, then the battered old Colosseum still standing there, floating behind that white sheet, more *bello* and more *brutto* than I ever dreamed. And you know what I felt right at that moment? That he had used his own son to see all this, by looking through my eyes that were his eyes. Aye, poor bones-in-the-water arranged it all! Never gives up, my drowned father. Woke his mother with his last cry, scared the wits out of his widow, haunted his son for years and years. And all of yesterday, his special day.

Let him be. As you say, I've probably lived a bit too much in his shadow. Time to get out from under, let go.

But I still have to complete the pilgrimage. One year from now, exactly twenty years on, I'll go south, take a boat to the island of Sicily and find Augusta harbour and look around. Maybe try a swim. Think of him, think long, then climb out on the sand and never look back. Then maybe I'll be good for something at last. And someone too, possibly.

That note you keep up your sleeve is right about his age but wrong about mine. One year out. I've not yet quite made it to twenty-two, he never made it to twenty-three. So now I'm wondering whether the puzzling words only mean to say something as simple as this. Soon I'll be free to live the years he never could. Maybe you heard me say something like that, when all them other weird words were in my mouth?

You know, when you started reading it was like you found a voice for me. After that I needed almost no help to speak. But never could I have made so much sense to myself alone. You launched me, you got us going, you set us thinking. And all along, even if you snoozed a while, I felt you there. And how much I needed that, my friend! Right at the start of this long bad year I lost the person I liked to talk with best. She loved to sit and chat, Nan was my education. Let it all out, hinny, she'd say, before it gets too dark in your head to see. And that's something I'd make a special point of passing on to my bairns, should ever I have one or two. Also I'd never let them forget the simple saying by which I know she lived. Think for yourself and say what you think.

I'd like to share with you just one other thing that today has made me more than ever tempted to believe. Everyone's head is in perpetual motion starting I suppose more or less from the day they're born, possibly even before, and although when asked we generally say it's a blank that's only because we're not actually attending to how it keeps on musing to itself. Same thing at night, isn't it, when it gets its free chance to dream, weaving a muddle of stories that if we never woke in the morning would likely never end. So one more thing this unusual experiment with you here today seems to be asking us never to forget, even though I've hardly begun to understand how my own mind works or even if it's any good at anything, is that having a brain really is a fantastic entertainment, awake or dreaming. And there I'm inclined to go along with her, possibly we make too big a distinction between the two. After all, it all comes from the same place, doesn't it? I'd like us both to drink to her.

Buona fortuna, lass, wherever you are, whatever it is you want from life!

Yes, all over now, all done and dusted, my friend. She led me a dance, I was out of my depth, I met my match, and I'm best shot of her. End of story. And how long have we been at it, all told? Seems an eternity. Way into injury time, that's for sure! Best call it a day and go back down and have ourselves something to eat like you suggested long ago.

Funny, I still catch myself wishing it could somehow all have had a different ending. Maybe there really is a chance she might wander into the Baffone one day. I'd have mixed feelings about that though, I think, if by luck she staged a comeback. Suddenly materialised. Grief no, why should I? The distrust, the resentment, the animosity, you have to believe that does fade. Aye, give her a bit to think about, wouldn't it, looking up and suddenly seeing who's blowing hot air through her milk coffee! Alternatively, someday I might find a way of giving her a ring.

It's not easy to find a sympathetic ear. All yesterday, the one thing I knew I had to do was sit down with someone and collect my thoughts. You knew it, and you were prepared to set aside all this time to hear us out, same as my imaginary dad. And this too I have to say, my kindly boss, I'll never forget your company and courtesy as long as I live. You've been a tower of strength, I give you my word. Goodness only knows what it all adds up to in the book of reckoning! We can never expect to make sense of everything, Nan said, but that is where the real interest lies. Always something unfathomable. Aye, who would ever want it all cut and dried! One minute you think you've stumbled on the secret of the entire bloody universe, next nothing could be farther. Still, still, when all's said and done I've mostly enjoyed the experience, speaking for myself. Of course I don't know about you, but I feel so much better for it! I've been right through the mincer and I can tell it's done a power of good. Restorative. But without you never could I have done it. I needed you a lot, such a lot.

Ah such a great lot, my mate! In you I am so fortunate.

Goodness, we're getting sentimental. Is it because between us we've finished off the whole fiasco? Bit of a shame really, because I was going to propose one last toast to the Sons of Temperance. But never mind that, time to go. Take a bath, have me a shave, then try that famous stew of yours. Afterwards, I seem to remember we have a kind of appointment with your son to go over to the Colosseum and pay our –

Here, hold on a moment, I must be dreaming! Man

alive, what is the world coming to? Look, there's still a drop left! Aye, I do believe there's just enough for each of us. Never say die, life's a blooming miracle. Let's share it. You first.

Cheerio!

And now tell us all about you.

CR, FR
(1977/ 2005)